THE RIGHT TO SILENCE

THE RIGHT TO SILENCE

Rankin Davis

LONDON NEW YORK SYDNEY TORONTO

This edition published 1996
by BCA
by arrangement with Hodder and Stoughton Ltd

First Reprint 1996

CN 9276

Printed and bound in Great Britain by
Mackays of Chatham PLC, Chatham, Kent

To all those who believed, you know who you are, and for all the children, everywhere.

ACKNOWLEDGEMENTS

No book is an island.

Without the following castaways this island would be a barren, inhospitable place.

Agents: Jon Thurley and Patricia Preece
Nanny and Sounding board: Barbara Laurie
Typists: Mike Shaw and Deborah
Copy Editor: Sara Peacock
Publisher and Midwife: Kate Lyall Grant, who discovered the true value of X

Thanks,

RD.

CHAPTER ONE

'He used her BAFTA award for part of the rape.'

Chief Inspector Boardman turned to stare at London's unforgiving skyline.

It never got any easier. He'd always thought it would but it hadn't. After thirty-four years on the force he was almost past caring. Now, instead of seeing the turbulence raging below him in the capital's dirty streets, he was gazing in his mind's eye at the deathly still purity of Loch Rannoch.

His intelligent, speckled grey eyes concealed thoughts of his retirement cottage as he nodded to his subordinate for more information.

The Detective Sergeant continued, 'At 9.15, before ten million viewers, she was presented with it. Between 11 and 1 a.m. it was re-presented at a private ceremony in her home.'

Boardman allowed the tasteless pun to escape. He'd been like that once, hiding fear with nonchalant sick humour. 'Will she live?' he asked matter-of-factly, still gazing into the night but watching his sergeant's reflection in the window. Osborne's bland features looked even more nondescript. If it hadn't been for the jagged scar along his cheekbone he would have resembled a blurred photograph.

The younger man nodded. 'She's lost a lot of blood. I hope her career's her life; she won't be having any children after this. It was certainly a big night for Beth Gamble.'

Boardman was familiar with the name. Who wasn't? Beth Gamble had exposed porn kings, emperors of fraud, and princes of deception with equal vigour and relentless enthusiasm. Her programme 'Take a Gamble' attracted a huge following. It was a simple format; take a sassy streetwise blonde and a public figure with a secret, stick a camera in his face, then blow the whole of his life into small nasty truths.

'Forensic's been through her like the clap: we have a hair sample,

1

dark brown, and there is sperm. All we need is someone to match it against.'

'Who reported it?' Boardman enquired, unimpressed by the swiftness of Osborne's conclusions. If only it was that easy. In his own experience things never were so simple: just hard graft, his old mentor had told him. As for luck, the concept never entered Boardman's logical mind. His father used to describe luck as the art of labouring under correct knowledge. Over the years, Boardman had come to realise that in criminal investigation there was no substitute for the step-by-solitary-step approach.

'A boyfriend, some TV guy – an American, Edward Maxwell – he produces Miss Gamble's programme. There'd been an argument earlier. He went round when he'd sobered up. Found the door open and her on the bedroom floor,' Osborne replied, flicking the pages of his incident notebook.

Boardman noted these details. 'Any chance he did it then changed his mind?'

The Sergeant considered. 'From what I saw, if he's acting he deserves an award more than Beth.'

It was always the way, whether it was an unidentified murder victim or a known rape victim. Within five minutes they became a person with a Christian name: a crusade.

'Has she come round yet?'

'No, Boss. I've got Grieves at the hospital. She's been into surgery for repairs; they do better stitch work than the Serious Crime Squad. As soon as she's awake he'll call it in. Do you want to handle it yourself?'

It was obviously important to someone that he did. It wasn't every night that a Chief Inspector was dragged from his North London bed to the Yard. But then it wasn't every night that a celebrity was raped in her own home. Boardman looked towards his Sergeant and cast one of his 'Is the Pope a Catholic?' looks before continuing.

'What about the Scenes of Crime Unit, do they know how he got in?'

Sgt Osborne hesitated. 'That's the problem. We've got our best lads on this one. They've been over the place twice. There's no sign of forced entry, not a loose window or slack sash in the entire place. Strangest thing of all though, guv, she doesn't live alone.'

Boardman raised thick eyebrows.

'So where was her flatmate?'

'No flatmate, guv – her father. She lives with her old man,' exclaimed Osborne.

'So where was her father then?' Boardman persisted, only just managing to contain his anger at this tooth-pulling exercise.

'In bed. Couldn't hear a thing even if she did scream,' Osborne replied cryptically.

'Get on with it,' demanded Boardman, 'this isn't a pub quiz.'

'Sorry, guv, he's got some sort of disease. She looks after him, apparently, with the help of a daily nurse, a Mrs Richardson. It was her night off. In any event, she's been spoken to and said that the father had been sedated earlier, which normally knocks him out until morning. Our boys found him still asleep.'

'What do you mean, "even if she did scream"?'

'Neighbours heard nothing unusual and no evidence of a gag. Either she can't even have heard him get into her room or she was quite happy until he smacked her out.'

Boardman doodled on the pad; it was a habit he was renowned for. 'So it's either someone she knows, and knows well, or it's a class burglar who's going to repeat if we don't stop him.' There was another angle that had sprung to Boardman's mind. 'Alternatively, Sergeant Osborne, Mrs Boardman may have this one taped before we've got the microphone in place.'

Osborne looked puzzled at the guv's reference to his wife. Boardman went on, 'Have you ever watched Beth Gamble's programme?'

Osborne shook his head, then offered, 'Well, once or twice. It's all politicians caught with their hands in the till or down a hooker's pants, isn't it?'

Boardman continued to draw the concentric circles he favoured upon the pad. 'Miss Gamble is in no way prejudiced. She's exposed people from doctor to social worker, priest to banker. The programme takes on any subject that guarantees viewers. It's the rapist's use of the award . . . somebody could have a grudge. It's not the fact he screwed her, it's what he screwed her with.' Boardman recalled the reaction of his wife Fiona after their slumber was abruptly curtailed. She, like him, had developed an immunity over the years to the sickness of violent crime and although her sympathy was implicit she nevertheless expressed surprise that something like this hadn't happened before to that poor young girl.

He let the thought hover. 'Is there anything else I need to know? Has she said anything since she was picked up?'

Osborne shuffled through the small but growing file of preliminary statements on the desk, eventually retrieving a single piece of paper.

'There was this, boss.' Boardman nodded for him to continue. 'The ambulance crew arrived at 1.27 a.m. Beth had been placed in the recovery position by the boyfriend, so she wasn't moving about, but when she was put on the stretcher she muttered something about, "Crawling, he was crawling," then that was it. She was straight into surgery after that; not another word.'

Boardman considered the information. Was the attacker crippled in some way? Had she injured him during the attack? He leant forward. 'Osborne, how do we know the boyfriend? What's his name?' He picked up his notes, searching for the information. 'Maxwell. Teddy Maxwell. Is he telling the truth about going home? Have we checked it out?'

Osborne looked annoyingly smug: it was one of his many irredeemable features. 'Already done. The driver of the limo checks the story out. He dropped Maxwell off, went back to the restaurant, picked her up, left her at home at 11.30 p.m., saw nothing suspicious. The limo was checked back in at 2 a.m. We've got the statement. A bloke called Middleton. Been driving for the limo firm for a couple of years.'

Boardman rubbed his chin. Already a harvest of stubble was pushing through his skin. 'I still want a further word with the boyfriend. Where is he?'

Osborne stood up, aware that for now his usefulness was concluded. 'Where he should have been at one o'clock this morning – at her bedside.'

Boardman picked up the telephone and asked his driver to wait at the front of the building.

Within five minutes the briefing was complete; there would be time for analysis later. Now he had to try to speak to Beth Gamble. As he straightened from behind his regulation teak desk his left knee cracked loudly, reminding him that the invitation he'd received from the consultant orthopaedic surgeon was long overdue. Hospitals! He hated them. He limped across the jaded green carpet, ignoring Osborne's ingratiating frowns of sympathy, in the knowledge that the canteen grapevine would later hear his health was deteriorating faster than the department's budget. He limped a little harder, hoping the news would reach Mrs Wilson, the cook: after all, her sympathy manifested itself in those little chocolate doughnuts made especially for him. There were some privileges that came with rank after all.

Anyone viewing the slight, well-dressed man limping along the greying corridors of the Yard might have thought him too soft around the edges to belong in this place. Lately Boardman had thought the same.

The car cut through the hammers and nails of another capital-city rainfall. The night was peopled only with late adulterers who'd stayed too late, and were now whisking home before discovery. Osborne for once was quiet. Boardman watched the moving picture show through the rivulets of rain mapping their way across the window. They passed over the triumphantly glowing Battersea Bridge where it straddled the Thames. A boat party was in progress below: he could see dancing bodies, framed through the condensation on the vessel's large windows against the brash fluorescent disco lights. On the south bank the formidable old power station stood out against the inky blue backdrop like an ancient fortress.

The car made its way through the streets quickly, not having to contend with the daytime traffic, and soon they were approaching the hospital's entrance. The driver broke the journey's silence, leaning forward to speak into the radio. Boardman wiped a space on the window with the back of his hand.

'The front or the back, guv?' Osborne queried. Someone's blabbed it already. Grievesy reckons one of the ambulance crews earned themselves a few quid. There's a dozen tabloids there already.'

The vehicle slowed to accommodate his answer. Boardman sank back in the seat.

'Osborne, you go in the front. It's a no-comment entrance. Give your rank and confirm that she's OK. Drop me off at the back first. I don't want this to have any higher profile that it already has.' He was aware that his involvement might cause panicked speculation. Boardman had put away the M25 Bad Samaritan for life, and the Blackheath Beast had received a recommendation of forty-five years minimum. No, if they saw him they'd jump on the serial bandwagon. The car pulled up smoothly at the hospital's decaying back entrance. Grieves, waiting in the shadows, flapped his arms, attempting to shrug off the freezing rain.

'Over here, sir.'

Boardman stepped out of the car and muttered to the red-faced Constable, 'Be quiet, man. If I can see you so can any journalist with a single neutron for a brain. Has she woken up yet?'

The young officer, a porcine victim to his love of fried food, dropped his voice to a conspiratorial whisper. 'She's been stirring for a bit, sir, but she's doped up. The doctors say we can't speak to her till morning.'

Boardman pushed open the doors that led to the kitchen; he'd been through this place more times than its patients had had hot dinners. 'She'll speak to me if I ask the right questions.'

They continued on to the service lift, having grappled with several sets of drooping, clear-plastic door ribbons, hanging like forlorn Christmas decorations. Eventually they came to a private ward where a uniformed officer stood and saluted.

'Who's in there with her?' Boardman asked, impressed with the officer's smartness.

'Mr Maxwell, the boyfriend, sir.'

'You mean Mr Maxwell, the suspect,' Boardman murmured as he forced the door open.

Inside, the antiseptic anonymity of the ward was broken only by the large burly figure of a man, dressed in a loose-fitting slubbed silk suit and black turtleneck, the stubble on his oversized chin more deliberate than incidental to the time of day. He held a pillow in his hands, and was bending over the still figure on the bed. He turned at the noise the door had made. 'I was trying to make her more comfortable.' The transatlantic yawn of his voice was a story in itself.

'That's what the nurses are here for, Mr Maxwell,' said Boardman curtly to the American.

Maxwell placed the pillow carefully under his girlfriend's head. The face that had turned so many remote controls to her programme was as swollen as a gargoyle. The lividity of the extensive bruising resembled a suicide by hanging. Boardman moved closer and examined her features. He made a promise to himself this was his last investigation and he would ensure its success. The room was silent until a voice croaked out from behind the hideous mask, 'Teddy, Teddy, is that you?'

CHAPTER TWO

The sides of her mouth felt as thick as T-bone steaks. It was as if a berserk plastic surgeon had grafted ugly pounds of fat to her usually delicate cheekbones, downward to the sore point of her chin. God knows what she looked like. From the other side of a long room she could hear Teddy's voice, increasing in volume! '. . . more comfortable.' She wished she was. The crust around her eyes separated and light, harsh and uncaring, poured in, stinging like acid. Her eyelids snapped together again with the force of a determined clam.

'Beth, oh Beth, Jesus, I . . .' Maxwell began and then trailed off. The silence made her force the lids apart, revealing familiar deep-set marine-blue eyes which now were cracked like broken porcelain around the irises. He sat, barely suppressing the spasms that contorted his large frame.

She tried to speak. 'It's all right, Teddy.' Her lips ignored the commands of her brain to articulate properly and the words rolled into one. Maxwell's eyes glanced briefly towards her, then away to his feet like an embarrassed child – or was it a guilty schoolboy? Boardman couldn't be sure from his angle. Beth attempted to ori-entate herself. The whiteness was a clue to a hospital, the drip in her arm evidence of a doctor's involvement; she knew where, but how?

'Miss Gamble.' She turned her head painfully, as a small, dapper, slightly greying man blurred into view. 'Miss Gamble, my name is Boardman, Chief Inspector Boardman. Do you feel well enough to answer any questions?' Beth stared at the man, and wondered why the police were involved. Suddenly an image thrust through her searching mind. She blinked hard and long, trying to force the vision away, but it surged on, blinding to her but unseen by the faces around her. She gazed vacantly and helplessly into Boardman's broad and honest features. 'My father,' she whispered but it didn't sound like her own voice.

7

Boardman continued, 'It's very important we speak to you as soon as possible if we're to catch the person responsible for this. You know how vital time can be with an investigation.' He nodded, trying to force her to respond in the same way. 'You don't have to speak, just indicate yes or no with your head, all right?'

Beth indicated she understood.

'Do you know what happened tonight?'

Beth moved slightly, then felt the fiery pain between her legs. Tears sprang to her eyes as she recollected. She nodded.

'How many were there? Tell me to stop when I get it right,' Boardman persisted. 'One?'

She moved, nodding her head painfully. A tress of golden hair fell across her face, the ends matted with blood. Maxwell quickly moved to her and flicked it gently over her ear. She flinched away from him. Boardman continued speaking, never shifting his eyes from hers.

'One man, and did you let him in?'

Beth remembered being in bed, just drifting off, thoughts full of the awards ceremony and another argument with Teddy. Lying with her head turned away from the bedroom door then feeling a rush of movement, a hard blow to her face as she attempted to turn around. She shook her head vigorously.

'Did you know him, Miss Gamble?' She watched as the policeman turned towards Teddy. 'If you did, there's nothing to be afraid of. Now, did you know the man who attacked you?' Maxwell looked sharply at Boardman before they both turned to Beth for a response.

She thought about the question. During her conscious moments throughout the attack, she could remember some guttural comments as he was thrusting into her, about 'ruining things' and 'leaving well enough alone', and a tone in the voice, a familiar timbre of menace, she had heard before. But where?

She moved her head in a neutral way and tried, despite the pain, to shrug her shoulders. Boardman quickly interpreted her confusion and pushed further.

'You're not sure. Did he know you? Did he say anything to indicate that?'

He had laughed. The bastard had laughed. She was face down on the bed and could see a gloved hand – an expensive glove – reach over her head and pick up the award.

'You fucked people to get this, now it's pay-back time.' Beth shuddered at the memory and the pain. She began to nod harder and harder, a thin whimpering began deep down; the words came out in a scream. 'Yesh, yesh.' The thin, white linen sheet wafted upwards with her sudden movement, uncovering her slender, tanned legs etched with the rapist's frantic scratches.

'Stop it, stop it now!' Teddy shouted at her side, leaning towards the policeman. Boardman swallowed hard, then looked into her eyes.

'I'm sorry, Beth. I've got to ask these questions. Was he from one of your programmes? Could he have been? Just answer me that and I'll leave.'

Teddy Maxwell spoke again. 'Boardman, you've pushed this as far as I'm gonna let it go. Now get out. I know a lot of very important people, they're gonna know about you. That's it, end of interview.'

He ignored Maxwell, concentrating instead on holding Beth's gaze. 'Come on, Beth, give us a lead. Did you expose him?'

She thought about it. There had been so many over the three years the show had run. Clergymen, boy-scout leaders, trades union officials and teachers; it had to be someone from the programme. She forced her painful lips apart.

'I shink sho.' Her tongue felt the front of her mouth where her even, white teeth felt slack. She closed her eyes as the door burst open and a furious-looking nurse barked for them all to get out. As her visitors departed, Beth tried to catch the nurse with an appreciative smile as she gently and expertly went about straightening the bed. Whilst the nurse cooed soothing words Beth could see the look in her face; it was not one that she was used to. Normally people stared when she walked down the street or ate at a restaurant, but no longer. Her status didn't matter to this woman.

Shortly after, Boardman stood in the corridor with Osborne, holding a handkerchief to his face in an attempt to obliterate the strong smell of harsh disinfectant rising from a stainless steel bucket at their feet. A disinterested cleaner stood idly by gossiping with a brown-overalled porter. The policeman glanced in their direction from above his temporary mask. The door to the ward sister's office opened and Boardman's number one suspect emerged and strode aggressively towards the two policemen.

'You'll pay for that, do you hear? I'll make you pay for it.'

Boardman turned to the large, red-faced American. 'Don't you want this man picked up, Mr Maxwell, or are your feelings of guilt clouding your judgement?'

He side-stepped as Maxwell loomed towards him and two uniformed officers appeared swiftly and took Teddy by the arms.

'Now if you'll be good enough to calm down, we may be able to eliminate you from our enquiries. If you'll just answer a few questions,' Boardman said in confidently measured tones. Teddy Maxwell looked stunned that he could even figure in their enquiry to begin with.

'That's better, Mr Maxwell. Now,' said Boardman, turning to the nurse who had joined the growing crowd with a frown of disapproval plastered over her shiny black forehead, 'if you can lend us the use of a room for half an hour, we'll get out of your hair.'

The sister led the way, shaking her head. 'You know I don't know what this city is coming to,' she muttered. 'I'd be safer back with the Yardies in Jamaica.' Boardman turned towards her. She ignored him, talking more for her own benefit and practising the story she would tell her friend the next day. 'She's the second woman we've had in tonight, who wasn't safe in her own home.' She didn't wait for a response as she threw open the door to a tatty medical storeroom. 'This'll have to do for you.'

Inside, the wastage of a hundred inaccurate supply requisitions leant against the walls.

'Have a stool, Mr Maxwell.' Boardman looked around at the slightly unstable black vinyl and chrome affairs in the corner of the room, placed precariously close to a bulging shelf. He selected what appeared to be the most comfortable and Osborne turned the remaining chair with its back towards their guest and straddled it.

'Now, Mr Maxwell,' said Boardman, leaning back. 'You were with Beth at the awards ceremony then you both went to a restaurant, correct?' The American nodded. 'Then you had an argument, a very public disagreement. What was it about?'

'Am I under arrest or something? Aren't you guys supposed to caution me or beat me up until I confess to something I didn't do? That is the English way, isn't it? But then again I'm a Yank not a mick.' Maxwell's face coloured.

'The argument?' insisted Boardman.

The American put his hands in his pockets, and raised himself to his full height, then walked to the back of the room and leaned against the wall.

'Look,' he shrugged, 'it was just a TV thing. A presenter gets an award, all of a sudden she thinks she's the best producer in town. It was – how would the British put it? – an artistic difference.'

'We might also call it professional jealousy. Did you receive an award last night?'

The furious producer pulled away from the wall.

'It wasn't like that. I know what you're suggesting. Beth's award was for the whole team.' Boardman took out a packet of cigarettes and offered one to Teddy. Gratefully he took one, fished a lighter out of his pocket, then turned the packet towards Boardman.

'No, thanks, disgusting habit. Did you and Beth have sex last night, before you went to the ceremony?'

Teddy inhaled lengthily before smiling slightly. 'Though it's got damn' all to do with you, the answer is no, we did not.'

'And the driver can confirm when he dropped you off?'

Maxwell let the cigarette fall to the floor. 'You'd better ask him. But then again, you already have, haven't you? Otherwise I'd be down at the station now whilst you and Pugsley here double-team me. Jesus, sometimes I'm so stupid.' He opened the door to leave.

'Mr Maxwell, I do hope you've told us the truth. I know how flexible that concept is in your line of work. It could be very messy if you've misled us.' The door closed on the last syllable.

Boardman stood, walked to the offending cigarette, picked it up with a sigh, and placed it in the small grey bin.

'He's hiding something about last night. I'm not sure what, but it'll come out, these things do.' The two men vacated the gloomy conference room, and emerged into the even gloomier corridor. 'Osborne, leave Grieves here to keep an eye on things. Ring the forensic lab for me in the morning. I want them to run a check on the semen sample.'

Osborne started to speak but Boardman continued, 'I'm aware we have nothing to match it against yet, but the question is, how many samples of semen have they found?'

CHAPTER THREE

Andrew Buchan had never been a heavy sleeper and last night had been even worse than usual. He opened his eyes and checked the insipid glow of the digital alarm clock, one of the few concessions he had made towards the rampant march of home technology. It was 5.15 a.m. and the neatly stacked pile of papers next to his bed glared at him mockingly. His recent elevation to Permanent Private Secretary had brought with it the long dreamed of privileges and responsibilities of high office but the obligatory bedtime reading did little to cure his insomnia. He stretched out and retrieved one of the blue folders, indicating high priority by Home Office criteria, switched on the lamp and re-read the summary page he had prepared for the Home Secretary.

The perennial problem of overcrowding in Britain's prisons and young offender institutions occupied the first lengthy paragraph of his report. The remainder outlined recent intelligence either intercepted through the screening of inmates' mail or gathered from the Association of Prison Officers. The conclusion predicted a winter of discontent, something that the Government – and in particular his superior, Anthony Palmer-Dent – could ill afford whilst riding a strong law-and-order manifesto into the election next year.

Buchan signed the document, replaced the folder, took another from the pile, and made his way through to the meticulously over-designed galley kitchen of his Westminster flat. He prepared his usual sickly yellow egg-nog and flipped through the pages of his detailed schedule for the day ahead: a 7 a.m. meeting with Palmer-Dent was first on the list.

Since his Minister's appointment almost a year ago, Buchan had tipped him to be next leader of the country. A relentless energy coupled with an innate instinct for political survival marked the Home Secretary as a statesman bound for the world stage. He was not a man to be interrupted. Often, when conversation with him was

13

teased in a certain direction which might displease or offend, he had the ability subtly to disengage and penetrate beyond his inquisitor's stare, with his deep-set brown eyes. Buchan had been present on many occasions when Palmer-Dent was described as a visionary or a font of inspiration; mainly by the party faithful, but occasionally and begrudgingly by his contemporaries in Parliament.

The great man's idiosyncratic nature was perhaps best illustrated by the ancient chest that travelled with him wherever he spoke: he stood astride its iron hinges, delivering alternate doses of oily rhetoric and genuine intent. It was that intent which worried Buchan as he glanced through the agenda. What would the Home Secretary's reaction be to the deepening crisis in the prison system against a background which included a Treasury determinedly seeking further cutbacks, and Palmer-Dent's own publicly declared war on crime?

Buchan slipped into his regulation grey chalk-stripe and eased into his second cup of Earl Grey at precisely 6.20 a.m. It normally took him ten minutes to complete the *Telegraph* crossword before leaving for Westminster, but this morning something caught his attention: a small paragraph in the *News in Brief* column. It read, SERIAL KILLER: POLICE PROBE BUT NOT TOO DEEP. Instinctively, he turned to the piece on page three penned by Jon Preece, a notoriously drunken hack whose self-declared sole purpose in journalism was to embarrass the Home Office.

Deep furrows appeared across Buchan's brow as he began scanning the article:

Evidence emerging from police forces as far afield as Humberside and Bristol suggests that the country is set to witness the reign of a brutal vigilante-style killer.

The bodies of the victims, all male and of varying ages, were found in a severely mutilated condition. One senior detective involved in the investigation described the crime scenes as the worst he had witnessed in over twenty years on the force.

The strikingly similar nature of the attacks almost certainly points to the work of one killer.

Although the identities of the murdered men have not yet been released it is thought that they all carried substantial criminal records involving violence and dishonesty. Police sources have revealed they are baffled by the murders and are appealing for public support to bring the perpetrator to justice.

In startling contrast, the Home Office, when asked for comments, appeared to be treating the matter with supreme indifference. Whilst stressing that it is not policy to comment upon any individual case, a junior minister suggested that this was not the sort of situation which would ordinarily arouse interest at the higher levels, given the status of the victims.

Detective Inspector Paul Richardson, who is co-ordinating the investigation, endorsed the Home Office attitude when confiding that he has been allocated 'less than the usual complement' of manpower to deal with the case and admitted that so far the public response had been 'underwhelming'.

Buchan made a mental note to contact Scotland Yard after he had spoken to the Home Secretary; Sop he might be but Preece did have an uncanny knack for creating scandal.

Seven days later a lifeless grey October sky hung heavily around the concrete and glass tower of Metropolitan Police Headquarters. The office of the Head of Intelligence Gathering and Pro-active Policing was situated on the fourteenth floor of Scotland Yard. The outer door opened straight into a small reception area used occasionally for gatherings. The door beyond that was strictly off limits to all but a select few. Today that door was firmly closed. The room behind it was packed: Commander Gerald Molineux – the Head of IGPAP – was in a meeting with his three assistants, two nameless MI6 agents and Andrew Buchan. The mood was intense and the room quiet for several minutes at a time, the silence interrupted only by the constant hum of traffic and the occasional insistent car alarm.

Molineux was perfectly suited to his position, being blessed with the patience of a chess player and the calmness of a priest. His black hair glistened with Brylcreem. Although his fifty-one years had left the odd wrinkle his olive skin, at a lean six foot he looked in good shape. Though he was married with a child he conceded only a passing interest in family life. His deeply recessed eyes, almost black when in focus, intent on the importance of his mission. This was his life: operating at the highest level of the British police force, commanding the covert operations team of IGPAP, an autonomous group of highly skilled intelligence officers which he had spent years manipulating into position. He had handpicked every member of his squad, physical prowess often giving place to high-brow intellectualism. The major responsibility of IGPAP was, as the name implied, to fight crime by using intelligence analysis, and then act positively upon conclusions reached. Only the most senior of police officers around the country were aware of the facilities at his disposal and most of these resented not only Molineux's arrogance but also the size of his budget.

He hadn't expected the telephone call from Buchan but considered the latter's interest to be a prime opportunity to demonstrate the effectiveness of his team. Buchan had informed him that the Home Office was very interested in a swift end to the vigilante killers. Whoever it was couldn't be allowed to take the law into their own hands and would receive a high-profile prosecution. That was music to Molineux's ears.

The morning's papers had been flooded with speculative comment and the hackneyed moral rantings of various commentators, resurrecting the arguments for and against cleaning up the streets. The political dilemma, he concluded, was that most right-minded individuals wouldn't care whether some toerags were being wiped out; perhaps a few of them would actually applaud the deed. After all, it was a great deal cheaper than spending countless millions keeping the criminal fraternity incarcerated for years on end. Nevertheless, Molineux had a job to do and as long as it raised his own profile the politics of it were a matter of supreme indifference to him.

It was a difficult meeting; progress on the investigations was slow. Molineux continued to brief the politician's emissary, making no effort to hide his growing anxiety as he outlined the intelligence received so far.

'In the previous three months we have recorded three murders with such strikingly similar features that Special Branch decided to involve us to consolidate and ventilate theories. Firstly, we are dealing with a nationwide problem: Bristol, Edinburgh, the last a week ago in Hull. Whilst it is probable that all victims have died at the hands of one assailant, we have not ruled out the possibility of several individuals being involved.'

'Why several?' Buchan enquired in his clipped Oxbridge tones, taking notes for his meeting with the HS later.

'A lone assassin could have carried out the murders, their timing and geographical spread allow for that scenario, but it is the sheer professionalism of the entire enterprise that marks this as a collaboration.'

'You mean there is more?'

'I'll come to that in a moment,' Molineux answered.

'What about the victims? Do they tie together?' asked Buchan.

Molineux nodded to one of his assistants, Bill Lever. He'd been with Molineux for three years: tall to the point of gianthood his gargantuan appearance masked a quick and nimble brain. Lever reached into the black filing cabinet behind him and began distributing hand-outs with photographs. Buchan caught his breath quickly as he glimpsed the first black and white print. A naked man lay prostrate on the ground with a hole where once there had been genitalia. A single black orchid was placed beside the hole in his head. The other two victims showed an identical *modus operandi*: the flower, the single bullet hole and the mutilation.

'So what's the proposition then? Two or three perverts working together?' Buchan enquired.

'Improbable,' interrupted Lever. 'Serial killers very rarely work in packs. Only ever been one recorded case, in El Salvador in 1984, when two transvestite lovers with a passion for kiddies' flesh . . .'

'All right, that's enough, Lever,' interrupted Molineux sharply. He had never relished the details his eager assistant so loved to regurgitate. 'The people we're dealing with are sophisticated. They have a detailed knowledge of police procedures and forensics. No witnesses and hardly any physical evidence at the murder scenes.'

'There must be something,' said Buchan, eyeing the summary on the desk before him. 'What about the flower? Surely there's an angle on that?'

'Afraid not. We've had it analysed and it's a common variety spray-painted black. We believe it is meant to resemble the infamous poisonous Peruvian black orchid.'

'Some calling card,' Buchan replied. 'Anything else?'

'Only the MO,' replied Molineux, closing his eyes and rubbing his temples slowly. 'Though each victim was known to have a criminal record for violence and dishonesty, none had previous convictions for sexual offences, which was our first line of enquiry.'

'And what was your next?' asked Buchan.

'Take a look at these.' Molineux nodded to Phil Anderson who rocked forward out of his chair and indicated to Lever to dim the lights and close the vertical blinds. The soft humming of the overhead projector began and on to the plain white wall appeared the image of page 32 of *The Times* dated 20 August.

Under Births, Deaths and Announcements the following passage had been highlighted in fluorescent marker pen:

Dunn, Patrick Michael
2 September 1954–2 August 1994, 10.22 p.m. RIP.
'Give not the power of thy soul to a woman
lest she enter upon thy strength and thou
be confounded'

Ecclesiasticus 9:2

'Each of these classifieds was placed the day before the victim's death,' Molineux continued from the darkness. 'We can find no record of any other Patrick Michael Dunn with the same date of birth. The early announcement of his murder indicates the suspects are confident of their abilities.' The image flicked rapidly to a similar page, dated 17 September 1994:

Phillips, Martin Charles
4 May 1961–18 September 1994, 3.19 p.m. RIP.
'Depart not from a wise and good wife whom thou
has gotten in the fear of the Lord; for the grace of
her modesty is above Gold'

Ecclesiasticus 7:21

Molineux spoke again. 'Phillips was found dead by his wife at 3.30 p.m. that day.'

'What did the local CID find out?' Buchan enquired.

'They ruled out the wife. She had a solid alibi,' Lever interjected.

'They found nothing at the scene, not even a fibre lift,' Molineux continued.

'What about ballistics?' Buchan pressed.

'Nothing amazing. A 45 high-impact bullet manufactured by Smith & Wesson. They sell thousands of them.'

'So we have a problem,' Buchan stated.

'You could say that,' murmured Molineux and continued smoothly, 'To indicate how much of a problem, I've instructed an outsider.' He glanced around the room, daring a response to this unusual event. IGPAP was known primarily for its secretive nature and the very concept of civilian assistance was alien to its ethos. Molineux, however, prided himself on innovatory thinking and the introduction of more brain power to the unit would only serve to enhance his own reputation. Results were all that mattered to him, whatever the cost.

He turned to his intercom and spoke to his secretary. 'Send in our visitor, Miss Wagnall.' He turned back to the gathering before rising from behind his desk. 'Gentlemen, meet Mr Ivan De Haus, criminal psychologist with the University of Oxford.' Lever opened the door and a thin man, with the smallest round eyes, walked nervously into the room. He wore the uniform of academia: corduroy jacket fastened high to the neck, with worn and faded elbow patches, stone-washed denims, black Doc Martens and tortoiseshell round-rim glasses. He glanced furtively around the room and nodded his greetings. De Haus had been puzzled when he received the invitation from Scotland Yard. Unlike many of his colleagues at universities around the country, he had never courted a professional liaison with the police, but when he had first spoken with Molineux forty-eight hours before his appetite had been well and truly whetted. His specialism was religious cults, a topic which had fascinated him ever since, as a student, he'd witnessed the growing numbers of zealots practising their oratorical prowess among the liberated love-children of sixties England.

'Mr De Haus, I'm afraid, is not the bearer of good tidings. Gentlemen, I'm sure you'll find his assessment of the situation enlightening. Mr De Haus.' Molineux invited the small man to stand in front of the conference desk where he assumed a balletic and donnish pose, gently squeaking a cloth over his spectacles.

'Who understands women?' De Haus asked abruptly. The room remained silent. His eyes narrowed when no one volunteered an answer. 'I didn't expect a response.' He paused. 'You may have thought the question flippant but there is a reason. Both the quotations you have just seen are directly relevant to the issue of men's attitude to women. Take a look at the third.'

'It was dated 15 October.

Gallagher, Ronald George

21 January 1956 – 16 October 1994, 8.43 p.m. RIP.

'And love is the keeping of her laws;

and the giving heed unto her laws

is the assurance of incorruption'

Book of Wisdom 6:19

'Whoever is responsible for these crimes is clearly of the belief that they are acting under a religious mandate. This indicates only one thing – that the killing will go on and will not stop until it is forced to. The motivation is neither financial nor for sexual gratification. It is simply for justice.' He continued, filling the silence, 'They believe only in a higher morality based upon ideals of divine justice. Their law is their own.'

'What are you saying? That these people are some sort of vigilante God Squad?' Buchan sneered folding his arms.

'More or less, Mr Buchan, although I trust my own explanation wasn't so crude. A serial killer does not know when to stop. A serial killer cannot stop. Once the first venture is successful, he or she believes themself invincible to detection.'

'I was led to believe that your speciality was religious cults.' Buchan waited for a reply.

'Many mass murderers have claimed a mandate from God. The Yorkshire Ripper saw himself as a messenger from the Almighty. To this day he insists that his actions were inspired from above. I have studied several similar cases: in those the slayings continued. This is a *Jihad*, a holy war if you like, against a specific group of men.'

Molineux took up the briefing:

'The common denominator is that the victims had all recently been acquitted of rape where the defence was consensual sexual intercourse. This coincidence cannot be ignored.'

'And?' Buchan pushed.

'And so at least we know the target group.'

'How many people are currently awaiting trial on a rape charge?' Buchan asked.

'Hundreds, and rising every day,' replied Molineux. 'There are presently 956 of them claiming consent. We simply don't have the resources to cover them all if they're acquitted.'

'Your budget is stretched already, Molineux,' reminded Buchan.

'Exactly, sir, that's why we need our own target.' Molineux hated referring to the insignificant civil servant as 'sir', but whilst he held the cords of the puppets, Buchan clenched the purse strings. He wasn't sure how Buchan would respond to the idea of setting up a target; it was close to the political bone, breach of civil rights being a hot issue these days. Nevertheless, he had to ensure that Buchan was in agreement; after all, he was the one who would have to sell the idea to the Home Secretary later. Molineux was pleased with Buchan's reply.

'Live bait,' he responded. 'Interesting. Out of the 956 are there any certainties?'

'Even if I were a gambling man, I wouldn't bet on a jury's verdict,' said Molineux, thrusting home his case.

'Explain,' Buchan demanded curtly.

Before replying, the Commander looked around the room, knowing once this boat was pushed out he would either sail or sink with it. He answered, 'We must take the matter out of the jury's hands.'

CHAPTER FOUR

Since childhood, De Haus had hated trains and the whole macho myth of growing up to be an engine driver. He had never wished to open a toy locomotive to see what made it tick. But people . . . they were a different matter.

He sat on the London to Oxford train watching the level of his coffee move in tandem with the undulations of the standard class carriage. He jotted his thoughts on the portable personal computer he now favoured after decades of scribbling on the corpses of dead trees. De Haus had placed himself on the inside seat, his overcoat bundled in the one opposite. [The two remaining seats were uninviting enough; if not, then an unsmiling glance would solve the problem of unwanted companionship.] His journey was taking him back to his bachelor rooms within the college.

When he had been approached by Molineux to join the think tank on the murders, he had been secretly delighted that his capabilities had been acknowledged by such serious-minded men. The briefing had been adequate if a little trite. He was asked to view the available data on the case with an eye to the religious connotations of the newspaper advertisements. It was his task to discover the intent behind their selection and to attempt to project what it was that the murderer sought. He was meant to climb inside the killer's brain.

His response had been one of reluctance until the matter of remuneration had been adequately ventilated in that embarrassed English way. De Haus used the true Englishman's distaste for plain speaking as a weapon in the negotiations, and used it to great effect. His reward was not money, it was worth much more than that: there were many documents on religious sects that were classified and so beyond his reach; but not any more. The promise that he could wallow in this forbidden research material to his heart's content was a heady brew for a man who trawled the computer internets of the

23

world, searching for the story or tragedy that would make his name internationally known.

That was before he had read the files on the present case: this was the one, he knew it. De Haus had worked feverishly on his appraisal of the killer's morals and intentions. It was not done out of any personal duty he felt owing to Molineux, but because it would form the very vertebrae of his finest published piece of work.

De Haus sipped the cooling caffeine from the Styrofoam cup, noting the similarity in taste between the coffee and its container.

They would refuse permission to publish his findings, but only if he asked first. The Official Secrets Act would be waved in his face, but that ill-considered piece of legislation would only project his work more firmly into the public eye and mind. Flicking a search command on the slim portable, he accessed his private conclusions on the case material the murders had provided.

The quotations were a sideswipe at man's mistreatment of women. They also highlighted the wrath that such treatment would incur. That did not necessarily mean that it was a woman at the heart of these murders: it could be a transsexual who saw himself as a woman or a schizophrenic whose other half raged at the beastliness of men's darker side, but De Haus had discounted both of these theories, at least for the moment. He would accept at face value the feminine basis of the murders. For now the safest premise was that a woman was responsible for these grisly deaths. The gender of the killer mattered little to him; what he sought was why they were happening at all. If he could discover the traumatic event that triggered the killings then the rest would fall into place.

The guard announced the train's arrival at Oxford. De Haus gathered his possessions up in his arms, then made his way to the very front of the snaking passenger train, so that he would not have a tiresome wait at the taxi stand.

He smiled to himself as he passed them in the snug, musty interior of the taxi: all the wet people, the silly people, those who thought they knew things, real things, important things about the world; secrets. De Haus had a secret, a big secret, and he was going to share it with a friend – at least, he hoped she would become one.

Back at the college, he climbed the creaking stairs to his rooms. The college porter granted him a surly nod from the ancient bulldog features that topped his skinny frame. The man had loathed De Haus since he had been a hard-working undergraduate. Even his subsequent pre-eminence in the college failed to meet with approval from the snobbish, bowler-hatted guardian of the college's standards. That would change.

De Haus removed the door key from its jingling companions and opened the aged oak door to his rooms. Reaching to his right he felt for the light switch and illuminated his home. From the outside, the blackened wood of the entrance promised the tasteful, comfy environment of a bachelor don: the shabby dressing gown, pipe and whisky decanter; the withered pot plants and dirty plates of another absentminded professor. But as the light bit into the darkness, De Haus looked with pride at the vast bank of computers that reflected his interest in their multi-hued screens. They were always running, always searching. Dutiful and obliging, they gave the scientist a sense of safety. They nestled neatly on the hand-crafted ash-blond work stations that he had ordered from Sweden the year before. Cursor keys winked lewdly at him with the promise of discovery. The rest of his rooms too reflected his preference for modernist functionalism.

He removed his coat and set to his task. At the briefing, De Haus had noted with interest the method used to access *The Times*' database. He had jotted the access codes down from the open file on the table in Molineux's office. Now he entered them on to the computer screen in front of him. The paper's 'menu' appeared. De Haus realised he could not afford to attempt contact through the Births, Deaths and Marriages section that the killers had used for their gruesome announcements. Instead, he flicked around until he found what he was searching for: the Personal columns.

He clicked his commands into the terminal, then read with satisfaction the accepted result from the newspaper's own computer. He had assumed that this woman, whoever she was, scanned the news, and hoped that her interest extended to the lonely hearts column. In order to maximise this possibility he ordered the advertisement to run for three weeks. If she did not read it personally then he anticipated that somebody close to her might. It was an unhappy compromise for such a conscientious man; it did, however, lessen the prospect of discovery by Molineux. Just before he switched the computer to another task he read over the details of the advertisement he had placed: 'Benign, Loyal Author, Considerate, Kind, Over (40), Rebellious, Caring, Horticulturist, Intelligent, Dependable, Beckons Enigmatic Woman. Any Replies, E-mail.'

De Haus doodled the first letter of each word into its true meaning. If this did not attract her, then she was not, and never would be, interested.

At 5.30 p.m., back in London, Buchan was in the process of formulating the following day's schedule with the Home Secretary who had just returned from the House of Commons, having endured Prime Minister's question time. The day had been as tough as they came on the political helter-skelter.

Buchan shifted uncomfortably in the green leather armchair and watched Anthony Palmer-Dent pacing up and down in front of the huge window. The Home Secretary raised his hand, tanned fingers contrasted sharply with the starched whiteness of his Gieves and Hawkes shirt collar as he rubbed the nape of his neck. It always seemed odd to Buchan when he witnessed private moments such as these from a man who had never publicly shown even the slightest indication of pressure or fatigue despite the enormity of his responsibility. At the moment, it seemed as if his burden was about to become heavier in the most unexpected manner.

'I watched him very closely throughout this afternoon's session in the House: he looked pale, and when we shook hands I could feel his skin was cold and clammy, like death cooled down. I'm sure he doesn't have long,' Palmer-Dent stated, staring out of the window at the graceful movement of the Thames below.

'Did you mention anything to him?' asked Buchan.

'Come on, Andrew, be sensible. You know as well as I do that the Prime Minister would be the last person to admit his health was failing.'

'I could speak to Tim Greenway,' offered Buchan, referring to the Prime Minister's Private Secretary.

'What, and have the entire Party think that I'm some sort of ambulance chaser? I'm trying to build castles, not dig graves,' Palmer-Dent exploded as he turned to face Buchan.

'All right, but surely someone should speak to the Party Chairman? We've only got eleven months to the election and there's no chance the voters will back him if they think he's about to die on them.'

'Do you think I don't know that? The point is some of his supporters weren't happy when he appointed me, but didn't envisage a situation like this at the time. If it becomes common knowledge that he is stepping aside then there's bound to be a leadership election. The 1922 aren't happy with the way this department's being run as it is,' Palmer-Dent said wearily, his usually calm expression etched with worry.

'I don't expect that they'll be much happier if the prisons blow up either. Did you get a chance to read my report?'

'Yes, set up a meeting with Her Majesty's Inspector, will you? We've got to ensure that our backs are covered if your scenario proves correct.'

'Already done: tomorrow at 1.30.'

'Good, you're getting the hang of things. Don't forget that if I do go upstairs Greenway will want to stay put. I'll do my best, of course, but a great deal depends upon how you handle the next few months.' Palmer-Dent looked directly at Buchan when delivering this blatant challenge. Buchan knew all too well that if Palmer-Dent became Prime Minister the incumbent top civil servant would fight to the death to stay at Number 10 and, not for the first time, Buchan felt the double-barrelled action of ambition and fear simultaneously pounding in his heart.

Palmer-Dent signalled the end of their meeting by reaching for his private telephone.

'There was something else, sir.'

'Yes?'

'It may not be important, but there's a bit of a stir going on about some sort of vigilante on the loose. A couple of hacks are asking questions. I've seen Molineux at Scotland Yard this morning: seems that they believe a woman or group of women are responsible, but as yet there's very little to go on.'

'That's all we need. What is he proposing to do about it?' Palmer-Dent asked distractedly.

'I'm not sure as yet, They're waiting for more intelligence.'

'It's about time he started to earn his keep. Tell him to do whatever it takes; we don't need any help to clean this country up. Now, if you'll excuse me, I'm going to take some soundings. Keep me posted.'

Buchan left the Home Secretary and headed back to his own office with a briefcase full of scorching political potatoes. One thing was for sure: if it all went sour he had to make sure that people knew he was only the waiter and not the chef.

CHAPTER FIVE

I t was Beth's fourth day in hospital when the clatter of cups and saucers pulled her from the dream. Her eyes were crusted with sleep and still oozing from their injuries. It was as if she was in a deep, childhood sleep, not having the strength nor the will to lift her head from the pillow. She tried harder, if not for herself for her father. I'll be fine, she told herself, willing the pain to a far-away place. She longed for the comforts of home, to be left alone, to be normal again: to wake up in the morning and know that she had something to do; to walk into her father's room and gently rouse him, then wait for the moment he would respond. To anyone else the flicker of his eyelashes would be imperceptible, but to Beth it was a reason to go on. Thinking of him made her nightmare seem less real and less important.

An auxiliary woke her 'sleeping policeman' with a tepid brew, then placed another by her side: 6 a.m. Teddy had gone an hour before, leaving her with a mirror. 'You might as well see the damage.' He refused to look at her for longer than a second or two before guilt dragged his gaze away. Poor Teddy. When the chips were down he would always be in Monte Carlo.

The argument hadn't really been about any one thing; it was a symptom of their dying affair. In reality he wanted the award more than he wanted her. A tear of self-pity swelled in her eye when she thought about him. Whatever it was that had happened that night, she couldn't help but feel that it was meant to happen. She toyed briefly with the idea that it was a punishment from above but quickly discarded the notion. She couldn't remember having done anything that would induce such furious retribution. Blaming Teddy wasn't going to help. When she had looked into his eyes earlier she knew it would never be the same again; they both knew it. The years they had spent working and loving together now seemed like part of someone else's life.

'How are you feeling this morning?' Grieves stretched his back as he spoke, forcing an expanse of stomach to his shirt buttons' busting point. Beth's eyelids flickered. She wasn't sure how she felt about anything at the moment. 'Have you remembered anything else?' His hazel eyes fixed for a moment on her swollen features, then swept away. 'All these flowers have come for you.' Beth moved her head slowly to the side. Several bouquets broke the drabness of the room.

Grieves moved a little closer, brushing past the cellophane wrapping, crinkling crisply. The sound seemed to amplify in the stillness of the room. Years of combat on the rugby field gave him the look of a nightclub doorman which belied the kind and gentle police officer that he was. He adopted his friendliest expression, cocking his head to one side, and said, 'Mr Boardman would like to speak to you again.' He could see the displeasure on her face. It was obvious this girl had been through a living nightmare. He quickly went on, retrieving his crumpled jacket, 'That's when you feel up to it. Just let me know. Now I'm gonna get some breakfast,' he added as cheerfully as possible before leaving the room in pursuit of his daily intake of high cholesterol.

Beth tried to sit up; the stitching stopped her in the attempt. She slumped back. What was the use of a cup of tea if you couldn't drink it? Looking around the room again she felt a warm sense of appreciation that so many friends and well-wishers had bothered at least to brighten her waking hours with such beautiful bouquets and cards. Her memories of hospital now, however, would never change. Only twice before had she dwelt in their antiseptic interiors and both visits retained a special place in her mind. The first had been as a very young child, having swallowed a dose of household detergent. In fact she hadn't swallowed it, she had simply pretended to do so in order to follow Lucy, her best friend, who had been admitted for a tonsil operation. She half-smiled at the memory of her mother's expression when her ruse had been discovered. Beth's crocodile tears had turned to real ones when her father smacked her for the first and only time. Her mother had told her later that she was bound to end up on the stage. Not a bad guess, Mum, she thought. Help me now while you look down from above.

Her other experience of hospital virtually robbed her of her father. A negligent surgeon, operating to correct a simple intestinal problem, had left him paralysed and cerebrally impaired. With the determination that had become her trademark as an investigative reporter Beth doggedly pursued the medical profession until it was forced to admit liability. Poor brain-damaged Daddy would know nothing of her present predicament, just as he would have heard nothing on the night it happened.

Thoughts of her family disappeared as quickly as they had arrived and the memory of that night intruded painfully once more. It had started so well. The Armani dress paid for by Paxton TV, the limousine ride, champagne and Teddy. It was all so right. She had believed herself invincible, but her rapist had put a stop to that. Beth shook at the thought of him, of what he had done. Before her mind could dwell on it any further, the door opened and Grieves reappeared with a doctor who looked painfully young.

'Miss Gamble. Did you manage to get any sleep last night?' She nodded. She had. 'You're going to be in pain for some time. We'll do what we can to ease that for you, but whatever we do it's still going to hurt. Now I want you to take this pill, then rest again.' He turned to the eating policeman. 'Can you sit outside? She'll be able to sleep better if you're not here.' Beth shook her head painfully.

The drug was already kicking in. The doctor's concerned face began to pulse and retract as her lids started to droop, and she fell into a deep sleep.

There was no telling how much time the narcotic had stolen from her when she felt a downward pressure on the mattress to her side.

'Beth? Beth, can you hear me?' Her eyes opened in response to the familiar sound; her nose told her it was lunchtime. His big bearded face held a gentle smile. 'Jesus, you look terrible, Beth.' Typical Fergus Finn. He'd been her cameraman since the start. Maybe it was looking through a lens all his life that made him so blunt. He always said that, like a camera, he never lied. God, it was good to see him. His heavy black eyelashes blinked away the suggestion of a tear from emerald-green eyes as he turned away. She smiled at him as he made a point of examining the monitors at her bedside.

'It's like Kew Gardens in here,' he said over his shoulder. The flowers seemed to have multiplied during her sleep. 'That copper's been on to me this morning. Reckons it could have been one of our punters. If it is, we'll find him.' Fergus had special dispensation from Beth's doctor to stay as long as her strength allowed; if it had been up to him then that would have been for good. He reached down to a large black holdall and began extracting wires and black boxes. Within a very short time he had set up a portable video and screen.

'Fancy a trip down memory lane?' he said before emptying the rest of the bag's contents over the floor. 'The life and times of Bethany Gamble. A hundred hours in the pursuit of truth, justice and a few quid in the bank. Are you hungry? I brought you a sandwich.' She shook her head. 'A drink then?' He pulled out a hip flask the size of a thermos and took a sip. 'Are the drugs any good in here? I could do with a blast of Valium.'

He continued to chatter as he placed the first tape in the slot. 'I've got the lot, start to finish.' He began to sing: '"Let's start at the very beginning, a very good place to start."' Fergus pushed the play button, the screen flickered, and a fresh-faced girl, in yesterday's fashions, introduced the programme.

'Good evening. This is Beth Gamble. Tonight we are going to show you the life crawling beneath the stone. Child pornography: the purveyors, the customers, and the innocent lives they crush.'

It had been a tremendous opening show. The debate it caused had led Parliament to double the maximum sentence for the possession of pornographic material. Not a bad introduction for a fearless young presenter. That was three years ago. Beth gazed at the screen, remembering the excitement she had felt in those early days of the programme. She had fought hard to persuade the studio to take a chance on her and eventually they had agreed, allowing her a small budget with a young American producer and no guarantee of a slot. The first six shows were meant to drive to the very heart of issues that other programmes dared not. Lawyers at the studio, she had later discovered, were strongly opposed to screening the pilot show for fear of libel action. Fortunately the Chief Executive, Donald Pierce, had ridden roughshod over them, and 'Take a Gamble' entered the nation's living rooms, at first in a late-night slot then very quickly afterwards in a prime-time listing.

'Now, I reckon this bastard is a lone hunter,' Fergus said, catapulting her back into the present. 'I've pulled out the companies and the institutions we've done a number on. It's a sex thing this, got to be, so the fraudsters and con merchants have gone to the back of the queue. We'll go for the smut first.' She knew that Fergus was right; whoever had done this to her had to be motivated by hatred. It must be someone whom she had publicly disgraced.

After five hours, Beth's head was starting to droop. The catalogue of sex cases and perversions had ranged from bestiality to orgasm by asphyxiation. Her eyes began to wander away from the monitor.

'I love this one, do you remember? We got hell from the police for it,' Fergus said; his appetite for watching the fruits of their labours obviously hadn't waned.

Beth focused afresh. They'd made this one two years ago. She saw herself on the screen. 'As more husbands become unemployed, as mortgage payments and credit card obligations cripple the family unit, some – it could be your next-door neighbours – have turned to prostitution to keep their homes together. The murky world of sex for sale has moved in next door, bringing with it the sordid men who will pay for it. These mobile monsters are crawling suburban streets asking innocent housewives and mothers for their price range. The outrage caused by this practice has led to the formation of the police unit we will follow and film today.'

It had been Teddy's idea to follow this one up. Complaints from the public had forced the Chief Constable's hand, and he had wanted to milk it dry. Their instructions were to remain in the van and film any arrest, on the understanding that the film could only be used after conviction. The video showed a normal London street. It was only the slow speeds of a number of cars that marked them as unusual. 'Do you remember this fella?' She watched as a Volvo estate rolled along at no more than five miles an hour. This was Fergus's own copy, unedited.

Beth listened to him talk as the car came to a halt and a girl in the tiniest of skirts approached its driver. 'Oh God, let it be him,' Fergus had muttered as the two plainclothes officers approached the driver. 'Jesus, it *is* him, there is a God!' She remembered asking who it was and Fergus's reply: 'He was my bank manager until he had me drummed out, the mean-spirited bastard.'

The tape showed the camera crew's van door slide aside; she heard his voice: 'I'm going for a close-up.'

Beth had only had a moment to decide, then found herself alongside the cameraman. 'We could lose our jobs for this, Fergus,' she'd warned on tape.

He had continued moving forward to the front of the car. 'It'll be worth it, Beth.' The screen told the rest of the story. She watched as the lens pulled in tight on the driver and heard his scream of anger: 'Get that fucking camera out of my face.'

Beth urinated involuntarily at the sound of that voice. It was *him*. The tone, the fury, the violence as his fist moved towards the camera, then obliterated the screen completely. Those eyes; the same ones that had stared at her four nights before through the slits of a ski-mask. 'Stop it,' she shouted. The pain tore through her.

'God, it's him, Beth, isn't it?' Fergus demanded, his fingers scrambling frantically for the controls of the video.

She could only nod weakly as the dampness spread down her legs and on to the sheets. 'Fergus, get me a nurse.' The tears bled down her fattened cheeks. 'I've wet myself.' Just like the night she was wet with her own blood, foetal on the paramedics stretcher. She tried to say it then. 'Crawling, he was kerb crawling. Had they heard her properly? Why hadn't she remembered until now?

Fergus put an arm around her, squeezing her to him. 'Sshh, girl, it's all right. I do it every night, it's nothing. Is it him, Beth? Was it that bastard Middleton? I'll kill him.' A flurry of footsteps could be heard outside her room before she had a chance to answer. Grieves pushed open the door. 'Get the doctor, man, hurry up! I think she's in shock,' Fergus shouted at the policeman. Grieves looked from Fergus to Beth and back again before slinging his sausage sandwich to one side, and rushing out.

Beth felt the room turn into a fairground ride as she spun down and down and down inside herself.

Grieves careered into the duty sister's office and summoned assistance; he was soon back in Beth's room taking a statement from Fergus Finn. Several minutes later he dialled the station.

'Boardman,' the voice on the phone answered tersely.

'It's Grieves, sir. She thinks she's found him. He was on the tape of a programme shown a couple of years ago. Guess what it was about?' He waited for the response. 'Remember what the ambulanceman said?' he said, prompting his boss.

Boardman made the connection. 'Crawling. Kerb crawling?'

'Spot on,' said Grieves. 'A bloke called Middleton. He was a bank manager. They got him on film trying to pick up a tart. He's got a real temper. He smashed the video camera and his knuckles, lost his job as a result. The cameraman, Finn, reckons he was fined by the magistrates, but tried and convicted on television.'

'What's his Christian name, Grieves?'

'I've pushed them on that. It begins with an A – Albert, Andrew, they can't be sure.'

As the officer was speaking, Boardman opened the case file and thumbed through the statements. There was silence until he found what he was looking for. 'It's Arthur. Arthur Middleton.'

Grieves began to speak. 'How do you know?'

Boardman answered, 'Do you know what Arthur was doing that night, apart from raping Beth Gamble?' The silence on the other end of the line was his answer. 'He drove her to the awards, then to a restaurant, then finally to her home.'

'What are you talking about, boss? She was chauffeur-driven last night.' Grieves's tone was perplexed.

Boardman smiled. 'Guess who the chauffeur was? I have a statement from him in front of me. Arthur Middleton of 45 Acacia Avenue. Good work, Grieves. Keep her calm. I'll handle everything from this end but don't let her see the video again. I don't want any smart barrister getting evidence excluded because we've breached any rules.'

'She's seen it twice already,' said Grieves.

Boardman sighed.

'Well, that can't be helped. Just take it off her, but softly, softly.'

The call ended, Boardman turned to the computer console in front of him. He switched on and keyed in the command. In response he was accessed to the Criminal Records Office, and the entry marked 'Arthur Gilbert Middleton'. The address sealed the matter: 45 Acacia Avenue. The information provided a thumbnail sketch of his crimes to date: two, and two only. On 20 October 1992, at the Horseferry Magistrates' Court, he had pleaded guilty to two offences: one for criminal damage to a camera; the other under the Public Order Act – a euphemism for 'kerb crawling'. Present employment – driver for a limousine company. He was their man.

Boardman printed out a copy of the report, then telephoned Middleton's employers. Eventually he was put through to the MD. 'Yes, I'm the officer investigating the rape of Beth Gamble.'

'What can we do for you?'

'Your driver, Middleton. Is he at work today?' He could hear papers being shuffled on the other end of the line.

There was a slight delay. 'No, he's not on the roster. What's wrong? Is he in some kind of trouble? I'd like to know.'

Boardman continued, 'Could you check the mileage on the car against the log of his journey last Saturday evening? It could be important.'

The man ignored the request. 'What is this all about? This company runs on its reputation. Any scandal could ruin us.'

'Mr Carruthers, do as I say,' Boardman ordered. 'An obstruction charge against its Managing Director will not assist the future of your company. Now how long has he worked for you?'

The man's voice was meek in response. 'Two years or so, part-time at first then an opportunity came along when we expanded so he became full-time.'

'Have there ever been any complaints about him, from women passengers in particular?'

'Well, not from clients. I do know the female staff in the office aren't too keen, but that's just a personality thing. Then there are the rumours about his wife.' Boardman waited for the man to continue. 'He's supposed to be a little heavy-handed with her.'

Boardman breathed out slowly. It was looking better all the time. 'Just do as I ask with the car mileage, then call me back.' He gave the number. 'But not a word to Middleton about this.'

Ten minutes later the call came through. Boardman was informed that the tally was correct, it checked out the journey log.

'Does he own a car?'

'Yes, of course. He drives it to work, parks it up when he's on a job, then drives home at the end of his shift.'

Or round to Beth's house, thought Boardman.

CHAPTER SIX

cacia Avenue, 9 a.m., the lair of Arthur Middleton. How would he play the arrest? Boardman wondered. In his time he'd seen it all, everything from indignant denials to spluttering sobbing confessions, but he doubted whether he'd witness either of these approaches today. It was the cold violence of the rape that marked Middleton as a dispassionate criminal: he expected to get away with it. It wouldn't be easy to convict him, but Boardman did not give up on criminals easily.

Boardman knocked on the front door. This was any street, anywhere. He turned to Osborne and the uniformed officer, indicating a sign affixed to the porch window. 'He's a member of the Neighbourhood Watch. I wonder who watches him.' The house was typical of its generation: 1930s, square and unobtrusive, like a million other homes in London's vast suburbia. Some schoolchildren passed by the front gate, and their attendant mothers looked over curiously at the two plain-clothes officers. Boardman nodded a good morning, determined to make as many tongues as possible wag like mad dogs' tails with this arrest. A line of neatly trimmed dwarf conifers hugged what looked to be a recently laid path. The whole garden was testimony to the care and attention of its owner. Boardman wondered who was the gardener in the house. If it was Middleton then he would have plenty of time to read all about horticultural pursuits when Boardman banged him up. The rattle of a security chain behind him made him spin around instantly.

As Boardman turned, a twiglet of a woman peered nervously around the door. 'Mrs Middleton? Mrs Arthur Middleton?' He produced his warrant card. 'Is your husband in? We'd like a word with him.'

The woman didn't say anything; she simply allowed the UPVC door to swing slowly open on its hinges. As she stood back to let them pass, Boardman could see her face was layered with thick

make-up; timid mouse-brown eyes flicked rapidly from face to
face as they entered her home. It looked as though the rumours
from Middleton's workplace were true. The woman closed the door
behind them and fidgeted with the net curtain in the porch window.
It was an odd moment; almost as if she knew what they had come for
but didn't want to say anything. Boardman coughed from the hall as
Osborne craned his neck into the kitchen.

'Mrs Middleton,' he persisted, 'your husband, please.'

'I'll get him for you,' she said meekly.

'There's no need for that, dear,' a voice announced as its owner
descended the stairs. His barrel chest was covered by a blue and
grey towelling dressing gown, through which sprigs of grey hair
peeked. Boardman could see at a glance that he was a fit man, easily
capable of the offence against Beth. He didn't bother with any more
introductions, just glared at his prime suspect with the naked disgust
of a priest in a porn shop. Pale blue SS Commandant eyes in a hard,
square face latched on to Boardman and refused to drop.

'Mr Middleton, you gave us a statement about the night you drove
Miss Gamble,' Boardman stated bluntly.

The suspect forced a friendly smile to his lips. 'Yes. Anything I
can do to help. Terrible thing. I told Agnes all about it.' He nodded
to his wife who appeared to be fascinated by the carpet. 'A woman
isn't safe in her own home.'

The Chief Inspector turned on his heel and fingered a small
photograph on the mahogany telephone table. He glanced back at
Middleton to judge whether his apparent sincerity had held. It was
plain to see it had not. Middleton was fumbling with the cord of
his dressing gown. Slippery bastard, thought Boardman. Osborne
shuffled towards the lounge, peering around the door.

Boardman turned to the fidgeting woman who was busily
rearranging the family snapshots. 'I wonder, could we put upon
you for a cup of tea, Mrs Middleton?' She disappeared towards the
kitchen, nodding in apparent relief to be out of the way. Boardman
turned to the suspect and eyeballed him.

'Arthur, we know about the show she did on you,' he whispered.
'You should have told us you knew her.'

'That was years ago,' he replied fiercely. 'Anyway, if I had, you
would have accused me of it straight away. I didn't do it. I was
here with Agnes. She'll confirm it.' They both turned to the small,
tired-looking woman who had reappeared holding a teaspoon in her

hand, to find her staring back at her husband, her free hand clasped to the area with the heaviest concentration of make-up. 'One lump or two, Mr Boardman?' she said vacantly.

Boardman smiled to himself: he didn't need any more. 'Arthur Middleton,' he began the caution, 'you are not obliged to say anything . . .'

He was interrupted by his suspect. 'I've heard all this before. Look, just let me dress, then we can sort this out.' He turned to his wife and flicked his eyes in the direction of the ceiling. Without argument, Agnes Middleton immediately made her way to the stairs and began to climb them quickly. God, thought Boardman sadly, Pavlov's battered wife. Middleton dropped his voice. 'I'll tell you the truth. I'll come clean. But will Beth?'

Beth slept badly. After all the excitement it was impossible to achieve any real rest. Fergus had stayed with her. Teddy had telephoned to inform her he couldn't.

'They should have picked him up by now, the evil bastard,' Fergus said as he stared out of the window.

Some of the swelling to her face had decreased, allowing her to talk, but with difficulty. 'You should go home, get some sleep. I'm fine, honestly. Please Fergus, you've been more than a friend; be a friend to yourself now.'

The Irishman spun round. 'You need someone with you and at the moment I'm the only candidate.' The criticism of Teddy hung in the air between them.

It was all too much. Her groin was on fire, the rest of her body throbbed like a fleshy super-nova, and now Fergus was giving her a bad time about Teddy. He was right, but it wasn't his place to criticise her choice of partner, no matter how lousy that had turned out to be. She leaned over and rang a bell for assistance, Fergus stood and stared. A minute later a staff nurse bustled into the private room. 'What is it?'

Beth said abruptly, her eyes filled with tears, 'I need to be alone. I need rest. Can you persuade my friend that I'll be fine?'

The nurse looked towards the Irishman, waiting for a response. 'That's all right. I understand perfectly,' he said, moving towards the open door. 'You have my number. I know how busy Teddy is. Goodbye, Beth.'

He closed the door quietly.

'Your boyfriend?' the nurse asked. Beth shook her head. 'I'm not normally wrong,' the nurse muttered as she left the room.

At last Beth was alone. She felt the tiredness begin to overpower her as she dropped into a healing sleep. Only one event disturbed her. There was the noise of the door opening. She watched through heavy-lidded eyes as a dark-haired woman gently placed a china vase containing a single black orchid on the bedside table. She glanced at Beth's apparently sleeping form before smiling sadly and leaving the room. Beth drifted back to sleep, thinking she must find out who the woman was and thank her for the gesture.

Boardman left Osborne to deal with the formalities of registering Middleton's arrest with the Custody Sergeant at the station. He had to decide what to do next. He was sure that Middleton was lying. Should he hold an identification parade? If he did, would Beth be identifying her rapist, or the man on the video, or even just the driver of a limousine? His musing was interrupted by a sharp rap on the door.

Osborne entered the room. 'What about Middleton, guv?'

'You'd better pull in some lads for an ID parade. I'll need nine ski-masks. We're playing this one by the book; the fairer the better.'

Osborne raised his eyebrows, then left to arrange the parade. It was unlike the Governor to be so pedantic when he seemed so sure of his suspect. Boardman retrieved the telephone and rang the Forensic Laboratory. The ringing continued until his patience failed and the call was stopped. He'd have to return to that later.

The ID parade would take some time to organise. It would depend upon how fit Beth was to attend and on Middleton's willingness to co-operate. If he refused they would be forced to hold a confrontation between the parties; just him and Beth. Is this the man who raped you? It would be as stark and blunt as that, and her response could free him or send him to prison for fifteen years at least. No, he hoped that Middleton would see sense. At the moment he was seeing his solicitor; it wasn't always the same thing.

Boardman left his office to speak to the Custody Sergeant. He found Banks busily scrawling something in chalk across the board outside cell number one; its inhabitant another drunken teenager. Boardman had always admired Banks and had been instrumental in his recent promotion.

'He's still in there with his brief, sir.'

'Give them another five minutes, then I want an interview room. Can that be arranged?'

'No problem. I've had number two set up for you, sir. Is he the one then?'

'Probably,' replied Boardman. He wasn't in the mood for speculation. At least not yet; something told him there was a lot more to come. The Sergeant watched the Chief Inspector open the door to the interview room and disappear inside.

Five minutes later there was a knock as Osborne, Middleton, and his solicitor Claude Milton entered the room. Milton had the swagger of success. His corpulent features had all but swallowed pink eyes that blinked through bottle-lensed spectacles. They took their seats, a tape was inserted in the recorder, and the interview commenced. Boardman watched intently. Middleton looked relaxed; his solicitor rich and confident. If Boardman could have his way he would automatically charge all briefs with conspiracy to pervert the course of justice simply for belonging to the profession they did. He nodded to Osborne to conduct the formalities for the purposes of the interview which later would be played at court, if the matter ever got that far. Boardman silently promised Beth that it would and hoped secretly that Middleton's appearance before a judge would be to enter a guilty plea and not to swear in a jury.

'This is the record of an interview with Arthur Middleton of 45 Acacia Avenue Finchley. Are you he?' asked Osborne.

'I am,' Middleton replied. Osborne went on to name the persons present in the room, then recautioned him.

The solicitor spoke 'Mr Boardman, it's been brought to my attention that you wish my client to attend an identification parade.' Boardman agreed. 'That will not be necessary and when you hear his account I'm sure you will agree. Now, Mr Middleton, if you'd be good enough to tell the Inspector?'

'Chief Inspector,' said Boardman.

'Whatever,' he shrugged, 'the details of that night.' Boardman folded his arms across his chest, ignoring all the body language seminars he'd attended over the years. He knew he wasn't going to like what he was about to be told.

Middleton leant forward. 'This will mean the end of my marriage, but I have to tell the truth. I recognised Beth Gamble as soon as Mr

Maxwell opened the door to let her in. She didn't look at me then, but she looked high on something: excitement, adrenaline, drugs; I don't know. I dropped them at the hotel for the awards and waited.'

'How did you feel about seeing her after what she'd done to you?' asked Boardman.

'Confused, I suppose, but it was all such a long time ago. It was a different life, a different me. After about three hours I was told to pick them up. Of course, they weren't ready. I could see all the flash bulbs when they came to the car. And that wasn't all I saw.' He paused before continuing.

'The limo has a smoked glass screen between the driver and the passengers. What they don't know is that there's a switch on the fascia that makes it transparent from the driver's side. They'd been quiet for a while until my curiosity got the better of me. I wish it hadn't: when I looked, there they were. At it. Screwing in the back of the sedan.'

Boardman winced. Now he knew what Maxwell had been lying about at the hospital.

'Well, you just don't expect that kind of thing . . .'

'How long did you watch them?' Boardman asked.

'She's a very attractive woman, I watched as long as I could. But I was driving as well, Mr Boardman. I didn't want to cause any problems for other road users.'

Boardman stared into Middleton's eyes, to see if he was serious; he looked utterly convincing.

'It didn't take that long. Anyway, they're finished, and he's lit a cigar before the argument starts.'

'What was the argument about, Mr Middleton?' interjected Boardman as he stood to pace the back of the bare room.

'I didn't really understand it. He was telling her to remember her place and that he was the power behind the programme. Mr Maxwell seemed very angry, then so did Miss Gamble. I suppose that's why she did what she did.'

'Did what? What did Miss Gamble do?' Boardman pushed, his voice rising.

'Well, let me take it all in order. Mr Maxwell asked me to wait outside the restaurant. He said he'd be about an hour. She'd gone inside already. Well, it wasn't twenty minutes before he stormed up to the car and ordered me to take him home. He was furious and muttering to himself about the award and what a fucking bitch she was. I took him to the mews. He was very drunk. I asked what I should do about the young lady. He told me to let her hitch-hike home and that she was a tramp anyway. I radioed back to headquarters to ask for instructions. They'll have the log of it. They told me to go back for her. Apparently this was a pretty regular occurrence. I went back and sent a message in that her car was ready.'

'But why? Look at what she did to your life!' said Boardman, incredulity leaking from his tone.

'She saved my life and my marriage, Mr Boardman. If it hadn't been for the truth coming out I would have lost Agnes by now. No, it was the least I could do, in the circumstances. She started to talk to me on the way back, saying how kind it was of me to come back for her. She said she never dreamed she would be alone on the night of an awards ceremony and would I like to come in for a drink? I said that I had to get the car back and then get home. She said, why didn't I come back after that? She's a beautiful woman. I'm just a normal man. Would you have refused?'

Boardman could not believe what he was hearing. The bastard was setting up a consent defence. 'But what about Agnes and your marriage? You know, the one you were so grateful to Beth for saving?' he snapped back.

Middleton shook his head. 'I'm afraid I'll have to answer to my maker for that one, Mr Boardman.' They waited for him to continue.

'I went back, she was very drunk. She told me she was tired of the fights with Mr Maxwell and would I cuddle up with her? Well, what could I say? We made love, unprotected as well. I don't know what came over me, you know. It lasted about an hour then I left. I felt terrible about what happened.'

'So,' said Boardman, raising his voice, 'how did she come by her injuries?'

'What injuries? She was fine when I left her.' Middleton looked around their faces then to the floor. He began shaking his head slowly before exclaiming, 'I thought it was him, but I couldn't be sure. You see, when I was pulling away from the door I thought I saw Mr Maxwell getting out of a cab. I wondered why at the time. Now I know. I don't want to say any more until I've taken advice.'

Boardman had heard enough anyway.

Two hours later he and Osborne were in the same room, a different couple sitting opposite. It hadn't taken long to track down Maxwell; the delay had been caused by his insistence on having a legal advisor present. Gone were the days when Boardman could have just asked him and gone ahead without a brief.

'I wish to point out,' said Teddy Maxwell's solicitor, 'that my client has attended the police station voluntarily.'

The man was tape-worm thin. His thousand-pound Savile Row suit flapped around his emaciated body like a washing line in the wind. Solicitor to the rich and famous, he would not be here on a legal aid brief.

Boardman's eyes swept across the Formica table, and connected with the sullen features of the TV producer. He didn't look like a volunteer. The whirring of the spools recorded the solicitor's empty comment.

'And we are grateful.' Boardman's voice was rife with insincerity. The torrent of expletives he'd received, on telephoning Maxwell to request this meeting, still rang in his ears. The man had a vicious temper.

'Mr Maxwell,' Boardman began, 'you are not obliged to say anything, but . . .'

'What is this, for Christ's sake?' Teddy demanded.

'Yes,' interrupted his solicitor smoothly, 'what exactly is this? We were not informed that this would be under caution.'

Boardman paused. 'I am cautioning your client for his own good. I am reminding him that he need not say anything unless he wishes to. I can inform you,' he turned to the solicitor, 'that I believe your client has already lied to me once. I would caution him against repeating that error.'

The solicitor looked towards Teddy for a denial. He remained silent, but shifty-eyed.

'Mr Maxwell,' the solicitor said quietly, 'I advise you to listen to the questions carefully and reply in the same fashion, if you wish to reply at all.'

Teddy nodded angrily.

Boardman concluded the words of the caution, before continuing, 'Beth Gamble, your girlfriend and colleague, was raped and assaulted in her home. You had been with her that night, is that correct?'

Teddy nodded.

'Mr Maxwell,' Boardman chided, 'the tape will not pick up the shaking of your head. Please reply.'

'Yes,' he replied churlishly, 'I was with her until we had an argument in a restaurant and I left.'

'Did anything happen between your leaving the awards ceremony and arriving at the restaurant?'

Maxwell raised his eyebrows.

'You know exactly what I'm referring to, don't you, Mr Maxwell? I asked the same question at the hospital.'

'It wasn't the same question. You asked me if we'd screwed *before* the ceremony, and I said no. That was the truth.'

Boardman tapped his fingers on the table's white top, waiting for his question to be answered. Eventually it was.

'OK, so we screwed in the car on the way to the restaurant. What about it?'

'You could have saved a forensic scientist twelve hours' work if you'd told me that at first.'

Maxwell shrugged his shoulders. 'So what?' He looked smug in his small victory.

'Perhaps you will care more about this, Mr Maxwell. The argument with Beth was a heated one. Would you agree you are a man with a violent temper?'

'It depends on the provocation,' he answered flatly, locking mean eyes on to Boardman's.

'The argument was about the award, was it not?'

'Not really. It was about Beth's overpowering ambition.'

'But it led to your storming out of the restaurant, and abandoning her to make her own way home.'

'So? She's a big girl, Boardman. It was what she deserved.'

He hesitated before the next question was asked. His voice was heavy with insinuation. 'Was that all she deserved, Mr Maxwell, or was there to be more?'

Teddy's eyes flickered between Boardman and his solicitor. 'What do you mean? What does he mean?' he asked the thin man agitatedly.

'Explain,' the solicitor demanded.

'Why was it you went to her house, Mr Maxwell? To apologise?' Boardman's tone was flippant as he offered the suggestion. 'You don't strike me as the apologetic type. Well?'

Teddy looked down at his nails, examining their cuticles, as if to find an answer.

'Look, Boardman,' his tone was less aggressive, 'I sobered up and realised I was wrong. I couldn't drive so I ordered a . . .'

'Cab?' Boardman suggested. Teddy looked unnerved by his interruption.

'Why didn't you telephone her and explain? It would have been simpler.'

Maxwell shook his head. 'Nah, Beth would have known it was me, she wouldn't have answered. This wasn't the first time we'd argued like this.'

'So, you went round to apologise. Am I right in believing that would be well after midnight?'

'Yes, I didn't check my watch, but I think it would be a little later. What are you getting at Boardman?'

This was the first sign of respect Teddy had shown him throughout their dealings; the Chief Inspector believed he was getting somewhere. 'When you arrived, did you see anyone else?'

Maxwell looked puzzled. 'No. I went straight in. The door was open. That's when I figured there was something very wrong. Then I found her . . .' His voice trailed away, then he shook himself, as if to banish the memory of the discovery.

'Mr Maxwell, I have to inform you that an arrest has been made in the case. The suspect claims he left Beth in good health, and whilst leaving, saw you arrive.'

'What the hell is this?' he bellowed. 'Are you suggesting *I* did it to her? Jesus H. Christ, is this some kangaroo court?'

'Remain calm, Mr Maxwell,' his solicitor ordered. 'As yet he hasn't suggested anything; you have. Now *is* that what you are suggesting, Chief Inspector?'

Boardman sucked on his teeth.

'It is certainly what may be suggested at the trial by the defence,' he warned. 'I thought it only fair to allow Mr Maxwell to put his side of the story at the earliest opportunity.'

Nobody in the room, including Boardman himself, believed the explanation he had just given. This was all designed to bring the brash American down a peg or ten. There were sharp stares from Maxwell and the solicitor as they left.

Boardman reflected thoughtfully on Teddy's attitude – if he was telling the truth, would a jury believe him?

CHAPTER SEVEN

B eth felt that her future lay covered in a Chernobyl-thick cloud of radioactive uncertainty. For the moment she had to concentrate on the good things in her life. The problem was there didn't seem to be any: it was an effort to get out of bed in the morning and a harder push to return when the night fell.

The trial would come and go, the memory would stay, but where did that leave her career?

In the two months since the attack, fresh flowers from Paxton TV had arrived every other day. For the first two weeks the hospital wards all shared in its offerings, then, after Beth returned home, she re-routed the delivery to a children's hospital. She didn't hold the company responsible; she'd known the risks. The obstetrician had told her she would be unlikely to have children. Beth already knew that. She could still feel the damage she had suffered. It wasn't as if she had ever really thought about having a family of her own before now. The reality of a childless future seemed strangely distant at the moment, but in time she would have to face it. For the present she could do no more than struggle from one hour to the next.

The pain was receding, but not the memory. Every night was the same. The slightest midnight sound would bring it back, him back. Nausea would hold her frozen until logic dispelled the fear and allowed her muscles and her brain to relax. She was thankful her father couldn't understand. When she had returned home, her face caked in surgical make-up, she believed there was a flicker of concern in his expression as he sat in the ancient leather chair staring out over the park below. He was once a handsome man with a strong jaw line and straight nose; now the withering of his flesh had accentuated his features to bony prominence. Beth had been forced to buy him smaller clothing as the wasting ate his shape away.

He had been told nothing of the attack – not that it would have registered had he been. Beth had allowed the nurse a holiday in

47

the hope that busying herself around the house and attending to her father's needs would obliterate the memories. How wrong she was. The swelling had taken a month to disappear, but she knew her recollection of that night would never recede.

Her friends had been supportive, if distant. It seemed the attack and its aftermath had set her aside, made her a cool object. Perhaps it was the thought of the VD and AIDS test, that steered them away, though both were negative. It was more likely that they shied away from her status as victim. Every time a visitor arrived she had tried earnestly to remain calm and unruffled. She responded appropriately to her friends' utterances of pity and support but they couldn't know, not really know, what it was like. The initial flurry had thankfully dwindled to a trickle as those around her rejoined the mainstream of their own lives.

The company had placed her on indefinite paid leave when all she wanted to do was work. Beth was as unsure as her employers what the future would hold. It seemed clear that the board of directors would be reviewing the situation after the trial. Instinctively, she realised that, whatever occurred, the company would consider itself first and her later, despite its outward display of support. Even the Chief Executive had spoken to her personally to warn her of the board's attitude: 'Let's wait and see what the lawyers have to say, shall we, Beth?' To Paxton the whole event was an embarrassment; they had discovered that she and Teddy Maxwell were likely to attract criticism whatever the outcome. Having their private lives plastered over the newspapers wasn't going to help Beth's position one bit.

Teddy had visited less as the weeks dragged on. He had never stayed overnight since it had happened; she almost understood now the trial was approaching. Teddy was the product of his own ambition. He would be busily attempting to consolidate his own position with the faceless 'suits' who signed the pay cheques at Paxton. She wasn't sure how she felt about that.

Beth remembered the day they'd met. His was a name she already knew; most people in the business did. There'd been an immediate attraction she now found difficult to understand. He was enthusiastic and direct. His energy was impressive, but so was his temper; she learned about that later when the thin veneer was rubbed away by familiarity. His journey from his native America had been the result of an unhappy nomadic childhood with battling parents. Their lives were a vortex of drink, violence and trial separations. Teddy always said that his trial was when they were together. Beth had been shocked to see the photograph of the pudgy child in bifocals grimacing unhappily through the metal fortress of braces on his teeth. It was that vulnerability that had first attracted her to the unquiet American.

Their relationship had been passionate at first. Plans and promises were made before the programme's success opened the world to him like a courtesan's thighs. They drifted apart. Occasional sex, like the incident on the night of the awards ceremony, was an irregular and increasingly less enjoyable pastime; and now it was over.

She must face Middleton alone. She had never really taken more than a passing interest in the cases of rape which frequently came before the courts. As a junior reporter she had sat through a number of them but then she'd had no idea what the victims were going through. If she had done her columns would have been full of the suffering they endured. Instead, she had only reported those where the evidence was sensational, and that was rare. She reflected on the lives of those women whose experiences had received no more than four lines of comment from her, and silently apologised. In the past she'd shaken her head when a rape victim had refused to give evidence against her attacker. Now she could sympathise with their dilemma. It wasn't going to be hers; no, she would tell them without shame what he had done and how he had done it. Every thrust of his filthy body penetrating her own as she lay helpless. She would tell it all. It was as if she couldn't progress until she had told her story and saw him convicted for what he had done. A purging of her mind and body.

There had been many offers to assist her during the last few weeks. The police had recommended that she should seek professional advice and she remembered their letter offering counselling. Counselling . . . God, what was the use of talking about it with a stranger?

She had rejected the offer, doubting its value to her. The only counselling she needed was a guilty verdict. The trial would not be easy, her conversations with Teddy had convinced her of that. He'd told her about Middleton's line of defence and the cross-examination they would face: that she was a lying whore and Teddy was a violent rapist. It didn't seem real, let alone fair. That Middleton would try to persuade the court that she had consented to sex with him rendered the trial a humourless farce. Never in a millennium could she find him attractive, nor did she have the remotest pity for his position. Beth had exposed him for the pervert he was. What had happened as a result was a matter of indifference to her; all she had done was her job.

The jury wouldn't believe him, how could they? Teddy had pointed out that she was drunk. So what! He had also reminded her that they had argued on one of the biggest nights of her career and that the jury could feel she'd been in the mood for company and . . . well.

'You bastard! You aren't going to say I'm a liar as well, are you? . . . Well, are you?' she'd challenged him.

Now Beth sat at her desk. The cards had ceased eventually, but all around her they winked from half-torn envelopes where she had stuffed them after glancing at the messages. The only one that stood on the top of the desk was home-made. Inside it Fergus had written 'I'm a believer'. He believed her, in her and for her. Besides, she knew he wouldn't ever have written to anyone else.

A cheery bowl of plum-red apples and her favourite bright orange satsumas sat invitingly before her. The whole room had been freshly decorated while she was in hospital. Fergus and her father's nurse had conspired with a Laura Ashley 'home fashion advisor' in the plan, but the memories a room held did not disappear with the old wallpaper. It was a transparent attempt to aid her recovery. Whilst she appreciated the effort, it merely served to heighten her own feelings of staleness.

A brown buff envelope from the Lord Chancellor's Department drew her attention. It was the communication she had been dreading. It informed her that in two days she would attend the trial of Arthur Middleton. The text was as stark and unfeeling as that. A warning was emblazoned across the bottom that should she fail to attend she would be compelled to do so under threat of imprisonment. How considerate. Let them try to keep her away! The telephone rang four times before it interrupted her thoughts.

'Beth? It's Boardman. I hoped I'd catch you. Have you opened the mail?'

'I'm afraid so,' she replied, half bitterly.

'I'm sorry.' His voice was disappointed and sincere. 'The idiots. I told them to inform me first. I intended to come round to tell you myself.'

'I haven't asked for special treatment,' she said quietly. 'It's just a pro forma letter.'

'I can only repeat that I'm very sorry you were informed like that.' There was a long pause before he spoke again. 'There was another matter. I don't want you to dwell on your stay in the hospital but do you remember the flowers you received?'

Beth was puzzled. What did they have to do with anything? 'Yes,' she replied uncertainly.

'One flower in particular, a black orchid?'

Beth did. It stood out in its singularity. All the others were bouquets. 'What about it?'

'I know it was a bad time for you, but do you remember who gave you it?' His tone was tense.

'No, not really.'

It was true. Beth thought back to the quiet of her hospital room. She had a vague memory, clouded by the painkillers. Through the haze she could see a blurred figure, a woman, a stranger, placing it on her bedside table and leaving with a smile. But it could have been a dream.

'I didn't know her. She just left it without a word. I was so drugged at the time that I could have hallucinated the whole thing, but I don't think so.'

Boardman seemed a little dissatisfied with her response. 'It could be important, Beth. I don't know why, but it could be. If you remember any more detail could you call me or speak to me at the trial?'

'Yes, of course.' She waited for him to continue.

'Try not to worry about the trial. I know that's easy for me to say, but don't.' The empty platitude did little to lift her spirits. After replacing the receiver, Beth sat down and could only fail to follow Boardman's advice.

The policeman turned his attention to the printout from the Holmes Computer System. The system was a nationwide database of information and requests for help across all Britain's police forces, carrying reports of serious crime. The request in this case was two weeks old. It must have arrived the day he left for his sailing holiday in the Hebrides. It was a request for information. It stipulated that any crime of murder or rape where a black orchid featured should be reported immediately to a Commander Molineux. No further information was given. Whoever this Commander was, he was playing his cards close to his chest. Normally, a request such as this would provide other background details as to why the information was sought. Whatever it was, it was serious. Boardman's hand hovered over the telephone for a minute before the decision was made. He removed the receiver from its cradle. As he dialled the number provided, he consoled himself with the thought that it couldn't do any harm.

Boardman had never been more wrong in his life.

Eve's flight from Geneva was short and convenient. The return journey would begin in five hours' time when her task was complete. Short strawberry-blonde hair framed a sharp vixen face that would have been beautiful if the cloud-grey eyes had not been so refrigerated. Her lithe body moved silkily through the phalanx of travellers. The small black aviator bag she carried contained her false documents; the other necessary items would be in the boot of the hire car located in the long-stay car park of Terminal Two. This was the way it was always arranged. Moving through the terminal, Eve entered a telephone booth. She quickly pressed the digits from memory. 'The wind hath blown me there,' she said simply.

She replaced the handset and moved swiftly to the newspaper stand. All she required was the final confirmation. Normally she would reach for The Times *but today, page 24 of the* Evening Standard *released her from her murderous starting block.*

She blended perfectly with the anonymity of the moving human cargo. It was Orchid time again.

CHAPTER EIGHT

Andrew Buchan perched uncomfortably on the edge of a
low-slung brown Draylon sofa which had seen better days.
His brightly polished Oxford brogues reflected what little
sunlight there was penetrating the dreary interior, and he made a
mental note to bring the condition of the briefing rooms at Scotland
Yard to the house committee's attention by way of a private chat
with the Commissioner. For the present, however, he was there to
enquire as to the progress of Molineux's investigation. Palmer-Dent
had taken particular interest in the series of articles penned by Jon
Preece and the reaction to them by the public.

Buchan was grim-faced as he spoke. 'It has been three months.
There have been two more deaths.'

'Three, sir,' Molineux corrected him.

'What? When was the third?' exclaimed Buchan. If there was
anything he hated, it was being left in the dark when it came to
exchange of information. How did people expect him to do the
job if they didn't tell him what was happening? He was about
to remonstrate with Molineux when the Commander took a deep
breath, smoothing down his hair and pulling himself to his full height
before delivering the latest.

'A relative found the body yesterday. Identical condition, the
same "Interflora" tribute. Pathology estimate about a week.' Buchan
eased himself back into the sofa. Digesting the facts, he glanced
towards Molineux who looked unusually tired. At the other side of
the table sat Bert Goodwin and Joe Knox, both intelligence officers
assigned to the case. They carried the anonymity of their profession
with consummate ease. Buchan had often thought these people were
recruited specifically for their instantly forgettable features.

The room's occupants waited for the Commander to continue.
'There was no announcement in *The Times*. It was in the *Evening
Standard*. The reference was from the *Song of Solomon 6:10*: "Who

is she that looketh forth as the morning, fair as the moon, clear as the sun, and terrible as an army with banners?" The date confirms the pathologist's conclusion.'

Buchan turned his attention to the two silent MI6 agents to his left. The older, bulkier one nodded. Buchan looked at the Commander. 'How has this been allowed to happen? You were granted the funding to scale a twenty-four-hour watch on all potential victims who had recently been acquitted of rape. Were your men asleep?'

Molineux frowned at the slur, then straightened his brow before replying. 'They have changed the rules, Mr Buchan. The three victims had been acquitted in the same way, and of the same charge.'

'So?' Buchan snapped.

'The difference was the time scale. The previous victims were murdered within three months of their court appearances. The recent slayings were of offenders of anywhere between six months and two years ago. They weren't guarded because they were not part of our target group.'

Molineux watched the civil servant reaching the inevitable and daunting conclusion.

'Then any acquitted rapist is now a target,' he hissed.

Molineux nodded slowly. The room fell into silence, before Buchan spoke again. 'What do you propose now, Commander?' His voice had a defeated quality.

'You heard my proposal the last time we met here. It's the only way.'

Molineux's voice carried a hard edge. From the moment he had formulated the idea of using an unwitting agent provocateur he had known that Buchan was against it. But it wasn't Buchan he was interested in; the person with the ultimate say was the Home Secretary. The only trouble was that to get him was only possible through Buchan. Catch bloody 22! De Haus had convinced him the killer wouldn't stop and, against the current political backdrop, Molineux was acutely aware that today's meeting represented the best opportunity to set his plan in motion.

Buchan exhaled slowly as he reached down to the red leather briefcase at his feet. Molineux persisted, moving closer.

'The operation has been planned. I sent you the command brief on the logistics, Mr Buchan.' He watched as the document was produced from the case and placed gingerly on the table in front of him.

'This,' Buchan waved a limp hand at the Commander's proposals, 'involves interference with the administration of justice. In a trial, for God's sake!'

'Sir, I understand all too well what I am proposing. The alternative is to allow these murders to continue indefinitely. We have no leads, no clues to follow. We still have to orchestrate a situation we can control and monitor. I cannot be responsible for the outcome if you refuse.'

Buchan looked lost between the horrors of future slayings, and his own tenuous command of his employer's loyalty. 'The matter is being considered,' he lied. 'In the meantime,' he glanced towards the bulky agent, 'there are matters you must be briefed on.'

He gathered up his papers. 'I must speak to the HS. Is there a secure line?' Buchan instinctively knew what Palmer-Dent's reaction would be. The last words of this morning's briefing had made it all too obvious: 'Do whatever it takes but make sure these people are caught and make certain that there is no link with this office.'

Molineux led him from the office to a recently 'swept' telephone, then returned to his room. The two agents were smoking silently when he walked in and resumed his seat. He felt reasonably satisfied that Buchan would come up with the answer he wanted. Joe Knox, the more memorable of the two intelligence officers because of his muscular frame, turned to face Molineux who responded with an expectant look. The bulky man took a long draw on his cigarette before beginning.

'Commander, I have to stress the secrecy of this information.'

Molineux nodded his head slowly, not wishing to stop the man's flow by speaking.

'A short time ago, a crime computer collator at Headquarters approached her section leader with some interesting information. She was attempting to trace captured armaments shipments to their destination. At every turn she reached a blank in the crossword. No clue. So, instead of tracing the end result, the collator turned the investigation on its head. It took months. Ships' lading forms, all false of course; bogus Panamanian inventories; the normal smoke-screen. Again, there seemed no way forward. Then a piece of pure luck. A Swiss banker on the run with a flight bag of his employer's negotiable bonds was picked up in transit by a routine check. Some of the documents he had were cross-referenced. They matched payments for the captured shipments. He was interrogated, and admitted he had been involved peripherally. He told us there had been talk at the bank about a woman. He did not know her identity, nor had he ever seen her. He did know she was English and immensely wealthy. Our operative then looked into the nature of the captured arms. One item stood apart from the rest: high-powered handguns with corresponding impact bullets. Normally terrorists are interested in more devastating ordnance – mortars, mines. Not so with these shipments.'

'Small arms are useful,' suggested Molineux.

'Yes,' the man agreed, 'but not for the Grand Gesture. Working with the weapon type, she checked the use of this calibre weapon against the ballistics laboratory's register. You can guess the rest.'

Molineux had; the same weapons as were used in the murder of the men.

'Your proposal is the only way forward. You have clearance. We are fully aware of the Home Secretary's attitude: Buchan is just a bit jumpy with this coming on the back of the Matrix Churchill fiasco. Any mention of ministerial sanctioning leaves him cold. Mind you, I can't blame him. If this one goes wrong it won't be Palmer-Dent's resignation letter sitting on the PM's desk.'

He waved the report in the air casually and, with some degree of satisfaction in his conspiratorial smile, went on: 'The problem as we see it is this, Commander. We have to have a case, a high-profile case, that will attract the attention of these people, whoever they are. It must be a rape case where the defence is one of consent. It must end in an acquittal; it's no use if the defendant is in prison. There will then be the opportunity to watch the victim and the defendant after the trial. You and I are pragmatic men. We know the reality of this situation, and here,' he tapped Molineux's plan, 'we have its solution. The only matter to be resolved now is the selection of the "bait".'

Molineux hesitated before responding. After he handed this over, there would be no going back. He cleared his throat before introducing the chosen dossier.

'After the last meeting I used the Holmes Computer System to circulate some scant information to Chief Constables in the UK. As you know, the system is monitored and updated on a daily basis to give a referencing point for the commission of serious crimes, so that similarities, if they exist, can be pin-pointed. I requested all

Chiefs to instruct their senior officers to key in information relating to serious rapes where the defence is consent. The more brutal, the more important it might be. I also referred to the existence of a black orchid. It is certain that this particular plant is being used as some sort of calling card by the organisation and we have received a response. A DCI called Boardman keyed in a vicious rape that had been committed on his patch. The defendant was arrested and gave a ludicrous account of the matter, but couldn't be budged on it. More importantly, when Boardman returned to the hospital to question the victim again, he noticed a single black orchid by her bedside. The girl was asked about it, but had no recollection of how she had come by it.'

The agent considered as his companion furiously scribbled down the information. 'So what do you conclude from that, Commander?'

'Well, we can safely reject coincidence, but as yet none of the other victims of the murdered men has received a similar flower. Therefore, either this woman is being singled out for special treatment or she is involved up to her neck. Whatever the significance, it seals the matter of selection for me.'

The door opened. Buchan, looking uncomfortable, entered and sat down. They waited for him to tell them what they already knew. After a few deep and unhappy breaths he did.

'But,' he concluded, 'if it should go wrong, your name is on the proposal. The Home Secretary has no knowledge of this operation.'

The Commander grimaced and removed a photograph from the dossier he had kept close to him.

Joe Knox spoke again. 'Commander, the matters we discussed in Mr Buchan's absence will be pursued by my collators. As the matter you raised has now been sanctioned, two of my units will be at your disposal during its currency. They are highly trained and dependable. All the equipment you have requested is yours, and all taps and wires are authorised as of this point. Now,' he turned to the photograph, 'who have you selected?'

There was no comment as he flipped it over to reveal a familiar face.

CHAPTER NINE

The 'casting' meeting was over. The star had been chosen, the script perfected, the show was ready to open. All they needed was the right audience. Alone again, Molineux asked his secretary to show De Haus into the room. The psychologist appeared tense as he entered. He took a chair, eyeing the file on the desk that gaped in his direction. The photograph stared back reproachfully. Molineux watched the man's eyes flicker in recognition as he removed his spectacles and polished their lenses on the tongue of his tweed tie.

'So you have chosen your "scape-girl",' De Haus muttered. Molineux turned the file towards the researcher,

'An admirable choice, I believe.'

'If such a concept can exist,' he replied disapprovingly.

Molineux removed a single sheet of paper headed 'Profile'; he pushed it in front of De Haus, who replaced his spectacles and read the name of the subject and a brief history of her life,

'Bethany Victoria Gamble,' he read aloud. '"Born 30 March 1969 at St Bartholomew's Hospital. Weight 7lbs 2 oz. Father Victor Gamble (RN retired), age 63, still alive. Mother Victoria (née Tremaine), deceased 30 March 1975." How traumatic,' De Haus remarked, 'for one's mother to die on one's sixth birthday.' He continued to read the typed script.

There followed a list of a school in every coastal town with a naval presence. '"Left school 12 June 1985. Qualifications: 10 O Levels. School report suggests rebellious attitude to authority figures. Described as bright and popular. Even after nomadic education still Captain of Hockey and Netball. First job, junior reporter with the *Blackheath Bugle*. Promoted to reporter within six months. Senior reporter by the end of the same year. Moved to Fleet Street as senior crime reporter with Syndicated Press. Employment terminated 13 May 1990. Reinstated after legal action 17 May 1990. Resigned 18

May to join Paxton TV as presenter of "Take a Gamble".' De Haus chuckled to himself.

'What is so amusing?' the Commander asked briskly.

De Haus put the brief report back on the table top. 'Are you sure you do not wish to reconsider your choice?' he asked the frowning policeman. Molineux shook his head. 'I should if I were you. You see,' he continued, 'this last incident in her life alone should make you wary of her. She was sacked, then she fought for her reinstatement, just so she could resign. She is a woman of principle; a fighter.' Molineux appeared unconvinced by this argument,

'Look a little further back. Deprived of her mother at a tender age and shipped around the world – still she survived. Not only that but also achieved. You are dealing with a remarkable personality; one that is not used to despair or failure. I wonder if she will play your little game with you?'

Molineux restacked the file without response. He withdrew a slimmer version from within the top drawer of his desk and handed it to De Haus. 'That's what I want you to tell us.'

De Haus accepted the documentation. 'Will it make any difference to your selection?'

'Not one jot.' Molineux rose to his feet, signifying the end of their meeting, 'though I would prefer to know how she will respond.' De Haus studied the tall policeman for a short time.

'Tell me, Commander, as a boy you will have played war games. I have no doubt that you commanded your troops with firm leadership, but was the casualty rate always a high one?'

Molineux allowed a brief, grim smile to escape his normal fixed expression.

'I shall expect the profile by tomorrow, De Haus. Goodbye.'

Two hours later he sat facing his computer screens. The meeting with Molineux had irritated him beyond expectation; the man was a philistine war-horse. He had no real intellect or compassion in his dry soul, just a margin for a brain where he fixed constant reminders of what he was attempting to achieve. De Haus was still damp following his walk from the station; his macintosh steamed quietly on the radiator. The kettle began to whistle. He shifted momentarily to switch it off; then, camomile tea in hand, returned to his beloved data. De Haus had been disappointed with the initial response to his personal ad. There had been a flurry of replies to the E-mail number he had used with some bizarre interpretations of his message. His spirits had begun to sink when the three-week run of the personal column came to an end. In the meantime he had busied himself with the humdrum passage of his academic career.

De Haus felt soiled by his experience with Molineux's group. It had acted to mar the excitement he had always felt towards his chosen research topic, as if it were too starchy, too far removed from an exciting hidden world where people died and others tried to catch their killers using the power of their brains. But then it had come. After a particularly dull lecture to a group of uninterested undergraduates, he had returned, deflated and depressed, to find an E-mail communication. He had by then given up hope of any contact with her. De Haus retrieved the message now to remind himself of its contents.

'*Woman, Horticulturist, Orchestrates A Ravishing Enterprise. Your Originality, Underestimated.*'

De Haus had been throbbing with excitement as he read the words:

'*Who are you?*'

There had been a corresponding E-mail number that he had accessed and replied with the same question. The winking of the cursor proved the recipient's reluctance to respond immediately. As he waited, De Haus had set off the pre-prepared programme to trace the origin of the E-mail. A response blinked up angrily, as if in direct reaction. '*Do not attempt to trace or communication will end.*' He felt as though he had been slapped across the hand with a ruler. He reached out and snapped off the previous programme.

'*Better,*' his screen responded.

He repeated his question; the reply this time was instantaneous.

'*Show me yours first.*'

He typed in his name and qualifications, then pushed the button to send the message on its way to her.

'*I know,*' the screen responded. '*At least you are being honest. So far.*'

'*What do you want?*' De Haus typed quickly.

'*Justice.*'

'*For whom?*'

'*For them all.*'

'*Does that include yourself?*' De Haus had hesitated before typing in this emotive question. It was ignored. Instead, an enquiry appeared on the screen in front of him:

'What should I beware of?'
'I don't know yet. Not properly. When I do I will contact you.'
'What do you want?' He had expected this enquiry,
'Knowledge. The end. What you seek and why.'
'You may pay a high price for such dangerous information. I shall contact you again. Repeat the advert if you have what we need.'

That had been three weeks ago. Now he had what she needed. De Haus repatched to *The Times* personal ads and repeated the dialogue from the previous lonely heart. He did not wish to risk her ignoring his attempt to re-establish contact. At the foot of its acronymic conclusion he typed, *'Beware the Trojan whore'*.

CHAPTER TEN

Beth had visited the Old Bailey on many occasions, but never in this capacity. The magnificent galleried hall seemed to have altered its demeanour to suit her status. The marble floor was colder and harsher underfoot than she remembered. The ceiling was higher and the space underneath noisier. Perhaps it was her imagination but everyone who stood around – lawyers, witnesses, defendants and clerks – seemed to have at least one eye on her. Beth brushed herself down more out of embarrassment than necessity, feeling uncomfortably conspicuous. Teddy had telephoned to say he would be along later; Fergus was waiting in the vestibule. 'On your own again,' he commented, following her inside and away from the gawps and sly glances of the crowds.

Beth started to follow the signs marked 'Victim Support Unit'. The VSU had been established to redress an imbalance in the law; the victim's plight as opposed to the defendant's rights. It offered help, assistance and advice. Those commodities had been less than constant in the run-up to this ordeal. Teddy had been comforting only at arms' length, Fergus too shy to share her nightmares, her friends alienated by the horror of the circumstances. She felt leprous; tainted. Perhaps this unit might help, at least with the nuts and bolts of getting through the day.

'Are you sure you want to go in there, Beth?' Fergus asked out of the side of his mouth as she stood at the door. 'They might be crop-haired dykes.' The door was opened to provide a complete contradiction. Two women, one short, one not, dressed in casually smart trouser suits and matching sympathetic smiles, answered her knock. The taller spoke. 'Beth Gamble. It's nice to meet you.' She turned to the shuffling figure of Fergus, inviting an explanation.

'Fergus is a very old friend, he's been very supportive,' Beth offered. Their smiles clicked naturally on to him.

'We all need friends,' said the shorter of the two, ushering Beth inside. Fergus began to move to the interior of the room. 'Beth,' the taller woman spoke. 'Would your friend mind if we had a chat with you on your own?'

Beth glanced towards Fergus who was looking for her to tell him it was all right; she smiled and nodded. 'I'll be in the canteen,' he said for her benefit alone.

In fact Fergus decided against a cup of tea, but in favour of scouring the courtroom where it would all happen.

He made his way into the body of the courtroom and walked along a small passageway behind the dock where Middleton would sit throughout the proceedings. The ancient wrought-iron bar around the edges of the judge's dais and witness box had a forbidding presence all of their own and Fergus gulped softly, visualising Beth giving her evidence raised above the court so that everyone would see her naked pain. The long, stepped oak benches rose up in front of him and he saw what he assumed to be a representative of the Crown Prosecution Service perched up on the top row, behind the ones marked for senior and junior counsel. The advocates themselves were absent. Fergus approached him. 'Will it be all right if I have a seat down here?'

The bespectacled civil servant looked up. 'Are you involved in the case?'

'I was. Some snot rang me yesterday to tell me I wouldn't have to give evidence any more.'

The man looked amused. 'You must be the cameraman.'

'And you?'

The man looked at him wryly. 'I'm the snot who spoke to you yesterday.' Fergus laughed self-consciously and apologised with a shrug of his burly shoulders. 'Don't worry about it. It was a bad day, I probably sounded a little offhand; this case has been a real problem.'

'What do you mean?'

'The barristers are in with the judge now. I'm afraid all the publicity that Miss Gamble's been attracting to the case has made everyone uneasy – the judge, the prosecution and D'Stevenson.'

'Who's he then?'

The clerk continued to scribble on the file in front of him. 'Fighter of lost causes that don't appear quite so lost when he's finished with them.'

Fergus considered this for a moment. 'So he's a slick smart-arse, this brief?'

The other man considered the accuracy of this description. 'Not at all. Let me put it this way: when a defendant is charged there is a race between the prosecution and the defence to see who can brief D'Stevenson to appear for them first.'

'So, you lost out?'

'No, the prosecutor, Miss Moncrieff, is a fighter. Once she gets Middleton into the box, it'll be worth selling tickets for.'

As Fergus calculated the cost to Beth he turned around at the rustle of gowns. Two barristers, a woman he assumed to be Miss Moncrieff and a man, entered from the doorway which was obviously off-limits to anyone who didn't have a wig. The man was shorter than the image created by his reputation. Fergus always imagined barristers to be hook-nosed and fierce-eyed or corpulent and corrupt. This man had kind brown eyes, like a Labrador puppy, surrounded by the wrinkles resulting from a thousand good jokes. Fergus heard his voice; friendly, almost laughing.

'Marianne, you know as well as I do that the point must be taken. It would be negligent not to. After all, the Court of Appeal may disagree with the judge.'

D'Stevenson smiled towards his opponent then winked. There was obviously a hidden joke Fergus didn't understand. He strained his ears in an attempt to catch the punchline.

'Of course it may, Giles. And I'll be riding Shergar in the point-to-point on Saturday!' The female barrister was tall and slender. She appeared to glide rather than walk as if her feet were on castors. Tendrils of black hair had escaped from a hairgrip's confinement and peeked from the tail of her white curled wig. An upturned nose unfairly suggested a spoiled nature but her full smile redressed the balance.

Fergus watched as D'Stevenson sat and removed his wig to display the lightly greying hair it concealed, and scratched his head. So this was the man who would call Beth a whore in public. Fergus dropped his voice and spoke to the scribbling civil servant, still eyeing D'Stevenson. 'So what happens now?'

The clerk put down his pen. 'Well, the defence are going to make a submission, that's an application in normal English, that the case shouldn't go ahead. They are going to allege that because of who Miss Gamble is, how well known she is and all the attention she's attracted to the issue of rape, Middleton will not get a fair trial.'

'But he's guilty anyway.'

'It's precisely because that might be the attitude of the jury without hearing any evidence that he's going to say it. I must say, for my own part, I have some sympathy with that view.'

Fergus pushed his fingers through his unusually clean hair. 'Will the judge do that? I mean, what about Beth?'

'Not this judge, but it may form part of the grounds for appeal if Middleton's convicted.

'What do you mean, if?'

The clerk merely raised one eyebrow as he retrieved his pen and returned his attention to the page. 'If you sit on the row behind me, they'll think you're one of the team. Do try to be quiet though. This judge won't hesitate to have you thrown out if you don't. Once he had the entire public gallery arrested for making a noise. They went straight off to prison for the night.'

A short time later, Fergus saw the clerk of the court take his seat in the well of the court, then saw a figure appear in the dock. He'd never forget that face. Arthur Middleton. 'Bastard,' he muttered.

Arthur looked towards him, then smirked. He beckoned his solicitor; there was a brief gesture in Fergus's direction and, Fergus assumed, an explanation as to who he was. The communication continued from the solicitor to D'Stevenson and from him to the female prosecutor. Eventually the clerk he'd spoken to earlier turned around.

'I'm sorry. Middleton's causing a fuss about you being down here. If you want to watch, you'll have to sit in the public gallery.'

Fergus turned to see the expectant audience, many of them women, staring back from the gallery's height. As he left the court well, a loud rap echoed throughout the large room.

'Court stand,' demanded an usher. Through the doorway entered a figure in a black robe, his ancient wig framing an expression of scowling aloofness.

The clerk of the court then spoke. 'Let all those having business before Her Majesty the Queen's Justices draw near and give their attendance.' The barristers bowed to the judge who gave a disdainful nod as he took his seat. The last words Fergus could hear through the closing door were from the clerk and the defendant.

'Are you Arthur Middleton?'

'I am, sir.'

'You, Arthur Middleton, stand charged with rape, the particulars of which are that on the 14th day of October you did rape Bethany Victoria Gamble. How do you plead, guilty or not guilty?'

'As God is my witness, I am not guilty, sir.'

CHAPTER ELEVEN

ergus, fortified by a quick pint, parked his van two streets away from the court. It stood on double yellow lines and was worth less than it would cost to free it from the inevitable clamp. The skies had opened and the pavement was wet as he pounded along. Rounding the corner, he checked his wallet for the tattered press pass he had lifted from a drunken hack a year ago. No one, especially Middleton, could stop him from being close to her when she gave her evidence. He knew that the legal arguments were likely to take up the morning session and, judging by the crowds outside, it looked as if the case was about to begin in earnest.

He stopped momentarily and watched the paparazzi light up the formidable frontage of the courthouse with their flashbulbs firing indiscriminately at anyone entering the building. He felt a swell of anger that Beth should be at the centre of this carnival, the irony of his own occupation lost in his affection for her.

Fergus slipped through the crowd of photographers, lenses hanging like fertility symbols around their necks, and was confronted by a bored security guard. Flashing his bogus card to the disinterested centurion, he barged his way into the overflowing press box. He glared at Middleton who sat, head down, in the dock. The journalists around him hushed as the clerk began swearing in the jury.

Forty-five minutes later, the prosecution were approaching the conclusion of their opening address. Fergus knew they were about to call Beth to give evidence.

Telling her story wasn't as awful as she had anticipated. Beth had been through it, over it and under it with her friends and the police, sometimes the level of interrogation was identical. She had lived through this moment in her dreams. They were the worst of all. Today she had decided to wear a clean-cut Chanel dress in dark blue. She had worn it for every successful meeting during its three-year tenure. It had acted like a talisman against evil; that came to an end during her cross-examination. What she was unprepared for was the ferocity. Middleton's mild-looking barrister fixed her with an intense gaze before he launched his attack.

'Tell me, Miss Gamble,' he began, his robes pulled tight around his relaxed figure, 'do you ever feel guilt or shame about them?' Beth felt puzzled by the obscurity of the question.

'Who do you mean?'

The barrister dropped his voice to a sad whisper. 'The people whose lives you destroy for the viewing public.' As the last word dropped from his mouth he turned slightly to the jury, and away from her. Beth felt angry; she was not the one on trial.

'They,' she began, her voice measured and assured, 'if by "they" you mean the subjects of the programmes, destroy their own lives by their actions towards other people.' She paused before continuing. 'They don't need any help from me.' The barrister smiled indulgently at her.

'Self-destruction is one thing,' he acknowledged. 'Public humiliation is another,' he added aggressively, all reason melting from his tone. 'The balance, the ratio between the wrong done and the punishment it receives, can be unfair. Does that bother you?' he asked, eyes wide with insincere interest; or at least it looked that way to Beth. She pulled herself up to a full standing position.

'I report: others make of it what they will.'

The barrister shook his head slowly before his voice dropped to a gentler tone. 'Please answer the question, it is a simple one. Does it bother you?' Beth shrugged her shoulders and immediately regretted it. It looked casual and she felt anything but that about her journalistic responsibility.

'Sometimes things, consequences, can get out of hand.' As she attempted to explain, her memory took her back to a darker time. Then, the consequences had been horrific: the subject of her programme had hanged himself before it was even broadcast. Beth shuddered as she remembered his blackened face and swollen tongue. He had set it up for her to find him. His tongue seemed to be sticking out at her. Beth could still see vividly the ligature bound tightly around the fat fraudster's neck. He had had his way, the programme was never shown, but Beth never forgot her discovery. The memory might recede but it would never disappear.

'I take it that you mean you occasionally regret what you have done?'

She nodded as that image of the hanged star of her 'show' returned in all its bloated horror, the dead man's feet no more than two inches from the safety of the ground.

'Very much so,' she conceded.

'What, if anything, can you do to make amends?' The question was accompanied by the raising of an eyebrow towards the male members of the jury. This was outrageous, Beth thought. She swivelled her attention to the judge, Mr Justice Woolmington. He had the courtroom pallor that Beth had seen on elderly judges before. A grizzly bear of a man, with gigantic hands, he had earned a reputation for severity and possessed a shorter fuse than a defective firework. For now, he sat blank-faced and unmoved by the lewd suggestion in the barrister's voice; he indicated with a slight dip of his wig that she should answer. Beth fought to retain control of her temper.

'There is very little I can do,' she answered through tightly clenched teeth.

'That is right, Miss Gamble, because in the vast majority of cases you do not have the opportunity to make amends. It must be heart-warming when the occasion does arise,' he leaned towards her, 'to redress the balance in your own personal way.' How dare he, she thought, colour suffusing her pale cheeks.

'I can see what you are getting at, and you are wrong.' She held her interrogator's gaze for a brief second before the judge's voice, grave with disinterest and cigar abuse, cut the cord.

'Miss Gamble.' Beth turned to face the wan complexion of the legal referee. 'Let the jury decide what he is getting at; that is why they are here.' He looked at them both and smiled. 'This is a court of law, not a television programme.'

Beth was stung by the partisanship of the last remark, but decided against a response.

'Thank you, my lord,' D'Stevenson uttered, nodding his head almost inperceptibly to the judge.

'Now, Miss Gamble, two different samples of semen were present in your body at the time you were examined, is that correct?'

'You know it is,' she snapped, annoyed at his smugness, 'but can I explain . . .' He raised a hand to quiet her response.

'All in good time, Miss Gamble. You didn't actually explain to the police until much later, did you?'

The insinuation in his voice was infuriating, but Beth had been warned that this would be an area of attack by the defence. She looked down towards her hands which were twisting with frustration.

'I was too embarrassed. At least at first.'

The stenographer entered the answer on to her phonetic pad, as the barrister looked sidelong at the jury as he spoke.

'But not too embarrassed to have sexual intercourse in the back of the limousine with your producer.'

She flushed again as she corrected him.

'My boyfriend,' she said, more calmly than she felt.

'Was anyone else present during the act of intercourse?' Beth fought with herself, attempting to stop her eyes following their course to the intent face of Arthur Middleton; the barrister followed their path theatrically.

'Exactly,' he commented. Beth could feel the barrister's delight at her response, the same delight she remembered feeling herself during a difficult interview when her prey's throat was unprotected and within her reach.

'You are . . . how can I describe it? . . . a modern woman; a woman of impulse; a creature of the moment?' Beth waited for him to ask a proper question. 'You decide what to do, then carry it through whatever the consequences. Would you agree with that précis of your character?'

Beth hesitated before she replied. She felt this was slipping away from her. The furious scribbling from the press box ceased momentarily.

'To an extent, but not in the way you are suggesting.'

'But *I* haven't suggested anything yet.' The jury were staring at the scene intently. Beth began to panic. 'You didn't care whether or not the driver could see you having sex?'

'I didn't think he could.'

'But he did: perhaps that was what you wanted, perhaps it excited you being watched by him?' Beth was too horrified by the suggestion to respond.

'When Mr Middleton was questioned by the police, he told them all about the incident in the car: he told the truth about it, and you now acknowledge that what he says did occur? Hmm? Hmm?'

'Yes.' Beth's tone was almost a whisper. The jury was agog for her reply. She could sense the icy fallout from the women members' eyes.

'So, you failed to tell a senior police officer, investigating your own,' he paused for the longest moment, 'alleged rape, that you had enjoyed,' his tongue rolled salaciously around the words, 'earlier sex?' The court held a collective breath. Beth felt dirty, and angry that she felt that way,

'It didn't seem important at the time,' she offered, then felt ridiculous at the inadequacy of the response. D'Stevenson merely shook his head at her reply; the action was more eloquent than any comment or further question he might have asked or uttered. The jury looked away, embarrassed for her; she dropped her eyes in response.

'Your relationship was not, how shall we say, as convivial in the restaurant as it was in the car. You had a public screaming match with your produ – I'm sorry, your boyfriend, at the table, isn't that so?'

'Look, couples argue all the time.'

'But not, apparently, when they are coupling,' he responded acidly.

The jury were still gazing at their laps.

The judge's voice interrupted the moment's tension.

'Mr D'Stevenson, please refrain from commenting on the evidence until your closing address to the jury.' He glanced disapprovingly towards Beth. 'Whatever the temptation.'

She felt impotent with fury. Her nails were cutting into the palm of her right hand; she had to keep control.

'Your disagreement was such,' the barrister continued, 'that he, that is Teddy Maxwell, stormed from the restaurant and left you to make your own way home.'

'No, that's not right.'

'No, it's not, is it?' he asked rhetorically. 'Out of the goodness of his heart, against the strict orders of Teddy Maxwell, risking his livelihood for a person who had stripped him of it once before, Arthur Middleton returned for you. You must have been very grateful?'

Beth steeled her voice to a menacing hiss.

'Not that grateful.' D'Stevenson smiled at her reply, though his eyes no longer danced with a good humour.

'Now we all know what we are talking about, do we not?' His face was as forbidding as a storm-swept crag.

'You must have been horrified when this monster,' he turned to glare at his client, who appeared genuinely startled, 'burst down your door and attacked you?'

Beth was expecting this question. 'He didn't burst down my door, but he did attack me,' she stated firmly.

'How then,' he asked, a pen at the ready, hovering over his notepad, 'did he get in? Two separate teams of Scenes of Crimes officers went over your flat with every modern scientific device. How,' he pulled himself to his full height, which, Beth thought unkindly, was not substantial, 'did he get in, if you didn't let him in voluntarily?'

'I don't know,' she replied, genuinely perplexed by the problem. 'I've thought about it. All I can suggest is that I'd left my handbag in the back of the car at the awards ceremony. He could have searched it, found the key, copied it then used it to get in.'

Beth watched Middleton. It was his turn to look down at his lap; Beth was now certain that was how it had happened.

'It's a lot easier just to open your own front door and invite tonight's second lover through it, don't you agree, Miss Gamble?'

'He wasn't my lover!'

'But his semen was found in, I emphasise *in*, your body.'

'He raped me!' Beth felt the meltdown of temper and frustration.

'His semen was not alone in your body. The sexual secretion of the man you had argued with so violently was also present. The man,' his tone plummeted to poisonous insinuation, 'who found you. The man who was covered in your blood when the ambulance arrived. The man, the powerful and influential man, who controls your career. He was jealous of your success, wasn't he?'

'It was the champagne that was to blame, not Teddy. He's not like that normally.'

'But this was no ordinary night. We know your attacker used your BAFTA award in the attack. Is it not correct that the award was central to your argument with Mr Maxwell?'

'It was more than that, it was . . .'

'More deep rooted? More serious?'

Her voice returned to a beaten whisper. 'More complex.'

'So, I suggest, are the facts of this case. It didn't take you very long to find Mr Middleton on your video records, did it? Rather a stroke of luck that. I have a document, a prosecution witness statement from your cameraman. It states that the video of Mr Middleton was found within five hours. Remarkable when we remember that he states that you had over a hundred of tapes to peruse. You knew exactly who you were looking for, didn't you?'

Beth was shaking her head, too furious to speak.

'Because when the two of you talked before sex occurred, he disclosed how your paths had crossed and in what circumstances. What you had done to him, how his career in the bank had been lost. You knew all too well where to look, how to attempt to protect Teddy from his own temper. After all, who's going to believe a taxi driver with a record for an offence like kerb crawling?'

The prosecutor jumped up. 'Is it time for closing speeches already? Have I slept through the rest of the case?'

The judge listened to the sarcasm. 'Mr D'Stevenson, do attempt to ask a question or two. It will speed the trial's progress.'

'How would it look to the world of the media,' he turned towards the bulging press box, 'if one of their own were accused of a crime of this nature? Why, they'd tear him to pieces before the case ever came to court. Much the same as your own programme has.'

'Teddy didn't do it! *He* did!' Beth pointed an accusing finger. She could see the women from the VSU nod appreciatively and Middleton shake his head in disbelief.

'May I congratulate you on your performance, Miss Gamble,' D'Stevenson commented slyly, pursing his lips with distaste at her outburst. This held her in check for the remainder of the unpleasant experience. Beth changed her answers to a dreary monotone, answering yes or no, as was appropriate. She felt cheapened by the experience. She didn't know why she felt that way; ashamed for an event that was neither of her making nor her fault.

Her ordeal continued for some time. Eventually, D'Stevenson smiled almost kindly at her. 'I have no further questions.' As he began to sit down, Beth relaxed, then he rose once more.

'One other matter, Miss Gamble, and I hope you can be as frank with the jury in this reply. Has your boyfriend slept with you since that night?'

Beth began to answer. The courtroom was a still vacuum of prurience.

'No, it's just . . .'

She was cut off. 'Thank you. A simple "no" will suffice.' He turned to Middleton, nodded gravely, then sat down.

'Do you have any re-examination, Miss Moncrieff?'

The prosecutor hesitated. The maxim 'Never ask a question you do not know the answer to' flitted briefly across her mind, but she pressed ahead.

'Why not?'

Beth swallowed hard then spoke.

'Teddy feels guilty about what happened.'

The scribbling of shorthand reporting sounded like a plague of locusts to her ears.

'I have no further questions,' said the female prosecutor.

D'Stevenson's voice could be heard, a stage-whispered comment 'Very sensible, you've done her enough damage with the last one.'

Beth made her way out of the courtroom to hear the usher commanding the court to rise until the afternoon sitting.

Fergus felt powerless. Waiting outside the courtroom, he pulled grimly on a withered hand-rolled cigarette. As Beth appeared he could see the desperation on her face. He glared at the onlookers in the corridor in that drab forum of legal misery, dropped the smoking butt to the floor as she moved slowly towards him and rested her heavy head against his chest.

'It was awful,' she gulped, trying to choke back the tremor in her voice. He could feel the losing battle as she shook under his touch. She felt too delicate for great ugly hands like his.

'The things they said about me, about Teddy . . .' Her fluttering began to subside as she regained the initiative in the fight against her emotions. 'Fergus, what do I do now?'

He gave her his best smile, the one he reserved for the most important people in his life.

'It's back to work for me and you, girl.'

Beth paused for a minute to consider his kindness. She smiled but couldn't speak.

'It's over.'

Beth considered the consequences of an acquittal on her future; she swallowed the rising bile from her stomach, then spoke quietly. 'Somehow I don't think so.'

She shook away the selfish nature of her preoccupation and thought about her father instead. He had always taught her to be honest; instilled in her an unshakeable loyalty to those who deserved it, and she lived by that credo. More than that, he had taught her to fight for what is right, not merely expedient. For once she was grateful that his illness prevented the trial and its sordid accusations from hurting him. She would do what was right by him, whatever happened: if only for the memory of a man who lay trapped in the decaying husk of his existence. She wiped away her last tears of self-pity and flashed Fergus her gutsiest grin.

'Whatever the jury say, I know the truth.' Beth's voice no longer sounded like that of a frightened girl. It had assumed a woman's strength. Looking about the court precinct she spotted Middleton's timid wife, easily recognised by her press photographs. Their eyes locked momentarily before Agnes cast her gaze to the ground and scurried away.

'And so do you, Agnes Middleton,' she whispered, 'so do you.'

Less than three hours later, Beth's evidence was laid out word for word, double spaced like the pages of a movie script, and held in hands with perfectly manicured nails. The eyes that skipped over the text were clear and unsmiling, set shallowly in an ageing face that had once carried flawless skin stretched over delicately arched cheekbones. Glossy black hair flecked with whispers of grey was scraped back from a broad forehead into a tight pleat.

She threw the document on to the mahogany table and looked out to the rolling countryside that surrounded the house. The landscape was littered with undisciplined copses and fragmentary areas of cultivated beauty; pockets of shrubbery promised secrets behind their bushy screens, but none so dark as the one she had locked in her formidable mind.

Her journey had begun and, as the good Lord had promised, the path of righteousness was becoming clearer by the day. No one could stop her now. She had been both impressed and surprised to discover a friend in De Haus and, although she could never allow his greed for knowledge to develop into intimacy, she realised her immense indebtedness to him. Now that she had found the 'Trojan whore', the question was not how to lead it to water but how to make it drink!

CHAPTER TWELVE

B oardman sat in the police room, its drabness lending a subdued air to his already sombre mood. A single abandoned pot plant stood in the corner, the last futile attempt to stem the tide of hopelessness these places exuded. He brushed aside its fallen leaves as he watched the other police witnesses chat about their cases, their evidence, their barristers. He didn't believe in the 'new' policemen, the ones who knew all about the law but nothing about its justice: collars were loosened, tunics unfastened, tongues loose and garrulous. Looking at the table in front of him, he saw cigarette ends submerged in the remains of slurped coffee and grey-blue tea. He didn't need to be a fortune teller to interpret their patterns as far as his case was concerned. Boardman closed his eyes to concentrate on the present position. Crossing his feet at the ankle, he took on the appearance of a middle-aged guru.

His evidence was not to be challenged by the defence, but it was important that the jury hear the interview with Middleton as spoken narrative, rather than endure the boredom of reading an agreed transcript. These were always the lowest moments; waiting in a grubby room to give grubby evidence in another grubby case.

The time passed quickly as he mentally reviewed the remaining evidence. He was barely conscious of the other waiting police witnesses being called from the room to the court to give their testimony, but he knew when he was alone; so did somebody else. The telephone rang. It was 1.45 p.m. Boardman glanced around the deserted room, double checking its status before responding to the call he had anticipated.

'Boardman,' he confirmed crisply, shifting his legs, straightening his back and waiting.

Familiar plummy self-satisfied tones responded. It was Molineux. 'I understand it's going well. He's done rather a good job on her.

Must keep an eye on him. There may be a little surprise this afternoon. Don't be alarmed.'

'What surprise?' All the news this man brought ranged from bad to appalling.

Molineux swallowed a bite of disappointment before replying angrily, 'Did you always ask what your presents were on Christmas Eve?' Boardman waited for the inevitable continuation. 'There may be a little low-flying flak, nothing a man like you can't duck. Cheerio, keep low.' He replaced the receiver. The news forced Boardman to rethink the coming evidence in the trial.

The evidence this afternoon was not in dispute. There was the forensic scientist, but Middleton had agreed through his solicitors and his interview with Boardman that his sperm was found. There was the ambulance crew, but again there was no challenge to their involvement. And there was himself. Surely the defence was not going to cross-examine him when his evidence supported the defence allegation of consent? He was troubled. They were going to throw a spanner in his works and he couldn't understand which piece of the machinery it was heading for.

Troubled, Boardman attempted to clear his mind of Molineux's interference by reminding himself of the whole point of this charade. From a well-secured briefcase he retrieved the details of the cases behind this operation. Several albums of photographs marked 'Pathology' leaked from the folder, covering the table in a dead sea of suffering. There was a ruthless murderer out there, he told himself almost hollowly, gazing down at the mutilated men before him. This had to be worthwhile, didn't it?

It was 2 p.m: the forensic scientist would be the next witness. Boardman had worked with him for years. Though effective, he was undoubtedly the rudest expert Boardman had ever used. Vain and demanding, prosecution-minded, he epitomised the scientist as tyrant of the laboratory. If it was Elliott they were intending to shake, they'd better be well away from the epicentre of his Quaker temper.

Fergus Finn was an Irishman who hated Guinness. With three pints of lager on board, he took a seat in the press box, and turned to a beery scribe whose breath held a darker menu of the lunch he'd drunk. 'How did she do in her evidence?'

The man's watery eyes twinkled in amusement. 'The gorgeous

pouting Beth was the victim of a legal hit and run.' He raised an eyebrow. 'The police are appealing for a "reliable" witness.'

'That bad then?'

'Worse. The jury think she's a whore out to protect her boyfriend. So far she hasn't made much of an effort.' Fergus scowled at the ease with which this stranger judged Beth and her life. He turned his attention away from the reporter's empty unpleasantness, towards the court's belly, as a voice interrupted his thoughts.

'My lord, the prosecution call Professor Elliott.' Fergus viewed the courtroom and its participants. The gallery and press box were depleted now that Beth's evidence was over; they would fill to bursting point when Middleton took the oath. The lawyers sat almost bored in their uniform black and white; the judge's blood-red robes cut across them like a sabre wound.

After a brief delay, a short, stern bantam cock of a man strutted into the courtroom, glared at the jury, then took the oath without any necessity for the printed card. 'Elliott, Home Office.' Then he went on to outline his impressive credentials in a flat, lifeless voice. It was obvious to all that he believed his attendance at the trial to be wholly pointless, and didn't care who knew it.

'Did you examine the samples of semen in this case and match them against the defendant's sample?' Miss Moncrieff asked her witness, gazing away absentmindedly to the ceiling. The judge's pointed interruption dragged her quickly back to earth.

'Miss Moncrieff, why are we hearing this evidence? It's my understanding that the defendant's case is consent, therefore this exercise is pointless.' The judge's face was beginning to colour; a waste of court time was a waste of his time.

The prosecutor appeared taken aback at the irritation in his voice. 'I have strict instructions from the Chief Prosecutor that this evidence should be given orally.' The judge pursed his lips.

'It is my court and I shall judge what evidence can and will be tendered. However, as he is here I'll allow you to continue, but it must be brief.'

She turned back to the witness, relieved that the judge wasn't going to pursue his attack on her running of the case. 'Do you have the original sample taken from the complainant, Miss Gamble?'

The scientist produced a sealed exhibit bag containing a small phial.

'I do. It's marked exhibit BG1. That stands for Bethany Gamble, and the sample removed from her,' he added, to help the jury understand.

'Did you also receive a voluntary sample from the defendant?'

The scientist looked bored with the matter. He reached back into the exhibit bag and removed another container. 'I did, it's marked . . .' He stopped to refresh his memory from the forensic report, then turned his attention once more towards the small package. 'This can't be right. I checked it yesterday.' The small man began to rub his thinning hair furiously. 'Something's gone wrong,' he muttered.

'To what are you referring, Mr Elliott?' asked the judge.

'There's been some kind of slip-up with the exhibits.' He held up the offending packet. 'This should be marked AM 1: that stands for Arthur Middleton's sample,' he added, this time in an attempt to help himself to understand. 'It's not. It's marked BM 1 and I have no idea to whom that sample refers.' He scratched his thin chin, re-checking the markings on the phials of evidence. The strands of sandy hair that covered his pointed head like a light web began to glue themselves with sweat to his corrugated brow.

'These exhibits are vital to many cases,' the judge warned. The note of menace returned to his voice. 'Luckily not so vital in this case. If this defendant's sample is elsewhere, to whom does BM 1 belong?' The judge was clearly thinking aloud. He continued, 'I'm going to adjourn this case until these enquiries are completed.' He paused only to shake his head at Elliott before addressing the jury. 'Members of the jury, you have heard what has transpired in this court. I have to ask you not to speak to anyone outside your number about the case. I shall keep you informed. Thank you.'

The puzzled jury made their way from the courtroom. The judge turned to the prosecution.

'The witness will make all proper enquiries as to the whereabouts of the original exhibit in this case and trace the file in relation to the other exhibit. I shall accept nothing less than a full explanation. Let us hope,' he said grimly, turning a cold stare on the sweating Elliott, 'that the other case does not rely upon identification by DNA alone. The consequences will be too terrible. For all,' he warned as he rose to leave the court. 'The defendant will be remanded in custody.'

Boardman turned as the door to the police room was pushed open and the prosecutor swept in. Hurriedly he packed the sensitive files together, then placed them face downwards. Her manner was slightly flustered. Boardman was surprised she had come to speak to him. He was aware that the evidence of one witness should never be discussed with another yet to be called.

'The defence have agreed I should speak to you.' She looked worried. 'There's been a cock-up with forensic. It's a bloody good thing this is a consent case or Middleton would have walked by now. There's been a switch with his sample – we don't know how. Elliott's trying to save his own arrogant neck by claiming tampering. The thing is, it's just not like him.'

Boardman knew exactly who it was like. 'What will be the effect on the case?' He was already well aware of the effect that seeing a slipshod prosecution was intended to have on the jury.

'Who really knows? But I don't get the impression that the jury are "Take a Gamble" fans now. It just makes the whole case seem seedy and badly prepared. I didn't want to call that sodding evidence in the first place. D'Stevenson had agreed that I could read it to the jury. Then out of the blue I'm ordered, I mean *ordered*, to call Elliott. I don't understand why.'

Boardman looked away, saddened by the knowledge that he did.

'It's almost as if it was planned that way. I know it sounds a little paranoid but I have a feeling that there's a game going on that I don't know the name of or the rules to.' She looked to him to illuminate her if he could.

'What about the link case? Have they found the source of the rogue sample yet?'

Boardman looked away from the flustered prosecutor, feeling guilty. He knew the answer to his question already; it had been part of Molineux's 'acceptable loss'.

She shook her head. 'It's in the pipeline. We're praying it's not a sex case. If it is, and it's the only evidence, then the prosecution are screwed.'

The silence between them confirmed the undeniable truth of the statement.

'I want to call Maxwell to give evidence,' she said quickly, as if coming to a conclusion she had wished to avoid.

Boardman looked up quickly. 'Why? The defence have agreed his statement.' She raised her eyebrows and lowered her voice, fully aware that this next disclosure went far beyond the agreement with Middleton's barrister.

'That may be so, but the defence have all but accused him of doing the whole thing himself. D'Stevenson has done a marvellous job on Beth. I know I shouldn't be discussing the evidence with you, but I have a terrible feeling we could lose this one. What is your impression of Maxwell?'

Boardman's reply was prompt. He'd made his decision on Maxwell at their meeting. 'Nasty, brutish and tall. But not a rapist. A womaniser, yes, but not capable of this. He will, however, make an appalling impression on the jury. They might disagree with my judgement of his potential.' The unhappy prosecutor nodded her head slowly at the middle ground Boardman was forced to take by her breach of ethics. She spoke to herself, as if to confirm acknowledgement of her breach.

'You're right, it's my call. I'll have to think about it. Thanks anyway.' Marianne Moncrieff rose from her chair with the heavy aura of responsibility clinging to her. Just at that moment there was a gentle rap on the door. 'Come in,' she called sharply. Brian Carr, the beleaguered prosecution clerk with whom Fergus had spoken earlier, walked gingerly into the room looking decidedly gloomy.

'Bad news, I'm afraid,' he opined as Marianne Moncrieff turned her eyes to the heavens. 'The link has been made. BM1 refers to a defendant called McCabe. Allegation rape, evidence DNA. Results are more fucked than his victim.'

Boardman exchanged glances with the woman lawyer, attempting to play a part he was never fitted for. She failed to notice the lack of genuine surprise on his face. 'They're chasing up the McCabe file now. Not too difficult really as the trial is listed before the same judge in a week's time. Are you going to give his lordship the good news?' the clerk asked as he slumped, unhappy and underpaid, into a vacant chair.

'God, he's going to reach critical mass when he hears this.' Moncrieff sighed. 'We'd better inform the Ministry of Defence that it's a judge not a terrorist bomb that's exploded.' Her gallows humour sparked little response from Boardman. 'I'd better let the defence know what is happening and then face the wrath of the righteous.'

Moncrieff and her sidekick excused themselves and left Boardman to contemplate what he had become involved in. He restacked the files, then replaced them in the briefcase and secured it. The anticipated phone call arrived a minute or two later.

'How do you know I'm alone?' He heard a chuckle from the other party.

'You wouldn't have asked the question if you were not. Besides, I'm very careful.'

'So was Professor Elliott.'

'A small casualty. Due for retirement any time now. It will save on the expense of a farewell party.'

'What about the linked case? Was that another acceptable loss?'

'Rather clever that, wasn't it? Remember, Boardman, you are one of many. Losses can occur in the most unexpected places, to the most unsuspecting people. Now that she wants to call Maxwell, what is your evaluation of him?'

Boardman did not bother to enquire how the caller had learnt this fact. 'He will be a bad witness if called but at least the defence will have to make their case clearer. It will give him an opportunity to deny it.'

'And if he isn't called?'

'Then the stink of suspicion will be overpowering. They'll say he's got something to hide.'

'I shall see to the arrangements.' The voice hesitated for a brief second before continuing. 'Boardman,' its tone had softened to a disappointing chiding, 'be glad it's not your neck on the block.' There was a click as the receiver was replaced.

He wondered how long that would remain true. A knock on the door and a black-gowned usher informed him the court was to reconvene and his presence had been requested. Draining the last of his cold coffee, he placed his jacket over his shoulders, straightened his Police Federation tie and walked out slowly. Whilst this wasn't his 'execution', he had just finished talking to the hangman.

CHAPTER THIRTEEN

'I want to speak to her and I want to speak to her *now*.' Teddy Maxwell's large bulk filled the doorway of the entrance to the Victim Support Unit's office. The two female representatives attempted, in a 'non-confrontational' way, to place themselves between the angry American and Beth. Teddy forced his way past them. The taller of the two pushed back in front of him and, standing tall, spoke. 'Mr Maxwell,' her voice was steady but strong, 'this is a private room and you do not have an invitation. Leave before I call Security.'

He looked her up and down. 'Beth, are these people some kind of joke? Gertrude Stein and a Munchkin! Is this the company you keep now?'

'Teddy, don't cause any trouble, please,' Beth begged him, all too aware of his temper and where that unruly beast had led him in the past. Maxwell stopped abruptly, as if the misery in her voice had pulled a string in his heart. He breathed deeply and glanced around the room's occupants: all but Beth held his gaze; hers was fixed by shame and unhappiness on the vase of tulips on the table in front of her.

'Yes, Teddy,' added the woman reasonably. 'Hasn't your temper caused Beth enough problems?'

He straightened his tie then pulled himself to his full height.

'Beth, what happened in there?' He waited for her reply. None was forthcoming. 'Look at me! What's happened to you? I've been approached by people on the inside. They tell me that I'm being blamed for all this and you're doing nothing to protect me.'

Beth felt her eyes fill. She answered the accusation. 'It wasn't like that, it was the way he made it sound. I told them it wasn't you.'

'Bethany, you know you're really not supposed to talk to other witnesses about your evidence,' the shorter woman said quietly. 'The judge did warn you.'

'Beth, please.' Maxwell's eyes brimmed with self-pity as he held out his hands, palms up. 'They're crucifying me in there and you're giving them the nails. Now what did you say?' He took hold of her shoulders.

He hadn't noticed the taller woman press the silent alarm button. Seconds later two sets of blue-clad arms pulled him roughly away, his own arms twisted forcibly up his back.

'Get off me! I'll sue you into early retirement!'

One of the policemen, whispered into his ear, 'You wouldn't be such a wanker with both arms broken. Calm down and we'll let you go.'

Teddy stopped struggling.

'Remove him. He's upsetting the key witness in a rape trial,' the taller woman informed them. She moved towards Beth, who was crumpled in an armchair, tears racing down her face. 'Now, you want him to leave, don't you?' It came as a command.

Beth felt too alone to disagree. 'Just don't hurt him. Teddy, please go. We'll talk later.'

Maxwell shrugged his acceptance as the policemen loosened their restraint. 'If you won't tell them the truth, I will,' he warned, as the three of them departed slowly through the door. It shut firmly behind them.

'He means it,' said Beth sadly. 'Teddy always get what he wants.'

Teddy was afraid, Beth could see that, smell it even. Not for her, not for the loss of whatever they had shared, but for what he himself stood to lose. Don't look for trouble, Teddy, she thought to herself. Beth had enough to cope with as it was. She shook her head, aware that he was incapable of accepting advice: he didn't walk away from trouble but courted it.

Maxwell was escorted down the main corridor under the stares of passers-by, widening his arms in an effort to disguise from the onlookers that he was under police escort. Eventually, the Sergeant accompanying him stopped applying the last vestige of pressure to the television producer's arm; the Police Constable followed his example. 'Now behave yourself,' said the Sergeant. 'If not, we'll arrest you for a public order offence.'

'On what grounds?' Teddy demanded, pushing back his ruffled hair.

The Sergeant smiled. 'On the grounds we don't need any offence or evidence to do so.' His fixed smile convinced Teddy of his seriousness. For once he decided to stay quiet. He had a right to silence like everyone else and now seemed a prudent time to exercise it.

He made his way to the office of the Crown Prosecution Service. The room had been newly decorated in civil-service grey. Sad pot plants were dotted around the desk's plastic tops in an effort to humanise what appeared to be no more than a processing plant. Inside, an unhappy CPS clerk was concluding a conversation with Miss Moncrieff.

'So we'd like you to take over the prosecution of the McCabe case.'

'If you can call it that.'

'Quite.' He coughed and the conversation ended abruptly as they both turned to face Teddy.

'I did knock.' The obvious lie was accepted by them in silence. His bulk moved quickly and uninvited into the privacy of their conference. He knew he was an intimidating man; that knowledge had served him in the impressionable world of television.

'I want to give evidence.'

The lawyers glanced at each other before the prosecutor returned her gaze to Teddy.

'That won't be necessary, Mr Maxwell. The prosecution is going to read your statement to the jury.'

Without invitation he pulled out a chair and sat down, leaning towards them. He smiled bitterly. 'You don't seem to understand. Nobody in this country seems to understand their own language. I'm going to give evidence.'

Marianne Moncrieff pulled in her chair a little way and smiled acidly. 'I decide who gives evidence for the prosecution, Mr Maxwell, and I have decided that you will not.' The clerk glanced slyly at her. A telephone call from the Chief Prosecutor had certainly helped her to reach a decision. 'You have no rights regarding giving evidence except in your own defence.'

'From what I'm hearing, that's precisely why I should.' His face was menacing.

'I meant in your own trial.'

'Isn't that precisely what this has become? They're trying to blame me for those terrible things. I have a right to tell the truth.'

The clerk spoke very quietly. The slight speech impediment

that had stopped him becoming a barrister was accentuated by the confrontation.

'How do you know what happened in court, Mr Maxwell?'

Moncrieff seized upon this and went into the attack. 'Yes. How do you know? You were warned not to speak to anyone about the case until you were formally released from giving evidence. You were instructed not, I repeat *not*, to enter the courtroom.'

Maxwell remained silent.

'You've spoken to Beth about it, haven't you? You stupid, arrogant man! I couldn't call you now even if I was allowed to.'

'What do you mean "allowed" to? You just said it was your decision. Who the hell is pulling your strings? What is this superior orders? Nuremberg! I have lawyers too, you know. Ones like you who do what they are told. I also have access to newspaper editors, influential ones.' He threw back his chair which lost the short battle with gravity and clattered to the floor.

The accidental violence hushed the room. When Moncrieff finally spoke, she did so quietly but with venom. 'For your own good, I'd better tell you that if you make any comment to the papers the judge will have no hesitation in locking you up.' Maxwell stared arrogantly out of the window. 'It will be contempt in the face of the court; in his face. He really doesn't take very kindly to a slap like that.'

He slammed his hand down hard against the window sill and spun round. 'This fucking country is upside down. It's a tea party that the hatter would refuse to attend. He's in the dock and I'm on trial – how do you square that one?'

They both stood, alerted by the violence of his outburst.

'On reflection, go ahead and speak to the press. I'd love to see a bully like you remanded to prison. You wouldn't last past your first shower.' This threat seemed to calm the angry American. He stared from one to the other of them for a long moment, picked up the chair and replaced it gently to its former position. 'Do you realise what they'll do to me after this? If he's acquitted, I'm finished. Perhaps not at first. Oh, no, they'll make sure there are a few expense errors, then they'll ask friendly accounts to allege they can't work with me. Then it's all over. The Income Support man cometh.'

The quiet desperation of his voice evoked Moncrieff's sympathy. 'I have a feeling we're all going to lose out one way or the other, Mr Maxwell. It's just a question of degree. There's nothing I can do. Please accept from me that in law there is nothing you can do either.'

She closed her brief, nodded at him, then made her way briskly towards the door.

'They'll be calling Middleton this afternoon. I'll do my best,' she said over her shoulder as she left.

'She doesn't look very confident.'

The clerk turned his gaze to his work then began to write. Realising the conversation was over, Teddy left for the nearest bar. It had been a very long time since he'd destroyed a few million brain cells. Who knew whether he would ever need them again?

The case for the prosecution concluded with Boardman's evidence of Arthur Middleton's police interview. He was not cross-examined by D'Stevenson. His evidence served to remind the jury that Middleton had made the same allegations at the time of his arrest: that Beth was a whore who was beaten by her boyfriend. On Boardman's withdrawal from the witness box, the judge turned to D'Stevenson and nodded for him to begin the defence case. The barrister rose to his feet and spoke.

'My lord, there is a question of law that I would seek your guidance upon. In the absence of the jury, of course.'

The judge appeared puzzled. He searched his considerable intellect for the existence of a point of law at this stage and could find none; the jury either believed the victim or they did not, it was as simple as that.

'Very well, the jury will retire until they are called again. Let me explain. I am the judge of the law, you are the judges of the facts. When a matter of law arises, I must deal with it in your absence.'

The jury were absent for an hour during D'Stevenson's submission that the judge should stop the case and order an acquittal.

'My lord,' he pleaded, 'the prosecution case is a shambles. The forensic evidence is worthless.'

'The forensic evidence was always worthless once your client decided his defence was consent, not identification. Now what is your point?' Mr Justice Woolmington was losing patience.

'The point is this,' D'Stevenson continued. 'The sum total of the prosecution case is her word against his. There is *no other* evidence that could convict him of this crime, and *that* evidence is flawed and inconsistent.' D'Stevenson was testing the water. He didn't expect the judge to stop the case, but wanted to see what he was thinking; how he would sum it up.

The judge shook his head. 'That's precisely why we have a jury, isn't it?' he enquired acidly. 'To decide issues of fact such as this. I will not usurp their function by interfering. Usher, will you ask the jury to come back into court and the case can then proceed?'

They were brought back in. The judge nodded to D'Stevenson to begin the defence case.

Beth sat flanked by her protectors from the VSU. The court waited. She felt like an actress in a black and white film of the 1930s: it was all so colourless and so polite. The cliché was cemented by the only sound she could hear – the court clock ticking its day to another end. Beth swivelled to look at the rapturous faces in the public gallery, held in silence by their anticipation of the drama to come.

D'Stevenson rose, turned and nodded to the jury, then swivelled and pointed to his client. 'I call Arthur Middleton to give evidence in his own defence.'

The defendant straightened his jacket as the prison officer escorted him to the witness box. The New Testament was offered and accepted as Middleton swore to his Maker to testify truthfully. His voice held nothing of the animal anger that Beth remembered from that terrible night, and which had filled her flat and her dreams ever since. His delivery was as reasonable and calm as D'Stevenson's questioning. Beth shuddered as he recounted the well-rehearsed litany of lies before the jury's hungry gaze. She screwed her eyes tightly shut as he told of the supposed frantic abandon of their sexual relations.

'Then, when I left,' he turned towards the jury, 'I felt so guilty about my wife Agnes, so ashamed. I shut the door quietly. Beth,' he spoke the name tenderly, 'I'm sorry, Miss Gamble, was asleep. She was exhausted. That's when I saw Mr Maxwell, at least I think it was him, making his way on foot. I thought, Best get out of here, Arthur. This could get messy. I wish I'd stayed. Perhaps I could have helped her, I don't know.'

D'Stevenson allowed the sad sincerity to wash across the court-room and over the jurors. Beth felt ashamed. It wasn't true, anyone could see that. She avoided the jury's questioning stares, feeling the hot flush of shame race unbidden to her cheeks; it was so unfair that he was allowed to say these things about her. She fought to control the warmth in her face but lost the battle.

D'Stevenson continued. 'Do you own a ski-mask?'

Middleton looked puzzled at first, then remembered the script. 'I've never been skiing in my life, sir, and no, I do not and never have owned a ski-mask.'

D'Stevenson turned to the judge and spoke. 'I would ask my learned friend to make a formal admission that no ski-mask was ever recovered from the defendant's home, my lord, and no fibres or blood found that could link the defendant with this crime.' The judge turned to the prosecutor.

With reluctance, but by agreement, she acknowledged these facts unchallenged. There was no forensic. D'Stevenson leant over the counsel's bench and stared unblinkingly into his client's face. 'Arthur Middleton, you are charged with rape. Are you a rapist?' His gaze did not waver from Middleton's face.

Middleton looked down at his hands, the nails of one biting into the palm of the other. He stared first at his barrister, then at Beth, and shook his head from side to side. 'I committed adultery that night and for that I must ask Agnes's forgiveness. But rape . . .' He paused, almost saddened by the accusation. 'Not that, no.'

Beth could stand it no longer. She rose quickly from her position in the court and shuffled past the various occupants. The jury turned to see the cause of the minor disturbance. As she made her way from the court, a loud stage-whisper was directed towards the jury from D'Stevenson. 'No stomach for the truth.' It was heard by all. The door was held open for her by a disapproving court official.

Fergus had witnessed her ignominious exit from the room. He found her in the canteen. She sat alone. The only other people in the room sat at tables far away from the hunched and shaking figure of Beth Gamble. Fergus placed a reassuring hand on her shoulder. She flinched and spun around, before focusing on his face. She quickly turned her attention to where her lightly polished nails had cut through the back of her left hand and drawn blood. Gently Fergus took the offending hand in his as he sat down opposite. 'Take it easy,' he soothed. She pulled her hand away slowly from his and buried it beneath her legs.

'I didn't want to go back to the Victim Support Room.'

He lit a cigarette. 'It didn't look so good, leaving like that.'

'It wasn't meant to. I don't know what I meant. I had to leave before I screamed at the bastard to tell the truth. It's funny. They tell you at the police station that you will be protected, yet all the time they know it's impossible. It's just what they say to get what they want.'

Beth felt bitter and angry and impotent; it was an explosive combination.

'All those people in the court, listening to his lies – they were so ready to believe the worst of me. Just because you are on television, you are a slut to them. It's typical. The English public only ever build you up to knock you down.'

He waited until her anger had evaporated. A man was watching her, his slack, sneering face an all too visual confirmation of her recent remarks,

'What are you looking at?' Beth snarled. 'This isn't a freak show.' The stranger dropped his gaze, another social voyeur challenged away from his hobby.

Fergus whistled through his teeth, pushing a ring of smoke from his mouth. He spoke slowly.

'A good lawyer could convince me that I'm a teetotaller, at least for a while. Then I'd look at the evidence – no money, bad breath, eyes like a Jamaican sunset – I'd use my common-sense just like the jury will, and see through all the smooth talk. They'll come to the right result, just like me.'

He reached out his hand again, this time she took it and squeezed.

'Hey, hey, I don't want a Chinese burn,' he warned.

She relaxed her grip. 'They say the jury will go out tomorrow, after the summing up. What if he's acquitted?' Beth sounded lost and afraid.

Fergus searched for an adequate reply. There was none. The late-morning sunlight cut through the canteen's smoke-ridden atmosphere, reminding them of the world outside. 'We'll know tomorrow, won't we?' she whispered.

He could only nod his agreement and draw on the dying embers of his cigarette.

CHAPTER FOURTEEN

The courtroom was as packed as a tin of sardines. People had queued for hours with thermos flasks and sleeping bags; it was like the Harrod's sale. Now, jostling for an extra inch of space and comfort, they awaited the moment of truth; or not, Beth concluded bitterly. The judge's voice summoned her away from her thoughts; he was concluding his summing up of the trial.

'So those are the issues for you, as members of the jury, to resolve. It comes down to a very simple question: who is telling the truth. Remember, it is for the prosecution to prove its case. The defendant need prove nothing. If, having heard all of the evidence, both defence and prosecution you are satisfied so that you are sure – which is the same as beyond reasonable doubt – that the attack occurred in the way that Miss Gamble described, then you will convict. If you are not, it is your duty to acquit. I can only accept a verdict, at this stage, which is the verdict of you all. You will find it useful to appoint a "chairperson" to regulate your discussions. Swear the jury bailiffs in.'

The court officials swore the oath to protect the jury from outside interference, then escorted them from the courtroom.

The women from the VSU had suggested Beth sit at the end of the bench, so that the jury might see her better. She suspected this was to avoid any repetition of yesterday's abrupt exit.

'What happens now?' she asked. 'I suppose we just wait?' The woman from the unit nodded.

The press had attempted to outbid each other for a story that she would never sell. Teddy and the Paxton executives had tentatively suggested a repeat showing of the Middleton programme with an update on her feelings during the trial. This was, of course, dependent upon a conviction. The question of any other scenario had never been discussed. Beth left the courtroom.

Teddy was waiting outside, on Beth's route to the Victim Support

Room. 'Well, Beth, they'll nail him soon enough. I have a table booked for this evening at Marco's new place. A perfect spot to celebrate.' His smile was as broad as his shoulders, and his nerve.

She turned to him without slackening her pace. 'Whatever happens there's nothing to celebrate, and if there were I wouldn't choose you to celebrate with.'

Where had he been when she . . . Beth stopped herself. She didn't need him, she'd just thought she did; now she knew the truth of it. He had kept his distance. Was it his guilt about the argument that kept him from facing her? Or was it that he didn't want to catch a dose of failure? Victims felt like failures; rape victims like sexual plague carriers, unable to shift the conviction that they had caused it to happen. Teddy probably believed that once the trial was over her victim status would fade away along with the jury's verdict. Beth wouldn't let that happen. This had changed her, was changing her, and as yet she had no idea what the metamorphosis would bring.

She knew that others needed constant reminders that these things, these horrors, were real. Like the Holocaust survivors' insistence that the nature of evil should not be diluted by the passage of time, she would not, could not forget. They were all examples of the base nature of others' perceived needs. Beth realised she had been staring at Teddy Maxwell all this time, as if he were a stuffed buffalo or caribou, something misplaced, outdated, extinct. It appeared Teddy could read her thoughts. His large figure seemed to implode, as though he could see himself through her eyes. He looked like the fat unhappy boy in the family picture. Whilst the weight had dropped away, the glasses been replaced with contact lenses and the teeth straightened by the metal brace, he was still the same unhappy child underneath. Teddy shrugged his shoulders and walked away.

As Beth continued her route, a call could be heard from inside the court room: 'The case of the Crown against McCabe.' She stopped. Two grey-faced police officers made their way into the room she had just left. They escorted a slim, brown-haired woman between them. Her build was almost identical to Beth's, her height not noticeably different. Her clothing however was dowdy by comparison: Beth rebuked herself for the unkindness of that last thought. Her features – finely chiselled with good bone structure – reflected Beth's own, but there was little strength in them. Her desperate eyes looked fixed in the full beam of the Old Bailey's headlights. She appeared as light and fragile as a tissue. Her escort was for support, not restraint.

'Isn't that the case that was mentioned in our trial? The one where the samples were mixed?' Beth asked herself aloud.

'It is,' Boardman confirmed. She had not heard him approach and turned to face him. She was surprised to see doubt and unhappiness etched on his face. 'I'm sorry to say that young woman has some very bad news coming her way. She was the victim of BM 1, or at least for the next few moments she is. After that she's just another crimeless victim.'

His words were brimming with pity for the woman about to confront her rapist, or her ex-rapist as he would soon become. Beth watched her disappear into the open maw of the courtroom.

'I want to see what happens,' she said, and quickly returned inside.

A rat-faced boy was lounging over the front of the dock rail, his razor thin face openly contemptuous.

'Stand up straight!' shouted the judge's clerk. With a grin towards the public gallery, exposing ruined teeth, the defendant moderated his posture by a few degrees.

'Are you William McCabe?'

He nodded.

'Say "yes",' commanded the clerk.

'Yes!' he snapped in response.

The clerk turned towards the judge, who was regarding the youth with undisguised contempt. 'The defendant has previously pleaded not guilty to an offence of rape and has been remanded in custody,' informed the clerk.

'Any change in the plea?' asked the judge optimistically.

'None, my lord,' said Stott, his barrister, a half-smile on his face.

'Very well, Miss Moncrieff,' continued Mr Justice Woolmington. 'I understand that you now appear to prosecute this case. This matter is linked, purely by negligence, to the other matter before the court. The same order applies. It will be contempt of this court for any person to publish, print or otherwise to disclose the identity of the complainant in this case.' He looked towards the depleted ranks of the press box. 'What is the prosecution's position?'

'Might I point out that I have only just been given conduct of this case?' The judge nodded. 'As you are aware, there was an inexplicable error. The case against McCabe was based on a

97

sample matched against that taken from beneath the claws of the complainant's cat. The animal attacked the rapist after he had attacked the victim. After his arrest a sample match was made. McCabe denied the offence. The sample was somehow switched with the Middleton sample.'

The judge interrupted her. 'The net result being that the prosecution cannot prove there was no contamination between the samples, or even whether the correct samples were tested.' This was for the benefit of the court; he himself understood the consequences all too well.

'Your lordship puts it so much better than I.'

He ignored the ingratiating reply. 'So what does the Crown propose?'

Moncrieff offered her gravest voice. 'We have no other evidence to offer to a jury, therefore with reluctance we must discontinue the proceedings.' She sat down, dejectedly.

The judge sucked in his cheeks, then exhaled. 'Very well.' He turned to the boy in the dock. 'McCabe, you have heard what has occurred. The charge has been discontinued. That means you are free to go.'

The thin youth glared round the court aggressively. 'That's it, is it? I spend nine months on the rule 'cos of some crap scientist and that is all you have to say?'

Stott turned towards the youth, a finger held out to silence him. 'No, McCabe,' said Mr Justice Woolmington in a threatening whisper. 'It is because of a,' he hesitated from using the same expression, 'scientist that you are free to go. Get out of my court and consider this: I was to try your case and if you had been convicted by the jury, I would have imprisoned you for life!' He was puce with fury, and meant every syllable.

The prison officer removed the defendant before he could respond. He still found sufficient time however to grin in the direction of the group of people Beth had seen enter the court. The woman looked familiar; not famous, just familiar. Beth couldn't grasp from where or when, just experienced the fleeting impression of having met her before.

'Miss Moncrieff, is the complainant in court?' the judge enquired.

The barrister turned towards the huddled group as all eyes in court followed her gaze to the ashen-faced woman. The judge looked weary with the imperfections of the law. He had evidently witnessed too many obvious injustices, and had prepared himself for another. He dropped his head and his voice before speaking. 'Then I must on behalf of the administration of justice apologise and explain what has occurred. It is tragic that due to the incompetence of so-called experts, this should come to pass. We are sincere in our regret.' A note was passed to him by the court clerk; he seemed to brighten at the call to adjudicate further. He opened his notebook at the appropriate page and sat like a wrinkled, ancient schoolboy. The brief apology echoed hollowly in the court.

'Now, I am informed that the jury in the case of the Crown v. Middleton has sent out a note in the form of a question. Ask Mr D'Stevenson to return. Prison officers, produce your prisoner. I shall wait for the court to convene.'

Beth pulled down the hem of her skirt; for some reason it now felt too short and tight. Her make-up felt over-applied and caked on her face, though she knew it was all natural tones. She held her breath, terrified by the jury's abnormally swift return.

'A question? They've only been retired for fifteen minutes.' Beth felt panic-stricken.

The women from the unit each took a hand. 'It sometimes happens,' said the smaller. 'They often ask for help with the law. Most of the barristers don't understand it either.'

Beth wondered how many times these two had been through this situation. All her previous efforts to glean information had been deflected with kind words and warm tea. D'Stevenson arrived next and took his place in counsel's benches. She could hear the opening of a security door moments before Middleton was produced. Beth felt sick to her stomach. She swallowed hard, fighting not to regurgitate the coffee she'd just drunk. Eventually the revolt abated, then she concentrated on the judge's advice to the twelve strangers who would decide her future. There was a brief exchange between Middleton and his counsel. The defendant nodded as some explanation was proffered and accepted.

'I have a note from the jury which counsel are aware of,' said the judge. 'In it they frame the following question. "We have had read to us a statement from Mr Maxwell. Why didn't he give evidence to us? Can we hear him give evidence now? Can you help?" My own view, subject to your agreement, is this. Firstly, there can be no explanation given as to the prosecution's failure to call him; they must only look at the agreed evidence contained in his statement.

Secondly, that the case is closed and they cannot hear evidence once that position is reached. Thirdly, no, we cannot help them further. Does counsel agree with that direction?'

Beth could barely make out the quiet agreement from the prosecutor, and D'Stevenson indicated that he had no objections.

'Very well,' the judge concluded. 'Ask the jury to come in and I shall explain.'

A few stale minutes crawled by before the administrative task was complete. The judge reiterated his opinion. The jury looked confused.

'Now, if you will retire again and consider further?' he invited.

'Court rise,' demanded the clerk. The judge walked slowly along the raised dais that elevated him over the rest of the court. Beth thought he looked as perplexed as the jury.

'They think it was Teddy.' She felt the bile rise again from the curdling acidity of her stomach.

The VSU women's hands were withdrawn from her own as she spoke. The tall one produced some macramé work from her cane handbag and set to work further on its dull design.

'I'm going for a walk, get some air,' Beth sighed; she needed a respite from the sealed constraints of this room and its occupants.

'We'll go with you.'

She was already sidling away. Outside, she half-expected to see Teddy but he was conspicuously absent. The marble flooring accentuated the painful throbbing of her feet. Why had she worn such ridiculous shoes? She found a window. Hugging her arms across her breasts she viewed the traffic. Did she deserve it? Had D'Stevenson been right, that reporting without due care for the circumstances made her equally as guilty as her subjects?

'Well, it's in the lap of the jurors.' Deep in thought, she had failed to hear Boardman's approach. He continued, looking closely at her, 'I don't pretend to understand how you feel, but I always find the waiting the worst. If it's of any consolation, so do the barristers.' Boardman looked as though he had been caught with his hand in the proverbial till.

'It's odd,' said Beth. 'In all the cases I covered as a junior reporter, in all kinds of different courts, I was only interested in getting the best copy available. It never crossed my mind, at least not properly, that these weren't just stories – they were people's lives.'

Boardman looked sympathetic. He reminded her of her father at this moment. 'It's a job, Beth, that's all. What D'Stevenson does is the same. He doesn't have to believe in his client's innocence, just that the decision is not his – it's the jury's.'

'Why are they taking so long?' she asked bitterly.

Boardman looked slightly uncomfortable. 'I remember a case some years ago. It was as clear as I'd ever seen. The jury were out for three hours. After that they returned a guilty verdict and nobody was surprised. The usher asked why it had taken so long. Apparently it had taken two and a half hours to elect a foreman, twenty minutes for a cup of tea, and ten minutes to convict. The point is, you never know.'

She considered the story for a moment. 'Thanks,' she said, grateful that he should take the trouble to tell her an apocryphal tale.

'Look, I've a few things to attend to. Once that's done, what about . . .'

'For God's sake, please don't say a cup of tea.'

'A drop of the good stuff. There's always a bottle in the police room.' They walked slowly together, not touching, but she found his presence comforting. He opened the door and asked if she would sit with him. Beth smiled gratefully before replying, 'No. Thank you, but no. I have to see this thing through by myself.'

A tannoy announcement interrupted: 'The jury in court two are returning with a verdict.'

Beth shuddered.

'Come on, we'll go back together,' said Boardman.

He offered his arm. She refused with a watery smile. If this was how she reacted, how was Middleton feeling at this moment?

Inside the court, anticipation silenced any idle talk. Even the press, forever ready to witness the downfall of others, were mute.

D'Stevenson sat with his hand supporting his head; Miss Moncrieff had adopted a similar posture. The command to rise was obeyed with uniform solemnity. The judge strode on to his bench, opened his notebook, then spoke. 'Produce the prisoner, then bring back the jury.'

The court clock appeared to breach some rule of relativity, the second hand refusing to obey the machinery's command to rotate at the normal rate. Then Middleton appeared, turning to his wife. The jury entered the room. The twelve moved distractedly towards their box. Beth could see their blank faces reflected in the courtroom's harsh sodium lighting. All of them were smartly dressed for the final day of the trial. One middle-aged man risked a quick glance in Beth's direction before the herd's momentum propelled him towards his seat. Shuffling rather than moving, all heads now averted, they found their allotted places.

The clerk spoke. 'Would your foreman please stand?'

Boardman took Beth's hand in his as a suburban matron in a once-fashionable frock rose to her feet.

'Have the jury reached a verdict upon which they are all agreed?' asked the clerk of the court, barking out the question to the uncomfortable chairwoman.

She looked around to her fellow members for final confirmation. All nodded in the affirmative, one or two braving a glance at Beth.

'And how say you? On the count of rape, do you find the defendant Arthur Middleton guilty or not guilty?'

She pushed out her chin before replying firmly, 'We find the defendant not guilty.'

CHAPTER FIFTEEN

The suggestion of a smile quirked the corners of her mouth as she gently replaced the receiver in its cradle. Irrespective of the many women she would continue to help, the countdown to her Perfect Day had truly begun.

She walked to the far end of the study and knelt down, pulling back the fringes of a brightly coloured Chinese rug. She carefully picked at the corner of a false section of the highly polished beechwood flooring and punched in the combination of the digital locking mechanism. The hydraulic door of the safe hissed open and she reached inside, retrieving a hefty file. Returning to the chaise-longue, she curled her legs beneath her and sat clutching the concealed treasure with the satisfied grin of a well-fed cat.

By ensuring the acquittal of Arthur Middleton, her pursuers had unwittingly created the perfect martyr for her cause.

The mail had continued to arrive in an even flow in the month since Middleton's acquittal. During the trial there had been a bar on publicity; that restraint no longer ensured Beth's protection. Neither could her home, or at least it felt that way. She looked at the contents of her living room. Two elegant 'Scoppos' couches split the drawing room into acceptable proportions; one facing inward to the marble Adam fire surround. The day was cold, but Beth had felt cold ever since it had happened. The walls displayed none of the showbusiness trappings of self-congratulation. Instead, tasteful prints and an original Chagalle marked her wish to be separate and apart from her career. She looked towards the now-abandoned bedroom where it had all taken place. Sleeping in the guest bedroom was not ideal, but she was closer to her father should he ever cry out and further away from the memories her room contained.

Beth returned her attention to the mail. As she did so she felt the physical manifestation of the attack; a pulling at her groin when she moved too quickly. It was a minor ailment compared with her dreams. Beth shuddered as she forced away images of him, his freedom, his ability to do it again. She looked down at the messages from 'wellwishers'. The letters of support, threats and promises of eternal damnation, found their way from the studio to her home. The mail seemed to be evenly split. Many argued the moral hell she had chosen to work within had led her down this path; others that she was a slut getting everything she deserved.

Beth decided to reply to each and every one. Her only limit was the amount she could take on in any given day. Teddy had been keeping away and she was as welcome as a bad smell around the TV studio. They had insisted that a lengthy rest was in order, and 'best for all concerned'. Several newspapers had offered increasingly large bribes for her to tell her story. No doubt she would be asked to pose in her underwear to do so. Only Fergus had been solid throughout. Fergus, now working with another crew, telephoned regularly, filling her in on station gossip.

'It's me, doll. Things are tighter than a nun's arse down here. No one is talking about the show any more, not even Teddy. He's been put in charge of a kids' TV show. The women in the office, well, most of them, are treating him like herpes on the Pope's ring. I'll keep you informed.'

Today a package marked 'private' attracted her attention. It was A4 size, bulky, containing what felt like documentation. She retrieved her silver paper knife, a 'present' from Paxton TV, slit the side of the package and reached into the folder. Beth was being careful. The police had counselled extreme caution. They knew of instances where razor blades had been left taped down on the flap to slice open an unsuspecting thumb or sever a fingernail.

The file offered up its contents. A pink legal folder bore the name 'Arthur Middleton' and underneath in bold capitals the word RAPIST. Beth turned to the first page. There was a professional photo inside. It was recent and taken with the aid of a telephoto lens. The result was high quality – there was minimal break-up of the picture. Whoever had shot it possessed top-grade equipment.

Middleton was leaving a sex shop, its neon sign naming it for what it was. Beth began to breathe more swiftly, the anger ballooning inside her. She took a little time, sipping Evian water and thinking cool thoughts, before turning her attention to the next document: an order form to a Danish importer of violent pornography. Middleton had requested *Hit and Fuck, Schindler's Lust* (the rape and murder of the Jews) and *Nasty Bastard*. How appropriate. The date of the order corresponded with the date of the trial. A small photocopy was annexed to a blank piece of paper. Rotating it sideways, she saw it was his five-year membership of the Nymph Adult Cinema. Beth knew of its reputation.

The rest of the documentation was bulky. It contained papers on Arthur's marriage: not his marriage certificate but the true history of his union with Agnes Middleton. Numerous documents, affidavits, statements and applications to the court to protect her from yet another beating. The catalogue of injuries was awful. Three broken noses, numerous black eyes and countless bruises formed the basis of the applications. The court's stamp at the foot of every pathetic plea for help completed the picture. 'Application withdrawn by Plaintiff.' On five separate occasions she had *almost* been strong enough to call a halt to the abuse. Each time, her courage had obviously failed. Recalling Arthur's performance during the trial, Beth could understand why.

Finally, a separate piece of paper written in the most cultured of hands. It was meant for her, Beth felt sure. It was as delicate and beautiful as the contents of its message. The paper was Chinese silk and the characters upon it more than matched its richness. Beth sensed this message was the real point of the package. It was a quotation from the *Book of Ezekiel*, 16:44

'As is the Mother so is the Daughter.'

There was nothing else. No clue, no name, just this reference. How had anyone managed to obtain this information? It could be Agnes, yet Beth doubted it. The legal documents revealed the domination Middleton held over her. Her attendance at the trial confirmed that it remained. If it wasn't her, then who could it be?

Beth studied the papers for some time. They proved nothing in themselves. The court cases were a matter of public record, the porn club membership was dubious but not illegal, the application for the videos was no more than that. The biblical reference was unfathomable. Her own mother had died when she was six: Beth did not believe it could refer to her. It was meant to be symbolic, she concluded, but of what?

The heading of the bundle marked its sender as knowing the truth about the night of the attack. If so, why hadn't he or she come forward? The day was wearing Beth down. These last months had taken a toll. She felt the ragged scraping of a migraine, crawling along the base of her neck. She repackaged the papers within their folder and placed it in the floor safe.

The flat she had felt so at peace in was alien to her now. Fergus had suggested a move but that was precluded by her father's special needs. It had taken months of work to install the special equipment he required to get through the day without complete loss of dignity. She knew she would have to stick it out for her father's sake and so she must work the weary hours away. Losing herself in a wilderness of work was now her path through the days.

Hours later the telephone's insistence interrupted her scant concentration. Beth moved to the answerphone. It automatically vetted calls by a time delay sequence, allowing her to intercept and end another torrent of abuse from a 'well-wisher'. She depressed the play button.

'Beth, it's Teddy.' His voice sounded heavy with seriousness. 'We have to meet. There are things to attend to, urgent things to discuss. I've booked a table at Marco's for eight-thirty. If I don't hear to the contrary I'll expect you there. 'Bye.'

There was little warmth in the words. She knew him well enough to conclude that it wasn't going to be about them, just her. The call had done nothing to alleviate her headache. Should she go? When she had last seen him, shortly before the verdict, his suggestion of dinner appalled her. Now after the months had dragged by, she felt it right to tell him exactly what his failure to support her had meant. Besides, his tone was ominous; she recognised it as his business manner. That meant it concerned the television station and must involve her future with it: that was, if one existed after this bloody mess. Beth knew she would regret going, but felt unable to refuse the intrigue in his voice. Teddy knew her well, but that was the old, flighty Beth, the one who'd died the day Middleton violated her body. She would go, but on her own terms. There would be no scenes, no arguments, just a hard-nosed meeting about her career.

She just hoped she could hold it together and avoid another screaming competition: the last one had ended in her rape.

Checking her watch, she saw she had four hours before the meeting and needed some rest. Pulling her dressing gown around her, she quietly opened the door to her sleeping father's room. He lay, grey and still, breathing shallowly. He had been like this for months now. The specialists said there was nothing they could do: the disease was degenerative and irreversible. He had not been expected to last this long.

Folding the duvet back to allow him to cool, she wiped the spittle from his chin then left for her own room to attempt to sleep.

She didn't need the alarm clock's aid; she had not slept and the time had been like heavy water dripping. As she rose, Beth could hear Lottie, her father's nurse, chattering to him in the knowledge that his condition would allow no meaningful response.

'Lottie, I'm going out for the evening. Leave the listening device on. I've got my bleeper if anything happens.' The nurse babysat for a French diplomat most evenings. The nearness of their flat in the same building made it an ideal arrangement.

'Yes, Beth, your father and I are just debating women's rights,' Lottie shouted. 'Has he always been so argumentative?' Beth smiled, knowing the debate had been one-sided. The shower relaxed the nape of her neck as she rubbed herself with Chanel gel. If she was going to be sacked then at least she was going to smell irresistible.

The rain hammered a tattoo of insistence on the black cab's roof. The driver had guessed Beth's mood correctly; the journey was concluded in silence. It deposited her at the restaurant's Georgian frontage. Beth moved quickly from the damp of the outside air and into the pink glow of the foyer. Fashionable people sat around on Chesterfields, paying homage to the brilliance of the chef though they had not yet tasted a morsel of his food. 'Not that it would make any difference,' she whispered to herself. As the maître d' took her cream Burberry she checked her watch, delighted to see that she was unfashionably prompt. Beth was escorted to the table. The maître d' walked with the fluidity of mercury. His clipped matinee moustache twitched as he spoke. 'Mr Maxwell is here already, madam.'

She saw him from behind. He was leaning forward, hunched shoulders almost hugging his ears.

'Your table, madam.' The maître d' looked towards Teddy who simply stared. The waiter tutted at his reluctance to rise to his feet to greet her, then strutted away, muttering *'Bon appetit'*, his insincerity louder than his words.

'Well, Teddy, let's get right to it.' Beth was going to be business-like.

She waited as he removed the complimentary matches from their holder and lit several of them, staring into their brief ignition. 'They've got me on a kids' programme.' He was full of pity, but only for himself. The matches formed a thin grey smouldering bonfire. 'A kids' programme . . . me, a BAFTA winner! Jugglers and acne-pitted singers and presenters. A 5 a.m. start. They know I don't normally go to bed till 3.'

'We have all had to adapt to what has happened,' snapped Beth, feeling her earlier resolve to remain calm leak away in the company of this self-obsessed boor.

He looked up quickly, alarmed by the harshness of her tone. 'But it wasn't my fault.'

So that was it. Beth breathed in slowly before speaking. 'And whose fault was it, Teddy? Because there is only one other candidate at this table. Is that what all this is about, you self-pitying bastard? You're worse than the weirdos and fanatics who write to me. You can't handle what's happened so you want to blame me.' Her voice had been rising steadily.

Teddy offered a weak grin of apology to the other diners. 'This isn't the place,' he muttered.

'The place for what? Guilt transference? A letter of dismissal?' She heard the hoarse bark of distress in her voice. 'Because I've been through a lot, Teddy. We were close, not marriage or anything, but we were once a team, at work and in bed.'

'Keep your voice down, damn it!' he ordered through lightly clenched teeth. 'Do you know how difficult it is to get a table in here?'

Beth glanced at her ex-lover. 'You don't need a table, Teddy, you need a life. Do you know how difficult *that* is to get?' The tears had come at last. After all she had promised herself, after the deep breathing in the back of the black cab, she had crumpled when he acted exactly as she had expected. Beth was furious with herself for being such a soft target. She needed to be somewhere else, away from him. She was a fool for coming, and a pathetic fool for crying. As she stood, her napkin fell to the floor. Teddy attempted to break its fall, but only succeeded in knocking his glass on to the porcelain plate where it smashed loudly in the sudden quietness of the dining room. She turned quickly and walked away.

The disapproving glances of their fellow diners accompanied her to the ladies' room. Inside, heavy Venetian marble framed a too

108

large vanity mirror. What Beth saw in it did nothing to enhance her own vanity. She snapped open her bag, then realised she'd forgotten to pack a tissue.

Beth reached towards the stack of pure cotton hand-towels piled next to the handbasin. 'They're too rough for your skin,' a soft Home Counties voice murmured. A silk handkerchief was passed to her. Taking it, she dabbed at her eyes. As she removed smeared mascara her vision began to clear. Standing in the mirror's reflection was a woman, smiling shyly. Blonde hair and blue eyes topped a body of similar proportions to Beth's own, their taste in clothing seemed to be a common one. Though the woman's voice was steady her body's involuntary swaying spoke of her discomfiture with the situation. There seemed an almost colt-like skittishness to this stranger.

'It's kind of you. It is so embarrassing, arguing in public.'

'Some things have to be done in the public eye, it's the only way,' the woman replied to Beth's apology. 'I don't mean to intrude, but is there anything I can do?' she asked.

'No, this is something I have to deal with alone.' Beth looked at the stained handkerchief. 'Look what I've done. Let me have it dry cleaned . . .'

The woman was shaking her head as she began to open the door, to leave. 'You don't have to deal with anything alone, Beth.' The door closed on the mention of her name.

Alarmed, Beth finished a hasty make-up repair then returned to the dining room. It could be that she'd recognised Beth from TV or the newspaper, but there'd been something knowing in her voice, an intimacy. Beth realised that the woman herself seemed familiar, but felt unable to make the connection. Teddy had not moved, despite the public humiliation. She resumed her seat and searched the room for the woman. There were several dining couples and a party of businessmen, who appeared to be looking in her direction, but no sign of the blonde.

Teddy was furious. He leaned his stubbled chin towards her; it was meant to introduce a note of intimacy but failed.

'Nice exit, Bethany. I have to warn you that you may soon be making a more permanent exit that that.'

She hardened her face.

'Teddy, if you mean you and I . . .'

He cut in, relaxing slightly. God, he wasn't going to be sincere after all this, was he?

'I didn't come here to talk about us, I came to warn you about your future with the company. You've caused a loss of confidence in the investors. Management is jittery and your contract's under review. I found out today they've sent it off for legal advice to see if your recent *problems* have breached any of the behavioural clauses. I don't think so myself, neither do they, that's why they've sent it to their lawyers. You can't afford another slip-up. Now, let's order.'

He handed her a menu. Placing it on the table, she realised she'd been clutching the handkerchief all along. Beth snapped open her handbag. Inside, a piece of white paper caught her eye. It hadn't been there when she was searching for a tissue. Teddy was hidden behind his menu, gloomily turning over the prospect of a life spent dealing with small furry animals and small obnoxious children. Beth slid the note from its resting place, then smoothed it out against her side of the menu.

> 'A bruised reed shall He not break,
> and the smoking flax shall He not quench.'
>
> *Isaiah 42:3*

The address of a gun club, and the time 10.30 a.m., were written underneath. She knew the handwriting from the file marked RAP-IST, but not the author, or at least not yet. Tomorrow, the gun club might provide the solution.

CHAPTER SIXTEEN

ve left him in the hall. The blood ran along the grip-free surface of her rubber suit down to the cheap flooring; there was always a lot of blood. He still shuddered where he lay between the table and the kitchen door. She knew these were death throes; she'd seen them a few times now. Eve felt a quiet detachment at these times, almost a peace rather than a passion, and she was getting better at it. This one had been easy, almost insultingly easy; she knew the Perfect Day would be more demanding. The cutting tool was wiped free of tissue, its saw-toothed edge snagging slightly against the lint cloth in her left hand. She allowed herself a wry smile when she thought about the rest of this portion of the operation.

'Clever,' she whispered. Eve stooped slightly to the jerking spasm of his body, lifted back his head to watch his final moment in the glaze of his fish eyes. As he slid away, two tears of blood dripped from the eyeball's ruptured capillaries. She moved her face towards his; her tongue flicked out, licking one then the other from his uninhabited body.

'Next,' she whispered, 'who's next?'

The shrill ring of the telephone pierced Molineux's sleep. Quickly turning over, he noticed it was 5 a.m. He reached to the phone and grunted his presence to the caller, careful not to disturb his wife's sleeping figure. 'Molineux. What is it?'

'We've had a warning shot from them, sir,' said the caller excitedly.

'Spit it out, Wilson.'

'We've just accessed the *Evening Standard* telesales databank and there's an announcement been hacked in and booked: got all the trademarks.'

'Fax it through.'

'On its way, sir.'

Molineux replaced the handset and quietly left the bedroom for his study. Gargantuan oak bookcases lined the walls. He quickly moved to the fax machine which was busily champing in the corner. It displayed that day's date: 15 January 1995.

Raymond Hunter

7 August 1960 – 15 January 1995, 7.24 p.m. RIP.

'Let He that is without sin among you,
be the first to cast a stone at her'

St John 8:7

He picked up the telephone and pressed the one-digit recall code. It was answered immediately.

'Yes, sir?'

'Have you run the name?'

'Yes, sir.'

'Does it correspond?'

'Yes, sir. Ray Hunter was acquitted at St Albans Crown Court 14 June 1992. Charge: rape.'

'OK, get a surveillance team on her, deploying a stand-by armed-response squad.'

'Yes, sir.'

Molineux could hear his instructions echoing through the conference facility and across the operations room. He went on, 'Profile of victim?'

'Ray Hunter, thirty-four, Caucasian, previous convictions for dishonesty, violence, and 'road traffic offences'. He is currently under observation by Herefordshire police on suspected car ringing: only daylight obs, sir.'

'Liaise with Assistant Chief Constable at Essex HQ. Tell him we're taking over full observation on Raymond Hunter until further notice and they are to abandon their operation. Any trouble, call me. Any reference to him in existing papers should be destroyed forthwith. Deploy three armed units *in situ* directed by Johnson, who should meet me there, And, Wilson, arrange my transport.'

'On its way, sir.'

'What about his victim? Was it his wife?'

'No, sir. One Michelle Roberts, nineteen years old, 6 Sellacomb Way, Greenford, London, current whereabouts unknown.'

'No parents?'

'Parents haven't heard from her since Hunter's trial.'

'Send someone round there. Get a statement from them. Sniff around.'

'Think we've got them, sir?' asked Wilson excitedly.

'I don't know about that, Wilson, but access Hunter's line and let's wait and see.'

'Anything else, sir?'

'Yeah, pray for my soul, Wilson.'

'Can't do that, sir.'

'Why not?'

'I'm a scientist, sir.'

'Later, Wilson.' Molineux replaced the handset and left the room. He showered quickly and couldn't hear the helicopter landing although his wife did. A cooling cup of Breakfast Blend tea had been left for him in the hallway with a note reminding him of their dinner engagement that evening; that seemed a very long way down his list of priorities. The chopper's blades fanned out the flaps of his raincoat like wings, as he ducked his head to avoid decapitation then clambered on board. Seconds later, when he was secured by his flight strap, it swooped up and away into the dark mouth of the early morning drizzle.

He emerged from the short journey to the RAF base, grey hair still damp at the roots. Wilson was there to greet him at the pad. They stooped under the rushing blades towards a waiting white transit. The metal rollers shuddered their way open and Molineux took his seat, one of three. Flashing lights resembled the workings of a hi-fi system.

The engine started and Molineux put the headphones on and nodded to the girl at his left. She flicked a button.

'All units report to Oracle. Lines are clear and free.' He turned his attention to the central screen which flickered messages.

'Unit one – quiet and calm. Unit two – quiet as the grave.'

Molineux responded. 'Mobile units stay in position, Oracle now moving into target. Zone time check 7.05 a.m.'

The girl silently typed in the message, relaying it to both mobile units on portable real-time PC Link. They arrived at the target zone with the minimum of fuss but maximum capability. Molineux viewed it as the professional he believed himself to be; it was 8.32 a.m.

The house was on the outskirts of St Albans, in a rundown street which turned off the ring road. There was a group of ancient trees on the corner that disguised the entrance to the shabby crescent of houses, all peeling paint and faded colours. Some children were playing on the semi-circular green. A woman flung open an upstairs window and leaned out to call something to them and they scattered like frightened starlings. In the other direction, towards the west entrance, there was a stream of traffic: fast cars, buses laden with sightseers bound for the cathedral, and noisy impatient motorbike couriers making their way to London. The wait began.

CHAPTER SEVENTEEN

The early light broke her fractured sleep completely. Last night's ugliness returned to focus: the sight of Teddy, at the end of the meal, drunk and complaining about the unfairness of it all; the strange woman in the ladies' room. Shuddering away the recollection of her parting from Teddy, Beth rose to dress. She slipped her feet into the snug fur moccasins her father had thrust at her when she had left home to work away for the first time. It wasn't that her home was cold, just that the footwear and the battered towelling bathrobe Beth drew around her shoulders gave her an anchor of familiarity and ordinariness.

She showered, scrubbing her body with a rough sea sponge, enjoying the tingle as her circulation left its starting block for the day ahead. As she washed herself thoroughly, Beth wondered, what did you wear at a gun club? A bandolier? A cowboy hat? Jeans? A checked shirt and a padded bodywarmer were her best estimate.

She ate a small mouthful of Greek yoghurt laced with a spoonful of smooth, sweet honey as she paced around unable to settle. It had always been the same. Whether it was a sports day or an exposé, Beth's adrenal gland beat out a tune that she was forced to acknowledge. She looked in on her father. It was obvious that he had hardly moved; he rarely did. Listening to the shallow draft of his breathing she closed the door quietly behind her. Teddy had once raised his eyebrows at her care not to disturb him by unnecessary noise. It made her father seem more sentient if she acted as though he could be disturbed by the squeaking of a door's hinge.

Beth's last act before leaving was to check the batteries on her dictaphone and load a fresh two-hour tape. If this woman had something to say then she wanted a record of it. Her father's nurse was tidying the front room. It wasn't a task included in her contract, but she was a busy woman, forever scurrying to fill her day with work and commitment. Beth watched her come to an abrupt halt in her work, then turn to face her. The nurse's wide flat face was etched with concern.

'I don't think he seems so well today, Beth. He seems very restless, as if he's worried about something.'

She had no idea on what plane her father's brain was working but the nurse had developed a sixth sense so far as her patient was concerned. Beth didn't know what to say, what she could do. Guiltily she hoped that his suffering would soon stop. 'I shouldn't be gone beyond the morning.' She slapped her waist to check the bleeper's presence. 'If anything does happen . . .' The nurse smiled understandingly as Beth said goodbye then left to keep her appointment.

The address was in Kent. Beth had decided to drive. The Volkswagen started first time. She set the vehicle forward and reviewed what she knew so far. Someone, or several people, were interested in the rape. They knew the true nature of her attacker and the truth of the allegation, but what did they want from Beth? They had gone to enormous lengths to gather the information on Middleton. This included access to membership books, the mailing lists of a pornographer, and County Court records. They must have known that she was meeting Teddy at the restaurant but Beth was unable to fathom how. The note that had been placed in her bag had not been written in haste. The perfection of the script showed care and attention to neatness. It had been written in preparation for making contact. What did she have that anyone could want or need?

Beth negotiated the dense early morning traffic, inching then ambling through the leaf-strewn lanes of the capital's perimeter. Eventually, with the aid of her *A to Z*, she found the Tarquil Estate and Gun Club. It resembled a folly more than an estate: as if several builders, each with a different view of aesthetics, had set to in an effort to outdo each other's excesses. Castellations ran rampant at the top of its entrance, giving it the appearance of a schoolboy's medieval fort, whilst Gothic spires and Byzantine domes fought for supremacy over each other; it was a mess. The drive took her in a full ellipse before the sign for the visitors' car park enabled her to get out and lock the door.

The reception area was an ugly throw-back to a beastly trophy-seeking age. Sightless kopi and springbok heads studded the mahogany-clad walls. The guns that had robbed the animals of life were braced between their stuffed and puzzled craniums. Beth always thought these bloody souvenirs looked terminally surprised, as if amazed that the men who stopped their gentle lives had been drunken butchers blasting at whatever crossed their path, rather than expert woodsmen.

She approached the reception desk. It was made from darkest African ebony and inlaid with shining primitive marquetry. Upon it an incongruously placed computer terminal sprouted leads to modems and fax machines. Hunched over its flickering cursor was an elderly man. Hair fanned out above the rims of his ears like ancient car indicators. A faded tweed jacket easily covered his thin frame; a white shirt sparkled against the dour brown of his frayed Gillies tie.

'I'm Bethany Gamble. Is there a message for me?'

He busied himself typing at a speed she would have found difficult to match. Eventually he placed the system on hold. 'Give me a moment,' he muttered in a harsh Kent accent. 'Yes.' He fished a visitor's day pass from the waiting pile. 'Wear this, and please don't remove it. She's waiting in site fifteen. That's through the doors. Follow the numbers, you'll find her there.'

'Who is she?' Beth asked, but already he had returned to his console.

She followed the directions, pausing to cover her ears with the regulation earmuffs that the shooting gallery's entrance sign had ordered her to wear. The ear protectors did little to deafen the cacophony in the large oblong room. The harsh plastic booth formations were joined smoothly but stood uneasily against the remnants of the ancient oak panelling. Eventually Beth found fifteen. A figure stood braced for firing, legs spread wide for better stability against the gun's recoil. It was as if she was aware, even through her preparation, that Beth was there. She squeezed six shots before jettisoning the spent cartridges from the pistol's chamber. She turned around, pushed her goggles up to her forehead and smiled. It was the woman from the restaurant the night before,

'Glad you could make it.'

'Make what?'

The woman looked at the pistol in her right hand, ignoring the inquiry. 'Did you ever fire one of these?' Beth shook her head.

The woman inserted more rounds into the stock and returned to her shooting. Beth saw her mouth something as she turned. It looked like: 'You will'.

She let off another volley of bullets before walking towards Beth and indicating with a nod that she should move off in the opposite direction from which she had come. The woman overtook her to lead the way. Beth began to follow then paused by the pulley wheel that stood at chest height at the booth's side. She turned the handle until the target was presented. The bullet-holes formed a circle around the groin of the cardboard commando. Whoever she was, she certainly knew how to shoot.

By the time Beth had entered the ante-room at the point furthest from the entrance, the woman was taking a sip from a plastic cup. A dispenser of iced water stood nearby. Beth reached into her bag, left open for easy access, and turned on the tape recorder.

'Did you enjoy your meal last night?'

The woman appeared amused by Beth's question. She smiled enigmatically without replying. Beth could now see her features properly. She was attractive and well turned out. The make-up she wore was not the mask of sophistication adopted at the restaurant the night before but more honest and wholesome. Beth had the impression that she was dressing for each particular role in the melodrama. She had to force the pace.

'How did you know I'd be there?'

The woman took another sip from the paper cup. 'Shouldn't you ask how I knew you'd come here?' She removed another paper cup and handed it to Beth.

'All right, how?'

The woman sat down on an over-stuffed Chesterfield. 'Intuition. Yes, let's call it that – a woman's intuition.'

Beth sat next to her, ensuring the tape recorder would pick up the conversation. 'What do you know about Middleton?'

The woman looked puzzled by Beth's question

'Middleton, Arthur Middleton, wife beater and rapist . . .'

The woman fixed her with an earnest stare. 'Beth, have you ever felt that things, odds, are not in your favour? That something is very wrong and you can't put your finger on why?'

'I feel that way at the moment. I deserve an explanation. You just presented yourself in my life, and I wonder why.'

'We,' the woman paused, then corrected herself, 'I, felt you needed help. I saw how your meeting was progressing. I thought we could talk about it, Beth. I know what you've been through.'

Her slip, her acknowledgement at first of the involvement of others, told Beth she was on the right trail.

'How could you know?' She demanded,

'I want to help. He's a snake. They both are.'

Beth wondered to whom she was referring. 'You prepared that note before you knew you'd have a chance to deliver it. When I went to the ladies', you saw your chance.'

The woman smiled knowingly before responding, 'If I'd approached you and pressed a note into your hand you would have had me thrown out.' She appraised Beth coolly for a few seconds. 'No, it's not that at all. You need to see things as they really are. I have some friends, sympathetic friends, who understand these things. They'd like to help if they can.' She looked earnestly at Beth.

'Who would like to help, and why?' She asked, moving the bag closer to the woman.

'In time. You've been through a great deal. Are you working on anything at the moment?' She glanced at the bag.

Beth just managed to stop her hand reaching out to protect the tape recorder.

'What does it mean, the message you left last night?' She retrieved the note from her bodywarmer's top flap pocket and read its contents aloud to her companion.

As her voice faded she watched the woman stare sidelong past her head at something Beth couldn't see. Seconds passed before she pulled herself back from the secret place she had visited momentarily; a place only she knew. She muttered something. Beth thought it sounded like, 'Bruise but don't break, smoke but don't burn'.

Beth pushed herself back into the woman's line of vision. 'Do I know you? You seem very familiar . . . But there's something different.' She paused to look at the woman. 'Has your hair always been that colour?' The question went unanswered. The woman swept back her hair and resumed her eye protectors but could not disguise her unease.

'There's something for you at reception. It's under G. I have to shoot some more rounds.'

They retraced their route in silence. The smell of cordite rose up to welcome them back to the gallery.

'Thanks for the pass,' Beth shouted through the increasing din. A man approached. He wore the gun apparel that Beth had anticipated so accurately. As he approached he smiled at the woman in the shooting gallery head gear, then appeared puzzled as he looked at Beth. He returned his gaze to her companion, shook his head in confusion then walked away without comment. Beth wondered why. Then it struck her. It was more than a casual likeness. From behind, Beth could see where the roots of the woman's natural hair colour had begun to reappear on the crown. Her clothes had a cut that Beth favoured, her shoes were the same soft Italian leather loafers. This woman didn't share Beth's taste, she had stolen it. They had reached booth fifteen.

Beth tapped the woman on her back as they entered its relative privacy. 'And you, what's your name?'

She turned slightly, and smiled innocently. 'You'll be told when the time is right.' Her voice was firm but not unkind, as if she were obeying an order she dared not countermand. 'I think we can help each other but trust . . . we need to trust each other.' She loaded the gun and took off the safety catch. 'Here, this is a Smith & Wesson. It's deadly from this range. Ideal, in fact.' She forced the gun into Beth's right hand. 'Trust, you see.' Beth stared at the weight of the weapon. The woman reached over and unhooked Beth's handbag. Beth swivelled towards her with the gun pointed.

'Trust, that's all,' the woman repeated, ignoring the potential danger of the outstretched gun in Beth's hands. She opened the bag. She didn't bother to remove the recorder, just its tape. 'It's a question of building it together. Go to reception. There are things you need to know, before you can understand. Beth, don't speak to anyone about this.' She took the gun carefully from Beth's hands.

The tape had been placed deep into a pocket. A loaded gun and a markswoman stood between Beth and it.

'Thanks for writing out my pass,' she ventured again, attempting to force the woman to acknowledge it was her handwriting. She hollered into her ear as the woman tensed, only to relax and deliver her bullets.

'That's OK,' she shouted as Beth left the shooting gallery.

The writing on the pass bore no similarity to the note from her handbag. Beth had been right. The note had been prepared in anticipation of delivery and the markswoman was just the messenger. She entered reception. Two men were moving away from the desk. They seemed inappropriately dressed for a visit to a gun club: limp Marks & Spencer double-breasted suits, crumpled by a journey, marked them out from the members she had noticed on her visit.

'Your tag please, miss,' the porter requested. She removed the day's identification and returned it.

'Those men,' she pointed to the departing figures, 'one of them looked familiar. Was he looking for me?'

The man shook his head.

'No, not you. They wanted to get a message to Miss Tremaine, or number fifteen as they called her. I didn't believe them for a moment. Are you a relative of Miss Tremaine's? You look very alike.'

Beth's voice was shaky as she spoke. 'There's a package for me under G.'

He looked concerned at the tone of her request, then turned for a second to retrieve a photographer's envelope. He placed it in front of her.

'If those men have been troubling you, miss, you tell me.'

Beth shook her head. No, it wasn't that that was troubling her, it was the fact that Tremaine was Beth's mother's maiden name. Nearby, an impressive copper-riveted armchair offered her a place to sit away from the eyes of the gun-club retainer. She needed to see the pictures; they wanted her to see the pictures. Feeling the inside of the envelope and testing its flexibility, she ran a polished thumbnail along its accessible edge. Beth removed the photographs. It was Teddy with a woman and they were making love. If you could call it that. The woman was one of the newer researchers on the show. That's what Fergus had meant when he'd said 'almost all of the women are avoiding him'. The bastard. The miserable, conniving bastard!

Beth pulled herself together. The pictures were a shock but it was the purpose of giving them to her that interested her. Why produce them unless they wanted to test the strength of her feelings for him? Or was it worse than that: were they attempting to push her over the edge? Their relationship had always included the prospect of his infidelity, and whilst she was shocked, she wasn't surprised. What did these people expect her to do? It seemed simple when she thought about it. Looking around the room at the stuffed heads, she imagined one to be his. That was what they wanted: they wanted her to confront him. Beth decided she wasn't going to disappoint them;

besides, she might even enjoy it. She thought through her expected response, rose quickly and began to return to the shooting gallery. They would expect her to demand an explanation from the woman inside. She stuffed the pictures back into the envelope and returned at speed to gallery fifteen. It was deserted. Beth pushed through to the ante-room. On inspection she discovered a heavy tapestry curtain. It led to a door then to a deserted rear car park.

She walked around the side of the large house, returned to her vehicle, climbed in then gunned the engine. It wasn't so much that Teddy had been screwing around, it was over between them anyway, but how did they get access to take the pictures? As she pulled away, considering the options presented to her that morning, she failed to notice a Vauxhall Cavalier pull in behind her on the trunk road.

Inside the Cavalier two men in crumpled Marks & Spencer suits watched her leave the premises they had themselves exited from minutes before.

'Target leaving, contact made. Exit through hidden escape. Possibility contamination. Contact five feet eight, blonde hair, slim, attractive. They did talk. Club refused to give access to members' details, did not disclose name. We'll have to go back in to dredge the details. No time now, we are on target's tail. There is possibility of receipt of documents at reception. Later check will reveal. I don't know what it is she may have been told or given but she's going to be stopped for speeding.'

Beth pushed the accelerator down to the floor. She wanted to confront Teddy before he left for an alleged business meeting.

'Heading towards Paxton TV. Will have to park nearby to avoid gate congestion. Will seek entry to studio with caution.'

Beth strode determinedly through the offices of Paxton TV. Many recognised her, but few offered any form of greeting as she walked speedily through their ranks. Teddy's secretary was too stunned by the suddenness of Beth's approach to ward her away from his door. She reached for it then thrust it open. He sat at his desk: it was as large and ostentatious as himself. He looked up, puzzled and surprised at her appearance.

'Beth, what a . . .'

'Explain these,' she said, her voice as calm as she had intended, dropping two of the more graphic illustrations of his activities on to the walnut grain in front of him. His eyes widened momentarily before they moved towards the room's other occupant and his smile thinned.

'You are a snake, Teddy, and you shed me like a skin.'

Beth's voice held the accumulated rage of months: she wasn't just shouting at him, she realised, she was shouting at Middleton, the judge, the police and the jury. It felt good.

'Does this poor girl have any idea what's in store for her?'

Eventually she followed the focus of his gaze as Teddy spoke. 'You know Miss Gamble, sir.'

Sir Donald Pierce, Head of Paxton TV, nodded grimly.

'All too well. But don't we all, *now*.' I'm pleased you're here, it will save us a letter, and this little performance will save us the litigation. You are dismissed, Miss Gamble. It is over. Your severance pay will be forwarded in due course. The contents of your desk, all that does not belong to Paxton TV, will be forwarded also. It's pleasing after all the trouble you have caused me that your latest behaviour is so accommodating.' His lizard tongue flicked over his words with a reptilian delight.

'So that's it? After all I've been through, you're just dumping me? You can't. I'll drag you through every industrial tribunal in the country. You're sacking me because I was raped: wait until that hits the papers. Every women's group in the western world will hound you for it. The compensation award will be massive.'

But Beth could see the oily creature was confident.

'Miss Gamble, this company has supported you throughout your tragic ordeal. I personally organised the delivery of flowers to the hospital and then your home. You have been on full pay since that terrible night. So it could not be said that Paxton TV has been anything but completely supportive to you in your time of need. You, on the other hand, have not returned that loyalty. An audit of your expenses over the last year has convinced me that your unsubstantiated claims for money spent could be viewed as a fraud on the company.'

Beth was speechless. She had never been asked formally to submit receipts for her claims. What she claimed was what she spent, but she realised how bad it could be made to look. Pierce looked, eyebrows raised, to Teddy for reinforcement.

'You've dumped yourself, Beth. This is all down to you.'

'And the photos?'

'Yes, that's exactly what I want to know. How did you get those?'

She turned to the station head. He only smirked.

'Are you going to leave or shall I have the doorman escort you?' he asked.

'You can kick me out but don't think I'm going to go away. By the way, Teddy, your pictures don't do you justice.' She turned to her ex-employer. 'He's even smaller in real life.'

'She's a very angry woman, Commander. If Maxwell ever had any balls they're in her handbag now. Further action?'

Molineux considered his reply. 'Good work, unit three. Continue relaxed surveillance. Miss Gamble's had a big day.'

He turned off the communication channel and turned to the notepad that lay on the van's console. Molineux felt confident that his well-designed plan would ensure him future promotion. They had taken her. He turned to his pad once more, his mind clear with the exhilaration of future success. On it was the rough sketch of a she-wolf, identifiable by the teats that hung down from a distended belly. He drew a jagged mantrap around its front paw, then whispered, 'Gotcha!'

He returned his attention to the quiet street: five hours had passed without any suspicious movement. The mood was tense. Molineux made fifteen-minute check-ins with central control.

'What's the news from the victim's parents?'

'Seems that she was a home-loving girl intent on going to London to study drama, sir. One day she meets Hunter at a bar in Euston Station. She'd been for an interview. He spun a line and ends up raping her. The mother said she lost it after the trial; they couldn't control her. Then the girl ups and leaves. Only been one communication since: postcard from Edinburgh, 28 July last year.'

'Copy it through, Edwards,' said Molineux.

'Transmitting now, sir.'

Instantaneously an image of Edinburgh Castle appeared on the central screen alongside the reverse of the card. Wilson read out loud: 'I'm sorry if I've caused you embarrassment and distress. I'm alive and well. At last I have found friends.

> 'For my thoughts are not your thoughts,
> neither are your ways my ways.'
>
> *Isaiah 55:8*

Molineux slid a little down the chair and turned towards Wilson. 'I hope we have caught them, but something tells me these people are . . .' Before he could complete his sentence his attention was drawn to a monitor above Wilson's head.

'Switch central to remote four.' The command was met with an immediate response. The central screen showed a young woman no older than twenty, Molineux guessed. She had bright yellow, peroxided hair, cut short, contrasting with the green of her windcheater. She seemed to be behind the trunk of a tree. After a few jerky movements she emerged into the drizzle and walked along the crescent. She wore neatly pressed chinos and chunky black footwear.

'All units. Female suspect now standing at south-western junction: confirm she is in sight,' Molineux barked.

The headset crackled and the response came from Johnson.

'Unit two has visual contact, sir. Proceed with instruction.'

'Nothing yet, just watch. Looks as if she may be moving to the telephone kiosk.'

The girl did just that within seconds of Molineux's caution. She opened the kiosk door.

'Trace!' bellowed Molineux and the girl next to him frantically keyed into the pad before her.

'Tracing, sir.'

The target stood motionless in the box after dialling the number. Three short clicks could be heard in the van then the amplified tone indicated they had intercepted.

Just at that moment the voice of Johnson interrupted. 'North-west corner entering now: blue saloon, foxtrot alpha mike, seven, nine, two bravo.'

Molineux swivelled his head towards monitor six like a quarterback surveying the play. A dark blue Mercedes pulled up just a short distance away from the telephone box. The door opened and an elegant woman fashionably dressed in a camel overcoat emerged, stopping briefly to talk to the driver. Her dark hair had a casual, expensive cut. She closed the door in a swift movement.

'Sir, suspect one has replaced handset. Number confirmed as taxi company. They have despatched a car.'

'Good. Intercept and pick her up.'

The woman with dark hair moved closer to the corner. She carried a pigskin briefcase.

'Unit two cover the vehicle,' Molineux ordered, 'and run a check on the car.'

'Already have, sir. It's registered to Jonathan Elliott, 4 Hampton Mews, Epping Forest.'

'Is the driver male, unit two?'

'Unable to assist, Oracle.'

'Description.'

'Can't tell from here, sir: windows are tinted.'

'Stay in position,' Molineux responded.

The two women spoke briefly; it was the confirmation he needed.

'Alert everyone,' he said over the airwaves. 'It's going down.'

The elegant woman gestured and the blonde girl pointed in the direction of another house before walking away. She would be apprehended by unit three.

Molineux saw the dark-haired woman check her watch. It was 2.14 p.m. exactly when she knocked on the door. The silence was morgue-like. He watched as she rapped the door for a second time. Then suddenly it swung open. She seemed to walk tentatively inside the hallway. Molineux didn't have time to react before the scream split the evening air.

Bewildered, he shouted on impulse, 'Go! go! go!' But he knew the difference between the scream of a man and the scream of a woman.

CHAPTER EIGHTEEN

'Stand still!' The command was bellowed from behind the garden wall. 'This is the police! You are surrounded by armed officers. Do not move!' The woman in the camel-coloured coat stood motionless, the briefcase on its side at her feet.

'Place your hands at the back of your neck and kneel.' Molineux watched from the van as the woman did as she was told.

A crowd was beginning to gather at the far end of the crescent alongside an ambulance and the flashing blue lights of several arriving patrol cars. Net curtains twitched along the street as neighbours spied on the proceedings.

'You're doing just fine. Now lie on the ground away from the briefcase.' As the woman turned, the camera zoomed in on her face. It was twisted with fear. Molineux felt the curdling doubt in the pit of his stomach.

'Something's not right here, Wilson.'

'What do you think, sir?'

'I don't know yet. What's happening with the blonde girl?'

'Harris has picked her up. She wants to go to a pub in the town centre.'

'We must ensure that she meets her contact if there is one. Radio Harris to stay with her.'

'OK.'

Molineux returned to the screen to see an officer with a hand gun pointing directly at the prostrate woman. He isolated the briefcase as another officer went to the woman and searched her; his task completed he turned to the camera position and gave a thumbs-down gesture.

'Unarmed suspect,' said Wilson.

'Curious,' replied Molineux. 'Check the case, Johnson.'

The order was obeyed. The officer delicately released the catches on the case. Molineux waited.

'Negative,' Johnson's voice sighed over the airwaves. A visible wave of relaxation followed with police officers now appearing from their hidden positions. The woman still lay on the ground. She was shaking as Molineux emerged from his control van.

The dark blue Mercedes was surrounded. Molineux gave the order. Its potential threat had to be neutralised immediately. He took up his position beside Johnson. The door of the house was still open but not wide enough for him to see in.

'What do you reckon?' Molineux asked.

'No movement inside, sir.'

'Has the woman said anything?'

'No. Did you hear her scream though?'

'Yes, but why?'

'We'll find out. Shall we secure the house?'

'Go ahead.'

Johnson began waving his arms in silent orders and the team of armed officers went about their operation with automaton efficiency. It was no more than thirty seconds before a shout emanated from the building. 'Premises secure. You'd better get in, quick.'

Molineux and Johnson sprinted up the garden path, side-stepping the woman who now appeared to be comatose. 'Get the paramedics. She's got some questions to answer,' Molineux said as he passed. Johnson pushed open the door and they were inside. The stink assaulted his nostrils, his shoe momentarily stuck to the floor. He looked down at the dark patch beneath him. There was no mistaking congealed blood. He noticed it was all around him, spattered beneath the dado rail and disguised upon the flock wallpaper. Molineux negotiated the passageway towards an officer, fighting the urge to vomit.

'All right, son?' enquired Molineux. 'There's been worse. Pull yourself together.' The officer looked at him with watery eyes that had seen a hundred dead bodies but never one like this. Molineux stood at the doorway to the living room and saw the mutilated corpse of a man lying beside the old velvet sofa.

The coppery smell was strong. Molineux blinked several times and his eyebrows rose. He turned to his left to survey the rest of the room: there was no evidence that a struggle had taken place. He moved closer to the body and peered down to inspect the bullet hole. 'Raymond Hunter, I presume,' he murmured and gently rolled the head to retrieve a single black orchid trapped between the neck and the dirty carpet beneath.

He stood upright and walked to the window. Outside the crowd had thickened, devouring the scene. Occasionally he shifted his weight but said nothing. The Scientific Aides and Scenes of Crime Officers went about their business in silence behind him, only disturbing the air with the sound of automatic winders repeating violently with every flash of a camera. For the second time that day Molineux felt the nervous acid climb his stomach wall. These people, whoever they were, were either very lucky or extremely well informed! As he watched the scene outside he began gently massaging his wrist, feeling the pulse race beneath. No one made a fool out of him. He could hear the questions being asked by his superiors when they discovered what had occurred, and his heart beat stepped up. He had never contemplated a leak, but it seemed that was the only way these people could have outplayed him.

'The woman's in the ambulance. She's come round. I think you'd better see this, sir.' Molineux's thoughts were interrupted by Wilson who handed him a slim white brief headed 'St Albans County Court between Angela Hunter Petitioner and Raymond Hunter Defendant, Notice of Application in respect of the Minors Catherine, Peter and Thomas Hunter.'

'It was recovered from the briefcase. She's a process server, sir, Mrs Joan Elliott, wife of Jonathan Elliott. We've got him, the driver, and he's not happy, shouting about all sorts of terrible things he's gonna do to you.'

'What about the blonde?'

'Harris dropped her at the Nag's Head. Looks like it's a regular haunt for the local fascists, skinheads that sort of thing. Stone cold, I'd say. I think we've been had.'

'Body's stiff,' said Molineux, ignoring his young assistant. 'Must have been dead for at least twelve hours.'

'You mean he's been here all the time we've been watching the house? The door was open the whole time?'

'That's right.'

'Jesus Christ!' said Wilson, genuinely astounded.

'Never mind the blasphemy, Wilson. Remember, you're a scientist. Let's get back to control and start picking through this mess. Lab reports will start coming in about fiveish.'

The pair tiptoed their way through the teams of personnel quietly exercising their skills and emerged into the street. A spectator from the rear of the crowd rushed towards them and thrust a microphone into Molineux's face.

'Are you in charge, sir?'

Molineux looked down at a young woman with a jet black bob, square cut to her jowls, with bushy eyebrows and lipstick heavily caking a full mouth. 'Samantha Pierce, BBC Television. What's happening here? Who are you?' The questions ran one into another.

'Commander Gerald Molineux in answer to your second question, and in answer to your first an armed operation has take place. The details I am not at liberty to disclose. I will only state that one, as yet unidentified, body has been recovered from these premises and we are treating the circumstances as suspicious.'

'Is it the owner of the house, Commander? Is that woman under arrest, sir? What about the man in the blue Mercedes?' The questions went on.

'No comment,' he replied. 'There will be an opportunity for all your questions to be answered in due course. Now if you'll excuse me!' and he hurried away from the unwelcome tirade.

At 1 a.m. Molineux was ensconced in his throne in the operations room, debriefing his team.

'So it appears, ladies and gentlemen, that our adversaries are more resourceful than we at first imagined. I anticipate a communication from them in the near future. There will be no press reports, we hit them with a gagging order, and Buchan has stayed the report from the BBC.' He looked around carefully at the collective body and continued, 'In the meantime we will concentrate on the reports from the murder scene and the interviews with Mr and Mrs Elliott.' The screen lit up and documents began appearing.

'Firstly – contents of briefcase, confirming status as enquiry agent operating from premises in Duke Street, St Albans,' he commented. 'So it appears she's been set up as much as we have. Seems she received a telephone call saying he would be in the house.' Suddenly Wilson entered the room with the lab reports. He marched up to Molineux saying, 'You'd better see this, chief,' and passed Molineux copy of the first print of the morning's *Times*. A ring of yellow marker pen outlined the notice: Molineux read its contents aloud.

APOLOGIES

Raymond Hunter

7 August 1960 – 14 January 1995, 7.24 p.m. RIP.

TO ALL FRIENDS AND OTHER INTERESTED PARTIES
WE APOLOGISE FOR YESTERDAY'S ERROR IN THE
DATE OF DEATH.

'God hath chosen the foolish things of the world to confound
the wise; and God hath chosen the weak things of the world to
confound things which are mighty'

Corinthians 6:2

CHAPTER NINETEEN

De Haus arrived at Scotland Yard at 7 a.m., bringing with him the early edition of *The Times*. He walked through the foyer to greet Wilson who proffered his hand. They shook clumsily and moved to the lift, an odd couple in animated conversation.

'You saw it then?' said Wilson, gesturing to the newspaper under De Haus's arm.

'Yes, I did. I expected your call.' He looked smug. 'I couldn't find a similar classified in yesterday's edition.'

'You wouldn't.'

'Why's that?'

'Because it wasn't in *The Times*, it was in the *Evening Standard*. They pulled the rug again,' replied Wilson, pushing the button by the lift. The doors opened immediately, they stepped inside, and Wilson pressed for the fourteenth floor. They descended instead of the expected ascent, giving De Haus a jolt. The younger man revealed a glimmer of schoolboy delight in his eye. De Haus ignored the prank. 'Clearly, therefore, today's apology was designed for our benefit.'

'Boss thinks so.'

'Did he say anything else?'

'Nothing so far. He's waiting for you.'

'Nice to feel wanted,' said the little man.

The elevator shuddered to a halt and they faced the familiar bland entrance to the operations room. Wilson conducted their guest across the threshold and headed for Molineux who sat holding court with a pensive frown on his face.

'Glad you could make it,' he said, directing his comment towards De Haus.

'I believe we have an opponent?' He responded, without replying to the greeting.

'Indeed we do, and what's more, we have an opponent who wants to talk business with us.' Molineux delivered the line slowly.

'What do you mean?' shot Wilson from behind. Everyone drew closer to the table.

'That's the trouble, working with scientists. Look at the quote, man.'

All eyes turned to the computer screen. Displayed upon it was *Corinthians* 6:2: 'Now is the accepted time.'

'The quote that appeared in today's edition of *The Times* had an incorrect reference. Before you is the actual quotation.'

Everyone turned to Molineux, awaiting his conclusion on the latest twist. He began, 'It doesn't take a genius to work out that these messages are designed for us.' He glanced round at the rapt faces in the room before continuing. 'I'm trying very hard not to believe that someone here has jumped into bed with these people, because that would have unthinkable consequences for the person involved, but it does seem highly unusual that they were able to set us up a full twenty-four hours in advance.'

'You mean they knew that we would be watching *The Times* announcements?' But that doesn't necessarily indicate that they are aware IGPAP exists. They were bound to know they were under investigation,' Wilson advanced.

'I know, but all the same I'd better warn you all that Internal Affairs will be sniffing around. This operation cannot afford to be compromised in any way.'

His words hung in the air like the darkest of clouds. Then suddenly his demeanour altered.

'There's only one way to deal with this situation. We have to acknowledge that they are worthy adversaries. It's pretty clear that they have state of the art technology easily capable of accessing any computer they wish, and right now I'm sure they will be expecting us to respond, so let's play, shall we?'

For a moment his audience looked bewildered until De Haus shrugged and asked, 'Who gets the first move?'

'They've already had it. Don't you see? If they can hack into *The Times*'s system and they expect us to see it, they know we can hack in also – and that leads me to the conclusion they have access to the same data banks as us, including Holmes. Wilson get on the central console. You're steering.'

'And me?' interjected De Haus, still puzzled.

'You're the navigator, Mr De Haus, the ship's navigator.' He invited De Haus to take his place. Once the exchange was complete, Molineux spoke. 'Mr Wilson, patch us into the Holmes System.'

Discs whirred and modems connected. The room went silent again.

'We're in, sir.'

The huge screen flickered.

'OK,' Wilson confirmed.

'Type in *"Corinthians, who are you??"*' commanded Molineux.

Wilson clattered away on the keyboard. The reply was instantaneously teleprinted on the screen.

'*St John 3:8*'

Wilson jolted back in astonishment. Molineux shouted, 'Get a trace on that line and for God's sake somebody tell me what *St John* 3:8 says. De Haus, stand by. We're gonna need you.'

The room burst into activity. No one had ever imagined, let alone challenged, an intellectual electronic cat-and-mouse game. If they could trace the origin of the line which was hacking into the Holmes System then they had a definite fix. The best bet was they had no more than twenty-four minutes to find the mouse hole. Molineux spoke as the answer to his enquiry flashed on the mainframe:

> 'The wind bloweth where it listeth and
> thou hearest the sound thereof, but canst
> not tell whence it cometh, and whither it go.'

De Haus rose forward to perch himself nervously on the edge of Molineux's great leather throne.

'Type in *"Who are you?"*'

All watched as the reply dotted out quickly: '*Genesis* 2:23

It was transposed instantaneously:

> 'This is now bone of my bones, and
> flesh of my flesh; she shall be called
> woman, because she was taken out of man.'

De Haus continued, 'Type in, *"What do women want?"*' He turned to Molineux. 'Let's try a bit of Freud on them.'

The screen stared blankly back at them. Only the intermittent flashing of the cursor in the left-hand corner signified the refusal to converse.

'Shit!' cried out Molineux. 'Why won't they answer?'

De Haus spoke calmly. Taking off his jacket and quickly rolling up his sleeves, he resumed his position. 'They won't answer because they only act by reference to God, so the only justification from their point of view can be found in the Bible, hence the references. They want us to question them not by our code but by theirs. It's absolutely astonishing.'

'Stuff the surprises, Professor, get on with the game. The clock's winding down and we're nowhere near them.'

'All right,' said De Haus. 'Try "*Who made thee a prince and a judge over us? Exodus 2:14*".'

The cursor blipped into action. '*Exodus 3:15 of course.*'

'What's it say?' cried Molineux. The quotation appeared.

'The Lord God of your fathers, the God
of Abraham, the God of Isaac and the God of Jacob.'

'Nineteen minutes,' a voice shouted across the room. De Haus loosened his tie. 'Try "*All is vanity and vexation of spirit, Ecclesiastes 1:14*".' He went on. 'Let's see if they want us to argue morality with them.'

The reply soon came: '*St Matthew 5:17*. Everyone read:

'Think not that I come to destroy the law of the
prophets; I am come not to destroy but to fulfil.'

'Eighteen minutes,' came the call.

'"*Thou shalt not kill, Exodus 20:13*",' shouted De Haus. Without time for a moment's blink of the cursor the reply confirmed their interest.

'*Naughty: Exodus 21:23.*'

'Don't tell me, I know. "*A life for a life, an eye for an eye, a tooth for a tooth, a hand for a hand, a foot for a foot, burning for burning, wound for wound, stripe for stripe.*"' Molineux's voice echoed the quotation which crawled its way across the screen.

'Fifteen minutes,' came the shout.

'Target area – south-east England.'

De Haus commanded, '*Isaiah 5:20 "Woe unto them that call evil good and good, evil."*'

Once more the reply was instantaneous.

'*Lamentations 3:59.*'

'Transpose,' shouted Molineux.

'Oh Lord thou hast seen my wrong; judge thou my case.'

De Haus contemplated for a moment. 'It confirms my original theory. These people refuse to acknowledge any other system of justice.'

Molineux anxiously monitored the scanner. 'Any closer?' he asked the operator.

'Looks like it's keyed in via Exeter main exchange. They're giving themselves every opportunity. There's over 100,000 lines to scan.'

'Nine minutes.' The cry precipitated a glowing dampness on De Haus's brow.

'Come on, come on: answer, De Haus,' urged Molineux. 'Keep them on the line.'

'"*Be not overcome of evil, but overcome evil with good, Romans 12:21*",' he cried.

The screen blipped. '*Silly, you forgot Romans 12:19.*'

'"*Vengeance is mine; I will repay, sayeth the Lord*"' De Haus whispered the words as they appeared on the screen. Before he could formulate a reply the cursor flickered again.

'*Kings 21:20?*'

They waited the few short moments motionless while their own computer searched its databanks then printed: 'Hast thou not found me, O mine enemy?'

'Fuck it!' exploded Molineux. 'They know we can trace them.'

'I think you'd better see this, sir,' interrupted the young scanner operator.

'What is it?'

'We've got a positive trace to a telephone sub-station on the outskirts of Exeter. Looks like a Ministry of Defence line.'

'Where to?'

'Only place it could be is Thonerton Airfield.'

'One minute.' All eyes turned to the screen.

'*Proverbs 18!*'

'Thirty seconds.'

'Line's gone blank, sir. Sorry, trace is dead.'

'What about the airfield?'

'No good. We can't track the air-to-ground signals. Air traffic wouldn't even notice them hacking in. Must have come through satellite link. These people certainly know what they're doing.'

As Molineux turned back to the grid of screens he saw the words appearing:

> 'The path of the just is as the shining
> light, that shineth more and more unto
> the *Perfect* Day.
>
> *Proverbs 4:18*

'What the hell does that mean?'

De Haus pondered for a few long moments before replying. Though he had no real need. She had used the phrase in their dialogue over the preceding weeks time and again. He had pushed her further and further in an attempt to force the true nature of the Perfect Day from the ever-flickering cursor that acted as their common tongue. Her replies had been too cryptic for even his esoteric intellect to fathom. It was the one question he sought the answer to. It was only that hunger for information that had allowed his conscience to justify his betrayal of this operation. After a little time De Haus realised the room's occupants were waiting for his response to the Commander's question. 'It means that their path cannot be deviated from and a pathway indicates a journey, as in the journey of faith for all Christians. However, I don't suppose they intend for one moment to tell us what will happen on the Perfect Day. For that matter, I don't suppose they're likely to tell us when that day will be.' He spoke in a croaking voice.

The room fell into silence once again.

Alone on the train back to Oxford, De Haus attempted to make some small measure of sense of what he had done. At the time he had instigated the dialogue with her, he had believed, naïvely as it transpired, that she would be warned away from Molineux's plan. He had hoped that he could turn the woman away from the poisoned meat that Beth Gamble had become under the auspices of the Commander's plan. The effect had been the opposite. Her response had chilled him more than anything he had read or heard to date about the murders. She was a games mistress. Not a woman who taught hockey to pre-pubescent girls but a mistress of mind games.

He saw his own reflection in the greasy window of the carriage. He looked a haunted man. Not haunted by what he had done but by the possible repercussions of his actions in causing the operation to be compromised so cheaply. After all, what had he gained? Some small degree of smugness that he was ahead of Molineux? A little tired self-satisfaction that he had engineered a meeting of minds with this ghoulish creature? The actual information he had gleaned from their console-based conversations was minimal. She had given him only what she chose to grant. His efforts to engage in an investigation of her peculiar morality had ended only in frustration. He felt cold and bewildered. Whilst he had not created a monster he had given it new life: Beth Gamble's.

CHAPTER TWENTY

F ergus sat in the seat opposite Beth in the comfortable kitchen of her home. He was now her ex-cameraman. He'd heard through the cannibalistic tom-toms of the TV jungle that she was out; he'd also heard how the execution had been carried through. At first he'd considered punching Maxwell, but he needed the work. He was probably living on borrowed time in any event, and decided he would wait until his own firing squad had loaded up before he settled with Teddy.

Beth was quiet, more quiet than he'd ever known her. She sat across from him, eyes downcast and puffy, smoking a cigarette for the first time in the two years since she'd kicked that 'dog' out on its end. After a few minutes of silence she outlined the bizarre events of the last few days, ending with her trip to the gun club. Fergus found himself regretting his earlier decision not to see to that treacherous bastard Maxwell.

'I don't know what's happening, but I'm going to find out,' Beth promised. Fergus looked over the rim of a steaming mug of coffee, his eyes for once serious.

'Why not tell the police? These people . . . this woman . . . is acting strangely. Isn't it time you let the police earn their wages? What's their purpose, Beth?' he concluded.

She looked up from her seat in the kitchen window. 'What do you mean, Finn?' She knew he had a nose for trouble, though it rarely kept him out of it.

'Well, it all sounds – intense, man-hating, like a religion almost. Have you asked yourself what they want from you?'

'I wish I knew. I *have* to know.' Beth paused. Fergus continued, 'The biblical quotes and the material on Middleton – may he roast in hell – what do they want from you?'

She considered the vexing question. 'Perhaps they want me to make a programme about them. I don't know. But what a great idea.'

'I know that tone. Have you forgotten you don't have a job?'

She gave him her drop-dead eyelash-bat, and lightened her voice to a schoolgirl lisp. 'But I still have a cameraman . . .'

'Ah, Beth, you've lost your *own* job, isn't that enough?'

She moved towards him, this time adopting an earnest expression.

'Fergus, have you any holidays left?' He nodded, not looking up from his drink. 'And can you borrow what we need? Camera, surveillance mikes, editing facilities? Just think about it. What a story! It's the way back for me, Fergus, I can feel it.' She was spilling her coffee as excitement swept over her,

'What about the lassie with the gun? What do you feel about her? Personally I'm terrified. That's what the Falls Road does for you,' he muttered.

'Just call it intuition, women's intuition. I don't believe she wanted to hurt me.'

'Are you sure this isn't some dyke thing? Those pictures of your man were meant to provoke a response. I mean, how do you feel about a shag at the moment?' He moved towards her. She parted her gown to reveal cleavage. They stared into each other's eyes then started to laugh. He took his seat.

'You're a real one, Beth. All right, you're not going to play hide the vacuum nozzle with the girls. So what are you going to do?'

'*We* are going back to the gun club.' Beth started placing her cup down with a bang on the oak kitchen table.

'You know how I feel about guns.'

'You can wait outside. She won't be there, but her address could be.'

Beth knew the way. The sun was high and round in the clear bright sky as Fergus's elderly van was steered towards the gun club. Beth felt she was doing the right thing. Recently she had allowed herself to be manipulated by those around her; this was the first time since that night that she had grasped the initiative and it felt good. Fergus lit a cigarette as they continued their journey in comfortable silence. In the calm of the van she could see him in profile. The inevitable leather jacket covered a lean body, hardened by work rather than exercise. His face – a kind, good face – still wore the camouflage of his ridiculous beard. She'd never known him not to have it and wondered how he would look if he ever took a razor to its unfashionable presence. He had always been there for her, never intrusive or pushy; just there with an open face and shy smile. Why is it, she thought to herself, that the best people are always the ones we take for granted?

The journey retraced her previous day's drive. On arrival, Beth got out of the van.

'I'm going to try the eyelid-batting first. I don't need you for that. If it doesn't work, then . . .'

He knew 'then'. 'Then I will be needed, I know. Be careful, Beth.' He reached forward and took a handful of her gaberdine windcheater. 'This isn't body armour.' He relaxed his grip, and she walked into the gun club.

The receptionist was not the old man of yesterday; it looked as though this was his wife.

'Good morning.'

Sour eyes glared at her over pink-rimmed spectacles; the overall impression was of an axe ready for battle. 'What is it?' she responded curtly, looking Beth up and down.

'I was here yesterday as a guest of Miss Tremaine.'

The woman waited for her to continue.

Beth removed her compact mirror from her handbag. 'I took this by mistake.' The woman reached forward to grasp it. Beth pulled away. 'No, it isn't that simple. You see, she has mine. It was a present and it means a lot to me. I'd like her address. I wouldn't want it to get lost.'

'We don't give out members' addresses. Anyway, how do I know you were here yesterday? I've never set eyes on you before.'

'Your husband did.' The woman considered her options.

'That may be so, but I still can't give that information to you. Anyway, if she's such a good friend, why don't you have her address?'

'I never said she was, that's why it's vital I find her. That compact was left to me in my mother's will.'

The old woman narrowed her eyes until they almost disappeared. 'You said before it was a present. That's different from a bequest.' She had confirmed her suspicions of Beth. 'No, miss, I'll leave a message for Miss Tremaine. If you'd be good enough to leave your name and address, I'll see she receives it.' Beth wrote out false particulars, handed them to the antagonistic receptionist then watched carefully to see where the note was placed.

As she returned to the van, Fergus stared at her face with mounting gloom; it obviously hadn't worked.

'Don't worry. What we want is miles away from the shooting gallery. You'll be in and out in seconds. Your van's beaten up already, another dent won't destroy its aesthetics,' she promised, They went straight into their planned manoeuvre.

Beth made her way to the side of the front door and stood back amongst the lush ivy covering the walls. She watched as Fergus reversed the van out of sight, but within earshot. Then she heard the deafening sound of the collision. The receptionist's shoes beat out a tattoo across the flooring as Fergus came running like a madman around the corner.

'I think she's dead! I didn't see her!'

The woman was at the entrance staring at him. Fergus took hold of her hand and began to lead her away. 'It's a woman – a young woman!' He sounded on the verge of tears. She was too bewildered by the speed of the occurrence to resist, and Fergus swept her away with him to view the carnage.

As soon as they were past, Beth slipped inside. She ran to the reception desk. Her note had been removed, she could see it lying in the bin. She identified the cubby hole where it had lain. The embossed sticker merely said 'B. Tremaine'. Beth knew she was short on time now. Even Fergus's blarney couldn't disguise the fact that there wasn't a corpse. In front of her was a thick ledger holding the members' names. She quickly threw open its pages. It was a payment of fees book. Quickly finding T, she scanned down the membership column. The sound of voices could be heard from outside.

'She must have crawled away into the bushes. We've got to find her. She could be dying, woman!' She could see him facing outward at the door, arms outstretched, to block the receptionist's entry.

'Get out of my way! I'll have you arrested! Bloody drunk!'

There was no time for subtlety. Beth ripped the sheet out complete, then thrust it into her pocket. She walked towards them.

'You almost hit me, you madman. I've reported you to the police.' She began to walk away.

'How did you get back in here?' the old woman demanded and began to follow Beth.

Beth turned around. 'There was a call for you. The owner. He wanted to know where you were and who I was. He's waiting on the line in reception.' Beth could see the woman couldn't be sure whether it was the truth or not. Then decided she couldn't take the risk.

'If I ever see either of you again, I'll call the police.' She scuttled away.

'Did you really report me to the police?' he asked as they ran back to the van.

Beth laughed. 'No, but we know someone who will.'

They jumped into the still-running vehicle and sped around the drive and out on to the open road.

'Did you get it?' he asked as the van negotiated a sharp bend at speed.

'Slow down,' Beth warned. 'A speeding van with its back bumper hanging off is very tempting to a traffic cop.' She produced the crumpled paper from the bag, then smoothed it out.

'Jesus, couldn't you just have copied it?' He looked sideways at the tattered document.

'I didn't have the time, Fergus. You and Ma Baker were wrestling in the foyer when I found it. Let's see.' She traced her finger down the list of members. 'Tremaine, B. She's been a member for two months.'

'Christ, they must have cracking instructors at that place.'

'And her membership is paid for the year. The copy receipt.' Beth picked off the small slip. '"With thanks, WCT".' Never heard of it. CT . . . That's normally "Charitable Trust". We'll have to check it out. The address is 23 Rickmansworth Road, EC.'

Fergus placed his foot hard agaisnt the accelerator.

Beth's escapades were described to Molineux by the occupants of the tail car. He had not expected the girl to return to the gun club so swiftly. She thought she was on to something and she was right. He removed his tailored jacket and placed it carefully on the beechwood hanger by the door. Removing the onyx cufflinks from his shirt sleeves, he doubled back the French cuffs and rubbed his palms together. This was more like it. Whilst it wasn't what he had expected, Beth Gamble's initiative might stir up the hornets' nest. He returned to his seat to follow the action. Before him lay a large-scale map of the area.

'Target proceeding east. She's a game girl that one. They pulled some kind of stunt on the receptionist. The speed they left, they must have found what they were looking for.'

Molineux heistated before replying. 'She went back for what we wanted yesterday. Has it been attended to?'

The crackle of the mobile handset interrupted the signal. 'Negative, Leader. Removal planned 1 a.m. tomorrow.'

'Do *not* lose her. I repeat, under *no circumstances* except discovery.'

De Haus was right, she was a very resourceful woman. She might now have the address of the mystery woman. Beth was ahead of them in this part of the game. That could be very dangerous, for her and for them. He wondered just how far she was willing to go. The beeping of the handset drew him away from his thoughts.

'Yes?'

'Van drawing up to Rickmansworth Road, driving slowly. They're looking for house numbers. They'll be lucky – all houses deserted, boarded up. Looks like a bogus address.'

Inside his van, Fergus risked a glance in Beth's direction. She was chewing the inside of her lip with focused concentration, but the disappointment registered openly on her face.

'No wonder the charity paid her fees.' His attempt at humour fell as flat as Beth's mood.

She flicked through the *A to Z* again, checking then double-checking for another similar sounding address. Eventually, Fergus spoke. 'Look, Beth, this is all a bit too sinister for me. Let's call it a day.' She sat still and stern in the passenger seat: Christ, he could almost hear her thinking. Beth pushed open the van's creaking door, climbed out, and walked towards the derelict dwelling. The fence around the unkempt garden was rusted, and sagged with neglect. There had been a gate once but that was long ago.

'You're wasting your time, Beth,' he shouted from the van as she disappeared from view. The front door had gone the same way as the garden gate. It was difficult to imagine that a family must have lived here once, she mused, picking her way carefully through the shattered cider bottles and refuse. The house stank of tramp's urine and despair. The stairs looked unsteady, untrustworthy. Fergus was right, this wasn't anyone's home, but if she hadn't looked she would always have wondered. That was the rule her first editor had drummed into the sixteen-year-old junior reporter: take nothing for granted, check everything yourself, and take nobody's word for anything. Deflated by the lack of a discovery Beth returned to the welcome light of the outside world and climbed into the van. There would be no 'I told you so' from Fergus; there was no need. He turned the damaged van around and headed back.

On the return journey. Beth was preoccupied. What the hell did they want from her? Was she the only one they were playing this game with or were others being tantalised in the same way? Fergus had got it right earlier that same day as they sipped coffee in her kitchen.

'What do they want from you, Beth?'

Once she understood that, she would understand them. In order to do that she would have to wait for another contact to be made. That prospect didn't appeal to her. It gave them the advantage again, kept her off balance, and allowed them to dictate the nature and the pace of the intrigue. There had to be a way of forcing events along herself. Instead of reacting, she had to act. But how?

They were nearly back at her home before she spoke again.

'Charitable Trusts have to be registered, don't they? If we call the offices of the Charity Commissioners they'll be able to give us an address.'

Fergus pulled the van to a halt.

'Yes, and it'll be 23 Rickmansworth Road. Look I've got a few things to do, such as get my van repaired.' The subtle invitation for her to pay for the damage was ignored. 'I'll call you later.'

Beth felt flat but not beaten. These disappointments had occurred before; the thing was to keep moving, keep thinking. The flat was quiet. Her father was sitting up staring into space. She kissed him hello, then smoothed out the tartan rug that embraced his withered legs. It was pointless even to attempt to talk to him. Moving to the kitchen she switched on the kettle, then went to the living room to check the answerphone.

There was only one message. She pressed the play button. It was the woman from the restaurant and the shooting gallery.

'Trust! Weren't you listening? That was very silly, and what did it get you? A visit to a squat. We need to talk about this. I'll see you at Delcorroe's, Fleet Street, 9 p.m.'

The message came to an end. How had she found out about this so quickly? Beth deduced that the club must have telephoned the woman. That meant that the gun club had her number. They must have guessed that Beth had been searching for something, then conducted their own search until they came to the ledger. Beth knew that there was no option but to go along with the woman's suggestion. If her name wasn't Tremaine, what was it?

Inside the thick walls of IGPAP, Molineux sat behind his great desk. He viewed the flowchart of the operation to its current status. All was going well. There was one minor inconvenience, the problem of the tap on Middleton's phone. The Home Secretary had decided in a fit of uncharacteristic fairness to refuse its authorisation. He had claimed it was unconstitutional. Molineux knew by his dealings with Palmer-Dent that fairness was a long way down his totem pole of priorities. It was more likely to be the stink of discovery that he feared. If it were ever revealed that an acquitted man was hounded by the security services, it would look like victimisation and the outcry would wind a smelly trail back to the Home Secretary's own door. It was typical, thought Molineux: the man would rather risk Middleton's life than his own career. He smiled at the hypocritical irony of his conclusion. He and the Home Secretary were cut from the same tough cloth. Many believed Palmer-Dent, ambition wearing the scant clothing of disguise, to be the next leader of his party and the country.

Molineux continued to conduct an overview of the operation, taking pleasure in the contingency plans designed by his strategists. They had every eventuality, every possibility, every uncertainty catered for; it was a work of genius. A red light alerted him that information was awaiting his attention. He flipped a switch to the tannoy which stood alongside a photograph of his wife.

'Mr Molineux, we have an intercept call to the target's home.' The tape was played back to him. This must have been from the woman at the gun club. Their communication system was impressive. The time of the message was only fifteen minutes after Gamble and Finn had left.

'All right, I want that restaurant vetted and infiltrated. Two teams; mixed couples, and the reserved table covered. We want access to the reservations book. I want the restaurant covered from 7.30.'

Beth arrived early; forty minutes early. Fergus sat outside in his battered vehicle. As usual, he was illegally parked. Beth checked the tiny transmitter on the inside lapel of her Armani jacket. 'The food looks wonderful, Fergus, I'm looking forward to it. Have you eaten?' The deserted foyer echoed to her words. She knew he hadn't. All afternoon he'd been calling friends, attempting to appropriate this equipment. Eventually at 6 p.m. he struck uranium. It was expensive but necessary. Now Beth approached the maître d'.

'Good evening, madam. Have you a reservation?'

Beth looked perplexed. 'I do. Oh, this is so embarrassing. A work colleague at a seminar asked me to dinner. I only met her today. You see, I can't even remember her name.'

He smiled indulgently. 'And for what time?' His immaculate dinner suit and manner received her most grateful smile.

'She said in an embarrassed voice: 'At 9.'

'Ah, let me see, the second sitting. It's strange. There has been a late run on reservations.'

'Well, was the first one made by a woman?' Beth asked.

'I took all the reservations myself. There was only one woman, a Miss Madeline Milton.'

The name sounded familiar. 'Thank you.' Beth had a £5 note in her hand.

'Later, madam. This service was an honour not a chore.'

'She's been in, Commander. She pulled a neat one on the head waiter. She's found the woman's name. Target sitting in van with Finn: meeting time approaching, she's ten minutes late. No sign of the other woman as yet. Will continue surveillance.'

There was a break in conversation before another surveillance team cut in and across.

'Commander, this is unit three, we've been trying to break into your channel for ten minutes . . .'

Molineux heard the tension in the operative's voice.

'It, what is it?'

'One lone man at the bar, sir. One man. It is Satyr. I repeat, Satyr. It's a set-up. No time to intercept.'

Molineux ground his teeth before replying,

'Do not compromise operation unless either target's life threatened.'

Beth was greeted again warmly by the waiter. 'Ah, madam, what a pleasure to see you. You were not being completely honest with me about your host.' He winked conspiratorially, leading her through to the plush bar. Other diners sat in couples: they always overdressed for quality restaurants, she thought. As she approached the bar itself Beth saw a man sitting at it, turned away from her; the bulk of his shoulders was familiar, as was his face.

'Sir, your dinner companion,' the waiter said to attract the man's attention away from his whisky. He was successful. The figure turned towards her, his face at first open then contorting in fury as recognition dawned. Arthur Middleton slammed down his heavy-bottomed tumbler on the top of the mahogany bar.

'You!' he exploded, his face looming closer to hers. 'You! Can't you leave me alone?'

CHAPTER TWENTY-ONE

The post-mortem was ordered immediately. The mood was sombre inside Molineux's office. The left hand had not known what the right had been doing. The result was as 'they' had intended: the worlds of Beth Gamble and Arthur Middleton had collided. The office was full of fragile silence. It also held strategists, collators, and Molineux himself, but pride of place went to Ivan De Haus. The Commander had demanded that he travel from Oxford immediately after the restaurant débâcle and was surprised that De Haus had agreed so readily with the unreasonable request. There was a change in De Haus's attitude: Molineux watched the little man's newfound enthusiasm with characteristic suspicion. He had made De Haus aware of the events of the previous evening but the surveillance tape was yet to be played.

Molineux caught the scientist's watchful, hungry eyes: something had whetted his appetite, sharpened his palate; now he looked avaricious not just interested. Molineux made a personal note to monitor this apparent shift. Clearing his throat to heighten the mood further, he began, 'We are all aware of the events of last night.' Several of the field operatives from the clashing teams raised weak smiles that were immediately seen off the premises by the look on the Commander's face.

'Play the tape back again. Mr De Haus, I'd like you to listen to this carefully.'

The skinny scientist reclined in his chair slightly, crossed his arms then closed his eyes.

'Aren't you going to take notes?' asked Dobson, one of Molineux's assistants.

De Haus shook his head. 'The tape will still remain; a first impression can disappear, if you are not ready for it.'

The play button was pressed.

'You! Can't you leave me alone?'

'Has there been some kind of misunderstanding?'

'That's the waiter's voice,' Dobson added helpfully.

'There's no misunderstanding,' Middleton said coldly. 'You! You're making my life a misery. Can't I be left alone? The jury believed me!'

'Who asked you here, Mr Middleton?' Beth's voice was calm, considering the circumstances.

'Some news editor, if it's any of your business.'

'Please, madam, could you continue this elsewhere?' De Haus remembered the head waiter's voice.

'If it isn't bad enough your telephoning my house at all hours of the night, telling Agnes lies about me. Well, I've told the police about you and you're going to suffer.'

'This editor – was it a man or a woman? Tell me.' De Haus could hear the reasonable tone of her question.

'Someone you know, it must be. Offering money for my story.'

The sound of movement could be heard.

'Please restrain yourself, or I'll call the police.' The head waiter's voice held panic. He was obviously unused to this kind behaviour in his restaurant.

'I'm going to get an injunction against you. This is harassment.'

'Ask your wife about injunctions. She knows all about them,' Beth spat.

The sound of struggling could be heard.

'Gino! Joey! Quickly!'

'Lying bitch!' Arthur's scream erupted. The tape was momentarily quiet, apart from the sounds of scuffling.

'Our people were at the door; they saw him,' said Dobson. 'She tipped his drink over him at this point. The head waiter had hold of him. His sons can be heard coming through now.'

The tape continued, 'I advise you to leave, madam.'

'Let go of me,' Middleton screamed.

'And madam is requested not to book again.' The tape whirred on until it came to an abrupt halt at a click from the off button.

Dobson took up the story. 'Then, after five minutes or so, Middleton was seen nursing a bloody nose outside the back door. He stopped at a couple of pubs on the way home, arriving at 11.30 p.m.'

All eyes turned to the expert. He made small gnawing movements with his teeth over his bottom lip, then raised his eyebrows. Without opening his eyes he said, 'It's a punishment.'

The room waited in respectful silence.

'She has transgressed. This organisation is its own legislator. It decrees the law without telling its subjects what it is. Then, when there is what they deem a breaking of the rules, there is punishment. In the present case, being confronted with her undoubted rapist.' De Haus opened his eyes, and addressed this last comment to Molineux.

He returned the stare until the little man closed his eyes again.

'The rules are biblical and fascist. Beth was not told to avoid an investigation. They knew of her propensities from her recent behaviour. So do we. Yet they punished her.'

'What does that tell you about them, De Haus?' Molineux cut in.

'It tells me that their general aim is punishment, retribution, control. The need to put right what they see as wrong. That applies to their overall view. The killings of these unfortunate men fit an identical pattern. They see one man as all rapists, and all rapists as one man.'

'What about Beth?' asked Molineux, conscious that this was the first time he'd referred to her by her Christian name. The room went a little quieter.

De Haus raised an amused eyebrow at Molineux's slip. He had now embarked on a relationship with her by recognising her individuality.

'How will she react? Or how will she feel? They are quite different, when you think about it. She will feel angry, cheated almost. It was a cheap trick. But then so was cheating an elderly lady out of the ledger at the gun club. What will she do? It was remarkable the way she dealt with a potentially disastrous meeting with Middleton. Her pursuit was not for retribution, it was for information. She was attempting to make a link; she will continue with that aim. Even in immediate danger, she remained in control. And,' he said, raising his voice and swivelling towards Molineux, 'she is in danger. She will not give up. You must pull her out.'

Nobody had ever challenged his power by a plea to his humanity.

'Remember your brief, Mr De Haus.'

'Professor De Haus,' he chided, 'you always call me Mr I am not here as a Mr. That is for dinner parties. I am here because I am a Professor and you need me. You respect my expertise, therefore be guided by it. If you continue to play with Beth's life in this way, you become as bad as they are.' Molineux glared at the open challenge to his role.

He turned his chair to his chief research assistant. 'Dobson, Professor De Haus and I have matters to discuss. We know they had to have Middleton's number for the set-up. I want the full trace on anyone named Madeline Milton, particularly any one who matches the description of the woman at the gun club.'

One of the researchers darted forward. 'Commander, before we leave . . .'

'Yes, Toby?' He was young and too clever by three-quarters. He had been the analyst at Middleton's trial and had advised how a jury could be swayed to a given conclusion. It had worked.

'I've been running checks on that name since the booking at the restaurant was discovered. There are over a hundred. As yet their descriptions haven't come through, but I knew the name from somewhere. It was the case linked to the forensic switch we pulled. The name of the victim in the Crown versus McCabe was Madeline Milton.'

The room went silent whilst the information was absorbed.

'Professor?' asked Molineux. 'Your view?'

'Why not? We in this room also operate on many different levels in order to succeed.' There was something in his tone that Molineux did not care for. It held a certain superciliousness, almost a disregard for others. His demeanour suggested a superior knowledge, or insight; or both. No, that wasn't it – it sounded like a confession. Molineux's thoughts were disrupted as Toby pushed himself away from the console.

'It could be another false trail, like the restaurant. It may not be the same Madeline Milton.'

Molineux took command. 'Then we need to know all about this woman. Description, history, whereabouts. Toby, you got the lead, you chase it. Don't let it out of your sight.' Delighted by his instant promotion and smiling at Dobson, Toby left the command centre. 'Now, if the rest of you will leave us . . .' Molineux said, nodding towards De Haus.

They obeyed without demur. As the door closed, the Commander's face was grim.

'Whatever your views, Professor, I must ask you not to challenge my authority in front of the rest of the team.'

'Perhaps it will make them think a little about what they are involved in.'

'You are entitled, within certain boundaries, to appraise me of your personal view. It is my law; whether that be biblical or fascist, *my law*, and that will only be done in private. Do I make myself clear?'

The scientist shuffled his unused papers together. 'I could always walk away from all of this, Commander.'

'No, you couldn't. What? Walk away from the most fascinating case of your life?' De Haus was as trapped by his curiosity as Molineux by his duty. 'I'd like a full report of your findings logged by tomorrow. After all, at your insistence we are acting on your findings. We need to know who to applaud at our investigation's successful conclusion.'

He was now on his feet, guiding the scientist to the door.

'Or who to blame if it fails, Commander?'

Molineux smiled thinly. 'Risks, risks. You need an increase in your section's research budget and access to sensitive files; you take this risk. We need an expert analyst we can trust; we take risks.'

De Haus's small frame was dwarfed as, exasperated, he stood his ground in the doorway 'And what about Beth. You called her that yourself. We know what we are risking. Does she?' He allowed the question to hang as he turned away. 'Tomorrow, Mr Molineux.'

'Commander Molineux.'

De Haus was proving to be troublesome. There was something in his manner that deeply disturbed the Commander. Morality was not the issue in this investigation: he would only be judged by its success or failure, yet De Haus was appealing to his sense of right and wrong. What worked was right; what didn't was an error of judgement.

Molineux returned to the command desk, opened his intercom, then released the access code. 'Target's status?'

'She's parked up outside the Charity Commissioner's office, on a double yellow. Shall we keep the ticket jackals at bay?'

'No, if she's going to be in a while, she'll be suspicious if she doesn't get one.'

Molineux knew that the past few days would make Beth suspicious of everyone and everything that seemed slightly out of place.

'We need to be inside. Watch her as closely as you can, talk to anyone she talks to, record any document she even glimpses.'

'She's entering now, sir. Out.'

Beth made her way up to the Charities Office. An ancient cage lift eventually responded to her request for the third floor. It began its ascent with a sullen shudder. Beth pushed the collapsible brass door aside with some difficulty, then followed the wall-fixed directions to the ante-room of the main office. She approached the reception clerk.

'I called earlier. I have an appointment with a Mr Banks.'

'And you are?'

'Marsh, Teresa Marsh.' Beth handed over her credentials. The press card had been sent when she resigned from syndicated press for the TV job; she'd never filled it in until now.

'Yes, Miss Marsh. He is in room twelve. Straight down the corridor, it's the second door on your right. You look very familiar. Have you ever been on the telly?'

Beth retrieved her card. 'Oh, just once,' she said, beginning to walk away. The woman appeared unconvinced.

The room Beth entered seemed to be covered in moss. It looked as mildewed as the velvet collar on the occupant's day coat. The stooping man, who rose with no small difficulty from the green-covered desk before him, spoke. 'Ah, the press; always beagling about, snooping where they shouldn't be. To what great scandal are we privy today?' He blinked in delight. His ill-fitting teeth made his mouth seem more pinched than it was.

'Your list of registered charities, I'm interested in the entries under W.'

He leant forward, removing his round-rimmed spectacles from his large nose and wiping them against the hem of his Harris tweed jacket. 'Always in such a rush. Why do you need to see these documents?' His tongue rolled around this last and favourite word. 'And why can you not be more specific about the exact charity you wish to investigate?' He continued to rub, gazing fondly at the decaying books that were his oldest friends.

'Mr Banks, we have a lead and, I have to be frank, no more than that. It tells a terrible tale if it is correct.'

He smiled, urging her to continue.

'It seems, . . . I cannot and would not go further than that at present, I cannot prove this yet, but,' she hoped her gabbling would put him at his ease and show that she was not a threat, 'we, I,' she said modestly, 'believe they've been extending their role beyond the charity as claimed. They've been helping unmarried mothers. Many of us are highly religious. We find it totally unacceptable'

Beth's voice held the conviction of puritan virtue, enhanced by righteous indignation.

'Dear me, a charity going beyond its charitable charter! That's so refreshing. The complaint is normally the reverse. What marvellous news. It's rare, you see.' The Commissioner leaned forward to the decrepit intercom system. 'Miss Driscoll, can you bring the register, please?' He turned to Beth. 'I have had a photocopy made of the relevant pages.'

Within a few short moments the documents arrived and were presented to her.

'Miss Marsh, the copy. And you can rely upon us for the utmost co-operation.' His toothy smile was as full as the bookcases in his room.

Beth left the greenery of the office, the pages of the extract at the bottom of her backpack.

Molineux was swiftly updated on her visit.

'Target leaving Commissioner's offices taking next lift. Unit Two at only exit. They will follow.'

'What did she do?'

'Meeting with employee. Mr Banks. We listened courtesy of a helpful receptionist in next room. Beth has a document. Their conversation was vague, he knew of her request; it was granted. Apparently a charity acting beyond its charter. I have arranged for Banks to be questioned. Further instructions?'

'Good work. The document, just make sure you get it.'

The blue-suited leader of the unit headed for the Commissioner's office and walked straight in.

'I don't have an appointment now. What is this about?' the Commissioner asked.

'About the reporter,' the agent offered, as if this fact should have been self-evident.

'Very well,' the Commissioner said, scanning the ID offered by the agent.

'What about her?' His afternoon tranquillity felt shattered beyond hope of endurance.

'What did you give her? It's important.'

'Just a copy of the charities registered under W. She couldn't be more specific. She seemed so young, so keen, and we are always ready for some positive publicity.'

'Look, just give me what you gave her.'

The documents were produced a few moments later. The old man was left pondering his transgression, whatever it was. The agent looked over the list then contacted Molineux. 'Sir, document contains a list of charities beginning with the letter W. Action now, sir?'

'Fax it through then follow other units in pursuit of target one.' Having given the order, Molineux considered the options. They could investigate any common link between the numerous charities with the available evidence, which was very little, or they could concentrate on Beth, follow her lead, and use her for what she was best at.

Molineux now knew Beth might not be just *his* bait for them, she might be *their* bait for him. The stormy meeting with Middleton had set small bells of potential betrayal ringing through his conspiracy-hungry mind. The entire operation could have been compromised at that point. The fact that it wasn't seemed just good fortune; but that was a concept alien to his pragmatic nature. Molineux had lost all traces of the confidence he had felt twenty-four hours before. The truth was that Beth – he corrected himself, target one – now knew more than he and his entire team, even if she knew less than the killers who were toying with them all. Was she now his lure? Was that the point of her meeting with Middleton? If he was right there must be a leak, and a leak meant a search, and a search would throw doubt on his command.

Molineux calmed himself with the argument that at present there was no evidence; just a feeling, a strong one. He drafted a note of his suspicions and addressed it to Buchan, PPS to the Home Secretary. Of course it was never sent, it only appeared that it had been. They needed a break, but if it came could he trust it?

CHAPTER TWENTY-TWO

B eth laid out the photocopy on her newly cleared desk at home. She knew that she was looking for some similarity, some link, between all that had occurred and the charitable trust. Many trusts were true to their name, performing works that generally benefited a specific cause. Others were not. Beth had no doubt which category this one fitted. WCT . . . She could be wrong, of course. It might be that her supposition that the letters represented a charity was incorrect. Bearing in mind their behaviour it could stand for 'Weirdos' Commando Training', but she doubted it. They, whoever they were, had access to substantial funds and resources. The benefits of charitable trust status included huge tax concessions, and a quiet respectable life. If she was right it wouldn't be quiet or respectable for much longer.

Scanning the page, Beth soon narrowed the search down to a choice between three charities bearing the correct initials. The first was the Wingrove CT. It had been granted its status in 1917, and had been set up by Major Miles Wingrove after the death of his son at the Somme. Its general purpose was as an educational one: 'For the education of those young people robbed of their parents in times of war'. Whilst there was a tenuous link with firearms, Beth doubted any connection. Moving on she briefly glanced at the next, the Workers' CT. She dismissed it, but wasn't quite sure why.

The Women's Charitable Trust . . . now that *did* have a comforting sound. Granted its status in 1985, its charitable aims were alleged to be the enhancement of education for women and the re-education of those who had not fallen, but had been forced. Even to Beth's untrained eye that purpose seemed a little quirky. More helpfully there was an address and a telephone number. The list of trustees was the normal straw-hat-and-morning-coffee array: Lady Christine Buckle OBE, Lady Samantha Cox, Elizabeth Chalmoley, Lady Diana Eve . . . the list ran on for some time. There was something to detect in it. She stared at it for some time but the tumbler refused to click.

The telephone interrupted Beth's concentration. The intercept cut in. 'Beth, please pick up the phone. I don't have long.' Beth recognised the voice of the woman from the gun club.

'Is Madeline Milton your real name?'

'You had to face him at some time. You had to see him in his weakness, and you in your strength. It went well.'

'How did you . . . ?'

'I said I haven't much time. The *Blackheath Bugle*, Beth, that's where it started.'

The receiver lay buzzing in her hand, the dial tone telling her the conversation had ended.

The *Blackheath Bugle*. What could Beth's first newspaper job have to do with this? The only thing that had started there was her career. She hadn't thought about that paper in years. They had been happy times, innocent, in as much as the reporting of human suffering can be. It was clear that they wanted her to follow the trail back to Blackheath. That she would do, but on her own terms, not theirs.

Back at Molineux's headquarters the telephone call had set away another chase. They knew it would be another exercise in frustration.

'Any trace?' asked Molineux.

'Another public call-box.'

'Get me everything we know about, what was the name of it?'

'The *Blackheath Bugle*, boss. Shouldn't take long to find a detailed record of a *famous* newspaper like that,' Dobson added bitterly.

'Just lose the sarcasm and find me the information. We need to know what they are playing at now,' demanded Molineux, aware of the frosty attitude of Dobson since his public demotion in favour of Toby as the Commander's number one assistant.

'And they *are* playing,' De Haus added, arriving.

Molineux had not heard him enter the command centre. The scientist stood, blinking over the glasses that were both his prop and his weakness. 'With whom? Her or us?' Molineux challenged.

'Both, of course, and they really are rather good at it.' De Haus looked weary. His complexion had turned to sea-voyage grey over the last days of the enquiry. Molineux could sense the man's disquiet at his continued involvement in the project. He could also see that it had been some time since he had bothered to wash his hair or shave. De Haus placed his briefcase on the desk top, opened it then removed a document. 'Here, Commander, my report. Or is it your insurance?' He waited for Molineux's stony expression to show a crack. 'We shall see.'

Molineux took the document and locked it in his drawer.

'Aren't you going to read it?' De Haus looked irritated.

'I have it, that is enough. It exists.'

The little man looked around the room. All of the operators were before their modems, intent on the pursuit of more data. He moved closer to Molineux and dropped his voice to a low whisper. 'You really believe this is going to go wrong!'

Molineux was concentrating on other matters; at least he gave that impression. 'What will she do with her information, De Haus? If we approach her for it, will she run or stay?' He rested comfortably back in his padded seat.

Ivan De Haus appeared to be fighting some internal battle. His eyes had lost the excitement of the chase, and seemed to glaze like a dying fish under the blow of an angler's killing 'priest'.

'She will continue until she knows everything or is stopped in the attempt. She will collate until the full picture emerges, and then expose it to the public. What did you expect? At present she trusts nobody but her cameraman. She has no reason to. The system let her down badly. If we approached she would want to know what she had been selected for and how. Are you willing to explain why it was necessary to interfere in the trial?'

Molineux seemed unsurprised by his answer. 'I agree, it's too risky at this stage in the operation. We'll keep it under consideration. De Haus, some fresh information has come our way. The gun club woman's name checks out against the victim of the linked case. Apart from the hair colour, the general description matches. Key into twenty-seven, I'd like you to give me your impression of her.'

De Haus switched on the machine; its eerie sea-green glow painted him a graveyard hue. A file heading appeared: Milton, Madeline.

'Just skip the early stuff. She was raped on the same night as Beth Gamble,' Molineux said lightly.

De Haus clicked the mouse until he accessed the relevant file.

Police Report: The victim was attacked at 9.10 p.m. The attacker was masked and armed. The rape was brutal and included anal penetration and oral sex. The victim was cut on the inside of her thigh with a long-bladed knife. She was gagged for most of the assault. A suspect, McCabe, William, aged 19, came to light. The victim had reported McCabe to the police for the burglary of the blind school, where she taught. He was on a community-service scheme. The report led to McCabe's re-sentencing; he received twelve months in a Young Offenders' Institute. The defendant was arrested on suspicion of the rape. He denied involvement, claiming an alibi. The alibi witness committed suicide before the trial.

The evidence against McCabe was solely DNA. The source of this was the claws of the victim's cat which had attacked him during his assault on Milton. McCabe was arrested and remanded in custody. At his trial the prosecution offered no evidence due to a contamination of the forensic material. The present whereabouts of Milton, M. are unknown. Interview with her employers concludes no contact for several months. Victim resigned shortly after the rape.

No Social Security payments or registered income payments since that time. No application for benefit recorded. No record of exit from the country.

'So she's just disappeared. Can't say I blame her,' Molineux said. 'She has no previous criminal history. What would make a woman, a teacher in a blind school, become involved in this scheme? We know she can shoot: our men at the gun club picked up the target after she'd finished. We believe she is the same woman. It seems unreal. Why her?'

'Why not?' replied De Haus. 'She is perfectly qualified since you allowed her rapist to walk free.' It was further evidence of his glacial distaste. De Haus stood on one side and shouted about good and evil; Molineux on the opposite, acting for the greater good. They would never understand each other's point of view. The scientist had little more to say on the matter; what was the point? He made his way from the command centre without a farewell.

Molineux reviewed the security of his operation. He checked his watch, aware that he and his wife were due to attend a dinner of high-ranking police officers that night. He didn't have long before he would have to leave. There were one or two question marks against some of the team – there always were; it made them more reliable rather than less – but these incidents, all minor transgressions, had been stale news so far as internal security was concerned. Molineux had implemented additional enquiries into the women members of the squad, hoping that he could identify a leak and thereafter use it to further the enquiry by disinformation to their opponents. It had turned up nothing, apart from a young recruit sleeping with a Chief Superintendent; but that could be filed away for other, later use. No, the problem of the leak remained.

He wondered if De Haus's recent behaviour was a response to something other than the real stress of this operation and his own duties. His watch bleeped to indicate that he was about to begin running behind schedule. Molineux posted a private memo to himself to reconsider the Oxford don's involvement with the future of the enterprise. As he rose abruptly he failed to notice the yellow slip drift away from its inadequate mooring on the page's margin and glide to the floor as the file was snapped shut.

The *Blackheath Bugle* was a typical local free paper. Packed with local adverts for 'Tony's Butchers' and 'Ken's Motorcycles', it survived by trading news space for revenue. As nobody would buy it, the paper was 'distributed'. That didn't mean it was a bad paper, just a brief one. The time Beth spent there had taught her the beginnings of her craft, but what could it tell her now?

The *Bugle* had folded several years before. A Christmas card, with an RIP attached, illustrated the editor's attitude to the paper's loss. The offices were now home to yet another charity shop; they seemed to be taking over the world. The only starting place was the library. Beth had spent numerous hours there, laboriously wading through thick folders of mildewed news items. If government cuts hadn't forced its closure then at least there the search could begin. That was the real problem; she could look for ever and not know what she was looking for. But it must be discoverable, otherwise it would be pointless sending her back into her own past.

Blackheath was a place slow to change; only the increase in litter on the street and too many men skulking in groups in shop doorways told the tale of its typical decline. The library seemed smaller than she remembered, as if it had shrunk with the passing years. Shabby seating and a dying pot plant completed the depressing picture.

They're 'bound' to be on computer, Beth thought ironically. A young, bored, anorexic girl flicked the pages of a Simone De Beauvoir novel. 'Where do you keep the old newspaper reports from local papers?' Beth began.

'I only started yesterday,' the girl replied, without lifting her gaze from the book's dense print.

'Congratulations. You must be very pleased to have a job.'

The girl's eyes, over-large for the angular face they inhabited, focused on her then narrowed. 'Delighted. You wouldn't believe the options I sacrificed.' Her mouth remained set through their ping-pong match of sarcasm.

'Were you given the library plan?' Beth asked, half-pleasantly.

The girl reached over and removed a single-floor plan from the top drawer of her desk, then dangled it limp-wristedly as her eyes returned to her chosen literature.

'You can be sure of one thing,' said Beth. The girl's face showed a flicker of interest. 'I'll never return a library book late, if you have to decide the charge.'

A sickly, satisfied smile spread over the librarian's face, exposing the yellowed teeth her slimming disease had inflicted on her.

The plan was ancient and probably originally prepared by Mr Baker, the librarian, who for years, had pointed Beth's research in the right direction. That meant the plan would be accurate.

All the local history and news had been painstakingly collected and pasted up by the ancient librarian. His passion for chronicling the daily business of a small place would make her task a little simpler, though by no means easy. A check of the plan confirmed her suspicions: nothing had changed; the clippings were stored in the same place.Moving through the decaying aisles, she headed toward the back, left-hand side of the Victorian book-house. The files, fat, old and browning, slumped against each other for support. This would be a long day.

Clearing a working space, Beth began to order the files into local and national. Working, she reviewed what she knew. There must be something, an announcement or news item that was supposed to lead her to a conclusion. About what, she could only speculate, but the name Madeline Milton could be the link. Beth refused to believe that the choice of name, in booking the restaurant, was an error. They wanted her to discover it. This was almost a paper chase or, more accurately, test. Beth brushed away the accumulated dust and looked at the tower of material; there was a lot of paper to chase.

Molineux's head ached from the dinner the night before. It wasn't that he had too much to drink; he rarely did. No, it was a brown-nosing hangover, the kind he developed when too many inferiors wanted too many favours in too short a time. They all knew that there was no such thing as a free lunch, breakfast or dinner, not in his book; the book he kept his list of favours in. His wife had been at her Molineux-promoting best. Sometimes he believed that he wouldn't have climbed so far up this slippery pole without her undeniable influence.

'Miss Gamble's been in there all day again,' Molineux was informed. The agent continued, 'Left to buy a sandwich for her lunch, returned immediately. We've had a few forays in, using different team members. As anticipated, she's searching the local files.'

Molineux wished he knew what the object of the search was but Beth would lead them to it. Their own researches had proved all but useless. They had a date for the paper's launch and for its demise. The years in between were a mystery to the computer terminals and their operators. All they could do was wait and watch Beth Gamble.

CHAPTER TWENTY-THREE

She found it. It took two days but she found it. Beth's back ached as though she had been kidney-punched by a boxer. The hard-backed, hard-bottomed chairs in the library were not ergonomically designed. The night before, her dreams had been of skiing through an avalanche of documents. Beth could see the mass from the corners of her peripheral vision as she polled harder and harder to escape its crushing weight. As she hurtled along the piste of her dreamscape she felt the crush of the main bulk pushing against her back, and as she struggled to keep her tenuous balance woke up, sweating but half-amused by the content of the dream. Now she pushed aside the memory. She had found it. In amongst a thousand planning applications and countless tales of local notaries it commanded her attention immediately. Beth was angry. She should have remembered. It had been her first day at the Crown Court for the paper, filling the place of an absent colleague. The Crown v. Milton. The grey, smudged print, ignored since 16 October 1985; her own column contained the news of that day;

Milton Manslaughter Case Halted

The trial of Madeline Milton, age seventeen, was brought to a sensational end by the intervention of the trial judge, Mr Justice Hunt. The learned judge ruled that an allegation that the defendant had watched inactive whilst her father, Walter Milton, aged fifty-seven, died from a heart attack, was insufficient on which to found a conviction for manslaughter. In announcing his decision, the judge commented, 'Whatever moral laws this defendant has broken by her failure to call medical assistance for her father, she was under no legal duty to take that action. Why she chose to do nothing we will probably never know. There is no case for the jury to decide.'

A police source commented that had the jury been allowed to hear 'other' evidence, things might have gone differently.
Beth Gamble, crime reporter

After so long it was incredible how that day's events immediately clarified themselves in Beth's mind. O'Brien, her editor, had been furious with the copy she had filed. His attendance at a meeting had ensured the story went to print without a fair appraisal of it.

'All the balance of an excited toddler,' was the expression he had later used for her piece.

Beth considered the information. This woman, if it was the same one, had stood trial accused of her father's death and had been acquitted. But that was years ago; what relevance could these proceedings have to Arthur Middleton and the events of the last few days? Clearly there was more. The question was, where could she find it? The trail would be submerged by a decade of events. Had Madeline Milton remained in the area? She could have emigrated or even have died. What was it Beth was supposed to learn from this ten-year-old story?

She removed the item. The library's one acceptance of the march of progress was the bulky photocopier that squatted sulky and ignored in the adjacent corner. A twenty-pence piece paid for the copy, and Beth decided that any further search would be unlikely to yield results. She could always return if other leads became chilly. What other leads? It took a little time to return the vast piles of history to their rightful place. Where now? She knew that libraries were a fund of information; the trick was knowing where to look.

She began with the simplest source – the telephone directory. Locating the books she noted there were addresses for eighty-seven M. Miltons in the Greater London area. This was going to be time-consuming. Next Beth scoured the Electoral Register for the area. If this woman was still around it should locate her whereabouts. The musty documents threw up nine names at varying addresses. In 1985 Madeline was seventeen; she would be eligible to vote the next year. Though Beth knew the council elections might disclose the relevant information it was more likely that registration for the General Election would help her progress. This narrowed the list down to four. Acting on a hunch, she cross-referenced these four to the addresses disclosed by the telephone directories; three tallied, one did not. Moving to the pay-phone in the corridor she contacted the three numbers that matched. Three short phone calls later resulted in three names being excluded from her list.

The one remaining address, M. Milton, The Tivoli School, had no corresponding telephone number. Enquiries showed it to be ex-directory.

Beth knew all too well the intractability of telephonists with this confidential information. She returned to the heart of the library. The librarian showed all the animation of a still-life study; she was still searching for enlightenment in the pages of her novel. The only lead Beth had was the school.

A local *A to Z* provided its location, no more than two miles away. Beth had a feeling it was meant to be discovered; just another part of the chase through Madeline's life. She gathered her researches together and walked towards the exit. Her path steered her towards the attendant. Beth could see, by the thinness of the book's remaining pages she had nearly finished her labour of love.

'The Existentialists did it,' Beth whispered as she finally left to continue her own search.

It was quiet in the command centre. Molineux dealt with other clerical duties: they helped to drive away the demon of lethargy. He felt as though there was something important he had forgotten. He concentrated hard on the missing topic; for the moment he could not place its identity or importance. Molineux knew if he thought about it, it would never emerge; if he pushed it to the back of his list of priorities, it would spring up, unbidden at an inappropriate moment.

'You won't believe the amount of material she's been through, sir. What should we do?'

He considered. The last day and a half had taken them no further forward. 'I'll have a team sent to run tests on all the documents. You said she's used the photocopier?' The operative confirmed this as fact. 'We may be able to locate what we want through that: there should be infra-red traces. In the meantime keep with her. Call in any developments immediately.'

Molineux swivelled his chair around. 'Toby!' The operator turned his head slightly. 'Any more announcements?'

He shook his head. 'All quiet on the "wasting" front, sir. I'll keep you posted.'

'Good man,' the Commander said sincerely.

'Sir? They've already changed their format once.' Molineux was aware that Toby was referring to the inaccurate announcement of the last slaying, the change in time scale and in newspaper. 'What if they do it again? Our alert system is geared into the biblical references; they might drop them.'

'De Haus says no. This is part of a major strategy, planned from start to finish, and I agree. The references are part of it.' That was it, he congratulated himself: De Haus was the missing topic. His brain steered him around the ring road of his memory until he found himself at his required destination; but there was no sign of the yellow flag he had inserted. He rewrote the memo and posted its contents to IS, the internal security unit. It wouldn't do any harm to take a look at the man, he concluded.

Toby accepted the answer and returned to his work. Molineux checked his watch. Boardman was due in his office in fifteen minutes' time. The dapper policeman worried him. Whilst his deductive abilities were excellent, his performance in the field beyond reproach, Molineux sensed a hint of disapproval towards his selection of Beth Gamble as bait. It was for this reason he had been asked to play little part in the operation. Boardman had registered a complaint about the conduct of the trial in a confidential memo; this had since been shredded, along with Boardman's original. Molineux now wanted to plunder Boardman's own peculiar knowledge of Beth; after all, the rape investigation was his. She had surprised them all with her resourcefulness: he wondered if Boardman felt the same amazement.

The intercom buzzed. 'Commander, your visitor is here.'

Shuffling his notes into the waiting file, Molineux made his way from the computerised intestines of the command centre, up in the lift to the waiting policeman.

'Boardman, thanks for attending.' He walked past without offering his hand in welcome. 'Come in and sit down. Tea and biscuits for two.' He had pushed open the door to the office. He walked in, without holding the door open for his visitor, and then sat down.

'Things aren't going to plan, are they?' Boardman ventured, seating himself. 'If they were, you wouldn't have asked me back inside.'

'Miss Gamble has taken us a little by surprise. Does that surprise *you*?'

Molineux's face was unfathomable; Boardman read his voice

instead before smoothing back the hair around his right ear. Molineux recognised this trick from previous meetings; it indicated Boardman was about to be difficult.

'If you mean are *you* capable of underestimating intelligence, the answer is yes. More specifically concerning Beth, no, I'm not surprised in the least.'

'Explain.'

'Her attitude from the moment I first questioned her at the hospital, and thereafter at Middleton's trial, is the key. She showed great strength and clear thinking: her ability to put us on to him by reference to an old video is an example of her excellent memory. She won't give up.'

'Give up what?'

Boardman searched the Commander's eyes for a brief second before he spoke again. 'She's ahead of you.' His eyes sparkled. He was certain he was correct. Boardman looked around the room. 'All this and that beast downstairs—' Molineux's forehead wrinkled at the reference to the 'secret' command post '– and she's showing you how it's done.' There was undisguised delight in his voice.

'Remember your position, Boardman. Your attitude is disappointing. I have asked you here to help. Didn't you see the pictures of the last murder?' This sombre reference straightened Boardman's face. Molineux played his hand. 'She's on the trail of a woman called Milton – at least we think so. She was the victim in the linked trial.'

He watched as Boardman pursed his lips at the reference to the rapists' acquittals then continued, 'I'd like you to go in at grass-roots level and find out what you can about this Milton woman and what Beth knows about her. The databanks have given us a sketch but no more than that.' Boardman looked surprised. 'I want you to discover everything about her through people she knew.'

'What do you mean "knew"?'

'The problem is the Milton woman disappeared after McCabe's acquittal. She is the key to this as much as Beth Gamble. I have to warn you, she's not the only one who's ahead of us.'

'A leak?' the Chief Inspector asked.

Molineux shook his head, attempting to chase away that inevitable suspicion. 'We're trying to track it down. I'd kick all the women off the team if I could, but I don't believe the source is here, or not within the mainstream anyway. We have a double-strength team on

Beth. I think it's time the two of you had a chance meeting. Keep me informed – of everything!'

He watched the dapper policeman make his way from the office before removing the tape of their conversation from the hidden recorder and placing it in the safe. He then spoke through his communication system.

'This is Molineux. Target five "Dock Green" leaving. Keep on him. His name is Boardman. Lose his name, remember his code.'

He had been partially honest with Boardman when he had referred to the leak not springing from the immediate team. That meant he had to look to a peripheral player. So far he had De Haus and Boardman himself. And whoever it was stood to lose more than their pension.

The Tivoli School was more than the name suggested. The brass nameplate on its front gate gave a fuller description: 'School for the Blind'. A nearby road traffic sign indicated the likelihood of the unsighted passing across. The grounds were ordered and well cared for, the beauty of their colours unseen by the pupils who walked them. Beth had parked the car outside the gates. She walked the drive towards the gatehouse that stood surprisingly far away from the gate itself. She guessed the building to be Georgian, its box-like simplicity a counterpoint to the lushness of its surroundings. The entrance hall was simple but dignified, and judging by its emptiness the pupils were at their lessons. Braille and scripted signs led her to the school's receptionist. The middle-aged woman appeared as tranquil as the school.

'I'd like to see the headmistress please,' Beth requested.

'I don't have a record of an appointment. Is it an emergency?'

'It could be.' Her voice was hesitant and unsure. She decided to take a chance. 'It's about Madeline.'

The receptionist rose immediately. 'Have you seen her? Is she all right?' The woman's concern seemed genuine. 'We've been so worried since the trial. She just disappeared.'

What was she talking about? The trial was over ten years ago.

'The trial?'

'The rape trial . . . that awful McCabe boy. He's walking the streets again, you know.'

'No, I didn't know.' Beth's mind sprinted to make the connections. She'd heard the boy's name before. A synapse snapped and she was back at the Bailey; a case was called on, the Crown v. McCabe, and a woman with dark hair was being escorted on to the courtroom. The forensic link, the acquittal, Madeline's disappearance. She had either dyed her hair or was wearing a very impressive wig at the gun club; either way this was the track Beth was meant to follow. She gathered herself, aware that the kindly woman had lapsed into silence.

'And who is she to you, my dear?'

'She's my cousin.'

The receptionist regarded her for a moment. 'Yes, I can see the similarity, apart from the hair colour. Do you know where she is? All her things are here in storage.'

'I've been abroad for months,' Beth lied resourcefully. 'I knew very little about what was happening. I feel so guilty. Can you help me to find her?'

The fussy receptionist thought. 'The headmistress is busy at the moment; a governors' meeting. She'll be free in an hour, can you wait?'

'Of course,' Beth answered, then continued shyly. 'There is one thing. You mentioned her belongings . . . may I see them? It would mean a lot to me. Perhaps it will help me to find her.'

The woman looked unsure. Beth wore her most miserable expression, verging on the tearful. Eventually, checking her watch against the headmistress's availability, the receptionist relented.

'Yes, I suppose it can't hurt. Come this way.' Neatly stacking the mail, she led the way towards the back of the school. 'Were you very close?' the small busy woman asked as she located and unlocked a store room.

'We used to be a very long time ago. I've a feeling we will be again.'

With a kindly smile the woman indicated the meagre boxes that held the secrets of Madeline Milton's life.

'I do hope you can find her.'

Yes, thought Beth, so do I.

CHAPTER TWENTY-FOUR

T
he room smelt of old things. The items, randomly stacked, chronicled the history of a blind school. Old guide-dog harnesses lay discarded, their wearers long dead; an umbrella stand held several white sticks. Beth noted the absence of chipped hockey sticks or ancient wooden tennis rackets and frowned at herself. Of course there weren't any, what possible use could they have been to the blind? The room seeped disappointment. She shook away the depression the gloomy atmosphere evoked. In the storeroom with the door shut, Beth realised she had at least an hour before the head might interrupt. She had no idea of the relationship between Madeline and the headmistress. The woman might be aware that Maddy did not have a cousin, who knew? It was the first thing that had jumped into Beth's head. After all, hadn't people noted how similar they looked? Wasn't it time for her to play upon the likeness? She didn't believe Madeline's pursuit of her was not connected to their resemblance and that was a chilling conclusion.

The three boxes were laid out neatly. It was obvious she had little in the way of possessions. These three containers bore testament to the past of Madeline Milton but Beth needed a photograph to confirm her identity as the woman at the gun club.

The first box contained clothing: Marks & Spencer underwear seemed in stark contrast to the elegance of the woman from the restaurant. The patterned socks and brightly coloured winter gloves seemed to belong to another personality from the sophisticate Beth had met. Thick jumpers and woolly tights completed the assembly.

She turned to the second box. School certificates and confirmation of GCSE and A-level results began the history of Maddy's education. A first-class Honours degree in Music completed the picture. Beth expected to find shooting certificates or medals; there were none. Eventually the dog-eared corner of an ancient picture slid out from the various diplomas. Beth retrieved it. It was not a typical family snap. A girl, perhaps eleven or twelve, looked glumly at the photographer, her features nipped tightly by unhappiness. A frail woman sat next to her; her mood matched the girl's. The picture had been taken whilst they faced into the sun. It wasn't the narrowness of their eyes that alerted Beth to this, but the long shadow the photographer threw across the small group. It seemed a chilly moment frozen in family history. It was her, Beth was certain. The school receptionist was right; if the girl had been smiling there would have been a marked similarity. The back of the photograph was marked in a fine but careful hand, 'Mama, August 1980'.

Beth continued to rummage in the second container but could find little of interest. She felt no shame about this activity: Madeline had entered her life without invitation; she was repaying the favour. Besides, this was what she or they wanted Beth to know. But why? She checked her watch. The time had sped past. She'd taken over half an hour on these two boxes and, apart from the picture, was no further forward in her search for the woman.

The third container was smaller than the others, and locked. Rummaging in her handbag, Beth removed the Swiss Army knife her first editor had given her as a leaving present. 'You'll need it some day,' he'd promised. As usual he was right. The clasp on the box was built to withstand a full frontal assault, and a heavy padlock had been added as well. The hinges at the back of it were her way in. Working quickly, she selected an appropriate blade and began to unscrew the two securing pins. This had always surprised Beth. It was often easier to enter through the back door which was never as secure as the front.

Eventually, with gentle persuasion, the screws came away. Removing the lid, which now dangled loosely from the padlock, she looked inside. It was a diary for 1985: the year of Madeline's father's death. The Sound of sensible footwear on the polished wooden flooring outside stopped her in her search. There wasn't time to replace the pins; she pushed the last box against the others and plunged the diary down the back of her jeans.

'Who are you?' a woman demanded. The rough tweed of her suit told Beth all she needed to know.

'You must be the headmistress.'

The woman began to look about the room for any sign of disturbance, ignoring Beth's comment.

'Who are you? Certainly not Madeline's cousin! I've called the police, they'll be here shortly. Have you removed anything? These are private possessions of a member of staff – a valued member of staff.' The headmistress began to bend to the third box.

Beth remembered she still held the photograph. 'I'm sorry, I was going to borrow this. I need to find her,' She said, handing it to the unimpressed woman, hoping to distract her attention from the boxes.

'You won't mind if I search your bag?' The headmistress held out a hand the size of a lumberjack's. Beth shrugged her shoulders and passed the canvas bag across. She shifted uncomfortably, feeling the small bulk of the diary against the top of her backside. This woman would not insist on a body search; the police might. She began to inch towards the door and the furious teacher muttered to herself as she went through the bag's contents.

'Can we talk in your office?' Beth asked, walking away, conscious that she needed to avoid the discovery of the 'cracked' box.

'Now you wait right there!' The headmistress began to follow as Beth had hoped, pausing only to secure the storeroom. 'That foolish woman will believe anything,' she spat, remembering the receptionist's gullibility. 'Here.' She thrust the bag at Beth. 'We'll wait for the police together. Then we'll find out what you're after.'

She increased her pace. 'I need to find her.'

The headmistress must have been well into her sixties but dealt with the increase in speed with ease. 'That girl needs to be left alone!'

They were nearing the reception area. Beth was relieved to see it was empty apart from the worried receptionist. It was now or never. She knew she would regret it later, but was aware that an arrest for theft wasn't going to help. She paused for a moment, allowing the elderly woman to collide with her. A gentle shove to the teacher's back completed the manoeuvre; the headmistress toppled to the floor.

'Sorry,' Beth said as she sprinted past the startled receptionist, then out of the front door and on to the drive. There was no sign of the police, and no one around to witness her departure. At least it seemed that way. She didn't notice the blue saloon as she sprinted back to her own car.

One of the occupants picked up the handset. 'We intercepted a call, sir, to the local police about target one. She must have been told they are on their way. She ran out five minutes ago followed by a woman who looked like a wrestler. I would have run too.'

'Just the facts, unit two,' Molineux interrupted. He resented how his men had taken to Beth.

'Sir.' The agent coughed to return himself to some semblance of seriousness. 'She's proceeding due south, heading in the direction of home.'

'We need to speak to the woman from the school. Have one of unit one visit as a PC in response to her phone call and intercept local PC. Find out what she was looking for.'

He closed down the line, then switched on the intercom. 'Dobson, when we researched the Milton girl, did we visit her accommodation?'

'We did, Commander. A night search, nothing found in her flat.'

'Was the search limited to her flat?'

'Yes, Commander, the team followed its brief to the letter, as per command instruction 165.'

Molineux groaned. The days of initiative were long past. His bitterness came from the fact that '165' was one of his own; he was as guilty as the rest if Beth had been more thorough than them. Molineux sensed that the temporary halt in the slayings was for a reason. The Perfect Day must be demanding an enormous amount of silent effort from their opponents: all attempts to trace any lead had failed. Computer interfaces turned to steam with the overload of time and information.

His own team was still under internal security and so far the results had been negative; he wasn't surprised. They had been selected after the most rigorous of mental and physical tests. Their background had been researched for two generations. Now their private lives were under twenty-four-hour watch. But it was necessary. The leak could only be stopped at the source, wherever that was. He would find it eventually. The results of the IS investigation of De Haus and Boardman had not thrown up any obvious clues so far, but it was early days and had only concerned their financial dealings. He had not yet sought permission to push deeper into their lives but if the situation worsened he would.

Molineux walked to the computer designated for the trust search. Computers had a smell, he decided: they reeked of cold efficiency. He flipped the VDU to sight seen, and watched the pixels dance in the search for more information. The computer continued to canter through the Charitable Trusts programme. The numbers had been slashed to ninety-two. Whilst this was an improvement, it granted him little confidence that this was the way. In the early days it had been the foot soldiers who did the real investigative work: he had been one. They sifted and evaluated the evidence as it was discovered. But they, and he, had touch, taste and instinct; a computer had chips. The world had been a larger but much simpler place then. He returned from his reverie to the present problems.

He had two women, Beth and Madeline. The solution to the Perfect Day lay between them. The organisation intended these women to connect. When they did he would be there to watch, but not to interfere; not yet. Beth had information that he needed. There were two ways to acquire it: one, to make contact with Beth, though De Haus argued against this, or, two, to wait and interpret through her actions what information she had discovered. It seemed to him the latter course was the only proper one to adopt. Buchan agreed and had briefed the Home Secretary throughout – as if he didn't have enough political pressure on his shoulders with the prison riots.

All operations were in position or in progress – if it could be called that. He wondered what it was that Beth had found at the school that had caused her to leave so suddenly. He felt he knew her so well. It was unlikely she would leave the school without success. What have you got, Beth, and why?

Beth Gamble sat at her kitchen table, Madeline's diary sat in front of her, closed by a tiny clasp. She drummed her fingers on the table top and stared at the private document. As a girl, Beth had kept a diary of her private thoughts and would have been horrified if they had ever become public. Her reflections on boys, pop groups and the unhappiness of a nomadic life would have upset her father and mortified her. This was different. This was the year in Madeline Milton's life when she had been accused of her father's manslaughter. Beth didn't expect it to contain the naïve ramblings of a love-torn schoolgirl. But it was private. What gave her the right to steal it then plunder its contents like a tabloid hack? Maddy has, she concluded unhappily.

After some hesitation she snapped it open and turned the pages, searching for the first signs of penmanship. She found it two weeks into the book.

15 January 1985. It was the first entry in a new diary, Beth noted, and she read on.

'She is fading like the photograph. Her skin is like Kleenex; used Kleenex. Her cancer makes it look like tracing paper. Christmas was the normal silent route march through a "family" holiday. She's not going to see another one – she's lucky. Do I mean that?'

Beth flicked through the mostly empty pages of the book. Madeline was not a compulsive diary keeper.

'1 February. The wheelchair came today. It's horrid. Dull hard metal and a seat that offers no hope of comfort, just like this terrible place. He seems to suck the life away from both of us. Whilst she slumps on her commode or pretends she can see the garden through her myopia, he stalks about the house. I push her around the garden in it and she even smiled yesterday, but I can tell she feels guilty. So do I.'

Beth knew the hardship of an invalid relative but not at the age of seventeen. The girl's sad miserable life seemed understated, as though she had already given up, or would give up when her mother did. She flicked further ahead.

'1 April. A foolish day to die; she has. My poor, sad, ill, miserable, wretched, lovely, weak, beautiful, kind, ill-treated mother is dead. They rang to say they're coming for the wheelchair later. It's a resource apparently. He didn't even cry, just stuck out his chin and attempted to hold my hand. He said, "She'll be happy now." Perhaps.'

Beth didn't like what she was reading between the lines of this journal. In her diary Madeline was now alone with a man; the father she was later accused of killing. Maddy's feelings for him did not seem to be warm and his for her appeared discomfiting. She read on, anticipating the inevitable. Madeline's trial was October 1985; her father's death must have been some months before with the normal committals and case adjournments taken into account. She searched until she found the next desperate entry.

'22 May. It's only six weeks since Mama's death. I feel forty years old. Father makes me pray during *it*, it's his way of making it a "rite". He never looks me in the eye, he talks to me from behind. It's either him or me.

'It's time, I can feel it. His angina pills look like Hedex.'

There were no further entries. There didn't need to be. The story told itself if you read it properly. But Beth needed more details. She was meant to understand something through all Madeline's misery. There was more, much more; there had to be.

She removed her copy of the article she'd written at the conclusion of Madeline's trial, feeling the emptiness of the badly written bias it contained. Casting her mind back, Beth visualised the officer, the police 'source' who'd slanted the piece away from impartiality to his own whispered 'verdict'. Scruffy and chain smoking, he'd stood slouching outside the courtroom. The 'Cantonese' fingers on his inhaling hand flapped as he whined about 'other evidence'. His name surfaced, conjured by a trick of memory; DS Forsyth.

Beth glanced at the diary. The cover was a fading image of a country garden. It held a confession and despair. She placed it in the floor safe. At first it rested next to the file on Middleton. Then, without knowing why, she moved it away from his sordid biography to a resting place of its own.

CHAPTER TWENTY-FIVE

After several phone calls, Beth managed to get a lead on the whereabouts of former Detective Sergeant Forsyth. He had disappeared from the force after the conviction of an armed robber was overturned without hesitation by the Court of Appeal. The findings of the court coincided with a much-needed holiday and an unfortunate, but minor, accident in the Algarve. That left him with 'floating' back pain, which was sadly incompatible with his chosen career. Beth eventually managed to wrestle a contact number from a reluctant steward at the Police Club.

Forsyth was now a private investigator, writ server and enthusiastic bailiff. He had agreed to see Beth, but only if money changed hands. Having negotiated an extortionate 'consultancy' fee she now sat in his office. He was not a man to waste money on clients' comfort. Her orange plastic chair would have disgraced a derelict comprehensive, and the chipboard veneer of his desk glowed a pig-farm brown. It was an apt home for the man himself. No money had been spent on his own outfit. The light blue Crimplene suit must have fitted him once, there appeared no other reason he would pay money for it, but that must have been long ago, and long before the subsidised beer at the Police Club.

Beth had concocted a research story concerning the updating of unresolved cases. Forsyth had showed scant regard for her cover. Too busy enjoying his own sense of importance. Lounging back in a reclining seat he blew great clouds of rank cigarillo smoke towards her. Occasionally, his brown pudding-bowl haircut reflected the strip lighting from the ceiling. 'It was the threads, you see, they said it all.'

She watched him, cigarette ash losing out to gravity and blending neatly with the flooring. He'd aged criminally since his role as 'police source'. A Routier's map of France webbed his swollen nose; Beth could almost find Nice by his left nostril. Mr

Forsyth, as he had been since his 'early retirement', leant forward.

'A hundred you said?'

She nodded and tapped her handbag.

'A hundred and fifty. It's confidential stuff this. I could lose
my . . .'

'Reputation?' Beth enquired with mock innocence.

'Private investigator's licence. I've seen your show. Well-paid
work that.'

'It was. That's as far as I'll go. Now, get on with it.'

'I kept these as a memento.' He indicated an evidence file.
Opening it, he removed a well-read pathologist's report. 'Let's see.
Walter Milton, time of death 8–9 p.m. The pathologist couldn't be
more accurate; the heating had been on in the house. It slows up
rigor mortis.

'Angina sufferer. Died of a thrombosis. There was no evidence
that he'd taken his digitalis pills, from his stomach contents. Here's
the interesting bit.' He used a highlighter to mark as he read.
'"Examination of lungs and airways revealed microscopic fibres.
These appear to be cotton fibres."' He looked up. 'We matched
them. They were from his pillow.'

'So?'

'So he was found on the floor, not the bed. She gave him a helping
hand. "Smothered" him with affection.' He looked pleased with his
black joke.

'Why didn't the jury hear about it?'

'Barristers. The defence produced some lung expert. He reckons
that they could have been inhaled before the heart attack. The judge
excluded it.'

'He could have been correct.' Beth's voice was firm and caused
the investigator to pause.

'Friend of yours, is she?' he asked slyly. Beth stared at him. Why
was she so hostile? He nodded knowingly before replying. 'Yes,
I suppose the judge could have been, but you didn't see *her*. No
emotion when she told us about the attack. She could have lied, said
she was in the bath, reading, anything.' He shook his head in genuine
surprise that anybody could be stupid enough to tell the truth about
anything if they weren't forced to. Beth wondered how many prison-
ers were still wrongly inside due to this man's code of morality. He
searched for a document. 'Record of interview.' He read an extract.

'What happened, Madeline?'

  'We'd been arguing about the usual thing.'

'What was that?'

  'I have a place to study Music at university; he didn't want me to go. He said if I left he wouldn't pay a penny towards it.'

'Do you have any funds yourself?'

  'Only the trust fund from my mama's estate. That's held until I'm twenty-one. He was the principal trustee.'

'Go on.'

  'Then he started to breathe very heavily, and told me to get his pills. He went to his bedroom. I followed. He was thrashing about on the bed.'

'Which way was his head turned – towards the pillow or away from it?'

  'I can't remember.'

'Did you give him his pills?'

  'No.'

'Why not, Maddy? You must have known about his heart.'

  'No reply.'

Forsyth winked conspiratorially towards Beth, she grimaced at his familiarity. He continued to read aloud.

'Maddy, he was your father. You seem to be taking this all very calmly.'

  'Miss Milton is in shock. Isn't that obvious to you?'

'That's her solicitor talking,' explained Forsyth for Beth's benefit, then continued reading.

'Did you do anything to try to save him?'

  'Remember, Madeline, you don't have to say anything.'

  'But I want to. No, I didn't do anything to try to save him, and I'm glad I didn't.'

Forsyth allowed the last few words to strike home. 'But we reckon she did do something. We had the proof. If the jury had seen the way she answered our questions . . . who knows?'

  'Was there anything else?'

  'Isn't that enough? I think I've earned my money. Look, the one thing we looked for but could never establish was a motive. Can you supply one?'

Beth reached in to remove the money from her purse. Of course she could; she'd read the diary.

Molineux was being briefed by Toby on Beth's visit to Forsyth.

'He's an ex-copper – Detective Sergeant. Left the force five years ago, under a typhoon. He'd buried some evidence, hidden it from the defence. It came to light at the same time his back injury did, if you catch the coincidence, sir?'

'What's his connection with all this?'

'The records show nothing so far. Sir, request permission to approach Forsyth. He's a PI now, he'll need his licence. I'll enlist his help.'

'All right,' Molineux agreed before closing the channel down. 'He sounds dodgy. Don't give him anything to trade with.' He asked for an update on the school incident.

'She claimed a bogus relationship with the Milton woman. Tricked her way into a private store. A box was forced, by the looks of things. We don't know what was in it. We're in the dark again.'

'Where is she now?'

'At home, sir. Phoned the Irishman, and left a message.' He turned then bent down to a console, keying in the command. Molineux heard the content of the call.

'Fergus. This is serious, urgent. Some very weird things are happening. I need to speak to you. I need your help. Get in touch soon, if not sooner.'

'Have there been any other calls since her return?'

Toby checked the log of intercepted calls. 'Only one. It looks as though Beth is back on the charity trail again. There was a call to the Social Editor of *The Times*. She gave her own name for once and mentioned several titled people.' He passed his superior a list.

'She claimed to be planning a piece on the generosity of the aristocracy to charities. The editor said he'd ask around and see what he could do to help.'

'Have you run a programme on the names?'

'That's running at the moment. These people are either very wealthy or very bored. They're all members of numerous charities. It's attempting to correlate now.'

'Exclude all letters of the Alphabet but W. Pursue only those trusts starting with W. Let's see whether Beth's chasing the same rabbit as before.'

Toby moved away to carry out his instructions. He had noticed a weariness in his superior. They were all feeling the absence of a result.

Molineux felt it too. The white-knuckle ride of activity had lapsed into the helpless droop of impotence. It was always about picking up threads, then weaving them into a tapestry of evidence. The phone taps, warranted by the Home Secretary, could only be used for intelligence gathering and not as evidence in court. Even if the evidence were admissible, it still failed to establish any link with the murders. Molineux felt stubble's appearance on his chin, longer than it should have been; he had to keep up appearances and morale.

'I'm going to shower. Let's keep pushing this.'

He was barely acknowledged by the remnants of the team, who slumped in varying stages of lethargy around the command centre.

'Sharpen up, people. I want a full Team Briefing at 7.30.'

'What about Boardman?' asked Dobson, without turning his chair.

Strangely, Molineux had been wondering the same thing.

Boardman steered the pristine fifteen-year-old Daimler out of his drive. The evening had dropped away into inky blackness as he moved with stately care along the quiet streets. The communications system, attached like an amorous limpet to the vehicle's walnut dashboard, never ceased to grate on his peripheral vision and sense of good taste. Boardman was considering Molineux's orders: 'A chance meeting, arrange a chance meeting with her'.

Whatever Beth had been up to she had them worried. Molineux's intellectual arrogance had been challenged by this girl. He must have been desperate to haul Boardman back on board, though it was hardly a lifebelt to a drowning man. Boardman knew that his stance regarding their interference in the trial would ensure he would be overlooked for further promotion. So be it. He was a policeman, not a politician, with very little time to serve before retirement to his peaceful loch. His job was to catch criminals not votes. He had been allowed to delegate his existing investigations. No doubt this was an attempt to sweeten him as a 'team player'. He always had been; the only difference was his choice of team. Boardman had immediate access to Beth's whereabouts. But it wasn't her position on the national grid they wanted, it was what was in her head; the information they sought and which she possessed.

'Where is target one?' he enquired, steering the Daimler's path away from his leaf-strewn home patch.

'Eating. The first time in days, actually.'

'Where?'

'Frangino's restaurant, Maida Vale, the High Street.'

'Alone?'

'She's got company, the cameraman. They've ordered. One team inside.'

Boardman altered the car's course to accommodate these directions. He spoke into the communication console. 'Can you hear what they're talking about?' He glanced in his rear-view mirror. A dark blue Ford Escort travelled a similar route to his own.

'Not enough notice, and too much noise inside.'

He approached a set of traffic lights, showing red. 'Book me a table. Do you have a female operative on duty? Not too attractive?'

'Basic qualification, sir.' He could hear the man's snigger. 'We'll have her waiting outside. ETA?'

Boardman moved the vehicle as the lights changed, indicated left, then turned sharply right. He watched the blue car glide past in his rear-view mirror, two men staring straight ahead. 'You tell me,' he whispered, having previously severed the line.

Inside Frangino's Beth looked tense but also excited. She and Fergus had arrived simultaneously and had been shown to a quiet table set for two within the restaurant's relaxed salmon pink-and-white decor. Her drink sat untouched before her, his was hurtling down his Fenian gullet. Beth was dressed in her eating-in-comfort clothing; Calvin Klein jeans and a black Katherine Hamnett blazer with a simple silk polo shirt. Fergus had made a real effort. Beth had believed his leather jacket to be welded to his back; now it was replaced by a simple sage green Harris tweed jacket. The fact that it had a button missing made her smile. Corduroy trousers and an almost-white shirt worn with a plain tie made this a remarkable transformation. There was something else. Beth stared at the Irishman until it dawned on her: he'd trimmed the hedgerow of his beard and even smelled of a tasteful aftershave.

'So what's been happening? Your message sounded urgent.'

Beth leant forward towards him. 'I feel like a grounded fox.'

His raised eyebrows urged her to explain.

'Like things are snapping at my heels.' The bread she'd removed from the basket sat in several pieces on her side plate. She continued to crumble it. 'Paranoid.'

He placed a warm hand over her busy anxious fingers.

'But are you right?' It was his directness in times of stress that appealed to her. She shrugged, then updated him on the strange events of the last few days.

'This woman . . . Milton, is it? Sounds screwy. Hardly Daddy's girl.'

'They couldn't prove it. They didn't have the diary.'

'I've never been one for the police myself but you should think about giving them what you've got. Let them do their job for once.'

'Give them what? An ancient diary and a bad piece of journalism. How do I explain I stole the diary? At the least, I've committed a criminal offence.'

'You need a holiday, or at least a break.'

'I need to know the truth, Fergus. If I don't try I'll always wonder about . . .' Her voice trailed off in an attempt to describe the unknown.

The waiter arrived with their food, laying antipasti before Beth and steaming ravioli in front of the troubled Irishman. They ate in silence. She picked whilst he attacked hungrily. His eyes widened as they focused on something behind her shoulder.

'Miss Gamble, how nice to see you.'

She turned at the familiar voice.

Boardman smiled shyly, before gesturing to a stern woman, some years his junior, standing by his side. 'This is Mrs Boardman. It's our anniversary.'

The woman forced a surprised smile and a nod of acknowledgement.

'Congratulations,' said Fergus through a mouthful of food.

'I've been meaning to get in touch about something, Beth. I know now isn't the time or the place, but it's something you could help us to clear up.'

Beth watched the woman's face harden as he spoke. She switched her gaze to the third finger of her left hand. She was toying with the shining ring that stood out against the pale freckles on her skin. It looked uncomfortable.

'How long have you been married?'

There was a moment's hesitation before the woman replied, 'It seems like forever,' and took his hand. 'I'm sure these youngesters have their own topics to discuss. Come on, I'm hungry. Nice to meet you, Miss Gamble, Mr Finn.'

Boardman smiled at his partner's abruptness. 'Yes, of course, I'll call tomorrow.'

Beth could just discern the glare the woman gave Boardman as they moved away to their table. Fergus continued eating until his plate was clean, mopped with ciabatta from the bread basket.

'I think we've just been sniffed by the hounds, Beth. How did she know my surname?'

CHAPTER TWENTY-SIX

They took a cab to his home. Realisation had forced a watchful empty banter over the remains of their meal. She felt sick. Sick and tired. Fergus allowed three cabs to pass before hailing the fourth and giving his address. He took her hand in his to stop the trembling that had descended with the chill of the night air.

'It'll be fine, girl.' He winked. 'Just games, that's all, games and costumes, believe me.'

The journey was completed in edgy silence. He paid off the driver, and, standing in the shadows, searched the road. The tarmac was empty.

Moving to the house, he unlocked the basement flat and nodded for her to enter first. The flat was as dark as his hair. He touched her shoulder, indicating she should remain still. His bulky shadow moved towards the window. Half-hidden by the curtain, he stared along the still-deserted street. Long seconds passed before, satisfied, he drew the thin curtains across the bay. The light, dim and depressing, half illuminated the shambles of his front room.

Beth looked around, shocked. 'My God. Have you been burgled?'

He grinned sheepishly. 'No such luck. It would probably be tidier if I had. We need a drink, girl, and a talk.'

The room was as untidy as his beard though there was a smell of fresh disinfectant and all of the surfaces that were visible were polished. The rest were covered with cameras. They ranged from tired box brownies to a highly polished brass tripod with a sweeping cloak hanging from its apex. Everywhere Beth looked, lenses stared back at her: Fergus's living room was a private altar to the captured image. It was strange, thought Beth, in all the time they had worked together, she had never once set foot in his home.

She moved several misplaced items from the sofa and sat. She could hear him muttering in the kitchen about clean glasses.

'This stinks of the Security Services.' He placed a bottle of brandy down on the Art Deco coffee table between them. 'Have you noticed any delay on your phone calls? Any buzzing or clicking?'

Beth shook her head.

'It's only something I read in a book once,' he confessed. 'Probably an author's device to catch the bad men. But this doesn't look good, does it? We only decided to eat at that place shortly after we met up. That means you're being followed. If you're being followed, they've most likely put a tap on your phone too.' He poured out two vast measures of Spanish brandy, and handed her one. 'Back home, there was always a game between the boyos and the Government men. Wire taps and torture on both sides until someone made a mistake, like tonight. They know we know about them now.'

The harshness of the liquid made her gag slightly.

'Whoa, woman! Drink it, don't drown in it.'

She coughed to clear her scalded throat. 'Why, Fergus? What do they want from me?'

He thought for a moment, swilling the drink around his mouth.

'Something you've got. This file on Middleton . . . they'd have access to that if they wanted it. I don't think it's them who sent it to you. There's no reason why they would. They will know you've been to the school, but not what you found. If they've followed you after that, then the bent copper Forsyth will have spilled his guts about your meeting. They'll be on that trail by now, if they weren't already.'

She thought about this interpretation of the facts. 'You're right. Madeline isn't working for them. So who is she working for?'

'That's what we have to find out, Beth.'

'We?'

He lifted his glass. 'We. The team. Gamble and Finn. There's got to be something else you have that the Government don't. Now think.'

Beth looked into her drink for inspiration, and after some moments found it.

'I was side-tracked. They were furious about the gun club. They tried to scare me off with Middleton at the restaurant, then laid a trail to the school. It would have been simple to give me the information, just like they did with the file. They wanted it to take time.'

'What were you doing before that?'

'That scrap of paper, the receipt from the club. It must be that.'

'Well, you'd better keep searching. I'm going to take a holiday, but I won't be going far. The odds are they'll be looking for me now. That copper at the restaurant knew the game was up. Odd really, it seemed as though he was relieved when that woman copper blurted out my name. Did you see the look she gave him? Whoever is in control will be livid.' He pushed his hand through the comforting warmth of his facial hair. 'Without this my own mother wouldn't recognise me. They certainly won't.'

He reached for a holdall, ready-packed for an emergency assignment, and removed his passport to check its validity.

'They're going to think I'm out of harm's way for a while. I'll be watching, Beth. Don't take any risks.'

He scribbled down a number and handed it to her. 'It's better if you don't know where this is. Ask for Billy – you can trust him. Don't use your own phone, except to get them off your back with a red herring or two.'

She memorised the number, then handed it back to him. 'You're scaring me, Fergus.'

'I'm scaring myself, Bethany. There's a lot at stake here and we don't know what it is. It's getting late. I'll take the sofa. There's an early start to be had.'

She watched the shaggy man make himself comfortable on the badly sprung sofa. She forced the last of the fiery drink down, then crawled on to it next to him. Without opening his eyes, he placed a reassuring arm around her shoulder.

'Fergus, we're not imagining all this, are we?'

'I hope so, Beth, I really do.'

Molineux had ordered the woman officer to his room as soon as he heard the debriefing. He didn't want what he was going to say broadcast to the rest of the operatives; it would be bad for team spirit and her own standing within it. She stood to attention in front of his desk, arms held stiffly behind her back.

'Basics, sodding basics. Who you are, the role you're playing. You forgot the lot.'

'Yes, sir.'

'All that training and you couldn't think on your feet.' Molineux was hunched and furious

'Permission to speak, sir.'

'Granted, but it had better be worth it.'

'The senior officer was Mr Boardman. I was instructed by him to follow his lead.'

'And?'

'He didn't give me one, sir. There was no mention in the briefing outside about an anniversary celebration. He instructed me that I was just there as cover, not an active participant.'

Molineux sat back in his chair. The girl was good, her evaluations were of the highest calibre, her loyalty unquestionable.

'And what conclusion do you ask me to draw from that?'

'Whatever conclusion you see fit to draw from his behaviour, sir.'

Molineux sighed. This new breed was so pedantic, so precise.

'Very well, what conclusion have you drawn from the incident? Speak frankly.'

There was no hesitation in her response. 'He wanted her to know, sir.'

Molineux believed the same. 'What was your conversation during dinner?'

'He appeared distracted throughout. He asked about you, the team, and the prospects of success.'

'Your response?'

She looked pleased with herself as she replied, 'I informed the Chief Inspector that the information was classified and I had no indication of his security clearance level.'

'And what was his attitude to that?'

'Amusement, sir. He made no further effort to question me.'

Boardman would know Molineux would question this girl thoroughly. Boardman was baiting him. To an outside observer it was the girl who had cost them that portion of the operation; Molineux knew who was responsible, but was not in a position to convince a superior.

'Did he at any stage blame you for the slip?'

'No.'

Molineux dismissed the girl then spoke to Dobson. 'She'll have to be reassigned. They've seen her now. We'll have to speak to the PPS: he needs to be briefed.'

Dobson noted the orders. 'I'll ask Mr Buchan to attend, sir.'

The Commander wondered how serious the damage really was. Beth had returned to her home in the early hours and had remained there since. Her companion had boarded the shuttle flight to Dublin and gone to an address that proved to be his mother's home. Operatives had watched as closely as they dared; so far he hadn't budged. They knew. They knew and knew he knew. God, this was becoming a Feydeu farce. Dobson patiently stood his ground. 'Sir!'

Molineux was pulled back sharply from the complicated picture. 'Is De Haus still here?'

'In the library. Do you want him? He's aware of the occurrence.'

'The occurrence' was a euphemism for Boardman's treachery.

'Yes, as soon as he can present himself. Tell him I require an appraisal of what the girl will do now.'

He resented the scientist's continued input to the operation, but so far he'd been right at every turn. It almost seemed that De Haus had some inside fast track to his conclusions: they rattled from his mouth with machine pistol speed. The little scientist was beginning to irritate Molineux. His depressed, solemn air travelled with him like a personal rain cloud. His continual carping to abandon the operation seemed an about-face compared to the enthusiasm with which he had embraced the initial stages. So far, IS had only discovered a long-past, short-term tryst with an undergraduate, but the boy had attained his degree and gone his own way. Other than that De Haus appeared to be clean. Molineux's suspicious mind distrusted those who were too clean. Give him an unhealthy interest in rubber or genital piercing any time; then people could be controlled.

The pressing worry was that the 'organisation' had been dormant for some time. They would make a move soon; he had to be ready to counter it. Was it time for the Perfect Day?

Back at home, Beth was a little stiff from the night on the sofa with Fergus. But she did feel more human for the contact she'd had with him. Just to feel the warmth of another person after all this time was an unqualified bonus. She hadn't held or been held since before it happened. Beth felt a pleasant sensation of lightness that was inconsistent with her present situation. You're acting like a schoolgirl, she told herself. Then stopped a moment to think. The first time she'd met Fergus she'd known she could trust him. There was something solid and sure about his smile, his movements, his polite awkwardness when meeting new people. But put him behind a camera and he was a demon. No risk was too great for the ultimate footage. She had seen him the afternoon before the BAFTA awards at the TV studio's canteen. Beth had asked him what he was going to wear for the ceremony. He had looked down into his black coffee and said that something had come up and he couldn't attend. At the time she had accepted his decision not to go, but now remembered a look, a slightly disappointed glance in her direction before he wished her luck and left. The next time she had seen him had been at the hospital.

Beth showered quickly and was heading back towards the living room, hair dripping, when something caught her eye. It was a letter, nestling on the mat at the foot of the stripped-pine front door. It was hand delivered, the writing on the envelope immediately recognisable: Madeline's. A voice disturbed Beth. She slipped the envelope into her dressing gown's pocket.

Her father's nurse had been changing him for the day ahead. 'He seems a little better today, Beth.'

She sat by him, and took his hand in hers. The nurse banged about in the kitchen.

'Dad, I'm scared.'

She was aware that he would be unable to comprehend what she was about to say but she needed to tell somebody.

'I don't know what's going on, but it's serious. I'm the rope in a tug of war. I don't know what the sides are pulling me towards or away from; all I do know is that it's not a game. I wish you were here, really here. Then I'd know what to do.' She felt a slight pressure on her hand.

'If you can hear me, do that again, please.'

She waited, but there was no response. The movement was just another spasm of a worn-out motor neurone. Gently she placed his hand against the counterpane and pulled the letter from its envelope. It bore that day's date. Beth unfolded the document, nervous as to what trick or promise it held. She spread the letter out flat, noting that the writing was hurried, perhaps forced, as if a decision had been taken then acted upon quickly.

Beth, you know you can't trust them. Did you have the feeling you were being followed? We can help. We are the only ones who can. You will help us in return. There is somebody you must meet, a truly remarkable person. Only then will you know the truth, and you need to know, don't you?

There followed a complicated set of instructions and directions for her to follow.

Do not leave this in your home. Follow it implicitly. Do not deviate. We shall meet soon.

According to her instructions there was barely an hour before the first contact was to be made. There was no option; Beth had to do it. In a world where trust was as hollow as a car salesman's promises she could only trust herself and Fergus. Where was he now? She hadn't expected things to happen this quickly. Beth gathered her tape recorder and notepad. Having showered and dressed in jeans and a sweatshirt she kissed her father goodbye; for all she knew it could be for the last time. Her jeans' belt held his bleeper. She ran a test on the battery which was fully charged.

Then Beth picked up the telephone. She listened for any whirring or telltale ticks. Apart from the tone it was as quiet as her father's voice. Dialling in the one-key memory number she waited for Teddy's transatlantic drawl to inform her he wasn't in, then invite her to leave her name and number.

'I know you're there, you bastard. I'm coming round to collect my things, and tell you a few things about yourself if you've forgotten. Stay there.' She slammed down the receiver, hoping she would deafen the prying listeners who were violating her life. Then she followed the rest of the instructions.

Firstly, she arranged for a cab to collect her from the back of the building in five minutes. She put on a beige jacket and matching headscarf and looked out of the window for a minute or so. Moving away from the front of the flat she removed them, changing into a long trenchcoat and beret; timing was all now. She shouted goodbye to her father's nurse, then pressed the call button for the service lift when she reached the back stairs. The lift arrived. Beth sent it down empty to the basement that gave access to the back of the premises. Then she ran down the front stairs. Looking at her watch, she saw she was on schedule. The porter's office was deserted, as promised. From the corner window Beth could see the cab drive past then round to the back. A car moved forward slowly, gliding in the same direction. After it had moved from her view a laundry van drew up by the lower downstairs entrance, its doors flung wide; she jumped in. Maddy pulled the doors closed behind her as the van proceeded at a lazy pace, into the streets and away.

'What now?' Beth asked her travelling companion, who could only shrug.

'Who knows?'

CHAPTER TWENTY-SEVEN

It had been tight, but Fergus made it, just. His ma didn't ask too many questions; she was too familiar with 'the troubles'. His face and jowls felt alien to the touch and red raw from the razor's unfamiliar scrape. The turn-around had taken an hour. His elder brother Rory had booked the return flight in his own name. Rory's eight-year-old, clean-shaven passport photograph was sufficiently similar to fool the authorities. The hire car had been waiting at the airport; the camera equipment at a friend's house nearby. Fergus knew it was too dangerous to call Beth. He could only watch and hope not to be seen.

The mews were quiet: he could see one of the few remaining elms that had withstood its own form of AIDS sway from the top of its thick trunk in the cold breeze that had met him at the airport. A movement adjacent to the bending leaves caught his attention. He could see Beth in the window, headscarf on; it looked as though she was showing herself deliberately It couldn't have been for his benefit. There was obviously something up.

Fergus tightened his watch and extended it to the whole of the area. There were several cars parked nearby. Only one had any occupants. In an area where a Mercedes was the family's second car, the Sierra Cosworth sat uneasily in its unfamiliar surroundings: he could not see the car's occupants clearly. Though the sun was a low milky sphere its pale light did not force the use of sun visors yet both visors were down. He was just able to make out the lower part of their faces, where the visors ended and their mouths began. Though they attempted to use the radio surreptitiously, their body movements, talking down instead of across, identified a status that made Fergus uncomfortable.

It had been a short time since Beth's window appearance. A black cab grumbled its diesel complaint as it lumbered past. The observation car began to move off. Fergus turned the ignition and pushed the accelerator hard. Nothing. He'd flooded the engine again. The Cosworth moved away towards the route the taxi had taken. Fergus was aware the car's engine would clear itself, but it would take time. He counted to twenty and tried again.

This time it growled into action. He attempted to pull out. A white laundry van sounded its horn angrily. He allowed it to pass, then followed. It drew to an abrupt halt outside the entrance to Beth's building and the doors were flung wide. This could waste vital minutes. He plunged the car into reverse then executed the first third of a three-point turn. As he swivelled his head back towards the van for an instinctive check on other cars, he saw her. The trench coat he knew, the beret was unfamiliar, the face was Beth's. He patted the steering wheel in thanks for the British car's awkwardness, then returned the vehicle's nose to its original direction. The doors were slammed shut behind Beth, then the van moved away slowly.

Fergus settled a short distance behind, aware that one bad change of lights and she'd be gone, one bad move and they'd know he was there. At the first lights he was sweating. Though he was only one car behind, the van was slow to move away. He only just pushed the hire car's nose through as the lights changed against him. Anxious minutes scuttled past as he continued the secret pursuit. Fergus took a note of the registration, for what that was worth, as the closeness of the city traffic began to relax in to leisurely Volvos and smart Golfs. The greyness of city homes gave way to the leafdom of suburbia, the road signs informing him that Kent was the destination.

He removed a fresh audio cassette, then placed it into the dictaphone. The journey continued as he spoke.

'Fergus Finn, 11 a.m., on the way to Kent and I don't know why. Beth's in a laundry van; always a cleanliness fanatic that one, though I don't think this is about dry-cleaning. I wish I knew what it was about. I hope to find out, perhaps today. The girl's terrified, I know her, but not too frightened to stay out of it. The countryside is pretty enough, but there's something ugly about all this. God, what am I waffling about? I've never been a talker; maybe that's why she's never really noticed me. It's always oily bastards like Maxwell that end up with the girl at the end of the film. I wonder where I'll be at the final reel? The car at her house looked like it was government issue. I don't believe they'd use a van though. This must be the other lot.' He clicked the off button.

That wasn't what he wanted to talk about. No, that wasn't it at all.

His ma had guessed, she always did. Though his visit to the family home had been a brief one, and whilst she never pried, she had made one comment: 'It'll be a woman then'. It needed her to make him see that it was a woman, this woman; it always had been.

The vehicle was now running at a steady 35 m.p.h., two cars behind the van. The van's superior height cleared the other vehicles' roofs and allowed him the luxury of permitting himself a gap as he pursued Beth. Fergus clicked the button on the dictaphone again.

'She never spoke about the rape, not properly I mean: not about how she felt, just what she felt. It was the pain, not the humiliation that she focused on. It'll have to come out sometime. I hope I'm there to put her back on her feet when it does. I've never been as close to her as I was last night. When she moved her body against me and held me I felt wonderful. It wasn't a sexual thing; it was warm, modest, trusting. I saw her hair fall across her face as the night took her and she lay in my arms. But it didn't last for long. I wonder if she remembers the nightmare? She was soaking wet and flailing about with her fists. I bet she put up a good fight. What *is* she doing in the back of that van?'

They'd travelled without speaking. The gun in Maddy's hand held Beth's tongue still for some time. The van held the smells of laundry and dry-cleaning. She caught stale wafts of the familiar chemical that clung to clothing after treatment, that lazy soporific odour that smelled warmer than it should. They sat opposite each other on the trellised wooden benches that ran along the side panelling of the vehicle. A single wire coat hanger lay loose and shifting with the vehicle's motion on the floor between them. It wasn't possible to tell their direction since the blanked windows denied her a back view of the areas they were travelling through. After about fifteen minutes she could remain silent no longer.

'I know about you, Madeline, and I'm sorry for everything.' The light blue eyes lifted towards her as she raised the weapon's barrel to her lips to invite further silence. 'You were alone. You did what you had to do.'

Maddy's eyes flashed to Beth. She pursed her lips, then pointed the gun towards Beth's bag. She draped it over the muzzle. Maddy opened it then removed the tape recorder, still turning its reels. She snapped it off, tutting to herself as she did so.

Beth exhaled slowly. 'Can't you tell me anything?'

Maddy shook her head, then indicated towards the front of the vehicle with her helpful prop.

'Well, I'll tell you what I know. Nothing you don't know already. I'm sorry. I'm nervous and frightened. Do you remember what that feels like?' Beth tried to hold Maddy's eyes with her own. She realised she was holding out her hands, palms upwards, in a gesture of honesty.

Maddy seemed to lose herself momentarily, screwing her eyes a little tighter in what seemed to be a concerted effort not to recollect.

'She couldn't have helped, you know, not really. I'm sure she knew you were strong, that you could cope.'

Beth waited for a response. Maddy's features appeared to slacken.

'She knew you loved her and she loved you. Some men are too strong in the wrong way.'

Maddy gazed down at her feet, nodding slightly.

'But all this,' Beth pointed to the gun in Maddy's hand, 'is it necessary? Aren't we on precisely the same side? Just think about what we've been through, what we've suffered. Aren't you violating me in almost the same way with that gun? Taking away my right to choose?'

A sharp rap sounded on the partition behind the driver.

Maddy spoke roughly. 'Look, shut up, will you? She'll be angry if I talk to you.' She checked her watch. 'I have to get out soon; you can ask as many questions as you want then. Here, put these on.' Beth was passed a pair of plastic 'cuffs. 'Pull them tight, or someone else will pull them tighter.'

Beth complied; there really wasn't any choice. She sensed the woman was unhappy with this treatment, but was more afraid of whoever waited than of any argument Beth might put forward.

The road felt bumpier than before. The noise from the outside suggested a remote area. Beth could hear birdsong with clear patches in between; the country somewhere, but where?

The command to bind herself had forced a silence she was now loth to fracture. All her efforts so far, appealing to their shared pain, had failed. It was worth one last effort to break through.

'Maddy, what he did was wrong. The law should have protected you. It didn't, so you protected yourself. But you were wrong too. You know that?'

Maddy sat quietly for a moment, and when she replied her voice was strong with self-justification. 'Who decides what is wrong and what is right? Not you, and certainly not me. They do. Just them, without reference and without consultation. It just is, the law.' She laughed. 'You saw the law, you suffered the law. So did I.'

'But, Madeline, the law acquitted you.'

'But it didn't protect me, not from him or the other one. It got it wrong in the end, that's all. It always gets it wrong where we're concerned.' Her voice had risen in volume and passion. It was as if she were repeating a well-learned mantra to reinforce her faith. Beth attempted one last gambit, one appeal to the gun-holding woman's reason.

'The law isn't perfect, nothing is. It let me down, but that's the cost of having a fair system.'

Maddy reached into her bag again and took out a gag. The vehicle began to slow as she fixed it around Beth's mouth, and as she did so she whispered into her ear, 'Fair to who?' She fixed the blindfold over Beth's eyes.

Beth heard Maddy scramble out of the van. Shortly after it pulled away, but to where?

Molineux knew something had gone wrong. The silence on the communication channel confirmed his worst suspicions. He caught himself drumming his fingers on the desktop in the command centre. The atmosphere was almost palpable, it intensified the tension on every face within the room. Toby fiddled with the gold sleeper that studded his ear, twisting it round and round. He was caught by Molineux's glance and drooped his hand to the space in front of his console.

'Commander,' a hesitant voice began, then paused. They could all hear the man's unease as he cleared his throat then continued, 'We've been had.'

'Explain,' Molineux spat, his voice rising in volume during his utterance of that one brief word.

'We followed the cab to the specified address. A woman got out. She waited outside Maxwell's place.' There was only a raging silence from Molineux. The operative continued.

'She took off the headscarf, then we knew. We moved in immediately, using police credentials. The woman was from an escort agency. She'd been told what to wear and where to go. I think she's up front.' In the command room they could almost see the embarrassed man shuffling from foot to foot as he turned on the rotisserie of the Commander's mute fury. Eventually Molineux spoke.

'You mean you've lost her, you bloody idiots! Send another team back to Gamble's home. I doubt she'll be there but we have to try. Jesus.' The command centre examined its collective footwear. Seconds dragged by. Molineux could hear himself breathing, harsh and deep! They'd done it again.

'Beth could be anywhere now; but she's with them. Question the woman and her agency. Tell them we'll slap on an immoral earnings if they don't co-operate.' He looked around the team; nobody would meet his stare. 'I want two teams. One on Middleton, the other at her home. I want to know the moment she gets back.' The line was severed without farewell. De Haus coughed and the echo danced around the room.

Molineux considered. Beth had co-operated in this. The set-up had been planned. He doubted that even she, with all her abilities, could have engineered this on her own. The Irishman was still sampling his mother's cooking, so it couldn't be laid at his door, and he doubted that even Boardman's sympathy extended to professional suicide. They had her, or she had them, or they had each other. Whatever way it was described his superiors would want an explanation – and a head. He spun the chair round to face De Haus. 'Will she join them?' He would suffer no criticism from the researcher at this moment; his tone was aggressive, menacing. De Haus had deteriorated further. His face was pinched as a mummy's, his tie loose at the neck, the ill-matching checked shirt half-loose at his waist.

The thin man assumed his familiar pose, eyes closed, arms folded across his skinny midriff. 'Should she join them? Perhaps. Will she join them? Who knows how persuasive they can be, what tactics, or techniques they may adopt? My own opinion is that Beth hates to be told what to do. Her record from school onward suggests a natural hostility to forced enrolment or acceptance. Let us hope they are headstrong and not cunning. They are, however, women.' He smiled sardonically at the inclusion of this broad sexual stereotype and his sharp teeth disappeared as he shut his mouth quickly. His eyes looked furtive, as if he had betrayed something or someone by his words. Molineux had seen and heard enough from De Haus. He had already received permission to investigate the man's lodgings in his Oxford college. Now he would order that to be carried out.

However, not even Molineux argued with De Haus's accuracy. They had all seen too much to disagree.

Fergus was sure they'd spotted him; they must have. Once he left the cloak of protection afforded by the city traffic, once they'd deserted the B roads for the winding roughened tracks, one glance would have alerted them to his presence.

So be it. He couldn't afford to lose her, in any way. He knew how to find the place again if he had to. The laundry van had indicated right along the straight road. He was travelling about half a mile behind. Fergus looked to his right as he manoeuvred the car past the entrance in time to see electronic gates close behind the disappearing laundry van. The entrance was set some fifty yards back from the road. There was no sign or name-plate, just a stark pair of high spiked gates. A continuous wall surrounded the perimeter. It too wore the spikes of enforced privacy.

A slightly uneven widening of the verge provided the first opportunity to park and take stock, though there wasn't a place to hide the grey Cavalier. His hands were wet and shaking. This wasn't the safety a camera's lens provided. Fergus considered his options. He could wait until she re-emerged – but how would he know if she was in the van? He could enter the grounds and find out what was happening. Unpleasant though the prospect was, he knew there was only one option. He was wasting time.

Fergus removed some items from the car boot: the binoculars he placed around his neck, the handheld mini-cam went into the poacher's pocket of the rust-coloured jacket. He checked the corresponding pocket of the coat for the comforting bulk of the can of Mace. He'd had it for years and hoped it didn't 'go off'. Finally he replaced the ignition keys. It all seemed melodramatic, unreal. He left the driver's door slightly ajar, then began to scout the perimeter.

Ancient oaks and ashes cut the available sunlight to a bare minimum, casting a sodium-flare effect, like the soldiers' nightscopes back in Ireland. Even the air seemed full of chlorophyll. The wall was at least ten feet high. The spikes upon it were not the rusted remains of Victorian paranoia; their points held the recent promise of sharpness and pain.

Fergus walked back towards the gate. He hoped there might be a break, a gap, an opportunity to enter without the danger of scaling the wall. He crawled the last few yards before rising, hidden by a pillar, to follow more closely the route Beth had taken. Through the binoculars he scanned the road from left to right, following the lazy arc of its path until it disappeared behind more massive trees. It was clear to him that whoever sat inside those walls had no intention of being watched.

In the time he'd taken to reconnoitre, not one vehicle had passed. This property's isolation was no accident of the landscape. Carefully he retraced his steps, hoping that he'd guessed the road's route accurately. After five minutes he passed the inviting open door of the hire car, walked two hundred yards further and looked for a likely tree to climb. Their limbs started too high for him to jump for one.

He needed a platform: the car was ideal. It wasn't built for off-road driving and the scratches to the paintwork would require some explanation; eventually he settled it underneath an ancient oak. Fergus was a lot heavier than the last time he'd climbed, looking for apples in an orchard as a shaver back home.

With some effort he found a branch from which to continue the surveillance. He guessed the house to be Georgian. It appeared to stare back, daring him to go further, large square windows reflecting the sun into the binoculars' eyepieces. There were two vans outside the front entrance. One, the laundry van that had carried Beth away; the other, parked diagonally to it, a florist's. Fergus checked his watch. She'd been in there for twenty-five minutes. There was no movement.

A sound drew his head to the left. Rubber crunched across loose chippings as a grey Bentley proceeded with formal dignity towards the house, then drew to a stately halt outside the stately home. The car was chauffeur-driven. Its liveried driver opened the back door to allow a tall, elegant woman to emerge from its interior. Fergus could see her hair colour, grey, and her suit colour, black, but wasn't able to see more than a profile; it looked familiar, but he could go no further toward placing the identity of its owner due to the distance between them. He strained his eyes in an attempt to sharpen the image, then swore at his own stupidity.

'Buggeration,' He'd committed the cameraman's cardinal sin: the video camera was still in his coat pocket.

Fergus filmed what could be seen. He knew that later image-enhancement might well show more than the naked eye could see.

He heard them before he saw them: dogs, and they were near.

They must have come through the gates. Thank God he'd moved the car or they would have come across it by now. The barking became insistent and closer, he didn't have much time. Voices could be heard, then a command: 'Find him!'

The whoosh of quick animals, unleashed and sprinting through the thick undergrowth, accompanied him down the tree. His camera dropped in the lush ground-cover as his feet thumped a dent into the car's roof. 'No time! No time!' he muttered in a panic, leaping the last few feet. Tearing open the door, he looked uncomprehendingly at the ignition switch. They were gone!

'Jesus!' He began to pat his pockets for the keys, like a man trying to put out a fire on his clothing. He hadn't replaced them when he'd moved the car.

'Slower, man, you could die here.' He forced himself to be methodical and heard the jangle of the keys against something metallic. He retrieved them as the first dog leapt.

CHAPTER TWENTY-EIGHT

With her blindfold and gag removed, Beth emerged from the van and crunched her way across the gravel forecourt, flanked by her silent driver. The house was magnificent in its simplicity; its perfectly symmetrical proportions were a three-dimensional testimony to a long-forgotten, grander age. The huge door opened as Beth stood under the portico and a rather intense-looking woman dressed simply in the country code of twin-set and tartan skirt smiled from the threshold.

'Miss Gamble, good afternoon.' Her gaze never shifted but her voice was kind, which added to Beth's confusion. 'Please do come in. Follow me.' As Beth started to move she heard a church clock strike the hour; it struck twice. She checked her watch to see that the peals were an hour ahead of themselves.

Beth was ushered across the square hallway and along a wide corridor with a worn, cool, stone floor. As she walked she noticed to the left a number of small rooms each containing several women gathered in clusters, some with heads bowed, others talking animatedly, others still and wild-eyed. The twin-setted woman registered Beth's interest and stated simply, 'Therapy groups. We have over thirty victims in counselling at the present time. This way, please.' She led on past a large kitchen before they emerged into a high-walled courtyard which Beth guessed was at the rear of the property.

A plain door was opened ahead of her, and two steps later Beth stood before a beautifully crafted Victorian hothouse with lush green foliage pressing against the glass. It seemed to extend forever ahead of her with its pinnacled dome reaching for the sky. Beth entered at the invitation and felt the humidity riding upon the warm still air press into her throat. The door closed behind her. She took a deep breath, allowing her lungs to adjust to the atmosphere. The wooden staging all around her spread as far as vision permitted until her eyes could no longer differentiate between the hundreds of vividly coloured blooms set randomly against the deep and fleshy leaves. The smell of moist wood mingled with the intensity of their perfume, providing a heady cocktail with each intake of breath. Suddenly she heard a gentle rustle and from the left, beyond the wall of colour, a voice spoke.

'Orchids are air plants, Miss Gamble. They devour moisture from the atmosphere. Some people do find it a little stifling. Please don't suffer in silence if you feel in any way uncomfortable. These are the most demanding of creatures to nurture.' The voice dripped like syrup through gaps in the confusion of greenery.

'Creatures?' It was the only thing she could think of to say.

'Most certainly. You see, words such as "plants" or "flowers" simply don't reflect the orchid's personality, its passion, and above all its purpose. But to achieve its purpose it must first have everything right.'

Beth's ears followed the voice along the aisle. Above her further deep and rich-coloured specimens hung suspended from their baskets like cartoon fireworks.

'Orchids are particular about all things. That's what makes them so interesting, Bethany. May I call you that?' Beth sensed an answer was not expected. 'Like people, they are unable to flourish and blossom until light, temperature and food are in perfect harmony.'

'It must take enormous patience to look after them.'

'I prefer to think of it as closer to love, Bethany.' With these words the woman behind the voice emerged around the corner.

The two of them stood opposite one another. Beth was unable to see the face of her hostess hidden behind a beautifully embroidered veil wound around a pale cream straw boater and gathered in layers at her neck and shoulders. After a moment the woman lightly touched the veil and said, 'The flies are so tiresome, and I spend so much of my time in here, I find this invaluable.' Beth suspected otherwise but didn't say so. The woman moved closer and Beth could see the shaded contours of her face with elegant, high cheekbones and a strong, broad forehead.

The woman's outstretched hand beckoned Beth towards her. 'Come closer.'

She obeyed instinctively. It didn't seem quite like a command: unassuming yet confident. She took the woman's outstretched hand and searched the veil for the colour of her skin or the fleeting glimpse of an eye. They stood toe to toe for several seconds in silence before the woman spoke again.

'You're even more beautiful in the flesh – the complexion of an angel and the eyes of St Joan. You are a truly brave woman, Bethany Gamble.'

'Why have I been brought here?'

'To help yourself.'

'Do I need help?'

'Everyone needs assistance at some time, but many are too proud or too scared to ask. Your life has altered its course.'

'You could say that.'

'And I confess to have taken more than a little interest in your more recent directions.'

'What do you mean?' asked Beth sharply, but the woman had already begun to turn away from her and drift slowly towards the centre of the greenhouse. Beth hurriedly followed. 'Did Madeline need your help?'

The woman glided to a halt and sighed. 'Poor Madeline. I'm afraid she still does, like many others. A lifetime shackled to the slavery of man's lust. It is a delicate operation to saw through those chains.' She shook her head sadly. 'For some, like Madeline, the gates of freedom cannot come quickly enough, and who am I to interfere with their path?'

'On the assumption that you're aware she's running around with a revolver hanging from her charm bracelet, I'd say it's a pretty fair guess that you've already interfered. Although God knows what kind of counselling that is.' Beth surprised herself with the sudden anger in her voice.

'You assume a great deal, but one thing you have said is accurate. God does have a name for it. Divine justice.'

The words hung in the hot still air. 'You mean, you're encouraging revenge. I know her story.' The woman raised her head slowly from the pink and violet bloom she had been inspecting. 'That depends on perspective. Yours may be different from mine. That's what you're here to find out, isn't it?'

'I don't know any more. Being brought here at gunpoint doesn't lend itself to particularly clear thinking,' Beth saw the suggestion of a kindly smile behind the veil.

'Yes, I'm sorry. I couldn't be sure that you would come.'

'A letter of invitation might have done the trick.'

'But, Bethany. You've already received my calling card,' the woman said, holding her gaze.

Suddenly Beth's mind raced back to the dossier she had received containing the truth behind the fabrication that was Arthur Middleton's life. She remembered the documents and asked bluntly, 'Where did you get access to those papers?'

'Isn't it journalists who are prepared to suffer incarceration before revealing a source?' Beth didn't respond. 'Now I'm your source, I expect the same loyalty from you. If ever a situation arises when you feel compelled to disclose some of the secrets I am about to entrust to you, be it on your own conscience. You will be judged by your own criteria, and at that point our lives will have parted for eternity.' The words loitered in the strange heat.

'What do you mean?'

'Who knows what the future holds?' came the reply in a light, almost glib, tone which left Beth feeling she was talking to someone who had always known precisely what the stars held in store for her. But, strangely, there was an undeniably genuine concern in the woman's voice, born from an emotion Beth couldn't quite put her finger on.

'And I suppose you have a different system of values.'

'My system?' The woman began to walk again. 'My system is the Lord's system. It is perfect in design. Unlike the procedures employed by those in authority, whereby the criminal justice system is left without protection from those who purport to administer it.'

'Who?'

'The police, the lawyers, the judges . . . sometimes even those who make the laws, the legislators. They all have access to, and frequently abuse, the system of justice. Don't you see that the law cannot function properly once it has been tampered with? Let me tell you the law I advocate. It is the law of God, both natural and divine. The right to protection, the right to privacy, the right of the sanctity of one's own body, the right to freedom, to walk streets and pavements without fear.'

'If you're saying what I think you are, it amounts to no more than you acting as judge and jury.'

'Incorrect, Bethany, for God is my judge. And what further evidence do you in particular require of the perversion of our system of justice? Look at the beast who raped you. Would he have walked free and you have been branded a whore had the truth been allowed in that courtroom?'

The statement shook Beth and she closed her eyes at the memory. When she opened them again, in front of her on the bench lay a single sheet of paper. She glanced at the woman who had turned her back and was reaching towards a high shelf. Beth heard her say over her shoulder, 'Read it if you like, you will find it interesting.'

Beth took the sheet and turned it over. It was headed with the Scotland Yard Metropolitan Police force crest and marked 'Top Secret'.

She scanned the four neatly printed paragraphs. It was the blue-print for the acquittal of Arthur Middleton, including references to herself and Teddy Maxwell. A swell of anger rose through her like a blast of helium. She spun around but the woman had gone.

Directly ahead of Beth was a narrow connecting door leading to a smaller hexagonal hothouse. Beth swung the door open and was struck immediately by the blistering heat inside. The woman stood to the right of her, stroking the trumpet contours of a frail white orchid.

'What the hell is going on?' Beth's shaking hand held the sheet in front of her.

'Sssh,' ordered the woman harshly. 'Close the door immediately.'

Beth controlled herself and reached for the door handle. As she did so, through the glass wall she spotted four dogs – Dobermans or Rottweilers, she couldn't be sure from this distance – thrashing across the lawns followed by several women. There was an underlying sense of menace in this place.

'You see, the very people who are responsible for protecting us from scum and evil are no better themselves. They act to change the course of justice, thereby bastardising its purpose and direction.' She grabbed the sheet of paper from Beth and folded it carefully before placing it on the pine dresser before them. Beth stared at it, trembling with anger. She had to have that memo but the way this conversation was going didn't seem to suggest that she would be allowed to leave with it, if she was allowed to leave at all. She considered making a quick grab and run for it but the look of those dogs soon dissuaded her.

'Why me? Why my case?'

'You were a trap, Bethany, and Middleton was a target.'

213

'A trap and a target for whom?'

'For me.'

'I don't understand.'

'The authorities dispute the validity of my system of justice and, true to their corrupt nature, they expected that you were too important an opportunity to miss for our cause, so they simply ensured that your rapist was acquitted. Can you believe that someone would want to do that to you after all you have suffered?'

'It can't be true.'

'Oh, but it is. All for the sake of ensuring that I am dragged into their mindless game without rules.'

'But why you? Have you assisted others like Madeline?'

The woman glanced in Beth's direction. 'I have gone further. I am a woman of substantial means and I have chosen to utilise those assets in pursuit of my own beliefs. The debate is closed, action has begun. I like to think of myself as a gatekeeper for women like yourself. I can open the gates to freedom, the kind of freedom which allows you to escape from the clutches of the guilt imposed upon you when the system failed you and said, "I don't believe you, Miss Gamble. You weren't raped, you were just another slut who asked for everything that you got . . ."'

'But Madeline . . .'

Before Beth could say any more the woman interrupted harshly.

'What about Madeline? She was simply another casualty of the system. They never considered her.' She softened. 'The day you were chosen meant Madeline would never stand even a remote chance of justice because her case was inextricably linked to yours. They overlooked that and now Madeline is a loose canon, ready to do anything. She is beyond even my control.'

'How do you know all this?'

'You're treading that line again, Bethany.'

'All right. If I accept that the police rigged Middleton's trial to force you into some sort of snare, why didn't you simply stay away from me?'

'Because you have a special role to play.'

'Don't get me wrong, but if you think I'm prepared to act as some sort of pawn, you'd better reappraise your strategy. It simply isn't going to happen.'

'But it already has, can't you see that? Choice was taken away from you by the authorities, not by me. It is they who are insistent upon interference. They who cannot allow our systems to co-exist. Their inability to acknowledge the purity of revenge is no longer reflected by society. I can hear the cries of desperation all around. No one is allowed to protect themselves from the hyenas of crime, whether it be the drug peddlers or the burglars or the car thieves. Act to stop them and you are punished. Well, no longer. The time has come and I shall lead the way with your help.'

'I don't think you heard me.'

'And I don't think you hear me: you have no choice.'

'What is "my special role"?'

'In time.'

'You talk in riddles. I want facts.'

'Are you sure you want to know?'

'Yes.'

'I once had a sister. I no longer have that sister. She was taken from me by a man who corrupted her values and turned her from me. Now he will pay for his sins.'

'I'm sorry but how does this affect me?'

'Soon enough.'

'Why not now?'

'Because first I must execute the Will of my sister.'

Suddenly the door behind them burst open and the same woman who had met Beth at the steps rushed in. The other woman looked up sharply.

'What?'

This was Beth's chance; she spotted an open bag of potting compost carelessly balanced against the base unit of the large old dresser. She turned her back to it and pushed the folded sheet along the dresser top, praying it would drop off the end and into the bag.

'There's been a breach of security.'

The twin-setted woman handed a passport to the other who glanced at it briefly then threw it towards Beth. She opened it and stood transfixed at the name Rory Patrick Finn.

'One of your friends, I presume?'

Beth shrugged in panic as her arms were grabbed from behind. What the hell was happening? It must be Fergus, what had happened to him? Her mind reeled in confusion.

'Take her away from here, and make sure her friend is dealt with permanently. Beth, it's nothing personal. Nothing is.'

She was dragged around and marched out of the hothouse by two strong women. As they approached the main house a hand was placed over her mouth and nose, wrapped in a linen handkerchief. There was a frantic shouting from behind.

'Search her before you drop her!'

CHAPTER TWENTY-NINE

The smell struck Beth's nostrils: flowers, strong and corrupt. Still blindfolded and bound, she forced hard against the leg and arm restraints. They would not move. They felt tighter after she had struggled. Beth had heard the doors slide open as she was placed in and secured. This must be a different vehicle from the one she'd arrived in. As the engine kicked into life its rumble sounded more asthmatic than the other.

The woman's last enigmatic statement tormented Beth's attempts to understand. 'Beth, it isn't personal. Nothing is.'

The smell was cloying, almost sickening. Every time the van turned sharply a new pulse of nausea swept over her.

Fergus! Oh, Fergus, what have they done to you? Beth was heartsick and tired. Had they really killed him? How did they know about him? How did he find her? The Orchid woman could have been lying about his death, yet his promise to watch over her had been private and, knowing him, binding. Fergus would never, had never, let her down. Yet she had let *him* down. This whole investigation had been a farce. She hadn't been following anything. She'd been led by the nose from the start, and had been betrayed by everyone but him. Even the trial had been fixed.

Her investigation, that was a laugh! How could you discover what was being handed to you on a plate?

Beth felt the first tears of hopeless defeat chart a course down her quivering face. This must have been how they felt, those desperate people counting the hours before her programme exposed the truth to the ones they cared about.

Now Fergus too. For what? The hope of climbing back up the TV ratings with another exposé of human inadequacy?

In the end the Orchid woman had used even intellectual bribery. She claimed that by making Maddy speak in the van, Beth had forced their hand; now they had rejected Maddy. Beth was responsible, she claimed, *she* must put it right, before Maddy went beyond the law. The choice was Beth's. When the van deposited her at the address she could, if she chose, merely walk away, but she must live with the consequences.

Beth dropped her head down on her chest and wept. She wept for herself and for Fergus, and all the others who walked this sad and disappointing road without hope. The van moved on.

All the operatives out in the field were on full alert. The various units sat at their designated locations, waiting for a call to further their pursuit. Operatives sat, redundant, outside Middleton's home and Beth's flat. Others were waiting outside Maxwell's address where the humiliating switch had come to light. They all waited on a single frequency for the call. Radio silence was maintained. The units extended that silence within their own member vehicles, each concentrating on their own explanation as to how it had gone wrong. It had been two hours since her disappearance. Then all car communications crackled simultaneously into life as an excited message crossed the air waves into their vehicles.

'All units – one, two, three, four, five – Code One Alert, repeat, Code One Alert. Target Beth Gamble sighted Heathrow Airport; armed and dangerous. Has hostage. Proceed with all haste, immediately abort operation, proceed to airport. You will be met and briefed. End message.' They had been trained to respond without question and did so without hesitation. The cars and their occupants sped away to answer their duty.

Rough hands forced Beth away from the loosened restraints. The van had been stationary for seconds only. Her hands were held by other gloved hands behind her back. She was taken round to where she guessed the driver's cabin would be before she was spun around and pushed to the ground. Beth fell against some bags, her hands instinctively reaching out to break her fall. The vehicle pulled away sharply as she removed the blindfold. Her eyes were flooded with the day's light as her focus fought against its glare. The haze moved slowly as she rubbed furiously at her eyelids. Her vision cleared; the vehicle was gone.

Beth climbed to her feet slowly, pushing herself away from the mound of decaying bin bags that had saved her from injury. She bent down, attempting to massage some life into her ankles where the strap's teeth had bitten. She rose to look around, repeating the same action on her painful wrists.

This was hell. If it wasn't then it shared the same landlord. Above her a huge tenement building loomed dull as brackish water over the wasted street. The sunlight seemed out of sync with the place; it illuminated its misery. So this was it. Was she really expected to believe that Maddy lived here? Amongst all this? It was decision time. Did she go, or did she stay? Beth didn't owe Madeline anything. What was so wrong with walking away? It was Madeline who had broken into and entered Beth's life, not the reverse. Then she remembered the diary. This girl had never been given a chance, yet against the misery of her life she had given herself to teaching the blind until another man had shattered her hope again. Even the woman with the orchids had abandoned her to her fate. Could Beth?

Now it wasn't a difficult question to answer. Flat 88. The eighth floor, she guessed, but not through the back. That's what they wanted, why they'd dropped her here in the first place. If she was going in she was going in through the front door.

Cautiously Beth made her way to the shattered entrance of Hope House. She searched in vain for a mail box bearing the number in her head, hoping to find a name to match against it. She found the wreckage of the stacked system next to the long dead lift, packed with refuse and used condoms.

Eyeing the stairs, Beth began her climb to the eighth floor. During her ascent she viewed the gaping doors with mounting suspicion. This was not one of her better ideas. The few remaining lopsided numbers confirmed her guess; only one more floor to go. The numbers skipped, like gaps in a seaman's teeth, 81, 84, 86 then 88.

Moving quietly, Beth pushed herself hard against the wall, then slid along it until she was within touching distance of the handle. The door was open. Her breathing echoed around the silence of the corridor. Debris lay scattered along its length. A rusted pram, missing its wheels lay in the half shadows at the furthest point of the corridor. Light was scant and insufficient. Beth closed her eyes to accustom them to the semi-darkness. After counting to ten she opened them again to find her vision improved though the view of the discarded nappies and ripped bin bags forced a grimace of distaste across her face. She took a deep breath and held it. She could hear voices, a man's and a woman's. The woman's was Maddy's.

'Eat some more, now! NOW, and SWALLOW, you prick!' Her command was reinforced. 'Or it'll happen now. Do you understand?'

Beth pushed herself until she was adjacent to the door, then began to open it a centimetre at a time.

'It wasn't me,' another voice whined. 'They said it wasn't. You heard them.' Beth could hear his mucus through the words.

'Then they were wrong. We know the truth, don't we, Billy?'

The door opened to reveal the contents of the room. Maddy's rapist, a sharp-faced youth, his crotch soaked with urine and fear, stood next to a window, forcing a handful of white tablets down his throat, gagging as he tried again and again to swallow. Maddy held a gun, lengthened by a silencer. It was aimed at his genitals. The boy's eyes, blood vessels already ruptured by fear or drugs, swivelled pitifully in her direction. 'Please! Please!'

His knees were beginning to buckle. A dull thump from the weapon hurled a bullet that spat into the decaying woodwork inches from his hips.

'Stand up straight, Billy,' Maddy whispered, then flicked her gaze towards Beth. A further gush of urine spread the wet patch further down his legs.

Maddy nodded towards the trembling boy.

'This is Billy. He raped and buggered me. Say hello, Billy.'

The rapist's sobs drowned out her command. 'Not me, not me.' His voice sounded unsure, even as the words spilled out.

'It doesn't matter, nothing personal. But what is?' said Maddy bitterly.

Beth swivelled her face to Maddy as she heard the last words of the Orchid woman issued from her lips. This was all meant to happen. They knew Beth would come here; they knew her. This was part of it and so was she, and Madeline, and the terrified boy in the soaking jeans. Beth had never been in such close proximity to animal violence before. The flat seemed alive with unexploded fury; it smelt of murder.

When he had heard nothing for some time Molineux decided to break radio silence with his teams units in the field. He patched into the single frequency, but addressed his attention to unit one, one of the two at Beth's home, 'any sign of target one?' After a slight radio crackle, a response was transmitted.

'Negative, Commander, but the airport perimeter is sealed.'
Molineux screamed into the mouthpiece.

'What the hell are you talking about, man? What airport?'

'Your command, patched through an hour ago. All units abort present operation and regroup at Heathrow. Target one seen armed, with hostage.'

Molineux's face drained of all colour and he began to breathe rapidly, 'Oh, God. Return,' he shouted. 'Return immediately. Break the speed limits, break the law, just fucking get back!'

Molineux sat wide-mouthed. His operation was crumbling into dust around him. Nobody would look at him. He glanced towards De Haus who sat with his head in his hand, whispering.

'No, no.'

'You can't, Maddy: it's wrong, it's immoral.'

'And rape isn't?'

The boy's eyeballs were rolling to the back of his head, then returning.

'This isn't the way. They've got you believing it is, but it's not. I swear, it's not.'

'If the policeman hadn't called around to see me that night he would have killed me. Wouldn't you, you little shit? Even when he escaped he still stabbed my cat to death. Poor Wolfy, he was brave; he tried to protect me. That's how they caught him, you know.' She waved the gun towards Billy's face. He cringed.

'Stand still,' she screamed. 'Medical science. Underneath his claws, DNA, and it matched, until the police became involved. There was a lot of blood, where he cut me, you see.' She seemed to be explaining to a child. 'A lot of it. My nightgown was ruined. It was hers, my mother's. She left me it, when she went away.'

Her vagueness terrified Beth more than her ranting. The boy was swaying. He began to shuffle to one side, without seeming to know where he was heading.

'Maddy, she didn't go away, she didn't leave you. She died, that's all. It happens to us all,' Beth said soothingly.

Billy was still sufficiently in touch to begin whimpering afresh at the mention of death.

'She died and you went on living, as she wanted you to. It wasn't her fault.'

Maddy turned sharply. 'What do you know about fault? He would

221

have gone to prison for ever, if they hadn't wanted you; hadn't interfered.'

The boy's eyes seemed to be focusing with more clarity. He began to edge a little closer to them.

'What about me, Maddy? I didn't choose to be a victim either.'

Maddy's eyes followed Beth's to the boy. She reaffirmed her grip on the pistol and he moved back a step. The smell of urine began to drift towards them, drying with the heat of his fear.

'I saw the photograph, Maddy, did you know that? I saw her too, your mother, her pain. I saw your father's shadow. It's still covering you, even now. Get out of that picture; find your own. But not like this.' Beth dropped her voice. If she could only get a little closer to her. 'If you did this, what would your mother think?'

Maddy froze at the question.

'She wasn't to blame and neither are you. Forgive yourself.'

At last she seemed to strike a chord in Maddy's mind. She looked down at the gun in her hand as if unsure of its purpose.

In the moments of her uncertainty Billy had moved back and was now perched alongside the open window, reaching for the fire escape. Maddy raised the weapon to take aim, and Beth made a desperate grasp towards her arm. The gun recoiled. Beth felt its warmth as the slug slammed into the woodwork next to the boy.

He flailed his arms before his face to protect himself. Beth watched in horrified fascination as gravity exerted its pull on his badly balanced body and took him for its own. His scream followed his trajectory, then stopped.

The overwhelming silence threw the shabbiness into sharp relief, until a quiet repetitive tone punctured it. They stared at each other, neither daring to seek its source, until Beth felt the gentle throbbing of her father's bleeper at her lower back.

'She'll kill us, you know. She doesn't forgive,' Maddy said, terrified.

Beth was already moving away. 'Go to the police. Tell them everything.' As soon as she'd said it she realised the futility of her advice. Maddy had come to kill and Billy McCabe was dead. 'Look, we're in this together now. You have to trust me.' She took the shaking woman's face in her hands. 'Do you trust me?'

Maddy shook her head. 'I don't have anyone else to trust after this. She didn't tell me to kill him, she wouldn't let me. I stole the gun.'

Her eyes were dilated in terror.

'She'll kill me.'

'Will you do whatever I ask you to? Will you, Maddy?' She nodded dumbly. 'Give me your phone number. We'll work this out, decide what to do. I can tell them it was an accident,' Beth promised the shaking girl.

The bleeper's insistence spurred her to movement once more. 'I have to get home now. My father. Go home. Stay there. I'll call you later.'

With the number in her pocket, she sprinted down the depressing staircase, and out of the building. This time she took the back stairs. She could hear the echo of Maddy's steps following the same route.

Outside she searched for a phone box. Nothing. Cars were stopped at a traffic light. A Ford Orion contained a driver deep in a telephone deal that had demanded all his attention. He didn't notice until Beth was sitting next to him.

'I'm a doctor.' She produced her bleeper. 'There's an emergency. May I use your mobile?' She didn't wait for his shock to subside before keying in her home number. The phone rang and rang. There was no reply.

'Get out of the car now! If you're a doctor, where's your medical bag?'

'Look, all right, I'm not. It's my father, he's in trouble. Can you at least get me to a phone box that works? I'll ring a cab.'

Reluctantly, he set off at speed. Three hundred yards down the road a silver cubicle stopped their journey. Beth leapt out and checked the dial tone. Thank God!

'Thank you,' she shouted at the car's disappearing tailpipe. Beth quickly dialled the ambulance service and demanded the dispatch of an ambulance to her home.

'One has already been dispatched twenty minutes ago,' the operator replied. 'Isn't it there yet? I'll check.' Beth drummed her fingers on the booth's counter. 'Yes, it's there now.'

She slammed down the phone without apology. Then she saw the cab. Jumping into the middle of the road, waving her arms furiously, she brought the taxi to a halt.

'Are you off your head, darling?'

'My father – an attack – they've bleeped me.' Taking out the bleeper as evidence of the truth.

'Don't you worry, I'll have you there before you know it.' Once he had the address, the black cab sped along the street towards her home. It took twenty precious minutes. She thrust a £20 note at him which she had hidden in the back pocket of her 501's, three hundred yards from home, when traffic brought them to a halt. Beth saw the lights of the ambulance first, then the police cars, four of them. She sprinted towards her home. There was no rush, no urgency to the outside activity.

Beth burst past a policeman at the door. Inside Boardman stood, grave-faced and solemn. He was finishing a conversation on a shortband radio. 'I'll do it my way, Molineux, do you hear me!' He turned to her. 'Beth, I'm sorry. I'm sorry about it all. It's your father, I'm afraid he's dead.' He put an arm on her shoulder and she looked at his face, incomprehension and bewilderment coursed through her. What was Boardman talking about? She looked at the bleak concern on his tired face. He chewed his bottom lip for a few minutes before continuing.

'There is something else. Bethany Gamble, I am arresting you for the murder of Arthur Middleton. You do not have to say anything, but what you say . . .'

CHAPTER THIRTY

'They took your bait, then spat it back at you.' Buchan was furious. 'The Home Secretary wants heads.'

Everyone in the room, apart from Boardman, flinched. Molineux had no reply; all this had been expected since the discovery of Middleton's corpse.

'What action do you intend to take, Commander?' It was twelve hours since the girl's arrest.

'Boardman, could you outline the evidence for Mr Buchan?' His tone was civil; he seemed beaten.

Boardman turned to the mandarin. 'It looks bad for her. The search of her home threw up a file on the deceased, marked RAPIST; it contained detailed research on him. The prosecution will be able to use it well at the trial. We all know she had a motive for the killing. So far she's refusing to talk to us at all.'

'Any alibi?' Buchan enquired.

'If there is, she's not willing to disclose it at the moment. The preliminary forensic report shows she has recent powder burns on her coat sleeve. She got access to him by a phone call to his wife, luring her away from the house.'

Buchan considered for a moment. 'Well, thank God we didn't approach her. All we need is another *security scandal* to bring the Government down. Is there anything to link the girl with this department?'

Molineux shook his head. 'No. We've severed surveillance links and removed the equipment.'

Buchan noted this on his pad. 'Then she's on her own. The sooner she's convicted the better. That is the view, though it is not for repetition. Is she to be charged with all the murders?'

The room dropped into a deeper silence. Nobody had considered this aspect.

Boardman punctured the uncomfortable quiet. 'Isn't she in deep enough? Besides we know she didn't, couldn't have committed them, sir.' He fought to control his temper. 'Aren't we forgetting the whole purpose of this team? It's obvious that she's been set up. They've been ahead of us from the beginning. Everywhere we've looked for them they've been there waiting with two fingers up.' The entire room had shared the same view, but thinking was not saying. 'How did they know the code and frequency to get the teams away from Middleton's home? Instead of taking heads, shouldn't we be taking stock?'

They were all embarrassed by his outburst.

'Internal security will investigate that aspect, Boardman.' Buchan's voice was measured and threatening. 'As of this moment this unit's operations are suspended until the enquiry is concluded. I need hardly remind you that any breaches of security . . .'

'Further breaches,' muttered Boardman.

'*Any* breaches,' he spat out, glaring at the policeman, 'will be traced and dealt with severely. The girl has made her own bed . . .'

He allowed the remains of the familiar phrase to be inserted individually.

'But we gave her the materials,' said De Haus. 'Morally we owe her a duty to care about her future.'

'Morally she is a murderess who will spend the rest of her life in prison. Where is the morality in castration?' He snapped his briefcase shut. 'This, Professor De Haus, is not a student seminar. I suggest you return to your own students if you wish to bandy undergraduate philosophy. This has been a costly operation and we are all accountable.'

Boardman doubted Buchan would be accountable for anything. 'What about the Perfect Day? Are we going to sit back and let it happen?'

Buchan rose to his feet, alerting them that the debate was concluded. 'That's no longer your concern.' He paused, then smiled maliciously. 'Your concern, Chief Inspector Boardman, is to make the case against her stick. You are a policeman, she is a suspect: do your duty.'

With that order he nodded to Molineux. 'There is a matter I would like to discuss with you in private. I shall wait in your office upstairs.' He then stalked from the command centre.

'Well, that looks like it,' said Dobson, reaching for the off switch on his computer terminal.

'Let the programmes run,' ordered Molineux. 'We may be suspended from the operation; he said nothing about closing off the computer searches. Keep me informed if anything pops up.'

'Sort of accidentally?' asked the grinning researcher, turning back to the console.

'Boardman, you have your orders. Keep me informed about Beth. She needs to think she can trust you.'

The policeman was deep in thought. He hesitated before looking directly into the Commander's eyes. 'And can she?'

The question was left unanswered as the room's other occupants began to follow their orders.

In Molineux's office Buchan glared reproachfully out of the window.

'I never liked this scenario one bit. You have overreached yourself. It has been noted.'

'It isn't over yet,' Molineux responded bitterly.

'But it is. Has it crossed your mind yet to wonder how they knew the code to send the teams away from the killing zone?' It had, but Molineux had been unable to figure a response to the conundrum. 'Shortly after yesterday's débâcle occurred, I ordered your request for a covert operation to be made operational. They searched Boardman's house. Nothing was found: that did not surprise me. He, of course, did not have access to the codes, or involvement at the initial stages of the operation when the first leak was suspected.'

Buchan removed a file from his briefcase, and threw it down on the desk. 'This man did. In De Haus's rooms we found numerous items of E-mail dialogue. Just read some of the contents.'

Molineux's heart plummeted as he flicked through the chronicle of the operation's betrayal. He swallowed hard before speaking again.

'Why did you allow him to remain in the debriefing?'

Buchan clicked his tongue in genuine disappointment at the question.

'You have lost your edge, Molineux. We are going to allow our little viper to tell them that this operation has come to an end. That should serve to end his involvement with us, once and for all.'

'The Official Secrets Act?' Molineux offered as his contribution to the De Haus problem.

'Too messy. He would splash the details of the whole sorry

venture across the press. Tell me,' Buchan asked quietly, 'what does his college despise most – buggery or bankruptcy?'

'We can't even police ourselves,' exploded Anthony Palmer-Dent. 'We are riding a policy of pro-active policing and you tell me the country's crack police unit has a traitor in its midst.' He paced the teak floor of his private room, his MCC tie flying to the side as he turned abruptly.

'I told you to deal with this whole matter yourself, Buchan. You have failed me.'

He sat stern-faced, a chastened schoolboy before his furious headmaster.

'The matter is in hand, Home Secretary,' he offered timidly. Palmer-Dent seated himself in his favoured captain's chair then steepled his fingers before him.

'I do not wish to know the details. As long as there will not be any publicity, and the matter is resolved with finality.'

Buchan nodded. His prospects of an early knighthood were disappearing in the heat of Palmer-Dent's fury. He watched the Minister remove a bundle of faxes from a pristine blue file.

'Andrew, the security problem is a minor matter compared to the others we face.' Buchan knew, by the use of his Christian name, that the subject of the leak would be shelved for the moment, but only for the moment. He also realised, by the friendly plural, that his help was needed on another topic.

'Our prisons are chronically saturated. Intelligence reports suggest that Wandsworth and Durham could explode at any moment. We have people on the inside who are terrified of the consequences if they do. The problem is always the sex offenders: the rest like someone to despise and they are the obvious choice.'

Buchan could see that the Home Secretary's impressive rationality had resurfaced.

'I believe we can use the situation to the Government's advantage.' Buchan smiled at the statement: Palmer-Dent meant his own, of course. 'If we remove the cause of their anger then we defuse the bomb.' He looked up and flashed the enigmatic smile that had met the applause of the party conference. 'A sex-offenders' prison.'

'Brilliant, Home Secretary,' beamed Buchan, aware that assidu-ous fawning might yet have him on bended knee before the Queen, and at the next Prime Minister's side. Palmer-Dent nodded his own approval at the appropriate response.

'I want you to set up a working party on the matter: the right people with the right attitude.' Buchan noted his tasks. 'Andrew, about the other matter – just have it taken care of. Make sure the Gamble woman is convicted, there's a good chap. Pity about her; attractive little piece. Wouldn't have minded taking a Gamble myself.'

Buchan tittered to the proper extent, fully aware of his superior's predilection for the fleshy side of life.

'No further mistakes,' said the next Prime Minister in waiting, as Buchan closed the door behind him.

Beth shivered in the confines of the stark police station cell. She felt displaced in time and space. Her father was dead. When Boardman had given her the terrible news she had stood rooted to the spot. She had failed to grasp anything else he had said. He had mentioned murder. At the time, in her confusion, she had believed she was accused of killing him, her own father. Boardman had allowed her to see him. He was on the floor. Though he hadn't moved more than inches in the past few years, he had died on the floor. How, for God's sake?

Boardman had been gentle when he drew back the shroud that covered him, but no amount of gentleness could prepare Beth for the ordeal of seeing her father dead. Someone had closed his eyes. She could see the scar across his face where years before he had fallen from a stepladder and gashed his cheek. Beth remembered his concern at her upset, smiling whilst the blood ran into a handkerchief, telling her it was all right. It wasn't: it never would be now.

They said it was a heart attack. He hadn't shown any of the signs until the minutes before he died. Now he appeared at peace for the first time in many long painful years.

The nurse had been hysterical. She was gabbling in shock about how it had only been a few minutes, just a few minutes, that was all. Tearful eyes begged for forgiveness, but Beth didn't blame her, she blamed herself, and now her father was dead. That was the past; this was now.

Beth shifted on the uncomfortable cot. She had caused all this: she should have been with him. Was he afraid at the end? His face, cold and still, showed no signs of terror at his fate. Eventually,

Boardman had pulled her away, his arms taking her shoulders, raising her up and away from her last vestige of family. When the silent dumb journey had passed and she arrived at the police station, she still felt numbed by the surreal quality of the day's events. Her handcuffs were removed as the Custody Sergeant was informed of the reason for her arrest. Boardman appeared almost apologetic as he recounted the name of her alleged victim. What was she supposed to have done?

She needed time to think. It wasn't easy. The simple white smock, given in exchange for her clothing, was a reminder of the last time she'd worn a similar garment; the night of the rape. She knew that at this moment the scientists would be poring over her outfit, searching for further evidence; attempting to build the case, to lock her up for life.

She'd been so gullible, so arrogantly confident, and now her father and Fergus were dead. 'They' had outguessed her at every stage of the game. She knew it was a game but until today had never appreciated the stakes were so high. She thought of her dead father again:

The wall's blankness was as depressing as her predicament. She had to think. There was no one left to trust; only herself. Beth had been informed by the Custody Sergeant of her rights, including her right to silence. It was one she decided to exercise to the full. How could she give a statement of her whereabouts to the police, when she'd been present at the murder of another acquitted rapist? That would involve Maddy too and Beth needed her. The long hours alone had left her with an opportunity to think. She had believed that her earlier efforts were the result of careful planning. She had been wrong. Now even poor sweet Fergus had paid the penalty. There was nobody she cared for left to hurt, but she was going to hurt the rest, all of them: the police and the vile woman who had pulled her strings so easily and with such effect.

The seeds of the plan were sewn. It wasn't much, but Beth had always refused to lie down, and now wasn't the time to grieve; it was time to settle some scores. She needed Maddy and it wouldn't be easy. The woman had been hysterical at McCabe's flat but Beth had also seen a different side to her. She had witnessed some impressive role-playing by Maddy during this charade. She had seen her in restaurants, in a gun club, and in control of McCabe's future, until Beth touched something inside the woman that forced her to remember her humanity. She must reach it again, if it was going to work.

Beth had been informed of her right to a phone call, so she could inform a friend or relative of her arrest and whereabouts, but it would be foolish to squander a call that precious; besides, anyone who had read the newspapers would know precisely where she was and what she had done. The timing was crucial. So far Beth had refused to co-operate either in interview or in the 'friendly' chats forced upon her by the investigating officers. All they wanted was a confession. 'Who knows? You might even get away with a manslaughter plea.' Beth knew this for the self-serving nonsense it clearly was. Even the policemen seemed unconvinced of that prospect. And she hadn't done it; she wasn't guilty no matter how awful things looked.

They had removed her clothing, and the Police and Criminal handbook she had been given on her arrest outlined the rest of the procedure. They could hold her here for a maximum period of three days before either a charge or her production before the Magistrates' Court. The sooner she granted them her co-operation the sooner she would be transferred to a woman's prison. Bail was out of the question. The timing was critical; there were so many things that could go wrong . . .

A knock on the cell door before the metallic flap was thrown aside pulled her back to the room's sterile reality. Boardman's eyes looked at her through the slit. 'We need to talk, Beth. I understand you're refusing to be interviewed?'

She waved her copy of the Act at him. 'All interviews to be conducted as per the Act. You're in breach of the Code of Conduct.'

Boardman sighed. 'Not an interview, Beth, a talk, that's all. You've been through a lot. I've informed the Custody Sergeant that I'm coming to talk to you about the arrangements for the funeral. It's all recorded on the custody record.'

She stared angrily at him.

'I'm not trying to set you up.'

'Who is then? Isn't that what you should be investigating?'

'This is off the record, Beth, I swear. You might be able to help me; we may be able to help each other. Look, I don't know what's going on, but I want to try to find out. Can I open the door?'

Beth considered; if he was attempting to screw her even further, then he could invent a cell conversation, but she doubted it was his style. 'OK. You talk and I'll listen.'

She heard the familiar clunk of the lock as the door opened, and he entered the bleak cell.

'Not exactly comfortable.'

'No better than we criminals deserve from a humane society. I might as well get used to it.'

She raised her knees to her chest, then rested her chin on them, staring at him. She could see her gaze made him uncomfortable, and so continued to bore her eyes into him.

'Firstly, I'm sorry about your father's death. It was unfortunate that your arrest coincided with the discovery. But there are things you need to know.'

'When am I being moved to the prison?' The question seemed to knock him slightly off balance.

'Tomorrow, why?'

'I demand to be placed in solitary confinement. If it's not done voluntarily then I'll disrupt things until it is done. I'm serious.'

He studied her face for a few seconds before replying. 'I can see that. I'll recommend that it be done. Beth, you need to know things before you continue with this silent protest.'

She raised her eyebrows for him to continue.

'We've got the file from your safe.'

She looked startled. If they had that, they must also have discovered the diary.

'Is that all?'

He looked puzzled. 'Why? Should there be more?'

So they hadn't found it, and if they hadn't then who had? Or was he playing with her? If he asked about Maddy she would know the truth of it.

'Where did you get the information, Beth? I know you're good, but some of that would be buried deep and virtually untraceable. Did someone send it to you?'

'Next question.'

'The forensic team discovered powder burns, recent powder burns, on your sleeve. I don't believe you to be a killer. Were you there when it was done? Did you try to stop it?'

She dropped her voice as she replied, 'Off the record?'

He nodded.

'I wasn't there, but I can't say where I was. If I could have stopped it I would have.'

'If you weren't there, you must still have been in contact with a firearm. If you were, tell me and I'll check your story out. We know about the gun club. Maddy . . . is she part of this?'

Beth hesitated. She had to steer him away from Madeline. 'I didn't kill him. I have an idea who did, but I can't prove it, not yet.'

'Give me what you've got, and I'll do my best to help you find them.'

'Did you enjoy your anniversary meal with your wife, or whoever she was? She didn't look your type.'

Boardman smiled indulgently. 'She was neither my type nor my wife. I wanted you to know. Wasn't it obvious?'

It had been slap-dash and unprofessional when she looked back on it; perhaps he wasn't as untrustworthy as she had thought.

'Beth, I don't like what has been happening to you, and that's as far as I can safely go.' He glanced back to the cell door. The flap remained reassuringly shut. 'I can't stay much longer, or the Desk Sergeant will become suspicious. Don't you appreciate how serious all this is? Think about it, will you? Tell us where you really were.'

'Mr Boardman, I'm grateful for your time. I know only too well how bleak things are for me.'

'Then give them the blood sample, Beth. Middleton had some of the killer's blood on him. If it wasn't you, then fine; it weakens the case against you considerably. Give yourself a chance.'

I intend to do just that, she thought.

'Can I state, for the record, and please put this in your notebook, I refuse to co-operate with this investigation in any shape or form. I rely on my right to silence, and intend to exercise it until the proper time.'

He faithfully recorded her words, then offered the notebook to her to verify and sign.

'Can I ask you a favour?'

He indicated she could ask.

'I need to prepare myself for the transfer to prison. Can you tell me what time that will be?'

'It seems a reasonable request. What about 3 p.m? Will that allow you sufficient time?'

'One other thing. I understand that I can make a phone call. I would like to make it in private. It's personal; about the only personal thing left to me. Can it be arranged?'

'It's your right, and I'll ensure there is no listening in.'

'Does that include you?' she asked, demanding trust to be a two-way street.

'I'll arrange it now. Come with me.'

Beth followed him to the station desk, where the Sergeant sat keeping a record of all suspect movements within the complex. After a few words she was shown to an interview room with a single telephone.

'Dial nine for an outside line,' Boardman informed her. 'The shorter you keep the call, the less the chance of disturbance.'

He shut the door. Boardman admired this girl. After all she had been through, she was still fighting, still looking for an angle. He had given his word not to listen to the call. She had accepted his promise. Clearly she believed she had no choice; neither did he, if he was to help her. Boardman removed the receiver carefully and listened with mounting concern to the conversation between Beth and another woman. Beth was careful not to use the other woman's name. Her precision and persuasion impressed him further, her ingenuity amazed the experienced policeman. Eventually the receiver was replaced; he repeated the operation with his own.

Boardman steepled his fingers and closed his eyes. It would never work without outside help. Even then it was risky. He nodded his head once to some internal mentor then made his way back to where Beth waited patiently.

'Everything sorted out?' he enquired as she began to walk back to her cell.

Beth simply entered then closed the door. She hoped so.

De Haus stared at the screen's single eye; it stared back reproachfully. His game plan had fallen to pieces. He was going the same way, he could feel it. His rooms felt wrong, invaded, as if something had happened there and he was unaware of it. He closed his eyes and rubbed the throbbing vein inside his right temple. De Haus had felt anxious for weeks; the arrest of Beth had raised his anxiety above bearable levels. He had returned from the debriefing two hours earlier. The college porter had smirked at him as he walked up the stairs to his rooms. The antagonistic attitude of old was replaced by a nodding smugness that held secret knowledge; De Haus was afraid. It had been days since he had given the Orchid woman the communication code. She had lied about her intentions, claiming that she needed it to ensure Beth's safety, and now Beth was facing a murder charge. Since then, silence.

De Haus pushed his hand through his hair, feeling the thick grease that had accumulated in it; he didn't care, but he was afraid, and he didn't know why. The first barb of real fear had lodged at the debriefing. Buchan had looked at every person in the room at one time or another, except him. It seemed that the civil servant was trying so hard to give nothing away that he gave it all, or was it just De Haus's own paranoia gripping? He couldn't decide and had pushed the spectre of exposure to the middle of his mind; that was until the hated porter's knowing nod. De Haus looked around the room. It didn't feel right. Something had changed in his absence, something bad. Everything was in its correct place, but then again it would be, wouldn't it? he muttered to the accusing computer screen. The books were as they should be, the mail unopened and scattered as normal, the pictures on the walls flush and straight . . . that was it, the pictures. They were straight! De Haus could never hang a picture plumb with a room. It came from an astigmatism in his left eye that forced his sense of perspective awry; and now they hung perfectly.

His mouth began to dry to dust as the implications of his discovery took root. Someone had been here, not a burglar or a thief; an intruder, someone who didn't want him to know of their visit. Icy sweat seeped down his back to the waistband of his trousers, where it accumulated in a pool of terror around his bottom vertebrae. His breath was jittery and quick as he logged into his computer programme marked O.W. for her, his betrayer. De Haus had taken the precaution of engineering the computer equivalent of a trip-wire in the programme. If an intruder broke into it they would leave their mark. He searched the hidden log of his trap for their 'finger prints'. Nothing. Then again, he thought to himself, if they know enough to get in they might expect such a device and disarm it first.

He entered the hard disk memory of his vast information matrix, searching for the echo of such a command, praying that it would not exist. The confirmation took him like an arrow in the eye. It had been disarmed when he had been in London. Buchan knew at the debriefing, that was why he'd avoided eye contact with De Haus, that was why he had wanted to see Molineux privately; it was over. The little man breathed out a stale gasp of air and could smell the terror on his own breath. His agile brain grasped for a reason why he had not yet been exposed. After several minutes of frantic concentration he fixed on their purpose. He was meant to tell her that the operation had been abandoned.

De Haus considered his position as carefully as his fragile mental state would allow. They would come for him at some stage, in some way; his treachery would not be tolerated forever. They would have a trace on his E-mail and his movements, watching and listening until he had fulfilled his last deed of betrayal. He felt almost relieved that it was soon to end as he typed in the last message he would send to her. She had cheated him. She had breached the promise of shared knowledge by refusing to give him the secret of the Perfect Day; he owed her nothing. De Haus looked down on to the screen for his last communication with her and read the terms of the message.

'*Tired Hybrid Exits Your Killing. Now, Orchid Woman, Seek Peace, Abandon Revenge Eternal. Bequeath Eden To Her.*'

He flushed the message through the E-mail system and waited for them to come.

CHAPTER THIRTY-ONE

I t was shortly after 7.30 a.m. when Fergus Finn entered the small village news agency. It seemed too beautiful a building just to sell newspapers. Then again the whole village looked straight out of *Horse and Hound*. He passed a man and his dog as they came out of the shop's front door. The man wore the gleaming wellingtons and crap-free Barbour of a 'true' country dweller. He paused for a moment to look Fergus up and down; his hound appeared to repeat the exercise.

'Christ,' he muttered, 'even the dogs are snobs.'

The shop was laid out in the self-conscious way of the amateur general dealer. It was a monument to good taste and a waste of it at the same time. The bright-cheeked proprietor behind its counter eyed him suspiciously; Fergus had looked in better shape, he knew that.

'Good morning to ye,' he ventured, simultaneously smoothing down his torn jumper. 'Do you have a phone I could use?'

Her eyes swept across the room to the old-fashioned instrument.

'It's out of order.' It was obvious to him that she was lying; perhaps he would have done the same in the circumstances. He drew down the sleeve of his jacket to cover the makeshift bandage on his wrist where the dog had gripped.

'That's a pity.' She looked relieved he'd allowed it to pass without apparent fuss. 'Is there a taxi firm, or a local who might give me a ride to the station? Is there a station around here?'

'It's a two-mile walk,' she replied, moving towards the door, then opening it. 'Go straight for the first mile, then second left, across the farm track. You can't miss it.' He wasn't welcome here. 'Have you been in some sort of accident?' She indicated with her hand the bloodied bandage.

'No, not an accident.' He'd been lucky. The search for the car keys was too little too late, but the chink of metal on a tin of Mace had saved him. The first dog's momentum had knocked

237

him breathless to the ground as it savaged his lower arm. It was excruciating. He had to hold the beast steady whilst he withdrew the canister of Mace from his pocket, flipped off the cap, then sprayed its contents into the animal's eyes. The second dog had been circling, looking for a bite point; Fergus had had to turn his dog around as it chomped on his wrist to ward off another attack.

The first dog had howled in pain as the gas bit into its eyes. Fergus had had no choice. Human voices were approaching at speed. The second dog got the rest full in the face. It was finished with a blow to the side of the head from the camcorder he'd recovered from the ground. The dogs went wild. Blinded by his attack, they attacked each other, ripping and snarling furiously. The battle took place next to the car door; he couldn't afford to be caught again. Fergus could hear their masters, or in this case mistresses, calling them. He'd made his way from the scene on foot, attempting to staunch the flow of blood. He reckoned there'd be other dogs at the house, others who'd smell the blood and find him; he wouldn't be that lucky twice.

The rest of the night had been spent wandering the country, always moving, always listening for the sounds of pursuit. His rucksack, containing his brother's passport and his own wallet, was in the car boot. All he had was some loose change and his thumb. His efforts at hitch-hiking were pointless: in his state Fergus looked like a vagrant from the American Dust Bowl. The night in the ditch was punctuated by dreams of the dogs' teeth and the painful throbbing in his arm.

'Are you all right?' The woman's question brought him back from his recollection. 'Do you want me to call the police?'

He raised his best smile. If he'd still had his beard, she would have called them the moment he walked in. As it was, she would call them the moment he walked out.

'No, I'm fine really. It was a stag night. It got a little out of hand. They left me and headed back to London.'

She clucked understandingly, as if a bleeding scarecrow could be understood if London people were involved.

As he was pushing past the smiling and relieved shopkeeper, his eyes registered a familiar name on the front page of a tabloid newspaper.

'Oh, no,' he muttered. Fumbling in his pockets, Fergus produced the small amount of loose change still in the bottom of them. 'I'll have this.' He picked up a copy, then with care offered the correct coins.

'That's all right, you look as though you need every penny you've got.' As an afterthought, she reached into the glass case that held a number of Clingfilm-wrapped sandwiches.

'Take this. If you come by . . .' she looked him up and down '. . . better circumstances, drop the money off then.'

Fergus would never understand the English. This woman was another example of how suspicion could change to kindness without any real explanation. 'I will, and thank you.'

She wouldn't call the police now, he knew that. Moving to a bench on the small village green, he opened his sandwich and the newspaper and read.

'Dear God, Beth, what have they done to you?'

A photograph of Beth in better times illustrated the news of her arrest for the murder of Arthur Middleton. He read the item twice, then sadly made his way to the train station. She was beyond his help now. He needed help himself, and the Irish club was the only place he would find it. Fergus bundled the paper up in disgust, then threw it into the waiting jaws of the waste-paper bin.

The train to London arrived an hour later. The morning sun had done little to eradicate the awful chill he felt through his sore bones as he climbed in, aware that he had no money, no passport, and no power to change what had happened. If he were arrested for fare dodging, then so be it; it was hardly the same as being arrested for murder.

The flowers comforted her. She attended to their refined needs, then checked the humidifier.

'Where is Madeline?' Her voice cut like a figure-skater's blade across virgin ice.

'She's disappeared.'

'She is dangerous. We cannot afford her any longer.'

The silence from the room's other occupant was an acknowledgement that the order would be carried out. The scent of the flowers pervaded the elegant conservatory.

'What about the McCabe boy?'

The other woman looked relieved that they had moved on to a topic that she knew something about. 'The police believe it was a drugs-related death. He was a known dealer; they're treating it as suspicious. Their scenario is a fall-out between dealers after which he was pushed to his death.'

The Orchid woman considered the information. 'What about the missing gun?' Her companion shrugged.

'Our source in the murder squad said nothing was found at McCabe's flat, apart from the bullets in the woodwork.'

'Did you retrieve Maddy's diary from Beth's home?'

'Yes, there was a slight problem, but that was taken care of. As it transpired it all worked well, he was dying anyway.'

She turned to smell the single orchid that hung like a tear drop over the lip of its delicate vase. 'And the Irishman?'

'Gone to ground. We have his home covered and his place of work. If he shows we will be ready for him.'

'What about our opponents?'

'De Haus tells me the operation has been abandoned. I have no reason to disbelieve him.' She leaned forward, and dropped her voice. 'We must keep a lid on these things. The Perfect Day is approaching. I will not allow anything to interfere with that.'

She returned her attention to the freshly-painted matt black orchid and stroked its velvet texture.

'Soon.'

It was now all about timing, and a measure of good luck. Boardman had been true to his word. Since his visit Beth had sat with her face away from the viewing hatch, and each time they checked upon her she merely waved her hand. The Custody Sergeant had informed the back of her head that at 2.30 p.m. she would be charged with the murder then at 3 p.m. she would be moved to the prison. The Governor had been informed of her request for solitary confinement and had reluctantly agreed to it. Her plan must be set in motion between those two events.

It was the gun club that had given her the idea; now she would have to see whether it would work. Beth had refused offers of cups of tea, preferring to keep her face to the wall before all the station personnel. At 2 p.m. the shift changed and a new Custody Sergeant made his rounds. She still kept her face to the wall, indicating in the same way that she was all right.

At 2.30 p.m., they came for her. Head bowed and hair loose and around her features, obscuring them almost completely, Beth listened to the charge being read. She was invited to respond but merely shook her head. She almost turned when she heard Boardman's voice order them to return her to the cell.

'The van will be here shortly. I have an interview to conduct at the men's prison.' She felt his hand on her shoulder, this time for reassurance. 'Good luck, Beth,' he said sincerely. 'If there is anything you need.' She shook her head; she needed only one person's assistance now.

Beth started the walk back quickly; time was running out. The door echoed as the lock engaged and she was once more inside. She estimated it was about 2.40 p.m. and prayed the van would not be early. Would she come? That was really the point. It was all a pipedream if her courage failed. Beth had explained it was safer for her in here than outside. She was panicky with fear. It might be that she had frightened Maddy off . . . Where was she? The unfamiliar sound of high heels on linoleum came closer. Beth retired to the familiar corner of the holding cell. The door was opened once more.

'Your solicitor to see you, Miss Gamble. Will you see her?' She guessed the Sergeant must have turned towards her 'solicitor' as he spoke again. 'She's refused to see everybody else. Mr Boardman okayed it.'

'I'll see her,' Beth whispered in a hoarse voice.

'Can we have some privacy?' the other woman asked. Beth could hear the voice was unsteady, ending on a request rather than a brusque command.

'That'll be all right, but she's being transferred shortly. Five minutes, that's all.'

'Thank you, Sergeant, you've been most helpful,' replied Madeline Milton.

The door was shut upon them.

'God,' Maddy gasped, dropping like a failed bungee jumper to the hard bed. 'My knees were going.' Her voice sank to a low whisper. 'Is this going to work?'

Beth's finger was raised to her lips, demanding silence. 'Yes. Now talk shop, nice and loud. You're angry with me.'

Maddy took off the brown wig, then loosened her own hair, its length and greasy condition as agreed. 'You know, Miss Gamble, you are more trouble to this firm than you are worth.'

Maddy removed the jacket of the black formal suit, and handed it to Beth. The skirt and hosiery were similarly exchanged with the now-naked reporter. 'We really wonder whether we wish to act for you at all.'

Beth smiled her encouragement at the nervous woman, who was removing her underwear.

'In fact, the Senior Partner has informed me that if you refuse to give us any instructions we are to part company.'

Beth watched as Maddy pulled the dishevelled smock around her now shivering form.

'Are you refusing to speak to me at all?'

Beth squeezed her feet into the shoes. This was going to be a little painful.

'I warn you, Miss Gamble, I am losing patience.'

Beth was furiously applying make-up in approximation of Maddy's just as she used the removal pad to cleanse her face.

'Well, you can lie there all day so far as this firm is concerned.'

Beth went to the woman and embraced her. 'You'll be safe in there. Remember, keep your head down and demand a coat to cover your face. You are going into solitary confinement. It will be hard and lonely, but you must not co-operate with them in any way. Don't give them anything at all. That includes visits and interviews. If anyone who knows me sees your face properly then it's all over. Trust me, Maddy.' She rearranged Maddy's hair, pulling it down around her face.

The girl took hold of her arm. 'Are you coming back?' she whispered.

Beth looked into her eyes. They were lost and afraid. 'Yes, I am. It may take a while, but they won't look for you in there. It's going to be tough, but you'll be alive. Now sack yourself as my lawyer.'

'That's it,' she shouted as Beth moved to the door, and banged on it. 'We are no longer your solicitors. Sergeant, can I be let out, please?'

Maddy moved to the back of the cell as the footsteps warned them of his arrival. She turned her head away so he would only catch a glimpse of her outfit. The hatch opened. He peered in.

'Told you you wouldn't have any luck. Anyway, the van's here for her.' He was distracted as she strode off. 'Hang on a minute, miss,' he shouted. Beth's feet felt glued to the tacky surface. 'You can't leave this with her.' The black briefcase was passed to her as she began to walk away.

'Thank you.'

'Strange one that, not as pretty as she was on the box.'

You wouldn't look pretty if you'd been through what I have, Beth thought. As she walked past the station desk, she saw a man watching her, just watching, unmoving, from an open doorway. Boardman smiled slightly, then returned his attention to the paper in front of him. As he did so, he raised one hand to his ear, mimicking a phone call. She walked out of the station.

A gaggle of photographers surrounded a prison van. Two burly wardresses made their way menacingly through them. The van would take Maddy to safety. Now there was work to do. They wouldn't be looking for her. Things had turned around. She would be looking for them.

CHAPTER THIRTY-TWO

B eth was as anonymous as the hotel she had chosen. Earls Court had an ever-changing population: young Kiwis and Australians working in the bars and hotels, financing another part of the obligatory European tour. They were friendly, but not intrusive. Beth kept her own counsel.

She had been here a week and was no further forward. Madeline's bag was a treasure trove of money, jewellery and cards. The first two would be useful, the credit cards much too dangerous to use in anything but an emergency. Maddy had written down the PIN number for her personal account, but Beth knew if she used that facility it would have to be far from where they would begin their search for Maddy.

The first task was to visit a chemist for hair dye and clear-lensed reading glasses. Having checked into the hotel, she chopped her hair and administered the henna. A plastic bathing cap hid the splendour of her new hair colour for longer than was suggested. When it was revealed she looked like a tart. Beth was delighted with the result. The glasses added a note of myopic winsomeness. Altogether she didn't recognise herself. Neither did she resemble Maddy. If she had to visit Maddy's flat, she would neither be mistaken for her nor recognised for herself.

Maddy must have withdrawn all her available savings. What would the Station Sergeant have thought if he'd looked inside the 'solicitor's' briefcase to find £5,000 in cash? Beth's own assets were untouchable. They would all be in police hands and under lock and key.

The TV in the hotel room showed her pictures of the prison transfer. She was news again. They had come from every station in the western world. Maddy wore the ubiquitous coat of anonymity over her face and shoulders during the transaction. The reporters were swarming like soldier ants around the restricted area. Arms were held high in an attempt to secure 'the shot'. Newspapers were full of conjecture. The camps were different and distinct. They were divided between the woman who had her convicted but justified what she had 'done' and the people who argued there was no place for vigilantism in a humane society. To date nobody had questioned her guilt. Beth had time before the trial began to force them to do so.

After a day or two of lying low she had visited the library of Gray's Inn. The Inn was one of four a prospective barrister could belong to in order to study for the Bar, and thereafter practise in the legal system; it also housed a formidable wealth of knowledge. It was vital that she discover the time scale that she would be forced to follow. Only then could she pace her enquiries properly.

The library was a magnificent centre of learning, its students from every race and religion in the world. Beth, like many, possessed a rudimentary knowledge of the law, but it was a more detailed study that was required to provide her with the answers she needed. The bright, Afro-American librarian was a contrast in every way to the last one she'd encountered in the grimness of Blackheath. Beth had written a series of questions; the woman provided her with the books that would give the answers. Large tomes with informative indexes guided her through the still-archaic language of litigation.

Beth received the heavy volumes gratefully. She climbed the staircase to the upstairs gallery, where a small table sat unused. She looked out of the window, down on to Gray's Inn Square. Students, both young and mature, made their way past her line of vision; she could have used their help too. Beth laid open the first book, entitled *Criminal Procedure*. She turned to the section on Magistrates' Courts' proceedings. Maddy would appear before them first.

This was the court that decided if there was sufficient evidence to 'commit' the accused to the Crown Court for trial. Murder could only be tried at the Crown Court. It appeared that there were two ways this could be done: either by accepting that there was sufficient evidence (a read-over), or by challenging the evidence through a legal adviser (an old-style committal). Beth hoped Maddy would say nothing, that she wouldn't challenge the evidence; neither should she agree to appear in court. Beth knew that a defendant could not be forced into the dock. She had once followed a case where the defendant refused to attend his own trial and had been amazed that the judge was powerless to order it. That information had been put to good use during her lengthy phone call with Maddy. After some further reading Beth discovered that the magistrates could commit her in her absence if there was evidence that she consented to it properly.

Her next task was to discover the time delay between such a legal order and its completion. There it was. A minimum period of one month between the order and its execution. This was to give the defence an opportunity to take the defendant's instructions on the evidence. However, she read with interest that the period could be shortened by the defence if they waived their right to it. Beth didn't want to have her stand-in languish for a day longer than she needed to.

The right to silence had been under threat for a considerable time. Even those once known to support that right above all others had been browbeaten and tempted by preferment to adopt a different attitude. All the law journals argued the case for and against. It seemed that whereas it had once been the prosecution's duty to prove their case, they now called it 'trial by ambush' if the defence didn't forewarn them. It didn't seem right to Beth, it couldn't be. But the right still held for the moment.

Finally, she researched the problem of non-attendance in court during a trial. This was a vital one. If Maddy were forced into the courtroom, any number of journalists would see it wasn't Beth. Her own rusty recollection needed shoring up by legal precedent. There were many cases documenting trials proceeding in the defendant's absence. Some had absented themselves during the course of the proceedings, aware that things were not going in their favour. Others flatly refused to come up at all. Her advice to Maddy had been correct. Beth was more than relieved. The photocopier duplicated the data she required.

Beth was about to leave through the library's front entrance when she saw him. The charcoal-grey suit, beautifully tailored, fitted his slim body well. D'Stevenson wore the bands and collar of a barrister walking with a colleague to his Inn of Court for lunch. During his cross-examination of her he had been impressive. In fact, she believed it was due to him that the jury had acquitted Middleton. He was the ideal man to defend her; after all a barrister had no morality in court, just a duty to perform. D'Stevenson had performed his with aplomb. Now he would perform it for her. Imagine his frustration: the plum celebrity murder case of the decade; the client he had represented gunned down by the woman he had vanquished. He would be unable to refuse. He would also be unable to visit his client. It would be the perfect lesson. Besides, if the worst came to the worst and she had no evidence of her innocence, D'Stevenson was the best barrister to have in her corner.

Beth had to find the house. The house where she had spoken with the Orchid woman was the key. The Orchid woman was central to the trial. But how? Beth had been blindfolded. The roads and their changing sounds had told her little of their location. The change from smooth tarmac to rough country lane could have been in any direction once she had left her home. Beth mentally transported herself back to the van and Maddy.

Then she wanted to kick herself. She had been so stupid. They wanted Maddy dead because she knew the location. Why hadn't Beth asked her? And now she could be in solitary confinement. It was impossible to regain contact. Beth had been too clever for her own good.

She had to find the house. If she could find it she could retrieve the document; without that she had no ammunition to fight the battle. But how? Beth sat on the Edwardian nursing chair by the hotel room window and relived her journey in the back of the laundry van. She was certain that they had travelled south across the expanse of the Thames. In her mind's ear she recalled the muffled static of a tourist river cruise guide pointing out places of interest to the passengers.

By her reckoning the journey had taken the best part of an hour. The first half had been the typical staccato movement through a busy capital city, the second half a smooth ride into the country. Beth estimated the van's speed as an average 30 m.p.h.: that gave a radius of travel at between 25 to 30 miles.

She shook her head; that was a vast area. Even if she could conduct such a huge search, she still didn't know what she was looking for. There had to be something else, a factor that would help to identify the property.

Beth looked down to her watch. It was almost 11 p.m. She turned on the radio to the BBC in order to check her watch's accuracy and waited for the time pips to sound. After fourty seconds they did. Beth was pleased that the twenty-first birthday present on her wrist was keeping good time.

Good time, that was it . . . Not good time but bad time. Beth recalled the inaccurate peal of the church clock when she had clambered from the back of the laundry van. The church had to be within hearing distance of the house, perhaps no more than a mile away. If she could identify the church then a search of the area would lead her to the house and the Orchid woman. How many churches had clocks? And more importantly how many had clocks that were an hour out?

There were some things she needed to further her searches. Beth switched off the radio and patted her pockets for her room key. She was on to something new.

Fergus could smell the fumes from the oil-fired heating system. He was tired of the incessant fiddle music already. His hand still ached. One of the Boyos had arranged for a tetanus shot. It was simple, unlike the more severe injuries they were used to. No questions were asked in this place. A man or woman spoke about problems only if they needed to, never if they were asked. If someone asked they were a stranger; if they were a stranger then they couldn't be trusted.

His room was next to the boiler in the basement. A simple cot bed that could be folded and hidden in a moment provided him with the sleep his body craved. He'd been in it for two days. They'd let him lie until his body was ready again.

Billy the barman and a bowl of warm broth waited until his long sleep had abated. 'Are ye with us again, Ferg? Get this down ye neck.' He pressed the warm bowl into Fergus's sweating hand.

'Ye know I hate this stuff. Have you no lasagne?'

The barman chuckled. 'That TV life is turning you into a jessie. Drink up, then we'll have a man's drink at the bar.' The crumpled figure made his way up the stairs that had the morning shakes worse than he did. 'Get yourself a wash. Ye smell like a dead dog.'

Fergus smelled himself; the old man was right. It was little wonder the other passengers on the train back from that terrible place had opened the windows and angled themselves away from him.

He'd been lucky with the guard. An Irishman himself, he'd asked Fergus out of the carriage with a wink, then taken him to his van for a brew and a chat. They'd spent the journey talking of the fine bars and women of their troubled homeland. He'd walked Fergus past the scowling commuters, smug in their cleanliness, at their destination then passed him a fiver.

'Get yourself a Jamieson's or three on British Rail.'

Fergus used the money for the tube, knowing that any cabbie would send him on his way with a boot up the arse. He didn't dare go home. He wasn't even supposed to be in the country. Now they had his brother's passport. He'd phoned home and advised the young 'un to report it stolen, it happened all the time, and since then he'd slept.

Fergus wondered if Beth was managing to cope with prison. She was a game girl right enough, but prison was another matter. He knew, he'd been there once.

Fergus moved up the rickety staircase to the body of the club. It wasn't a gentleman's club in the British sense, but it boasted more real gentlemen than Whites or the Garrick could muster at a blackballing. The club was quiet. Drab chairs that had held the backsides of a hundred wild men and boys spouted foam and sprang buttons. A quiet group in a corner stopped their talk until he came properly into view, then nodded and continued their business.

He moved towards the washroom, opened the door and entered. It was Victorian and spotlessly clean. Fergus still had the camcorder. After he'd brained the dog with it, he'd kept it. The film could have been ruined by the blow. Certainly the play-back was knackered. Fergus had to get hold of some facilities to view it properly. He had to find out who the woman in the limo was. He could find the house again, but they might expect that of him. They could be waiting and this time he wouldn't be so lucky. His wounds were seeping serous fluid: a good sign that they were on the mend. Using the clean towel that hung, as in all good bars, on a nail, he wiped away the residue of the soap from his face; his beard was returning.

Fergus re-entered the room. The railway station clock, liberated from its housing in King's Cross during the night the Republic qualified for its first World Cup, told him it was an hour before opening time. Business was usually done now. A pint and a nip were waiting on the bar for him.

'Do I know ye, Mister?' asked Billy, placing his own drink down on the bar. 'Well, sod me for a blind man, if it isn't Ferg Finn back from the gutter.'

'You should know, ye old bastard, ye've lived there long enough.'

The old man was delighted with the abusive banter. It was a way of greeting that held more affection than a thousand 'how are yous'.

'Has a girl called for me – an English girl?' Fergus asked, taking a sip.

'That's what it's about then? Should have known, shaving those fine whiskers off for a woman.'

Fergus looked steadily over the rim of his drink.

'Apologies,' Billy said, holding up his hands. 'No, there's been no message. I'm not going to ask, but a word to the unwise. If this is what her old man is capable of then ye'd best keep away.'

Fergus shrugged. He wished it were that simple.

'Fergus, you're welcome to stay here. I've cleared it as long as you can promise there'll be no trouble brought?'

Fergus nodded. It was as solemn as a promise sworn in church.

The silence was interrupted only by the murmuring of the group in the far corner. Each man paid deference to the other's right to silence.

Eventually Fergus spoke. 'I'll be needing a few things, Billy. A loan from the fund, some clothes.'

Billy was well used to this kind of request. 'Spending or real?'

The bar seemed to lapse into a deeper quiet as he considered. 'Real. It could be a while. I have some things to get.'

'How real? I take it this isn't official business?' Billy had now been invited into Fergus's troubles and was entitled to ask what he would. Whether he would be answered depended on the desperation factor.

'Real, a couple of thousand. It could be official, but I don't know why.'

Billy whistled at the amount, then nodded sagely at Fergus's description of his problem. 'It's a fact,' he ventured. 'I'll see what can be done. Your family called. The passport slip is in the hands of the responsible authorities.' His voice was heavy with sarcasm at this reference to the immigration men.

Until Fergus had the means to move about, there was nothing to be done but sit and think. And drink. He drank a toast to Beth. The silent raising of his glass caused the understanding barman to raise his own in response.

'Wherever she is,' Fergus whispered.

CHAPTER THIRTY-THREE

Beth retrieved the items from the carrier bags on the dressing table. She took the ordnance survey map from its protective plastic cover and spread it flat on the bed's counterpane. She took the compass from its carrying case, fixed a newly sharpened pencil into its holder then matched the points with precision. The map had a scale on the bottom left-hand side. Beth spread the compass point and pencil tip until it matched her equation. At an average of 30 m.p.h., a journey of one hour equalled a radius of thirty miles. She placed the compass point on the closest landmark to her home and drew the pencil in a perfect circle around it. Next, she divided the circle in half horizontally.

Beth was sure that she had crossed the river; that meant her search would be concentrated in the lower half of the circumference, south of the river. She removed the magnifying glass from its velvet case, cleaned the lens with a yellow lint pad and bent closer to the map to search for churches in the target zone. As she identified each church, Beth ringed them in red felt marker pen: there were twenty-three in all. There were no indications that any had a clock.

She then made a full list of the church and parish names and cross-referenced these against the copy of *Crockford's Church Directory* that she had purchased at a religious bookshop. That gave her the postal address, the identity of the clergy designated to that parish and the telephone number of the incumbent. Beth worked her way down the list with the aid of the hotel room's telephone. They must have thought she was very odd.

'Hello, does your church have a clock?' If not, then, 'Thank you and good morning.' If yes, then, 'Does it tell the right time?'

If yes, then, 'Thank you and good morning.' If not, 'Which way: ahead or behind?'

Eventually she narrowed the search down to two: Saint Martin's in Leavesham and Saint Peter's near Sevenoaks in Kent. Beth returned her attention to the map. The nearest large house to Saint Martin's was four miles away, but Saint Peter's boasted a National Trust property, Peagrove House, no more than a mile and a half away. Beth felt certain that was it. There was only one way to be really sure; she had to go and see. She felt herself shudder as she recalled the Orchid woman. Beth would go to Peagrove House, but would she return?

Fergus had £500 in used notes in his hands within minutes. There had been times in the past when his knowledge and expertise had been put at the disposal of the club and some of its more dubious members; they didn't forget – not a slight, not a favour. Billy's wardrobe was placed at his disposal. It would have graced the cast of *Waiting for Godot*. A short trip with his friend's money remedied the situation. A pair of suede walking boots, warm corduroys, a seaman's sweater and thick Aran socks could hardly be described as city attire but, then again, he wasn't intending to be in the city for much longer. Fergus returned to the club to take care of more serious business.

As it was later in the day, the premises had began to fill. A fine stopping-off point to or from the bookies, it provided an ideal, but transient, meeting place for talk of a 'cert' or a 'donkey'. Fergus had other things to discuss. A few familiar faces greeted him, after taking a second or two to adjust to a beardless Fergus Finn. They could see that there were pressing matters that forced him to shy away from an update on family and friends.

Billy wiped the bar's surface clean, or at least his version of it. 'Mountain-climbing, is it?' he enquired slyly, looking the intrepid figure up and down.

Fergus moved within whispering distance of his friend. 'Is Tommo at the back?'

Billy thought for some time before replying, 'It's like that, is it?' Fergus nodded.

'It must be a serious form of trouble you've caught then.'

This wasn't a question. Fergus knew of Tommo, knew what he was and what he was supposed to be responsible for. Right now that wasn't an issue. He'd heard of the 'back', by whispers and innuendo, but had never met a man who would admit he'd been there.

Billy watched his face with a measuring look. 'I'll check if he'll see you.' His eyes were imploring the young man to think again.

'Do it then,' Fergus said quietly. He reached over and under the oak bar, to where he suspected he would find Billy's working tot. He whisked the whisky out and down in one movement.

Billy returned, looking grim and burdened. 'Through there, second door on the right. You're not carrying, I take it?'

Fergus was already on his way. The sweat from his throat had already soaked the turtleneck of his new sweater. 'Calm, Fergus boy,' he whispered. The corridor was gloom-ridden and packed to bursting point with shadows; he thought it was just how Hollywood would shoot this scene. He reached the door. It bore no symbol or identification as to its contents. Warped wood bent slightly away from true, where it strained to meet the jamb.

He knocked. Sharp hands took his arm behind him and up: enough to hold but not to hurt.

'Steady, lad,' a heavy Ulster voice warned his ear. 'Precautions'. Another pair of hands patted his body thoroughly. 'He's fine, aren't you?'

His hands were released, and a slap on the back indicated he should move forward. Instinctively, he half-turned. A clamp like iron seized his shoulder. 'That would be a daft thing to do.'

He moved his head slowly in agreement, then reached for the door handle and entered the 'back'.

A simple wooden trestle table stood in the centre. Behind it a man's back presented itself to him. The lighting was dim and unpleasant; another Hollywood touch. The man didn't move or speak.

Fergus felt impelled to. 'Tommo, I don't want to trouble you. I know you're a busy man.'

The silent occupant raised a hand in a gesture to indicate he should get on with it.

'I need a weapon. I'm in danger and a friend, a close friend, is in desperate trouble. They've tried to kill me once; they'll try it again.'

The figure shrugged its shoulders.

'I have to help her. I'm going to, whether or not you help me. You can give me a fighting chance. That's all I ask – a fighting chance.'

Fergus didn't know what more to say. The silence angered him.

'They say you're a fighting man yourself. A man can't fight alone; he needs his friends. I'm on my own, and so is she. The authorities have her.'

He watched the shoulders stiffen at the reference.

'This is the only way. Will you help me? If so I'll promise never to set foot in this place again. I have family back there, family I love. There'll be no trouble from me if I'm caught. Just another Mad Mick on a solo mission.'

He was spent and realised how quickly the words had spewed from his dry lips.

After a long moment a head was shaken in the affirmative, and, realising the audience was over, Fergus left the room. Thanks seemed redundant. He'd bartered his life and his family's with an anonymous terrorist.

Inside the back, the anonymous figure swivelled into the light from the bulb. Billy Thompson the barman called to one of his men outside the door. He entered the room quietly. 'Yes, Tommo?'

The man's face held none of the congeniality of his other life, behind the bar. 'Give the boy what he wants. A pistol and twenty rounds. Make sure the serial number's gone. Get him a car and some more money.'

'Do you want him followed, Tommo?'

'No. He's on a strange journey, that boy, but it's not ours.'

In the bar, Fergus searched for Billy. After a few minutes he appeared from upstairs.

'Sorry to keep you, lad. A call of nature. What'll it be?'

'What did he say?'

The barman poured a large double and pressed it into Fergus's shaking fist. 'What did who say, lad?'

Fergus caught the drift quickly, almost as quickly as his drink disappeared. 'Billy, I'd like to thank you for your hospitality. The money will be forwarded when I'm straight. I'm going to go down to the boiler room and collect my things.'

The barman smiled as he spoke. 'I'll miss you around here, lad, but we'll meet again. We always do, we lads.'

They shook hands warmly. Fergus turned and descended into the bowels of the bar.

The gun sat up like a dog on top of his meagre possessions. A wax covering did nothing to disguise its shape or purpose. He could feel the dirty crinkle of the money as he loaded the items into a filthy backpack. No one turned to bid him farewell as he left the Irish club for ever.

The taxi journey to the outskirts of Peagrove House passed an hour and cost £65. There was no tip; Beth couldn't afford to waste any of Maddy's money.

Beth had no idea what to do next. She moved away from the open road and into the undergrowth. The wall was an obstacle she really didn't relish overcoming. The spikes intimated that she was right about the nature of the property. What market garden would seek to protect itself so thoroughly from prying eyes? She had to get inside.

It took her an hour to beat the boundary. Snagged by thorns and stung by nettles, she scouted its outer wall, searching for a way in. Eventually, she found herself back at the gate she had started from. The light was beginning to turn its back on the day. She needed the cover of darkness if she was to get inside. For now she lay in the dense grass and awaited her opportunity.

The driver of the van had telephoned as soon as she entered the safety of the house, the outer gates firmly shut behind her.

'Are you sure?' The driver shook her head. 'Not positive, but how many black cabs do you see around these lanes?'

Sitting at her desk, in her Mayfair apartment, she closed her journal for the day. 'Put the guards on alert. Then use the emergency exit to disappear. Take everything with you. There isn't much left.'

'Shall I put the dogs on the perimeter?'

The razor-faced woman smiled. 'No. If they want to come in, let them. They won't get out again. You know the contingency plan. Follow it to the letter.'

CHAPTER THIRTY-FOUR

B eth felt the creeping damp from the grass's moisture permeate through the cheap, thin clothing, forcing a wet chill through her bones. She had watched a patient spider weave a web of death for its future victims and marvelled at the single-minded endeavour that task demanded. It was too obvious a comparison but Beth was forced to gauge its labour alongside the Orchid woman's. Both had a purpose, both toiled to that end, both were killers. The difference lay in the spider's natural instinct to live by killing; the woman lived to kill. Beth could have swept the web away with a gentle movement of her hand, but that would have been a crime against the natural order of things. She wished the woman's web of murder could be destroyed so easily, and turned away as the arachnid approached its first guest.

Her back was stiff with cramp and enforced stillness. In the seven hours Beth had waiting in the grass nothing had moved in or out of the gate. The passing traffic had diminished as the day darkened. Now she could do something. Standing slowly, she stretched to straighten out her tortured vertebrae, then listened for the next vehicle. Through the evening's intermittent country sounds a car could be heard. Keeping low, she moved away from the entrance through a shrubbery and towards the approaching sound. The headlights lit the roadside in a full beam onslaught, throwing swiftly moving shadows to mark the car's progress towards her.

She could remain inactive no longer. She decided to flag down the vehicle. Her clothing was too dull to be noticed by the car's driver. She removed her coat, holding it by the collar in order to wave it. Moving closer to the verge, she prepared to leap into the road.

But something was wrong. Listening, Beth realised the sound now absent from the night was the engine; it had been cut. The lights went from full to main beam, to barely useful sidelights, then faded to blackness as the car glided from the road on to the verge then into the undergrowth. Beth didn't know what she had planned to say to the driver; that is if they had stopped. Now the driver had stopped; but not because of her.

A shiver teased her already painful spine. It could be a couple seeking the privacy of the bushes. In the headlight's beam she'd been unable to ascertain the number of occupants. It wasn't likely they'd welcome her company, but they might help if she had the right line to spin. Her fear was rising as she moved to the point where the car had left the road. What if it was one of them? The thought caused her feet to falter. No, she reasoned, if they came they'd come from the house not the road, and with less fuss and noise; it had to be an outsider. Moving one scared step at a time she made her way cautiously towards the vehicle. Every sound she made sounded louder than a heavy metal concert. Each fractured twig an ear-bursting fanfare of her arrival.

Beth heard a grunt emanate from the route the car had taken. They might be making love, she thought, then realised it was one sound, and one sound only that had cut across the silent night, and it sounded like one of pain, not pleasure. She moved cautiously to her destination. Beth pushed through the thick undergrowth as carefully as she could, holding aside each branch and twig, pushing through, then returning them gently to their proper places. The car was now in view. Why had it been driven so far into the bushes? It was barely a foot away from the wall. It was still and silent, the driver's door was ajar. She stared hard to distinguish the occupants.

Back here, the light was oily, melding shapes and shadows into a terrifying swamp of uncertainty. Then came another grunt, this time from the other side of the stone structure. Whoever it was was now inside the fortress. Beth approached the car and could see how it had been done. A rope-ladder had been thrown over the wall from the car's roof. Its last rung rested upon the vehicle's top. A bulky blanket, or padding of some kind, rested on the wall's top, covering the spikes. It must have been brought for that purpose. She deduced it was someone who'd been here before; the ladder confirmed that conclusion.

There was something else. The driver expected trouble. Inside the battered Metro a set of keys still swayed gently in the ignition. Her search of the rest of the vehicle was fruitless.

This was her way in. There was one thing she had to do first. Turning the key, she kept the revs as low as they would agree, and turned the car around; this might be her way of escape. Now the car faced the angle of least resistance; that was, if she was right about this place. She switched the engine off, left the keys in place and climbed on to the roof.

Beth had only ever used a rope-ladder once before and her skill had not increased with that experience. The trick was to place one foot either side and her weight centrally to overcome the natural swaying of the device. It was tricky. The pendulum effect pushed her from side to side along the wall, its metal rivets rasping a warning to those inside. She waited until it had subsided then, snake-like, scaled the wall.

At its apex Beth saw where one of the spikes had already stabbed through the padding of the child's Dunlopillo mattress. There was blood on its tip. That accounted for the first grunt, the drop from the corresponding end of the ladder, the other. It was another mantrap for anyone foolhardy enough to leap without looking. The levels at either side differed by a good six feet. Beth knew if she jumped down she wouldn't manage to walk away. She used her initiative. Straddling the wall, using the padding as protection, she pulled up the outer portion of the ladder, then hung it down to within a foot or so of the ground inside. She began her descent.

Inside, the trees' lofty branches robbed the night of all but the meanest light. Still she kept low. It was like playing 'Killer' as a child. She remembered the disadvantage of the darkness, her blindfold secure, and the advantage of the other player's light. This was just like 'Killer', that was the point. Beth clicked out, then held her Swiss Army knife blade in front of her as she started the search.

The cover was good. At these outer limits of the grounds, shrubs sprouted to chest height. Beth beetled from one to the next, holding her breath as she did then exhaling slowly as her target was reached. Her progress was slow, but safe. She wondered what progress the car's driver had made, as she headed inexorably towards the light.

It was the same bloody hand. The same painful bloody hand as before. This place didn't seem to like his hand. And the ground didn't seem to be too fond of his ankle; that too was throbbing. Fergus thought about the flashlight, but disregarded it as too dangerous. He replaced it, then patted his pocket for the terrifying reassurance of the revolver, still unsure as to whether he would use it.

The house was barely lit. Two upstairs lights at either end of the frontage indicated where the occupants might be; but he was listening for the dogs, and listening in vain. That scared him. Night was the usual time for hounds to patrol, but there was not a bark or growl to indicate their presence. He pushed forward with as much care as his injured ankle would allow. He should sue them for that bloody drop; someone could be badly injured . . . Stop raving man, he scolded himself. That was the whole point.

The house was square on to his approach. It looked well secured as far as he could see. The landscaped gardens were artfully planted around the lawn that covered the last fifty yards of his slow, limping progress. He deviated to the left and followed the curve of extravagant plant life towards the house's side, then stopped. He turned his head back to the point of entry. There was someone behind him. His heartbeat thundered to a new high as he quickly scanned the foliage for a place to hide. To his extreme left, the landscape's architect had looked for mass, rather than elegance; a clump of rhododendron bushes squatted together. He crawled into their chunky embrace and, waited, pistol in hand.

The figure scuttled into view after five or so minutes. It was a woman. She was slightly built, wearing inappropriate clothing for this kind of work. She also held a knife. It flashed dully in the meagre light. She seemed to be taking her time. She too had taken the view that the cover to the left was the best option, or was she following him? There was only one way to find out.

She moved ten yards past his hiding place, then he began to crawl after her. She seemed unaware of his presence. There was something naturally graceful about her movements, each step careful and measured, almost as if she were looking for landmines. This was no member of the household. Her progress took her to a willow tree that swept its branches broom-like to the ground; she disappeared beneath. Fergus took the other route, knowing, or hoping he knew, her plan. He acted swiftly. It was chancy, but worth the obvious risk. He sloped around the right-hand side of the tree's outer foliage and waited for its tell-tale rustle to pinpoint her exit.

She walked straight into him. He clamped a hand over the one that held the blade, then punched her in the face. She fell without a sound. He saw no sign of movement. He took the woman's feet and dragged her under cover of the tree. She was face down. Her bag was dragged with her. He opened it and looked for evidence of who she was. The woman began to murmur, distracting him from his task . . .

'Jesus, woman, be quiet will you?' he whispered through clenched teeth.

She went limp and still at the sound of his voice, then she spoke too.

'Fergus, is that you?'

He spun her over quickly, then crouched closer in the darkness.

'It can't be. Beth! Oh, shit.'

Blood from her split lip spread across her chin and dropped off its point to her khaki jacket. Fergus could see her hair colour and style had changed dramatically.

'Fergus, it's you!' She was shaking her head, attempting to clear it.

'Quiet, Beth.' His voice was gentle now. 'They said you were in prison.'

She pushed herself to a sitting position.

'Then I was lucky. They said *you* were dead.'

He pulled her up to her feet and wiped away the blood with his own grubby bandage. 'We haven't got time for this. Do you think anyone saw you, Beth?'

She removed a handkerchief, dabbed at her mouth and shook her head.

'You're the only person I've seen in seven hours. What's the plan?'

He shrugged. 'I wish I knew. I only came back 'cos this was the last place I saw you before . . .' He paused, not knowing how to finish the sentence.

'Before they set me up for Middleton's murder?' Beth concluded for him, looking through the hanging branches toward the menacing outline of the house. So she was right, this was the place with the hothouse and the murderous woman. 'We have to get inside, Fergus, it's the only way.'

She turned to the Irishman, who was looking quizzically at her.

'How did you get out of prison? Bail?' His voice was sceptical.

'Sort of,' she replied enigmatically. 'I'll tell you about it later.' And began to move off cautiously.

'If there is a later,' Beth heard him mutter as he began to follow the route she had taken.

They tracked silently around the side of the house, freezing at every natural night sound; their progress was slow. Then they came to a gravelled area. 'There should be a van parked here somewhere,' Beth whispered into his ear. A slow sweep of the area failed to disclose the van's whereabouts, but it led them to the hothouse. The sight, even from the relative safety of outside, still chilled her flesh close to zero.

'I spoke to this creepy woman inside here,' she explained quietly. 'I left something. I have to get it back.'

Fergus was in the dark, in every way. 'What are you on about, girl?'

Beth raised her finger to her lips, demanding his silence, then searched for a point of entry. 'I've got to find it, Fergus.'

The door to the hothouse was ominously unlocked; almost an invitation to enter.

'I don't like this one bit,' the Irishman muttered as she pushed open the door and entered the lair of the Orchid woman. Beth could see the empty staging. Not a single bloom remained.

'What are you looking for?'

'In the heat of the moment she forgot about it,' Beth said distractedly. He was none the wiser. Pulling open the door she stepped inside and revisited the smaller glass house. He pushed behind her as she spoke. 'She was so confident that she had won that she became careless.' Beth moved to the bag of potting compost and reached inside, hardly daring to breathe; if they had found the paper, then 'it' would never work. Her fumbling fingers pushed under the top layer of soil, then triumphantly snagged the corner of the tightly folded document.

'Gotcha,' she whispered, as she retrieved the evidence of the rigging of her rapist's acquittal.

'Do you smell that, Beth?' He had already taken her arm and was rushing her towards the door. Her feet were trailing as he began to push her through. In the excitement of the search she hadn't noticed the insidious smell; the air had become cloying, almost tangible, with the leaking smell of danger. Five yards beyond the door the explosion hurled them to the ground as the edifice behind disappeared into the night air, showering debris, ancient but still deadly, around and on to them and into the shocked silence.

CHAPTER THIRTY-FIVE

A siren pulled her back from oblivion. The night was illuminated by raging flames, hurling twisted spirals of smoke up into the waiting sky. Beth turned to look for Fergus. Battered masonry lay crumpled on the ground like discarded clothing. So did Fergus. Stiffly, holding her lower spine, she moved towards him, conscious that her entire body felt jolted by the impact of the blast.

At least he was breathing. A chunk of shrapnel had cut his lower leg open. There was blood; a lot of blood.

'Oh, Fergus,' she muttered as she attempted to staunch the flow. Even through unconsciousness he grimaced at the pain as she tied a tourniquet on to the upper part of the wound. She had to get him away. The rope-ladder was out of the question. Using all her remaining strength, she dragged him a few yards away from the blazing hothouse and into the bushes.

The first siren had been joined by others, creating a discordant choir. Beth could hear voices, men's voices, shouting orders through the crackle and snarl of the all-consuming fire. She removed her jacket and wrapped Fergus in it. The last thing he needed was to dissolve into shock. Finally she rolled him on his side, a precaution in case he vomited whilst she set about making their escape.

Looking down on to his soot-blackened face Beth could see there the strength and the goodness that she had taken for granted for three years. She bent to his side and kissed him lightly on the lips.

She cut through the bushes back towards the gate. If the fire engines and police cars had gained entry, then surely the gate must be open. She was right. From behind a tree she watched briefly as other fire tenders, ambulances and worried personnel rushed to the scene; the grounds were a hotbed of confusion. It was now cr never, she felt. She must use the confusion to get Fergus out. Once the situation was under control the area would be cordoned off.

Conscious that all eyes would be on the blazing house, she sprinted away from the dazzling bonfire and into darkness. She found the ladder with ease. Her climb was not quite so successful as before but eventually, her painful back ignored, she made her way up then over the wall. The car's roof accepted her weight as she dropped to it then off and on to the springy turf.

The vehicle started at the second attempt. She drove it cautiously through the woodland. A flat tyre would be a disaster.

She pushed forward without lights. The road was a teeming thoroughfare of activity. It wouldn't be long before the reporters and TV crews began to arrive. She had to act quickly.

To her astonishment there was nobody manning the gate. Beth drove the vehicle in darkness towards the Halloween red of the sky. The hothouse was beginning to implode. It seemed to be eating itself as the aged metal glazing bars and buttresses buckled and squirmed until there was no fight left in them and they perished where they had stood for so long. The little car was almost invisible in the cover of the massive fire-fighting tenders. She parked near to where she had hidden Fergus, left the engine running, then leapt out of the driver's seat.

She found him; he hadn't stirred. The only movement was the seeping of blood through the soaked tourniquet. She had parked the car as close as she could without running him over. Even then he was a big man and a dead weight. She paused to get her breath. That was what she would have been, a dead weight, if Fergus hadn't pushed her out of that place. Using what remained of her swiftly disappearing strength she pushed his body into the passenger side, fixed his seat belt round him then set the car in motion.

Beth crunched the complaining gear box into action then steered the vehicle in a tight circle towards their point of escape. She didn't want to attract attention by racing away from the inferno, so she drove to the splayed gates at a modest speed. Her mind was moving much more rapidly than the vehicle as she remembered the reason for their entry to the hothouse.

'The document!' she said to the drooping unconscious figure beside her, as she furiously patted her pockets. 'Calm, Beth, calm,' she instructed herself, as the search for the vital paper continued. 'Fergus, where is it? If it's in the fire then it's all over.' She felt her stomach tighten in the grip of panic. The car continued its slow progress to the open gate as she continued the hunt. Fergus began to stir. Beth hadn't noticed before but his right hand was clenched. It had been all the time. She started to pull his fingers away from the tight knotted bundle his hand had become. She could see the corner of the piece of paper. He had it; somehow that wonderful brave man had managed to safeguard both her and the vital document before the explosion. Even now, he was reluctant to relax his grip. She manoeuvred the car past the gate as another fleet of police cars darted towards the fire.

Beth turned on the car's lights and picked up speed. But where was she going? After a mile she pulled into a lay-by and examined her passenger as best she could. She began to loosen his jacket. The bulk of the weapon appalled her. Christ, what was Fergus Finn doing with a loaded gun?

He began to groan and flail about as if to ward away the force of the explosion. It caused his right hand to relax slightly. Beth saw her opportunity. She prised the fingers gently apart and retrieved the paper he had guarded so jealously. It was the right one. The evidence of the conspiracy, her way to fight them, and she would take it.

No. *They* would take it; Fergus and she.

Beth glanced across at his slumped figure, caught in the light reflected from other cars' headlights, his brave, honest face hurled into haggard relief.

'Oh, Fergus, what have I done to you?'

And what could she do now? Where could she go? The task that lay ahead was daunting, and what she planned had to be executed perfectly, the way her opponent worked.

All she needed was the last piece of information. With her gaze on the road ahead, Beth recalled the face of another person who had helped, who had taken a risk on her behalf. She knew there was only one place to go.

She had been in this awful place three weeks. It felt like three years.

Her polyester nightgown had run up her back again as she thrashed around on the prison cot, vainly attempting to find a comfortable position.

Madeline Milton had stopped crying the week before; it was only then that the terrible sameness of the days had exhausted her ability to find anything new to upset her.

She had read accounts of hostages filling their dull days with clever mind games. Her attempts at the exercise met the stone wall of her memory. Maddy didn't want to remember. Eventually, the boredom of her existence forced her to recollect dark events; these always concerned her father and McCabe. In a way, the two were interchangeable. Both had carried out depraved acts on and in her body, neither had the capacity for compassion or regret, and both of them were dead.

Maddy shifted again and flopped exhausted on to her back.

She was glad they were dead. What they had done was unforgivable. Her father's continual night-time assaults were incomprehensible to her even now; to the child they'd been terrifying. Maddy remembered the first. Her mother had been ill for some time; the sickness scythed her body to a skeletal husk. She attempted to cover her hair loss with a wig and hide the radiation marks with dense cosmetics. It didn't make her attractive to him; it barely made her look human. Maddy was just beginning to develop from a girl into a young woman when his first visit came. Had he been drunk she might have had some understanding of his weakness. When she saw his figure silhouetted against the pinkness of her reading light, and the fixed stare when he pulled back the bedspread, she couldn't understand anything. Maddy shuddered at the memory. He had spoiled her for ever. That's what men do, she told herself as she pulled the thin prison-issue cover over her body: spoil things. She didn't hate men in the way that others did. She just couldn't see how they could touch anything without soiling it.

McCabe was like that. All she had done was report a theft from the blind school: she wasn't the judge who had sent him to prison; she wasn't the social worker who had put him into care or the headmaster who might have expelled him; she was merely a teacher who attempted to protect the school's property. No, she reminded herself, she was a woman. That meant she was vulnerable to savage attack because biology had provided orifices for men to vent their hatred into.

She didn't hate men; she just hated what they did.

Maddy shifted again, lowering one of her legs on to the floor by the side of the bed. The smell of bleach from the open-doored toilet wafted across the room and made her gag. This was no way to treat people, no matter what they had done. If you beat them like bad dogs, how could they learn to be good ones? If you locked them away in vile, stinking cells, why should they respect the beauty of a stranger's house? If you made them defecate in a bucket, why not on a cherished Persian rug?

Something was wrong with the system. Now Maddy had experienced it she realised what it was. The public did not want justice, they wanted revenge.

She closed her eyes with the pain of her insight and attempted to find some peace in sleep.

CHAPTER THIRTY-SIX

Boardman pushed the weighty duvet away from his tired body. The room held the promise of sleep, but not for him. His wife slept on. Where was Beth? The question invaded his thoughts every day. All other business seemed trivial, almost pointless, by comparison. He moved quietly from the darkened bedroom, pausing momentarily to pull the door behind him, then padded silently to his study. He felt for the hammer switch on his desk's brass table light. It clicked on as he hitched up his pyjama trousers and reclined into the familiar cracked leather chair.

He rubbed his eyes, blinking them into use. They and he had seen too much. There were only three weeks of his career left for him to navigate. He used to love his job but the years had worn away the self-protective mechanism vital to anyone who faced the reality of death on an hourly basis. Whilst it wasn't his death, each autopsy, every black-and-white, felt like another nail through his heart. It was time to leave.

But there was unfinished business, and Boardman disliked open-ended problems. Where was she? The face of the brass clock informed the tired policeman that it was 2 a.m. He sat for some minutes mulling over the mess that was his last case.

All Molineux was really interested in was putting somebody, anybody, in the dock. They all knew that Beth hadn't, couldn't have, murdered Middleton. But that wasn't the point, Molineux had warned him; that wasn't relevant, he had wheedled in response to Boardman's complaints and demands for the real killer to be found. Then Boardman had been dropped from the investigation. Well, so be it, he had thought, but if I get a chance to help Beth Gamble, then I will, he had promised himself.

His feet took him down to the kitchen, where he sat feeling greyer, older, but no wiser as to how he could help Beth Gamble. He'd helped in the police station, helped her to escape from lawful

271

custody; that was some turn-around after thirty-five years' service. When they discovered that he had been the senior officer at the time, criminal proceedings would be levelled at him; the loss of his pension would be a relatively painfree experience by comparison. But what they had done was more wrong. Molineux should not have meddled in the trial. The system of justice only operated properly when the victim was embraced and cosseted like the defendant. Beth had the right to tell her own story without interference or fear of injustice. They had conspired to rob her of those rights, and for that there could be no proper reparation. What they had done was done for ever, fixed in the amber of his conscience.

He clicked on the kettle. Just who was the woman who had taken Beth's place inside the prison? Boardman's own guess was it was the one from the gun club and the restaurant. But why she would do it was a wholly different question. News at Ten had carried the story that Beth Gamble had been committed for trial at the Crown Court. The Magistrates' Court had remanded her in custody. But the real story was not the fact that she would go for trial at the Old Bailey, but that she had refused to stand in the dock to hear the charges against her. Boardman, of course, understood why. Only he, Beth and the other woman knew the truth of it.

The news also carried the story of the suicide of an Oxford don – Ivan De Haus. The newscaster had dropped his voice to a grave whisper as he relayed the facts. The Professor had been discovered in a fume-filled car in the Cotswolds. The newscaster went on to state that the researcher had been helping the police with their enquiries into a child pornography ring and that the death was not regarded as suspicious. Boardman didn't share that view. He had been mulling over what he had learned about De Haus from their brief encounters. The man had a first-class brain, and his piercing intellect brought him closer to madness than sanity; even so, he didn't seem the suicidal type. Who did? Boardman asked himself. But something troubled him, it was the reason he couldn't sleep: that and the nagging worry over Beth. Finally he managed to isolate what it was that was wrong. De Haus didn't have a car, he couldn't even drive. He remembered De Haus's delight in claiming that, as a personal protest against the world of modern transport, he'd always travelled by train or bicycle. So where did he get the car from? And when did he learn to drive? The policeman forced his naturally enquiring mind from the puzzle. He had other matters to attend to: Beth.

He looked towards the bland functionalism of the digital kitchen clock. It was 3.30 a.m., the 'graveyard' shift. He felt uneasy, almost jumpy, in anticipation of an expected event. It was a curious sensation, one he had experienced on only a handful of occasions during his sixty-three years.

On all the others he had been right, the shiver of anticipation had been accurate. Boardman marvelled at this instinctive ability but fought against the devil of over-analysis lest it should leave him without that rare gift. Patience, he whispered to himself. Whatever was coming his way would come at its own pace, not his. He made a cup of hot chocolate, sipped slowly at the scalding creamy mixture and waited.

Maddy lay in the still of the padlocked night. So the first 'court appearance' was over. Her refusal to attend had brought doom-laden letters from her solicitors; the phrases 'trial by media' and 'celebrity status' were intended to coerce her into cowering defeat and accept-ance. She could not co-operate: Beth had been very specific about that in particular. She trusted Beth; she had to, there was nobody else. What if something should happen to her? What if the Orchid woman managed to catch her, kill her? Where would Maddy be then? If only there had been more time to talk to Beth, to understand what it was that she was attempting to achieve, what her plan was . . . But it was silly to think that way, childishly attempting to wish herself away from all this back to happier times. The problem was she had difficulty recollecting any.

The hard bed had begun to give her back pains as she squirmed in a vain effort to bring some vestige of comfort from the night and everything it held. Where are you, Beth? she whispered.

Fergus groaned each time the car turned a new corner. The seat was soaked with blood, but at least the flow had slowed to a trickle.

The problem was how to find Boardman. The police station had refused to give her his home address when she had telephoned from a call box just outside central London. That had not surprised Beth but it had been worth a try. Now what?

She returned her eyes briefly to the ashen face of Fergus Finn. She'd thought she had lost him once. She wasn't going to go through that again. The traffic was light as she eased the battered car into the metropolis. Beth felt menaced by their very presence in this unkind city. This was a desperate situation, it required desperate measures. It was five minutes or so before she located another working call box. She locked Fergus inside the car then retrieved the number of the police station and made the call. She had to take this chance; there was no other alternative. The steady hum of the transference of electronic sound measured twelve beats of her racing heart before the call was answered.

'I need to get an urgent message to Boardman,' she informed the Station Sergeant.

'Do you realise what time it is, miss?' he asked, his voice chiding her.

'Of course I do,' she answered tiredly. 'It's urgent, a matter of life and death.'

The policeman clucked his tongue at such melodrama. 'Do you know how many times I've heard that trundled out?' he said almost kindly. 'These things always look pretty bleak at night. By the morning they have a way of working themselves out. Why don't you tell me about it, and I'll leave him a message?'

Beth had had enough. 'You must ring Chief Inspector Boardman at his home now. You will tell him that you have spoken to Beth, then tell him I know about the orchids. I want you to take this down.' She read off the number of the call box. 'Tell him I will wait for five minutes and only five minutes. If you do not do this I shall ensure that Boardman learns of your refusal to help. Your prospects of a quiet life are diminishing every moment you hesitate.'

She paused to allow the searing threat and the confident menace of her voice to persuade him how serious she was.

There was silence. Eventually the man's unhappy voice began to mutter: 'All right, but this had better not be a wind-up.'

'Five minutes,' was all she said as the phone was replaced on its hook. From the shelter of the phone box, and through the rain-spattered glass, she could see Fergus. At least he was still for the moment. She checked her watch. It was five minutes to four on a bleak morning in the capital of dirt and indifference. Beth knew she must remain inside the booth. It was unlikely that any other person would want to use the telephone at such an early hour but she just could not take that risk. The minutes refused to pass.

The second hand of her watch refused to circle the circumference of the face at the normal rate. She glared at the telephone. 'Ring, damn you!' she whispered. The long minutes passed. Four minutes gone, then five. Beth sighed, then pushed open the booth's door and began the depressing walk back to the car. She unlocked the driver's door and began to swing her legs inside as suddenly the silence of the night was slashed by the ringing of the telephone. Beth sprinted back and threw open the door, grasping frantically for the receiver. She ripped it from its cradle, and shouted, 'Yes?'

'Beth. It's Boardman. How serious is it?'

'Extremely, and I have a casualty,' she responded calmly, more calmly than she felt.

'Do you have transport?'

'Yes.'

'Scotland Yard isn't safe. You'll have to come to my house.'

Beth hesitated. 'Can I trust you, Boardman? I know Middleton's trial was rigged. Even if you weren't involved at the top level, you must have known about it.'

His silence was his acknowledgement of the truth.

'I don't have any option but to trust you, do I!'

Beth could almost feel him nodding his approval. Without further comment he gave her the address and directions to his home. There was a further hesitation.

'Beth,' he said, his voice gentle, 'the answer to your question is yes, you can trust me. There are a lot of things you need to know, to understand. I will tell you everything when you arrive.'

'Thanks,' she replied.

'No, don't thank me yet,' he said quietly. 'Wait until I've done something you can thank me for. Park at the back. I'll expect you in half an hour.'

She rushed back to the car. Fergus had been alone for longer than she had intended. She was delighted to see that he was awake. He rubbed his eyes, then groaned as he moved his leg.

'Keep still,' she ordered. He rolled his eyes heavenwards at her schoolteacher's tone.

'Where are we going now?' he asked, absentmindedly fingering the bandage around his leg as she moved the car forward into the still sparse traffic.

'We, Fergus, are going to interview a policeman.'

She flashed a smile at his puzzled face as the car accelerated away into the early-morning light.

CHAPTER THIRTY-SEVEN

Boardman was waiting at the back door. His hair was still damp from a hasty shower; his expression concerned as Fergus was helped from the car. He limped heavily and placed his weight on one leg. Boardman moved forward to take the bulk of the Irishman's body on to his own, feeling the click in his own weak leg, relieving Beth of more than just that burden; she could trust him. They moved in silence through the rose trellis that framed the entrance to the rear of his home. Beth could smell the promise of warm coffee and relative safety.

The passageway led to a comfortable kitchen, walls lined with family photographs displaying happiness and success. Beth noticed that when Boardman was featured his expression was one of uncomfortable shyness; he was not a man to court the camera. Whilst she looked around the private aspects of his life, Boardman was more concerned with investigating the extent of the injury to Fergus's leg.

'When did the bleeding stop?' he asked over his shoulder as he bent to pull the encrusted bandage gently away from Fergus's thigh.

'About an hour ago. I'm really not sure.'

At the sound of her hesitant, vaguely drifting voice, Boardman turned to appraise this remarkable young woman. The dark whorls around her eyes spoke more eloquently about her exhaustion than any remark she might make. Boardman had three sons; he and his wife had always longed for a daughter, but had never been fortunate enough to be granted that gift. But if he had . . .

'Beth, sit down before you fall asleep on your feet.' She looked startled by the command in his voice, then smiled when he added, 'Please.'

The chairs were as comfortable as the rest of the room. She felt herself begin to slide into semi-wakefulness, her eyes beginning to flicker, then close.

Fergus had remained silent throughout. With barely disguised contempt, he watched the policeman tend to his injuries. Fergus had read the document; he held them all responsible for what they had done to his Beth.

'It'll take more than a bandage to put that girl right,' he said through clenched teeth into the bending policeman's ears.

Boardman glanced up and into the Irishman's eyes, holding their steady, unwavering appraisal. 'I know,' he said quietly.

Fergus realised that there was nothing more to be said about that matter; it was an agreed fact. Boardman's wrinkled forehead told him this man was no actor.

'It's not as bad as it looked at first, but it should really be stitched, Finn.'

Fergus was tempted to add the words, 'Just like Beth,' but commonsense dictated that this uneasy truce must be allowed time to run its course.

'Thanks, Boardman,' he said, almost sincerely.

The sound of feet on the stairs drew their attention. Boardman pulled himself to his feet as a middle-aged woman wearing jeans and a Breton sweater walked calmly into the kitchen.

'Breakfast,' she said kindly and without questioning them. She offered an open smile to Fergus who could not refuse to return its genuine warmth. He watched this attractive woman pause quietly by the sleeping form of Beth Gamble, gently stroke her still-damp hair, then turn to her husband and nod gravely.

'I've made up the beds in the spare room,' she stated, making her way to the cooker and clicking the grill on to full. Within minutes, steaming mugs of coffee were passed around; one was placed before Beth. The clink of the cup against the table's oak top pulled her back from wherever she had been. She looked wildly around the room before her memory tripped in. She fixed her gaze upon the Irishman and managed a wry smile.

'Are you all right?'

He nodded before answering, 'Thanks to you, yes.' There would be time later for an explanation. For now there were other questions that required answering. Beth felt his reticence and understood its cause. She looked towards Boardman then to the woman that she assumed was his wife.

'Fiona and I have no secrets, Beth,' Boardman said with obvious pride. Beth saw the slim, kindly woman look away shyly towards the cooker.

The policeman moved slowly to a briefcase that sat on one of the work surfaces. Beth could see a moment's hesitation before he grasped it firmly by its handle; whatever last doubts Boardman had held had been resolved in those brief seconds. He brought it to the table top and opened the combination lock.

'Beth,' he began. 'For what it's worth, I'm sorry about what's happened. I can say no more than that. The problem is how we put it right.'

She sipped at the warming mug of coffee before replying. 'We?' she asked. He nodded without offering any other explanation. 'Aren't you compromising yourself?'

He busied himself removing a number of files from the case. 'I did that when I allowed these people to interfere with your trial.' Bitterness sliced through the cold morning air.

'Did you have any choice?' Fergus enquired, impressed by the man's sincerity.

Boardman's eyes met those of his wife. 'There is always a choice, Mr Finn, the point is being brave enough to make it.' The words, heavy with regret, forced a stillness on the room. Any lurking doubts Beth may have held were dismissed.

'Over the last eight months there have been several brutal murders of men up and down the country.' Boardman fanned out the files on the table top. 'There is a common thread: each of these men has been acquitted of rape. The issue at their respective trials was consent. The method of their murder was identical.' The sizzle of cooking bacon interrupted his flow for a moment. 'Castration and execution by a single bullet through the brain.'

By stark contrast to the horror of the description, Fiona could be heard humming to herself as the preparations continued. An amazing couple, Beth thought, as Boardman continued his explanation.

'A single flower brought me into the investigation,' he said, looking down at the photographs before him.

'The orchid in my hospital room,' Beth stated.

'Yes, a single bloom. At that time I had no idea what was happening. I received orders to contact a man called Molineux. I followed these orders, and he followed his. You were selected, Beth. Your trial was targeted. These people were too clever, too slick, too well informed to be caught any other way than by a trap.'

It was all too clear now. Beth looked out of the kitchen window where the grey sky matched her mood.

'All right so I was bait, but so was Middleton.' Her tone was one of quiet anger,

Fergus looked towards her, feeling bewildered; Arthur Middleton had raped her, yet she could still feel outrage that he had been rendered a victim by the interference of the police.

'They believed that every possibility had been covered. They were wrong. I believe that there was a leak inside the department, somebody with top clearance. I believe I now know who it was. He handed you and Middleton to them.'

Bacon sandwiches were passed around the table as Beth concentrated on the information.

'What about the orchids?' she asked, taking a bite from the sandwich in her hand.

'Obviously they are in some way symbolic to these people,' said Boardman, searching through the pile of documents.

'The problem we faced was that they could be grown anywhere by anyone with a hothouse, and there are thousands in this country alone. They are only black because they have been sprayed black. What we need to know is the identity of the grower, and the place they were grown, and that we do not know.'

'I do,' said Beth. 'I saw them, I saw the hothouse where they were grown, and the woman who grew them.'

'Explain,' Boardman said, his voice returning to its normal authoritative tone, hitherto absent. He was a professional; it was time to behave like one again.

Beth told them all that had transpired after the laundry van had spirited her away from her home to the explosion of the hothouse and their escape to the Boardman's home. They sat quietly as she told her tale without exaggeration, in a matter-of-fact voice.

Boardman considered the information before speaking again.

'There must be a way of tracing the occupancy of the house back to a name, or organisation.'

'Or Charitable Trust,' volunteered Beth. Boardman's face invited a further explanation which took some little time. The policeman chuckled as he heard how she had tricked her way into the information.

'Then that is the lead I must pursue,' he concluded.

'We,' Beth stated.

'I do not wish to remind you of the obvious, Bethany, but you force my hand. As an escaped prisoner, and a well-known one at that, your prospects of investigating anything are limited. As for you, Mr Finn, they have tried to kill you once already.'

'Twice,' he spat. They all looked to him for further information. 'Later,' he said, suddenly exhausted by recent events.

'All the more reason why you will both have to lie low for a while. I'm owed a week's holiday and Mrs Boardman is a better sleuth than the Chief of the Met.'

'I've met the Orchid woman. We've seen what she is capable of.'

'And we will be careful. Your concern is touching. After all . . .' He paused, obviously distressed by memories of his past involvement.

'There'll be time for self-recrimination later, Boardman,' said his wife kindly.

Beth studied this loving couple and feared for their safety at the hands of the adversary. There had been too many deaths already. Beth didn't feel strong enough to witness two more.

CHAPTER THIRTY-EIGHT

Maddy played with her food. Her fork moved the stew around in concentric circles, sloshing the brown Windsor wetness over the edge of the plastic plate. At least she had time to think; too much time. Previously she had filled her life with her studies, then her teaching, and now this. For the first time she realised why she had accepted the post in the blind school: to be invisible. At university there had been no scarf-swapping romance with a sincere undergraduate, no innocent wine-drinking pranks with her fellow students; only the work. Maddy had chosen that course but she would have loved to have been taken out of that by a life-lasting friendship. Instead there was only the keyboard of the piano to accompany three comparatively lonely years of study.

She replaced the white plastic fork on the table as she remembered the painful solitude of her graduation. All the hundreds of others with friends and family, hugging and smiling in a frenzy of pride, whilst she walked away, alone, without a witness. She thought how proud her mother would have been: even her father would have met the occasion with a facade of fatherly pride. It was the innocence of the students' shining faces she remembered most, all of them framed in a mortar board from the college hire shop, delighting in their own slightly ridiculous appearance; she had lost her innocence long before that.

Maddy slumped head down on the table. None of it was her fault. Now here she was, alone again. Her time at the blind school had been happily anonymous until McCabe. When he had thrust into her, he had thrust her back into the grimness of the real world, a world of chain-smoking policemen and hard-faced female doctors; then Diana had invited her in. There was something about the letter that spoke of secrets to her, an undertow of concealed experience, a current of acceptance. Maddy had thought about the offer of help for weeks. Eventually – when her GP had refused her further Valium prescriptions, when the dreams began to lodge in her open eyes – she had gone to them, and they had not failed her.

The counselling wasn't an academic exercise from therapists who had read books about rape. It was from women who knew their subject intimately; too intimately. After a while her reliance on the mind-numbing drugs eased as she began to accept her own reality. It had happened, and now she had to live with it. There had been relapses when the urge to shower countless times a day was purged by constant repetitions that it wasn't her fault. One of the women at the charity's sanctuary had scourged her breasts and genitalia to open wounds with a pumice stone, but they hadn't been angry with her, just with men. They had advocated the need for self-protection not self-harm.

Maddy recalled the self-defence classes in the hall of the sanctuary. Beaten women stood drooping before the instructress until her words drove them into a rage of potent flailing punches and well-aimed kicks to the suit-wearing male dummies before them. Maddy was surprised at her own level of anger, stopping the attack on the hapless blank-faced marionette only when exhaustion and the decreasing power of her assault forced her to her knees. Then they were taught control, discipline and self-reliance but the fury never went: it was the same fury she had felt when she had taken the gun from the sanctuary's safe and confronted McCabe. Then Beth had come along.

She was everything that Maddy wasn't. They stood, positive and negative, success and disaster, in the same room whilst she steeled herself to take her rapist's life. And she had. Whether he would have died if Beth hadn't made her abrupt entry she really couldn't say, but the fact remained that he had died, and Maddy wasn't sorry.

Beth despised lying low but the many questions that remained unanswered in her mind since Boardman had disclosed the truth made it bearable for the present. The safe house he had secured smelled damp and unoccupied but at least it was somewhere for Fergus to recover and for Beth to concentrate. Her experience drove her down a familiar route. She had to figure out how to bring this 'show' together. It was strange that, despite the horrifying reality, she still thought in those TV terms. It was as if this was someone else's movie.

In the time that Boardman had been gone, the growing pile of newspaper articles and Beth's scribbled notes had spread randomly over the cheap table. The press seemed content that the continuing Beth Gamble saga was providing enough copy to fill their pages several times over. She had to admit that had things been different there was no doubt she would have run with the pack: instead she was the prey.

The central question to have emerged during the raging debate was not whether Beth had murdered Arthur Middleton but whether she had the right to. Convicted already by the High Court of Media, she reflected upon the power of the industry she could never return to. Her enforced policy of silence through Maddy only served to fuel the reactor, as if the press had been given *carte blanche* to speculate at will upon her feelings. This written insight, allegedly gathered from sources close to Miss Gamble, was a revelation in itself. She hadn't realised she had so many friends who had spent their own lives dissecting her morality and motivation. One in particular caught her attention. A quotation in the *Daily Express* accredited to Teddy Maxwell read: 'Beth Gamble was my lover and my friend; she was rejected by the system in this country. I stood alongside her in that witness box and I witnessed the despair that followed. There is no doubt in my mind that what Beth has done is what many others would like to have done but never had the guts. Although I haven't talked with her since her arrest she knows that I still stand beside her.'

Over the other side of the canyon, thought Beth. She realised now that Teddy Maxwell was nothing more than a symptom of her diseased infatuation with the industry that had turned its back on her. Just then, her future shuffled across the room: it was becoming reassuringly familiar as the days passed by. She smiled at him as Fergus slumped in the chair and reached for a fresh bandage.

'Let me do that,' she offered.

'No, I'm all right,' he winced through gritted teeth. 'You carry on. The sooner you come up with something, the sooner we get out of here.' Fergus began fumbling with the tubigrip around his leg. Beth ignored him, knelt down at his feet and looked up into his eyes, saying nothing. The wound was healing quickly, more quickly than she had anticipated; it meant that they were mobile again. As the gauze was peeled from his leg she spoke.

'There's a piece in the *Sunday Telegraph* about Peagrove House in Kent being razed to the ground by a freak gas explosion.'

'Some freak,' replied Fergus, watching her carefully.

'Exactly, but the interesting thing is that the house belongs to the National Trust.'

'So?'

'So I rang the National Trust first thing this morning to pledge support for the restoration fund and guess who the house has been leased to for over five years?'

'Guy Fawkes.'

'Close. The Women's Charitable Trust.'

'Isn't that the same organisation who paid Maddy's gun club fees?'

'Yes.'

'Boardman told us to keep out of this.'

'No, he didn't, he told us to keep out of the way. He didn't say anything about phone calls.'

They looked at one another before Fergus relaxed once again, adopting the sounding-board pose that had become such a part of his life with Beth. She tied a knot in the new bandage and stood to pace the floor.

'What if the WCT has no idea that the Orchid woman advocates murder as the final therapy? What if she simply uses the umbrella of an otherwise respectable organisation to select cases, particularly severe cases where the rape victims themselves can't see a way through, and then offers them a way? Remember I told you she referred to herself at the gatekeeper?'

'It's possible,' replied Fergus, well aware that when Beth was in full flow there would be more to come. He was right.

'It's more than possible, Fergus. She was very disturbed about Madeline, almost as if she felt Maddy had let *her* down in some way.'

'What do you mean?'

'I don't know exactly, it's just a feeling.'

'Your feelings are usually pretty accurate. Try me,' he offered encouragingly.

'It was the way she talked, as if I had hit a nerve.'

'Go on.'

'She told me that the authorities never considered Maddy; she was a casualty. That's the way she put it, a casualty.'

'A casualty in what?'

'The war.'

'Her war?'

'Yes, that's the point. It was extremely personal.'

'But how does that reconcile itself with her attitude to Maddy? I thought Maddy was supposed to be part of all this. I mean, I thought she was on her side, a soldier if you like.'

'I did at first but now I'm not so sure. Maddy is a very frightened girl.'

'Aren't you?'

'Of course I am but that's not what I mean. I don't believe Maddy ever figured in the great plan.'

'You mean McCabe's murder wasn't planned.'

'Precisely.'

'How do you work that out?'

'The way I see it is this – she told me that for some women the gates of freedom can't come quickly enough and implied that Maddy was one of those women.'

'A sort of loose cannon then.'

'Something like that. Beth turned to the files handed over by Boardman before he had left and tapped the top one softly. 'The victims of all the murdered men had rock-solid alibis for their whereabouts when the murders took place. Maddy wouldn't even have considered that necessary; all she was interested in was killing McCabe. If the Orchid woman had anything to do with setting up his death, therefore, I'd be very surprised. You only have to read these to see how carefully the murders were planned and executed: so much so, that they could only be the work of a professional assassin.'

'So where does that take us?'

'It could mean that when I was set up by the authorities the Orchid woman had no choice but to get closer to Maddy. She had to demonstrate that she couldn't tolerate their disregard for Maddy's case.'

'So why not kill McCabe anyway?'

'I expect she would have done in time, but she likes the conditions to be perfect. Like growing an orchid. I believe that there are some women connected with the charitable trust who are aware of what she does and secretly applaud it but conventional counselling comes first. She was very proud to point out that she had developed a system of care. In it there must be steps and procedures which precede the ultimate gesture, just like the law.' Beth breathed out slowly.

'So you're saying Maddy didn't respond to initial counselling.'

'It's just a feeling, remember, but what if she responded all too willingly – the guns, the vigilantism, the ultimate revenge – all that exploding in her mind? She was probably too far down the road to stop.'

Beth felt the fog of confusion settling on her own mind again. It had been like this ever since Boardman's disclosures. The real focus of her anger escaped her like the approach to an unfamiliar roundabout; she didn't know which road to take. Men, powerful and supposedly principled, had changed her life so easily. It enraged her to the very core. Beth would make them regret their decision.

On the other hand, a woman had attempted to have her incarcerated for life for a murder she didn't commit. That too was an act of appalling arrogance. Fergus was right. The Orchid woman had to be stopped and Beth had to be the one to do it. It was as if she had been chosen to bring these two warped ideologies to a cataclysmic collision.

Beth longed to be part of the audience again, not a player on the stage. The only problem was that she had no strategy; she could only react to what was being forced upon her. Gaining control was the only answer. So far on this journey she'd been led like a blind dog, never knowing who was holding the leash. Until she discovered the identity of the Orchid woman it would be impossible to plan anything, but one thing was for sure: the answer lay with her.

CHAPTER THIRTY-NINE

Boardman's first mentor in the police force – a crusty, gruff-voiced Sergeant – taught him the most important technique in investigation: preparation. Without it he would never have taken the Blackheath Beast or Simon Thorndike, the Camden Car Rapist. It might be dull but it worked.

He glanced down at the computer printouts before him. Sergeant Dobson had accessed, quite illegally and much to the younger officers' delight, the available records of the WCT. For the most part they made stale but well-intentioned reading. They showed donations and the distribution of that money to the various linked organisations that the Trust patronised. Nothing seemed amiss.

Boardman's wife had accompanied him on this tedious mine-sweeping of the accumulated papers. After four days they were no further forward towards discovering the secret of Peagrove House. His enquiries with the National Trust had confirmed that the property had been leased to the charity three years before.

That led to the charity's solicitors who were bound by legal privilege not to disclose the names of any of those involved. The woman lawyer he had spoken to was tigerishly hostile in defence of that information. Boardman reckoned that she was either a very high-principled solicitor, which went against his experience, or that she had some knowledge of the parties concerned. Even with that suspicion he was not in a position to force a show-down with a lawyer who, on the face of it, was doing her job correctly. It was Fiona, as usual, who forced him to stop and evaluate what it was they were seeking.

'But isn't the point this?' she began, spreading copies of the dead men's files before him. 'We believe that this charity is involved with the murder of these men. The charity is involved with the victims of rape, whether or not the rapist is convicted. What if the names of the acquitted men's victims appear in their lists of beneficiaries? Out of all the rape victims in the country, wouldn't it be an amazing coincidence if they had been singled out for help?'

Boardman saw her point immediately. If he could prove a link between the two then that connection could not be ignored. It meant that they might have a way into the organisation. They set about the laborious job of retrieving the massive list of women the charity had helped over the past three years and marvelled at the breadth of their work. Before him sat the names of so many tragic women whose rapists had been acquitted. Fiona was right. They were all there, every one of them. Each had been given a grant to attend a therapy course at Peagrove House. Each of them had attended the course but none of them ever reappeared on the records as needing further help.

Boardman then cross-referenced one more name to the list: Madeline Milton. Again, the tally matched. It even confirmed the payment of her gun club fees under the heading of 'recreation'.

'That's all well and good,' he muttered to himself, 'we could be right but it isn't proof.' He turned his face to his smiling wife. 'If I approach any of these women they'll clam up. They've got little enough reason to trust the police.'

'I've always seen myself as a charity worker,' his wife confirmed, 'working tirelessly for the community and safeguarding my old man's pension.'

'We have to be careful. I'm not taking any risks with you.'

'They'll probably appreciate a visit from a Trust representative, just to see how they are getting along. Boardman, you select the target, nobody young and idealistic, and I'll wear my most caring outfit.'

As she left the room he scanned the case papers, searching for an ideal candidate. Patrick Michael Dunn had been found dead in his bedsit in Bristol on 21 August 1994. His ex-wife Teresa, aged forty-four, had been in the local Catholic church at the estimated time of death. Even the Bristol CID were not going to call a priest a lying alibi witness. This was the first of the murders. Boardman hoped that sufficient time had elapsed to ensure that she would not be suspicious of a visit. Noting the address, he checked his road atlas. They could be there in less than two hours.

Teresa Dunn, headscarf nipped tight around her prematurely greying hair, left the confessional booth for the third time that week. It was

290

only Tuesday. It wasn't that she had a voracious appetite for the commission of sins, it was the one large sin that she could not forgive herself. The priest had claimed that she was long forgiven by the Lord; Teresa did not share his confidence.

Pulling her thin mac around her, she braced against the sunshine of the Bristol sky. She had never felt warm since she'd heard the news from the police. She walked, eyes downcast, afraid that any stranger could see the dreadful guilt in her soul. There was time to stop at the fishmonger's for a small piece of haddock then she would trudge back to her council house and pray that she might forget what she had done. The walk from the church, to the fishmonger's then to her home was a well-trodden route. She had followed it every day since that one, with few exceptions. The last thing she expected was a visitor.

Fiona Boardman was hot inside the fusty clothes she had chosen. A twill skirt and matching jacket made her appear bulkier, homelier than she was. She heard the owner approach and turned to see a small thin woman, her face almost covered by her plain brown headscarf, with a house key in her hand.

'Mrs Dunn?'

The timid woman nodded her head without looking up as she inserted the key into the familiar lock.

'I'm not here to sell you anything, I'm here to help.'

'Are you from the benefit? I've told you about the cleaning job. I'm an honest woman, not like many round here.' As she spoke she raised her face to scan the neighbourhood. 'It doesn't do a decent woman any good, the likes of you, dressed like that, turning up at my door.'

Fiona noticed that her voice was not unkind. All she had said was merely a matter of fact, not opinion.

'No, I'm from Peagrove House.'

The woman's hand immediately reached towards her neck, where Fiona could see a rosary at the throat of her crocheted top. Teresa began to mutter.

'Really it's just for a chat, to see how you are getting along, that's all. There's nothing to be afraid of.'

'That's what she said.'

'What who said?'

'You know who, your boss.' She began to fumble with the lock and push past. 'Tell her this, that there are worse things to fear than her justice. I haven't told, the Lord forgive me, and I won't, but I'll have no further part in that wickedness.'

Fiona could see the woman's eyes were fierce.

'Tell Diana, tell my bloody lady, that I rue the day I listened to her hatred.'

The little woman bustled past with surprising strength then slammed the door with all the might her furious frame contained. Fiona considered knocking on the door, but common sense dictated that Teresa Dunn would be as deaf to her knock as she would be to any further questioning.

Back in the car, Boardman waited for his wife to resume her seat.

'I thought she was going to tear me apart. I'm glad I never made it inside. God knows what she would have put in the tea. That's if she bothered with the niceties and didn't go straight for the electric carving knife!'

Boardman listened to his wife's account as he drove them back to London.

'It was the hatred in her voice, as if she wasn't afraid of anything this world could do to make her life worse than it already was.'

'You are sure she referred to "Diana" as "my lady"?'

'Positive. She spat it out with such venom, as if she hated the fact of the title.'

'It must be somebody important in the Trust,' Boardman concluded. 'If she is titled then she will be named as a trustee. Beth has done some research on this already. Let's get back to her and see if we can make the pieces fit.'

He reached across and squeezed his wife's hand.

'Boardman, you're not patronising me, are you?'

'No, just being thankful.'

The car continued its journey from one desperate woman to another.

CHAPTER FORTY

Maddy ached from head to toe with the strain of her inertia. At increasingly frequent intervals she was swept with an urge to move quickly, violently, to shout or laugh, sing or cry – anything for the solace of action – but time crept slowly and unsympathetically on. It had been six weeks since she had been persuaded by Beth that the safest place for her was where Beth should have been: in prison. She sat on the only chair and stared at the badly painted cell walls that defined her world. She reached for the bulging but neatly arranged box of legal papers and was probed once again by the fingers of doubt.

Maddy had been notified that the trial was in fourteen days and she had heard nothing from her fugitive friend. Each passing day was cut into defined segments of monotony. Each morning, each evening, brought another crack of uncertainty that eroded her confidence. What if Beth couldn't find a way of proving their innocence? What if she decided never to come back? That couldn't happen, wouldn't happen, she repeated to herself. But the prospect of discovery was ever-present in her mind. She had thought of ending the dangerous charade they were playing but, as Beth had told her on the telephone, there was no one to trust anymore: not even the Orchid woman, and especially not the police.

The irony of her situation struck a dissonant chord. Here she was with dangerous people searching the country for her, never thinking to finger their enemies' pockets. Besides, the sleepless nights spent here in society's garbage can seemed to hold a strangely moral purpose for her. Although technically innocent of McCabe's murder, she knew if she hadn't pulled the trigger he would probably still be alive today. If she was ever to be judged guilty she estimated that the time she was doing now was sufficient to appease public abhorrence. She was glad McCabe was dead. She could only hope that Beth wasn't.

* * *

293

Beth wilted under the early-morning misery that precipitated another day of waiting for Boardman to contact them. This was their tenth day of pointless supposition and a thousand dead end lines of thought. The rain belted at the window and Beth drifted, not for the first time, to thoughts of Maddy. Her early surge of confidence in her ability to frustrate the Orchid woman's plan had withered with each relentless hour. Poor Maddy.

If Boardman couldn't get a breakthrough with less than two weeks left to the trial, Beth would be forced to acknowledge that she had been wrong and, Christ, what would happen then? Fergus had reminded her she was a fugitive from justice, an escapee, and walking into the nearest police station saying, 'I'm sorry' certainly wasn't going to be met with much sympathy.

She had the memo signed by Molineux, but given his behaviour so far it was debatable how long that particular document would remain intact once he knew that Beth had it. What would become of Maddy if they couldn't find the Orchid woman? Nothing was more certain than the prospect of long-term incarceration for conspiracy to pervert the course of justice, and worse still, she was still wanted for questioning in respect of McCabe's death.

Just then, through one of the rivulets streaming down the pane, she saw a car drive to a halt outside the house. Boardman stepped out of the vehicle and unfurled a blue umbrella. Beth's heart began to pound and she jumped to her feet. 'Fergus! Fergus! Boardman's back!' she shouted upstairs, only just remembering his instructions never to open the door. Within seconds all three of them were standing in the kitchen.

Boardman was shaking the umbrella vigorously at the back door; Fergus sat expectantly to Beth's left at the breakfast bench. She watched the policeman as he circled the room then sat down beside her. He looked tired.

'Well?' Beth eventually opened.

'Good and bad,' Boardman responded.

'Stop playing games.'

'Hardly, Beth.'

'I know, I'm sorry, it's not easy being cooped up here cut off from everything.'

'I understand, but you've got to remember it's for your own good.'

'All right, what's the bad news?'

'We still don't know who she is,' Boardman replied.

Beth's head dropped before the Chief Inspector gently lifted her chin with his index finger. 'I didn't say all was lost, did I?'

Beth looked into his eyes. 'What do you mean?' she said slowly, daring to hope.

Boardman began to recount the investigation in minute detail. They listened to each syllable, hanging on for whatever revelation lay at the end of his monologue. There had to be one, surely, as his voice chartered his exploits with rising enthusiasm. Beth got the impression that he hadn't enjoyed himself so much in years. Then he revealed to them the name that had emerged from his investigations.

'Diana,' Beth repeated slowly.

'Jesus, it could be anyone,' said Fergus dejectedly.

Beth rose from her seat and smiled to herself before rushing out of the kitchen. Boardman and Fergus looked at one another, utterly perplexed.

'Was it something I said?' Fergus muttered.

'I don't know,' Boardman replied as he too left the kitchen and found Beth rummaging through the pile of papers on the dining table.

'Excuse me,' he said, 'but are we to be enlightened as to what's going on in that mind of yours?'

'Sssh,' Beth replied as she continued to search the pile.

Suddenly she produced a sheet of paper filled with her own neat handwriting. She held it triumphantly in front of her and scanned the contents.

'What is it, Beth?'

'It's a list of the founders, friends and trustees of the Women's Charitable Trust. She must be on it somewhere,' Beth replied without looking up. Within minutes she had compiled a shorter list of nine names. She swept past the confused Boardman and reached for her coat hanging over the banister.

'Where do you think you are going?' he asked.

'I've got some research to do,' Beth responded matter-of-factly. The cobwebs of the past weeks' inactivity had been brushed away and she could feel the rush of adrenaline through her veins.

'Not without me, you're not,' Boardman stated, reaching the door behind Beth.

'Nor me,' said Fergus.

Beth looked at the two men and suddenly felt overwhelmed with gratitude to them both. True friends indeed.

'Where are we going?' enquired Fergus, pulling on his jacket.

'To find Diana,' Beth stated bluntly.

Boardman could only follow. This young woman was in control now.

CHAPTER FORTY-ONE

The British Library's familiar round reading hall felt like a warm comfort blanket to Beth. Boardman and Fergus sat either side of her as she opened the pages of *Who's Who*. The list of names she had compiled lay to her left. The one common denominator was the Christian name Diana. Flipping through the catalogue of fame she quickly located the first name on the list. Baroness Diana Marchant, date of birth 1908. No good. The woman she was looking for was, she guessed, somewhere between forty-five and sixty years old so anyone outside that range could be instantly discounted. Three names later she came across Dame Diana Birchall, born 1934, life peer, of Regent's Park, Greater London; but the many organisations to which she had lent her support aside from the WCT didn't seem right to Beth. Her Diana wouldn't for instance, she was sure, have any time for membership of the Committee on Review of Railway Finance. Another two names were instantly crossed from her list by virtue of geographical location, one residing in South Africa married to an ancient colonialist, and the other a committed archaeologist no doubt tunnelling her way to another lost tomb in the Valley of the Kings.

Then it sprang from the page like the backdraft from a burning building. Beth's body froze as she read: 'Lady Diana Eve Elizabeth Chalmoley, born 14 April 1948, d. of the late Charles and Alice, Lord and Lady Chalmoley. One d., Eve. Roedean and St Hilda's College Oxford. 1969: Panel, London Pregnancy Advisory Service. 1970–1: Harvard League for Penal Reform. 1972: Sister of Mercy Voluntary Mission Overseas, particularly South America. 1973: Stress Syndrome Foundation. 1973: Founding Trustee of WCT. Recreations: Gardening, politics, women's issues.' She copied the entry down quickly before passing the open volume to Boardman.

'That's her,' she whispered. Boardman whistled softly through his teeth as he read.

'Beth, you don't expect me to go crashing into this woman's life on your hunch, do you?'

'It's her and you know it.'

'Maybe, but there's no evidence, in case you've forgotten. Remember, you're a fugitive. Who's going to believe your word against that of a respected, titled philanthropist?'

Beth glared at Boardman's brutal but nonetheless truthful comment. He was right; she had to find out more. One thing about the entry struck her as being highly peculiar.

'Did you notice she never married?'

'So?' replied Boardman.

'So where does the daughter come from?'

Boardman re-read the potted biography and had to admit to himself it was strange indeed. Fergus was peering over their shoulders and interjected, 'I'd say a more pertinent question is, who is her sister?'

'Why?' asked Boardman.

'Well, it's clear that this Diana is motivated by something connected with her sister. Find that sister and we may find some answers.'

'But apart from the fact that her sister shared the same name at birth, she could be anyone. She probably married,' Beth said despondently.

'Only one thing for it then,' he responded brightly.

'What's that?' Boardman said, genuinely impressed by Fergus's positive attitude.

'Meg Sheldon.'

'Meg who?'

'Fergus, you're a genius,' said Beth, rather too loudly for the peace of the library.

'Who the hell are you talking about?' persisted Boardman.

'She used to be the gossip columnist on the *Tatler*, retired now. Mad as a milliner but what she doesn't know about high society isn't worth knowing. We used her when we did that piece about the Dirty Duke, converting his dungeons into a brothel. She's bound to be able to tell us something,' Beth explained.

'All right, but you can't let her see you. I'll do it,' Boardman said firmly.

'I don't have to. She lunches at the Ritz every day with her cronies. I can telephone. She'll be delighted to hear from me especially when I've not spoken with anyone else since I've been in prison.' Beth smiled.

They hurried through the foyer and out of the huge doors to Boardman's car. Three minutes later Beth could hear the high-pitched voice of Meg Sheldon over Boardman's mobile.

'Well, well, Beth Gamble speaks. I must be privileged, my dear.'

'Hello, Meg. I imagine this conversation may be enough to force you back into print.'

'Not even an interview with the Lord our creator would make me do such a thing. Now, I don't suppose this is just a social call, Beth, my love. Do you want to know who's saying what?'

'Not exactly.'

'You must be interested. Everyone is talking about you.'

'No, I need to know what you can tell me about Lady Diana Chalmoley,' Beth implored.

'Ah, a good friend to have in your predicament, I'd say.'

'Really?'

'Charming woman. Very influential but doesn't show herself in public too often.'

'I sort of gathered that, but more specifically I wondered if you knew who her sister is?'

'"Was" you mean.'

'Pardon?'

'Was, dear, as in the past tense, dead, no longer of this mortal merry-go-round.'

Beth's mind catapulted to her conversation with Diana in the hothouse. It was beginning to make sense. Diana had told her she must execute the Will of her sister. Beth was brought crashing back to real-time by Meg's next comment.

'They were inseparable once upon a time – known as the charming Chalmoleys on the circuit. Fun-loving girls, and so pretty. Either of them could have had the pick of the boys. Instead Juliet married that obsequious little groveller Palmer-Dent . . .'

Beth's grasp of the mobile telephone failed: it fell into her lap like an oversized cockroach. Meg's piercing voice could be heard, oblivious of the lightning bolt she had inadvertently dropped.

'. . . mind you, if you're thinking of contacting her I don't suppose you'll have much luck, lovey, she didn't speak with her sister for twenty-odd years. Good for her, I always said. Didn't attend the nuptials either – you'll find it all in the *Tat* – nobody ever knew why, but having him as a brother-in-law is a good enough excuse for me. Next thing you know she was a "convert"; went to South America for a year, came back a changed woman, adopted a child out there, been a virtual recluse ever since. Beth, are you still there?'

She slowly returned the crackling black mobile to her ear. 'Yes, Meg, thank you. I have to go. I'll speak to you soon.'

'I don't get up to Holloway too often, my dear, but keep your chin up and you never know.'

'No, you don't.'

'What's that, dear?'

'Never mind. Thanks again.'

'Toodle pip.'

The three of them sat in silence for several minutes before Boardman took command.

'I'll have to speak to Molineux, Beth. It's just too big.'

'I still can't believe it,' was all she could say. Boardman gunned the engine and the car joined the rush-hour mania.

CHAPTER FORTY-TWO

J esus Christ,' Fergus muttered for the seventh time, from the back seat of Boardman's car. Beth had sat for twenty minutes in the brittle silence of her discovery, whilst Boardman drove, occasionally shaking his head in utter disbelief.

'Stop the car,' Beth said suddenly.

'What for? We've got to get to Molineux,' Boardman replied insistently.

'Stop the car,' she repeated. 'I need some time.'

'We haven't got any. Trust me, we can work this out. You're holding all the right cards. Molineux will have to cut a deal now.'

'No, I'm not ready to play. Give me twenty-four hours.'

'What's got into you? This is not a fucking rehearsal, it's the real thing,' Fergus shouted from the back seat. 'We've got what we wanted, now let's kill this thing.'

'But that's just it. Everything we have is circumstantial.'

'So what! It's got to be enough to make Molineux think again. Besides, you've still got to lay the memo on him. If nothing else, that'll make him take it seriously.'

'Use your head, Fergus. The point is that even with Boardman standing beside us he could still refuse to listen. Remember, you're the one who keeps telling me I'm a fugitive, so what's my word against someone like Diana's? And that's assuming he's going to go right ahead and arrest her on suspicion of conspiracy to murder.'

'What do you suggest?' Boardman asked, pulling the car to a halt in a side street.'

'Like I said, give me twenty-four hours.'

'To do what?'

'I must find out what she meant when she said she must first execute the Will of her sister.'

'Why?'

'Because that's the only thing that matters to her. Don't you see?

301

She's been clever enough so far to avoid being caught. What makes you think that she is going to stop now? I have to find out what's in that Will.'

'And how do you suppose we're going to do that?' Fergus enquired.

'I hate to spoil your party, Beth, but I can't let you do that. Besides, there's no chance that anyone connected with Palmer-Dent's wife will talk to you,' Boardman concluded.

'Maybe not me, but I would have thought there's a fair chance that they'll talk to the deceased's niece.'

'You can't be serious! I suspected that you were a little unbalanced but not barking mad!'

'Just hear me out, Boardman.'

'I'd rather not.'

'Well, OK, don't, but I'm getting out here and I don't think you're really in any position to stop me!' Beth replied, the threat implicit in her voice. Boardman looked and felt inadequate. For, despite his complicity in all that had occurred, there was no getting away from the fact that he was in as deep as Molineux. They locked eyes unblinkingly until he smiled, more at the sheer nerve of this beautiful, brave young woman than at the ludicrously impossible situation he was placed in.

'All right, Beth, twenty-four hours. If you're not back to the safe house by then I'm going to speak to Molineux myself and I'm sure you don't want to miss that. Now, get out of my sight. And be careful.'

Beth stared at him for a brief moment before leaning over and gently kissing him on the cheek. Boardman blushed then fumbled in his inside jacket pocket retrieving his wallet. He pulled out a bank card and handed it to her. 'Here, you'll be needing some money. Take it out of this,' he said sheepishly. Beth beamed her best at him; words were unnecessary. She turned to Fergus who raised his eyebrows but felt the swell of excitement rush into his veins.

'Back to work then, Maestro?'

'Guess so, but let's go shopping first.' Beth smiled, feeling the same adrenalin pumping into her system. They opened the car doors and stepped on to the pavement. Beth stopped for a moment before leaning back into the vehicle. 'What's the card number, Boardman?'

'9999, what else?' he replied as he revved the Daimler's engine.

* * *

302

Fergus hadn't had much time or inclination for other women since Beth exploded into his life. So it was not without apprehension that he found himself at Beth's request hanging on the telephone waiting for the Glaswegian twang of Melanie Brennan. What had once been a love thing, turned convenience thing, was now definitely a hate thing.

'What do you want, you Fenian bastard?'

'Hey, nice to speak to you as well, Melanie.'

'Sod off, Finn.'

'Such grace, such charm.'

'What's the matter? Your pretty girl locked up and you've got no one to play with any more?'

'Yeah, something like that, Melanie, just thought you may be getting a bit lonely yourself.'

'Think again. Now, if this is just a social call . . .'

'Whoa, girl, hold your fire. I need a favour.' Fergus crossed his fingers and held the phone at arm's length.

'. . . pig-farming . . . Irish . . . pissant . . .'

Fergus screwed up his face, periodically bringing the telephone receiver back to his ear. He guessed that the entire news research department would be listening to the tirade of abuse by now. He gambled. 'Look, it's not my concern, but if Teddy Maxwell gets to hear that you're putting your personal life before your job then it's no big deal to me.' He waited like a Las Vegas hotshot, willing the dice to stop rolling.

'Bullshit.'

'No, serious shit, Melanie.'

'All right, what do you want?'

'That's my girl. Give me what you've got on Lady Palmer-Dent . . . deceased,' he added, but didn't need to.

'Why?'

'Because Maxwell's thinking about a new series on prominent politicians' wives. We thought she might be as good a start as anyone.' He threw the die once more.

'Sounds like Blarney to me but I'll send something up to you later.' Fergus knew that he wouldn't be there, but she had obviously accessed the computer already so he pushed ahead. 'When did she die, by the way?'

'On 19 September last year, after a short illness. She hadn't been seen in public for some years before that.'

'Is that right?' Fergus whistled, knowing full well that the aristocracy's euphemism for either mental breakdown or suicide was 'a short illness'. His thoughts were interrupted by a knock at the hotel room door. 'Gotta go, sweetheart. Thanks, I'll make sure that Maxwell gets to hear how helpful you've been. See you soon.'

'Not if I see you first, Finn!'

Fergus moved to the door after the second impatient bang and gawped at the vision standing on the threshold. Beth, with hair as black as Diana's orchid, stood clutching what seemed to be the entire stock of Harvey Nichols's carrier bags.

'Don't just stand there, darling,' she gasped in the plummiest voice he'd ever heard on stage or in real life. Quickly he dragged her into the room.

'What the hell!' he exclaimed as she was tipping the contents of the bags on to the bed.

'Haven't you heard of props?'

'Boardman is not going to be pleased,' Fergus said as he fingered the bottle of stage make-up.

Beth grabbed it off him and headed for the bathroom.

'There's a taxi coming in half an hour. Get my clothes ready, will you?'

'Where are you going?'

'With any luck,' she shouted over the extractor fan, 'the House of Lords.'

Fergus waited in the cab, passing no comment but several sighs as he listened to the driver's inanities on everything from the role of politicians to the drinking habits of the many peers he had had in the 'same place as you're sat, guv'.

It had been an hour and a half since they'd left the hotel in Bayswater and almost seven hours since Boardman had driven off into the London traffic. For the first time Fergus began to lose faith, until he saw Beth emerge from the main entrance, the door being held open deferentially by a green-liveried porter who doffed his hat as she casually waved a hand.

'Start her up, mate, shall I? Looks like your missus is back,' said the cabbie.

'Yes,' replied Fergus with a bemused grin on his face as Beth clambered ungracefully into the car, the tight and very short skirt restricting her progress.

304

'Well?' he asked expectantly.

'Barkley, Barkley, Lightfoot and Smedley, please. Chancery Lane,' Beth stated, her new voice beginning to grate on Fergus.

Thirty minutes later Fergus was unfurling his fingers from their habitually crossed position.

Beth was sitting opposite him, sipping an espresso and munching on a thick slice of chocolate pecan pie smothered with cream. It was a long time since he had seen her so animated. His own heart soon thumped along as Beth brought him up to speed.

'So far, so good,' she said with a satisfied smack of her red lips, contrasting sharply with her darkened skin and black hair. Fergus was past caring whether she was blonde, auburn, black or brunette. He reached over gently to wipe a smear of cream from her top lip.

'Are you sure you know what you're doing?'

She smiled at him.

'I've never heard you say that before, Fergus.'

'We've never been in this situation before, what do you expect?'

'I know, but we're close now, I can feel it.'

'Yeah, me too, only I've always had this uncanny knack for knowing when to pass the parcel, Beth. This whole thing is way out there.' He sent his finger spiralling upwards.

'But this time there's nobody to catch it, Fergus, don't you see that? This is my life and I've got to follow this through to the end. With or without you,' she added, glaring at him but almost instantly wishing she hadn't. 'I'm sorry,' she said softly.

'It's all right. I can't pretend to know how you feel but my head is bursting right now.'

'Well, pull it together and help me work out what to say in there.' She flicked her eyes towards a large black door across the street: the entrance to the Chalmoley family solicitors.

Beth had figured that if she could find out who was responsible for administering the legal affairs of the Chalmoley family it was entirely possible that they would have continued to act for Lady Palmer-Dent after her marriage.

'I don't get it,' Fergus said.

'She will have been a wealthy woman in her own right, Fergus. Her family money wouldn't have been put into Palmer-Dent's hands.'

'So you reckon that these solicitors dealt with her Will?'

'Now you're up to speed.'

'OK, but trying to convice them that you're the adopted daughter of Diana is pushing it a bit. I mean you don't even know anything about her. They may have already met her. It's too risky, Beth.'

'Is that likely? Meg Sheldon told me that Diana and her sister hadn't spoken for years. If the rift runs that deep I bet no one in there has clapped eyes on Diana, let alone her South American daughter, in the last twenty years.'

Fergus had to admit it seemed logical enough, especially in light of Diana's aloofness since her return from abroad.

'Are you sure these are the right solicitors?'

'I sincerely hope so, because I created mayhem in the House of Lords' general office.'

'Oh, no. Tell me you didn't, Beth?'

'Afraid so. I told them that Lord Chalmoley hadn't had the decency to reply to my letters regarding our recent car accident and that I was there to collect recompense in person. They didn't want to be held responsible for creating an embarrassment for his lordship and so we compromised on the name of the family's solicitors where I would no doubt be able to come to some amicable settlement.'

'Jesus, you've not lost the art of bullshitting, Beth.'

'Once a star, always a star!' she said, modestly.

Beth strode through the lobby of Barkley, Barkley, Lightfoot and Smedley. Several young men were sitting around the reception area dressed in varying shades of blue, giving the space a wall-to-wall pinstripe look. Without exception they stared after Beth's swaggering walk as she approached the receptionist who smiled dutifully. The name tag proclaimed her to be Sara Peacock.

'Good afternoon, madam. Can I help?' she enquired.

'I do hope so,' replied Beth, her accent cultured English with a hint of Latin mystery to match her looks. 'I am visiting you without an appointment.' Her legs felt like matchsticks ready to snap.

'Well, if you could tell me broadly what sort of advice you require I may be able to arrange for one of the lawyers to assist you, but I am afraid they are all very busy.'

'That's very kind of you, but you see I'm not really sure anyone will be able to help. I am Eve Chalmoley, daughter of Lady Diana.

It's rather delicate. I know that your firm acts on behalf of my uncle, Lord Chalmoley . . .'

'Oh, please accept my apologies, m'lady,' Sara interrupted. 'I am sure Mr Smedley would be horrified if he were not informed that you had visited us. He is the partner who looks after all family business,' she continued in an almost conspiratorial whisper.

Beth tried to conceal her own surprise, although her mouth was dry and her stomach beginning to curdle with the cream she had seen off in the coffee shop.

There was no turning back now. Sara was already on the telephone speaking with Smedley's secretary and within a couple of minutes Beth was ensconced on a comfortable green leather Chesterfield in Smedley's corner office, with its fine view over Lincoln's Inn gardens.

Smedley was an old-school solicitor with a froth of pure white hair surrounding the shiniest pate Beth had ever seen. He was stirring his tea slowly and deliberately whilst appraising her, perched as casually as decency would allow on the sofa.

'Let me get this right. It's extraordinary. I knew of course that Diana had adopted a young child when she was doing missionary work but because of the way things progressed I never dreamed that one day she would be sitting in my office and, may I be permitted to say, making it a much more agreeable place.'

'Thank you, Mr Smedley. You see, because my mother returned to England and I was left at the mission, I was totally unaware of the wider family – my mother never talks about them – and now she is suffering I just didn't know where to turn.'

'Yes, a real tragedy. I of course have not seen or heard from your mother for many, many years.'

'After – well, I suppose I should call her my late aunt – died it seemed that everything became so much of a struggle for my mother. She visited the mission only once this last year and could not have made the return alone, she is so confused.'

'Is she compos mentis?'

'What?'

'Is she in control of all her mental faculties?'

'Oh, no, quite the contrary, and that's the reason I have come to seek your advice. Lately, she has become very insistent that she should get on with her task as, how do you say, Execu . . .'

'Trix, my dear. Executrix. But I fear that your poor mother may be suffering more than you thought. You see, the Will of your late aunt has already been executed. In fact, I was one of the executors.'

'Oh,' said Beth in genuine surprise, 'then I have wasted your time.'

'Lady Diana was, of course, very surprisingly named as a beneficiary.'

Beth's mind galloped back with the trophy of hope.

'Was she really?'

'Yes. A rather curious bequest consisting of a key which seemed to be of the old gatehouse at Kleetsworth Hall, the family seat. But as that entire estate passed to the current Lord Chalmoley, your uncle, there was no way the property could be bequeathed by your aunt. Besides, it has stood empty for many years. I seem to remember that in their young days the girls spent many hours playing in there. We all assumed it was some sort of last message when the key was handed over. In fact, I sent it myself to your mother, care of Peagrove House. I do hope she received it, for what it was worth?'

'She never mentioned it to me.'

'I am afraid I can't help there. She did visit the gatehouse because the groundsman at Kleetsworth helped her carry out some old boxes of stuff about a year ago, but I don't think they were of any value.'

'I wonder,' Beth said, staring out on to the pretty gardens below. 'I wonder . . .'

CHAPTER FORTY-THREE

Beth watched as the man with dark, greased-back hair climbed out of the unmarked Rover motor car. He was quickly followed by two others, scrambling along after his lengthy and purposeful strides. She had spent so much of her time pondering what she would like to do to him that now the moment had arrived, she felt deflated. She continued to watch him enter the ground floor of the safe house. He was dressed in an anonymous grey suit but his demeanour told her that Molineux was a man used to getting his own way.

Boardman looked up at her. Nothing was said, there was no need; she realised she had just seen the man who had violated her life as surely as Arthur Middleton had violated her body. Boardman replaced the telephone and got up from behind his desk. Beth turned once more towards the window. The setting sun cast a strange orange hue over the evening sky and not for the first time she wondered how on earth it had come to this. She didn't even know how she would react when she could look into his eyes for the first time and hear him speak. Try to explain.

She leant forward and rubbed her temples. So much had happened she had almost forgotten the sequence, but most of all she realised that she had yet to grieve for her father. When this was all over she promised herself that much at least. His graveside would have been full but he wouldn't have cared less about the other onlookers; only her. The man she was about to meet had made sure that she was the most notable absentee from the funeral and for that alone she could never forgive him. She felt Fergus's hand on her neck, softly massaging the tension, and without looking placed her hand on top of his. The shadows in the car park below grew longer. There was a soft rap on the outer door. All three of them turned to face it. Boardman looked at Beth. 'Are you ready?' he enquired simply.

'As I'll ever be. Bring on the dancing bear,' she replied, forcing a smile, but they could both see how anxious she looked.

Boardman went to the door and stood to one side as Molineux strode in, flanked by his minders. He glared at Boardman as he took the seat opposite without invitation. One of his men stood, arms folded, at the door; the other walked towards Fergus and snarled, 'Get up, Finn, body search.' Boardman raised his hand.

'Commander, there is no need for this. I guarantee that no one is armed.'

Molineux appraised him coldly, then a slight nod of his head caused his man to back off and walk towards the window.

'I don't believe you will want your men to hear what we have to say,' Boardman continued. 'It is sensitive for you in particular. There are no other exits from this place, but of course you know that already.'

The air in the room was blood-thick with mutual distrust. Once again Molineux nodded his agreement. The highly trained duo turned as one and left the interior of the safe house. Safe for whom? Beth wondered.

Then she looked into his cold eyes. She had never seen a more calculating pair through her years of exposing some of the country's most skilled liars and cheats. They locked on each other like a pair of heat-seeking missiles before he was distracted by Boardman clearing his throat.

'Sir,' he began, 'this is Bethany Gamble.'

'I know who it is, I just didn't expect to be meeting her in circumstances quite like this. Now let's get on with it.'

Suddenly, Fergus lurched towards the Commander. 'You bastard! Is that all you've got to say for yourself?'

Molineux answered coldly, 'I trust you will remember who I am, Mr Finn, and more importantly who you are. The two of you are in very, very serious trouble, so if I were you I wouldn't lose my temper. You'll have plenty of time to do that inside.'

Boardman coughed again from the corner of the room. 'Sir, before we go any further I ought to show you this.' He reached into his inside pocket and drew out a copy of the internal memo signed by Molineux and watched the Commander's eyes as he scanned it in silence. After a few moments, Molineux placed the sheet of paper to one side and looked towards Beth.

'Where did you get this?'

'It doesn't matter, she stated bluntly.

'It's a total fabrication.' He was lying and she could see it.

'I don't think so, Mr Molineux, but you will have plenty of time to deny it to whoever has the pleasure of questioning you about it.'

'What do you mean?' he replied hesitantly.

'I have deposited the original with solicitors with instructions that, should I be convicted of the murder of Arthur Middleton, then it is to be released to the press.'

'Now wait a minute, you can't do that,' Molineux blustered.

'Mr Molineux, do you really believe that you are in any position to carry on calling the shots?' she retorted. Boardman lowered his head, trying to conceal his delight as Beth continued to glower at Molineux who stared back in disbelief.

'This is outrageous,' he stammered. 'Boardman, what the hell is going on here?'

'Oh, I'd say you've just been gazumped. The real question is, what happens next?'

Molineux shook his head in frustration and Beth could almost see the options being considered and discarded with the lightning speed of a computer inside his skull. She knew that he had no choice: the memo was his all right but it implicated so many other people he wouldn't dare acknowledge it.

'Are you feeling all right, Mr Molineux?' Beth grinned.

'Just tell me what you know, Miss Gamble,' he responded.

'I'll tell you what I know, and then you will listen to what I want.'

'I'm listening. Without prejudice, of course,' he added hastily.

Beth told him everything that she had discovered during her exploits, filling up Molineux's memory banks with all that he had been so desperate to discover himself through IGPAP. When she had finished, he raised his eyebrows. 'And what is it that you want, Miss Gamble?'

'First of all I want a guarantee of immunity from prosecution for my friends Fergus Finn and Madeline Milton, then I need the Home Secretary's itinerary and schedule of public appearances over the next three days.'

'The former, possibly. The second, why?'

'Because I know an assassin will try to kill him.'

'What if you're mistaken?'

'Then you've lost nothing, but I'm sure.'

'How can you be?'

Beth had asked herself the same question. The family connection had come as a shock to them all. Palmer-Dent could well be the next leader of the country but his sister-in-law obviously did not see it that way. Beth had seen very interesting information from the police computer. An inquest had been ordered into the death of Palmer-Dent's wife. The evidence from the coroner showed that she had spent the last five years of her life in a private nursing home which specialised in psychiatric disorders. She had killed herself by drinking weed killer. They found her in the hot-house surrounded by exotic blooms. There was no note. The coroner concluded that the death occurred when the balance of her mind was severely disturbed.

They were rapidly approaching the anniversary of that dreadful event. Beth was sure that Diana blamed Palmer-Dent for her sister's death and that the day of reckoning was near. All that had led up to this was her preparation for the Perfect Day.

'I am sure, Commander,' said Beth, 'that's all you need to know. I would be delighted if I were wrong.'

'Why the next three days?' said Molineux, staring at her with rapt attention.

When the Orchid woman said she had to execute the Will of her sister, what better time than on the anniversary of her death? For some reason it felt right. Beth did not expect this man to understand.

'There's no way I intend to go to the next Prime Minister of this country, young lady, and recount to him what you have just told me because there is not one jot of evidence to support it.'

'But what if I am right?' She held firm. His black eyes searched hers for any indication of self-doubt. Beth refused to drop her confident stare.

'All right, I will alert the Home Office that there is a crank on the loose just to cover my own back – we will increase security for a while also – but that still leaves the question, what do you want, Miss Gamble?'

'Me! I just want you to feel what I've been through for the rest of your life, Molineux. You used me and I want you to remember that so that you think twice every time you feel tempted to interfere again in someone's life.'

'What if you are convicted? Do you really intend to release your story?'

'I'm not guilty, Molineux, but I don't want you anywhere near my trial. You've done enough damage already.'

'You can't just leave me hanging on like that!' he exploded.

'Why not? You were prepared to do the same to me,' Beth shouted, feeling a sudden burst of fury. Molineux rose to his full height and made his way to the door. Fergus predicted his departure and nudged the wastepaper basket in his path. The large frame careered off balance as Molineux collided with it, stumbling against the wall. He glared at Fergus like a school prefect who'd lost control.

'Precisely where you belong, Molineux, with the rubbish,' said Fergus with a satisfied grin.

'I trust that you'll be in touch,' added Boardman as the compromised Commander stormed from the room.

'Will he go along with it?' asked Beth.

'He has no choice,' Boardman said, reaching into the desk drawer in front of him. He produced the tape recorder from its hiding place and clicked it off with a satisfied nod. 'He's not the only one who can play 007.'

He removed the small cassette and placed it in his top pocket.

'If he does nothing and Palmer-Dent dies, we have this to prove that we attempted to prevent it. We also have partial confession to Molineux's involvement in the whole affair. If we link that to the document then we have him.'

Beth sat smiling quietly to herself, then a frisson of doubt intervened.

'But what if we are wrong?'

Boardman could only shrug his shoulders. Beth already knew the answer to her own question.

Andrew Buchan had been dragged from his early-evening bath and his regular indulgence of a thimble of Bailey's over ice, to answer the insistent telephone. He cursed himself for failing to switch on the answering machine. Five minutes later he was cursing himself for becoming involved in Molineux's plan.

'How deeply are you compromised, Commander?'

He swallowed hard before replying. Buchan was already distancing himself from the whole sordid affair.

'We are all in deep, Mr Buchan, and that includes your superior.'

He grimaced at the barely disguised threat from the panicky policeman.

'Give them what they want. If the woman wishes to stand her own trial, so be it. I do not intend to brief my superior fully on the matter. You will command the protection units. The operation will be normal response to possible threat.'

'You mean, crank status. My God, Buchan, this is no sherry-soused phone call. If Beth Gamble is right then we are dealing with a trained assassin.'

The PPS to the Home Secretary pulled the cord of his damask silk dressing gown tighter around his waist.

'You have your orders, Molineux, carry them out.'

'But . . .'

'Good night, Commander.'

His evening was ruined. The calm he had felt when lounging in the rose-petal bubbles of his cast-iron Edwardian bath had dissolved into ineffectual anger. His delight at the public's response to Palmer-Dent's brutal handling of the recent Durham riot had disappeared. He could not order a full protection response for the Home Secretary. If he did then a detailed explanation would be required by the PM and Palmer-Dent. Buchan could not afford that.

He slumped down on the floral sofa in the tasteful, antique-packed drawing room. He and Palmer-Dent were close to the ultimate promotion. The PM's transparent efforts to cloak his failing health were confirmation of that fact. Once they were established at Number 10 then their power was limitless. He would not risk that cornucopia on the hunch of a murderess and a rogue policeman.

Reaching for the telephone, he keyed in a one-digit number that connected with the machine's small but agile memory. Brief seconds later the private line of Anthony Palmer-Dent, Prime Minister in waiting, was answered.

'Sorry to disturb you, Home Secretary. I'm afraid we have had another crank death threat . . .'

CHAPTER FORTY-FOUR

aving been sworn in, the jury in the trial of the Crown v. Bethany Gamble settled into their chairs in number two court, the Old Bailey. The High Court Judge, flanked by his clerk, opened his notebook, though he did not intend to use it with any regularity. The nostrils of his fierce patrician nose flared slightly as he considered the facts before him. It was a clear case. The woman's failure to co-operate in her own defence was evidence of that; her refusal to appear in his court compounded his view of her guilt. From his lofty perch he watched the barristers who would do battle in this one-sided contest. For the prosecution John Climb, tall, slim, smart in double-breasted suit and waistcoat just discernible underneath his black robes. Climb by name, climb by nature. He was the face of the new-age barrister. The watch fobs and pendulous stomachs were increasingly a thing of the past. The long lunchtime of the Bar was now over; it was time to return to work.

He turned his attention to the defence advocate. A curious choice this one. Though highly respected to a point, that point had been surpassed by the seriousness of this case, but the defendant had demanded D'Stevenson and that was who she was going to have. He wore the burden of the trial like a lead cloak around his shoulders, and nodded gravely to the jury as his opponent introduced him by name to them. D'Stevenson attempted not to wince as Beth Gamble's refusal to attend the trial was explained to them. Climb was fair but hard; D'Stevenson listened as he told them to disregard Beth Gamble's absence.

'It is,' he said, straight-backed and trustworthy, 'still for the prosecution to prove the case, so that you are sure. Miss Gamble has the right to silence and that includes her non-attendance. Please attempt to ignore that.'

D'Stevenson winced. Climb was burying Beth in an avalanche of fairness. Nothing was more likely than a fair prosecutor getting a fair result. D'Stevenson had always preferred doing battle against the odious swaggering bullies who enjoyed excess with everything but fairness; at least then the jury only convicted a defendant with some reluctance, but Climb was different.

'The facts are for you,' he informed them helpfully. 'What I tell you now is not the evidence, merely a brief outline of the case against Miss Gamble. And a tragic one it is.'

D'Stevenson sat impassive, looking neither to left nor right. The bloody man even sounded fair when he opened the facts! 'More in sorrow than in anger' was the phrase that leapt to the barrister's mind. He listened as raptly as the jurors as the basic facts of the allegation were laid before them. The rape trial was common knowledge after Middleton's acquittal; other facts were not. The file caused many an eyebrow to be raised; the powder burns more; the blood stains found at the scene and their matching by medical records to Beth Gamble had the jury shaking their heads; her refusal to offer up a sample of her own blood for analysis by DNA made them frown. They've made up their minds already, D'Stevenson thought. He could hardly blame them; a reasonable man from start to finish. Nevertheless, as he had told his solicitor, he had a job to do.

He heard Climb finish his address to the jury and announce the name of the first witness: Agnes Middleton. D'Stevenson unscrewed the top from his Mont Blanc pen and set about his onerous task.

Madeline Milton sat in the holding cell of the Old Bailey. Whilst she had refused to go into the courtroom, Beth's instructions had been for her to be at hand; for what reason she was still unsure. She trusted Beth, but things were getting close. Her lawyers had asked to see her on dozens of occasions; her denial was identical in each case. At least this cell was a change from the grim home she had occupied for the last eight weeks. It was a change rather than an improvement, but appreciated nonetheless. Her barrister, D'Stevenson, had informed her of the attacks he would make on the evidence, but his advices pleaded for her to see sense by seeing him. Without the sample of blood, he had warned in the opinions pages, she would be as good as convicted. It had crossed her mind to give the sample up – after all, it wasn't her blood at the scene of Middleton's murder – but again Beth had been specific.

'If I don't return before the end of the trial then do it, but I will be back. You must be patient and brave,' she had said, attempting to encourage Maddy's trust.

By her calculations, Beth had three days before the jury would be asked to retire and reach their verdict. Maddy needed Beth before that stage. She was frightened, still frightened. She had always been frightened, until she was pushed too far. Her father and McCabe had pushed, she had snapped, and they had died. Now, resting her head against the cold marble wall, enjoying the calm its icy surface lent her brow, she told herself to be brave and patient.

A prison officer punctured the quiet moment. It was lunchtime already. Placing a tray before her, the woman's face was almost kindly as she spoke. 'The prosecutor's finished opening the facts of the case against you.' She'd *almost* seen it all before.

'He called his first witness. Middleton's wife; she found the body.' For the first time someone inside the prison service was treating her with some compassion. Maddy watched the thin ram-rod figure of this woman.

'Thanks. Look, could you keep me informed about what's happening upstairs?'

The wardress considered this proposition before cocking her head to one side, and nodding sadly. 'Wouldn't you be better off up there where you can see for yourself what they're doing?' It was the first time Maddy had seen her move her body against the pull of the Home Office uniform she wore.

'Will you? Please?' Maddy begged.

The woman's face softened even further, hearing the note of desperation in her voice.

'I can't see that it will do any harm,' she concluded. 'Now you can do something for me.' She pushed the tray closer to Maddy. 'Eat this. Keep up your strength. You'll need it. You know the barristers are running a book on how long it will take the jury to convict you. Mr D'Stevenson is in for a fiver on an hour.'

It came as no surprise to Maddy. Her own intelligence had forced her to the same conclusion; the trial papers confirmed the truth of it.

The country had convicted Beth Gamble because it wanted to believe that such a savage, well-merited revenge had taken place.

Eve's hair had accepted its change of colour gracefully. The once blonde cut now sat black and seal-like around her vixen features. This flight was the last she would have to make. Immigration accepted her passport without scrutiny; just another of the hundreds of shuttle passengers from Amsterdam to Heathrow.

She had two days to set up the confrontation. Eve had always been taught to meet that which she feared most, to the extent that now she did not fear anything. There was only one obstacle before Diana too could share that exalted state.

She cut through the milling crowds like a laser through margarine, people moving aside as her advance continued, linear and unstoppable. The more self-confident of the men admired the strength and grace of her movement. It was towards Winchester. There were things to be done, matters to attend to, before the time and circumstances were exactly right.

Three hours later she arrived by train at the cathedral city. Her chosen accommodation had attracted her by its bland modernity. Eve required her surrounding to be efficient and functional in order to function herself. She had demanded that the television work properly. That was a necessity not for recreation.

She placed it in the very centre of the room, a focal point for the future of the enterprise. If there were any news items that might interfere with its execution then she would need to know of them immediately, and respond accordingly. From now until the end it would remain switched on.

The streets of Winchester were thronged with pilgrims and pocket cameras, all in their own way attempting to achieve a personal souvenir of their visit. The cathedral cut through a skyline of Georgian elegance, its spire grasping for recognition. Eve stalked the streets. At the cathedral she examined the car park at the building's rear, noting the turning space and exits. Research had been her surrogate mother during the years of isolation. On its knee she had learned that to fail to prepare was to prepare to fail. Winchester had been the capital of England in the ninth century. It had the longest Gothic cathedral in the world, the oldest public school in England and, more amusingly, the Domesday Book had been compiled within its walls – she had her own chapter to write in it. An epilogue.

Once inside the cathedral, Eve could see they had already roped off the area for the presentation of the programme. Heavy cords of velvet snaked through burnished brass eyelets and defined the first target area. The audience, sitting on the recently constructed platforms, would be able to see it all. Well, almost. She grinned at the thought. Eve paced to the exit from the stage, concentrating on each separate metre of that journey.

Back at the hotel she removed the grey hand-made outfit from its leather carrier. The hat sat in its protective case, red braid slashing across the muted predominance of grey. Other props would arrive by express delivery the next day, including the black bloom.

The television recapped the nation's day. Her interest was raised when she watched her target speak briefly to the Police Federation.

'They can't help you now,' she whispered to his picture. 'Nobody can.'

CHAPTER FORTY-FIVE

I t was the Perfect Day, Beth was sure of it. Inside Winchester Cathedral she could feel a lurch in her stomach. They must be right – or was this another of Diana's ploys to keep them off balance? Beth doubted it. All the facts pointed to this ancient monument as the stage for the fulfilment of the Orchid woman's plans, the anniversary of a loved one's death pinpointing the Day as Perfect. They had travelled by helicopter to the outskirts of the city, the journey a maelstrom of Molineux's clipped commands barely audible over the thunder of the chopper's spinning blades. The discredited Commander wore his anger like an impotent scar. Their eyes met across the cramped seating briefly but often; he always dropped his gaze before Beth's.

Fergus had held her hand during the journey but remained silent throughout. These months had worn him thin, both inside and out. Where there had once been a kindly face hidden behind the camouflage of a beard, there was now a handsome seasoned man, whose steady eyes and prominent cheekbones told the story of their journey.

Boardman sat close to Molineux: not by coincidence. The radio he held was tuned to the frequency of the Commander's, and ensured there would be no sting in the tail for Beth.

From the shelter of the monitor room, she watched as the 'Question Time' crew went about their final checks before the show went live to the public. Security was always vigilant with so many politicians present; tonight, security was all. She scanned the audience. She was looking for the idea of a face, a face twenty-five years older than the photograph they had discovered in the *Tatler*. She knew that tonight Diana would be there. The gathering of eager questioners shuffled their notes, awaiting the call before the viewing nation to ask for the answers the politicians believed only they could provide.

Boardman's face was grim as he too trained his gaze over the faces of the expectant crowd. The room had been transformed after special dispensation was sought from the Bishop. Camera wires snaked across the polished floor, lighting booms and radio microphones were there in profusion. There were two hundred in the invited audience. Boardman had read the list of names with care. Their applications to attend had been received months before. If it was to be tonight, then the planning must have been long-term and meticulous. That was what troubled him. Diana had been able to outwit them all, she'd shown them an aristocratic pair of clean heels from start to finish, why should tonight be any different? His crumpled grey suit matched his sombre mood.

Molineux and his men searched. They did not know what they were searching for. They had an idea but not all the facts. Boardman had advised that a full disclosure of what they knew would render them superfluous. They needed Molineux to need them or a double cross would be in the air. Now they had the world's most valuable item: knowledge. They also had the document. With that they had him dangling gently from their noose, waiting for the chair to be kicked away. But they had to watch him, he could so easily place the hemp around their own necks.

Fergus was unhappy. The presence of the cameras dragged him back to a simpler life, was it really only ten months ago? He slumped by one of the monitors, grumbling at the poorness of the camerawork as the shots appeared before him on the screen.

Palmer-Dent sat opposite Buchan in the ante-room to the main hall. The aged hard-backed chair pushed against his straight back as he levelled his gaze at his aide. 'And everyone has been thoroughly vetted?' he asked. The civil servant nodded confidently. 'On at least two occasions. They have all been searched for concealed weapons.'

Palmer-Dent smiled icily as he turned his attention to the file of topics for the programme.

'Cranks. Not the first time, not the last.'

'Quite,' Buchan agreed as he waited for the Home Secretary to continue. Palmer-Dent looked towards him, noticing for the first time a slight catch in the normally frosty delivery of Buchan's voice.

'You all right?' The small man nodded once. Palmer-Dent raised a quizzical eyebrow.

'I need a team I can rely upon. You are the support-team leader. I expect complete reliability. Or are things becoming too much for you? If so, say so. I don't expect to be Home Secretary forever, particularly with the Prime Minister's medical problems.' He paused. 'There's another rung to climb yet. Are you up to the altitude?'

Buchan pulled open his own file without replying. Palmer-Dent took that as his answer.

'Good. Now tell me what the ill-informed of Winchester are going to tax me with tonight. You know, Andrew,' Buchan raised his head from his papers, 'we need a good showing tonight, something strong and impressive.' Palmer-Dent shifted his eyes to some private horizon. 'The time is right. I can feel it.'

The light babble of the audience's voices rose slightly as the programme's producer walked, clipboard in hand, on to what was now the central stage. It nestled in the vastness of the soaring chamber, the lights casting weird shadows and rebounding up to the massive arches of its interior. He looked tiny in this place, they all did, diminished by the Gothic grandeur. He paused, waiting patiently for the murmuring to come to a natural end before he began to speak.

'Good evening, ladies and gentlemen.' His voice was business-like: a few echoed his greeting and he continued: 'In five minutes we will be going live to the nation. Could I ask you please to have your questions ready, to keep them succinct and not to ask them until you have been invited to. You may be asked to respond to the panel's answers: again, please be brief.' His tone was reasonable. 'Enjoy the programme.'

He moved away, listening to the floor director's words through his ear-piece. The final adjustments were made to the set and camera angles. Beth felt nervous. She watched as the panel made their way on to the stage. She saw a thin bespectacled man, dressed in light tweed make his way absentmindedly to his seat and guessed him to be Dr Colin Makepeace. The others she knew. Linda Bradford, Labour MP and Shadow Home Secretary; Colin Treat, Chairman of the Probation Service; and, eventually, the Home Secretary himself.

Palmer-Dent made his way with an assured step to his place; furthest from the opposition and nearest to the audience with whom

323

he claimed a long-standing rapport. Beth watch him nod greetings to the other panellists then sit facing the audience. Few returned his oily smile.

Beth watched Palmer-Dent through the bank of monitors. Their room was some distance from the Home Secretary, tucked away in the upper chamber. Now, for the first time she could see him for what he was: the person who had allowed Middleton's trial to be raped by Molineux. And more, much more.

'We could be wrong, Beth,' Fergus whispered in her ear.

She turned to him. His concerned face reflected the harsh overhead lighting.

'No. I don't know how she's going to do it, but I know she'll try.'

Boardman confirmed this as he stood behind them, peering into the shared screen for clues. That sixth sense that had warned him of Beth's arrival at his home after the explosion returned full force.

'It's got to be tonight,' he muttered to himself, 'but I can't see how . . .' Once again he checked the exits from the platform to the world outside.

The programme began. The floor manager orchestrated the applause that led to the participants' introduction. The presenter gave a brief, flippant description of the panellists, ending with a risible anecdote; but their careers were their passport to this programme.

'Tonight,' he continued, 'the topic is crime and punishment.' He paused to stare gravely into the camera's lens. 'Whether we as a nation care too much about the criminals and not enough about their victims.'

He watched the audience, listening to the producer's commands on his ear-piece. He followed instructions and pointed to a pensioner, his shiny campaign medals fixed regimentally to his blazer.

'Good evening, panel,' the pensioner began. The camera switched to grace the viewers with the empty indulgent smiles of the politicians, a real smile from the head of the Probation Service, and the flat gaze of Makepeace; he was only interested in the questions. 'Does the panel feel that the death penalty should be re-introduced for the slaying of police officers?'

The presenter relaxed slightly, the programme was going to plan. He allowed the debate to pass like a baton between the panellists.

Boardman reflected that a year ago he might have suggested the same solution to the rising toll of police deaths. Now? Events since then had taught him the corruptibility of the judicial system; if death was the sentence the system had to be perfect, and it wasn't. The topic was argued between the panellists, each with their different motivations and points to prove. The presenter looked delighted with the heated way the show was proceeding. What could go wrong?

Eve steered the hire car through Winchester's quiet streets. Her uniform fitted her slim athletic build perfectly, the trousers the final part of the disguise. She checked her Cartier watch; a rare indulgent present from her mother. It wouldn't be long now. The car was driven as close to the back of the chapel as she dared. There was the anticipated police and Special Branch presence, but they were expecting to keep something in, or out; she had been right, as ever. All eyes looked for the enemy within. The bag was heavy, but made no sound as she retrieved it from the hire car's boot. It wouldn't; each item had been carefully wrapped to deaden the sound. Lights reflected on to the damp of the pavement as she concluded her journey on foot.

From forty feet away she pulled the sodium night-scope from the inside pocket of her grey jacket. She lifted it to her eye, took a moment to adjust her sight then aimed it towards the Bentley. A man's figure could be seen from behind. An occasional flare and a plume of smoke showed his activity as he sat in the driver's seat of the vehicle. She scanned the rest of the area. The movement was minimal but they were there, and they were looking in the wrong direction. Eve carried the dead weight of the bag with ease and padded quietly to the car's smoking driver. 'Soon,' she whispered, 'soon.'

Halfway up the banked seating of the arena, opposite the stage where the object of her desire sat confidently in his place, Diana too calmed herself with the knowledge that the Perfect Day had arrived. Dressed in a twenty-five-year-old outfit from Coco Chanel's most celebrated collection she waited and listened until the moment was right. Palmer-Dent berated his opposite number for her naïveté. He knew what the people of this country really wanted.

'Criminals only understand one thing and that is punishment, harsh and swift. It is the only reaction this country can afford to give to the yob culture.'

A smattering of applause from the closet fascists in the audience was greeted with booing from those liberals who dared to react.

'Please, ladies and gentlemen,' the presenter interjected, wearing a frown of false concern, 'let us keep this civilised.'

Diana raised her arm.

He scanned the room for a figure to calm the debate. His eyes settled on a middle-aged lady in a still-smart suit. He pointed in her direction, giving a brief description so that the cameraman and sound boom might pick her out; Palmer-Dent's eyes flickered in a puzzled half-recognition.

'A question for the Home Secretary.'

Beth reeled at the sound. It was her, the Orchid woman, Diana. She dug Boardman in the ribs, eyes round with the excitement of discovery. Boardman, looked into her face, then, realisation dawning, gazed on Diana. A strong forehead framed a face full of intelligence and passion; lightly greying hair marked her as a trim and young fifty.

'How can the Home Secretary's own crimes allow him to take such a stance on savage retribution?'

The audience began to shuffle excitedly in their seats; the presenter attempted to switch the camera to another questioner. Beth could see Palmer-Dent's features; they were slack with incomprehension.

'I have all the evidence here,' Diana continued, business-like and commanding. The cameraman remained on her. 'Insider dealing on the Stock Exchange is only the beginning of it.' Her words held the audience silent, Palmer-Dent grey-faced. 'At least fifteen share issues during this Government's tenure Do you deny profiting from there?' She did not wait for his reply.

Palmer-Dent had begun to regain self-possession. He looked angrily towards the presenter who seemed transfixed by these events.

'Can't you control your bloody audience?' the Home Secretary barked.

Boardman looked to Beth who shook her head. Molineux burst into the monitor room as Diana continued her public interrogation of Palmer-Dent.

'Is it correct that whilst on the board of Distillers you opposed the payment of compensation to the victims of Thalidomide?'

Palmer-Dent seemed stunned again by this accusation. His face said it all to Beth, and everyone else who witnessed Diana's questioning. Molineux moved across from his own monitor and demanded, 'Is it her? For God's sake, tell me.'

Boardman turned towards Beth. 'It's gone too far already. Tell Molineux who she is.'

'No, it's time! Leave her to tell the truth.'

Molineux's urgent face awaited her confirmation. 'She's supposed to be one of the party faithful,' he shouted, looking down at the audience, plan in his hand. 'Margaret Neary, Conservative party fund-raiser. Who the hell is she, Beth? She's killing him out there.'

'Better in here than out there,' She muttered to herself.

Boardman shook his head again; security men were itching to be involved. The other panellists watched, their mouths gaping.

'Where is your wife?' Diana asked him, totally in command of the situation. Palmer-Dent stared at her for the longest moment, narrowing his eyes to see her better through the unkind studio lighting. He whispered one word. Beth could lipread its content and see the horror on his face.

'Diana.' The Home Secretary's face looked desperate as realisation struck him like a steel boot. He set his features into a stare.

'You know where she is, Diana. She's dead,' he shouted, beginning to search for his body mike with panicking hands.

'A year ago today, Anthony. Why didn't she want to live?' the woman said coldly, rising to her feet. Palmer-Dent's face was set in a death mask, his arrogance lost.

'Anthony,' Diana said quietly, 'you may as well have killed her the day you raped me.' It was delivered like a much-practised line into the startled lens of the camera. Her face held the certainty that this description would colour his memory for eternity. '*Rapist*. Nothing more, nothing less.'

The camera followed Palmer-Dent as he furiously sought the microphone in its place on his left lapel; it was found then hurled at his sister-in-law as he stormed out of the studio, past the still-stunned figures of his minders, and out of the back door of the cathedral.

'Oh my God, she's forced him out into the open,' Beth shouted

327

to Boardman. 'It was never meant to happen in here. That's what we were supposed to think!'

Boardman exited the room at speed, Molineux followed. Beth watched the monitor. It was fixed on a middle-aged woman who sat calmly as security men moved towards her. A grim smile played across her lips as she looked directly into the still filming cameras and said quietly, 'It's over.'

Palmer-Dent swept on, not stopping to wonder why the door was already open for him. He failed, in his humiliation, to notice the difference in build between the driver who had brought him and the one who shut the door on him as he sat in the rear of the car. The scarlet braiding of the driver's cap mirrored his own brief future.

'Take me home,' he demanded, looking down curiously at the black orchid lying beside him.

'Yes, Father,' said his daughter Eve, releasing the switch that locked the door on Palmer-Dent and sealed his fate.

The grey car sped away, the sound of a man's fists beating hollowly against his own security glass.

CHAPTER FORTY-SIX

Molineux's men found the unconscious figure of Palmer-Dent's real driver slumped in the back of a hire car. There was no sign of the Home Secretary. Special Branch and Special Services units arrived in Winchester within an hour; but Beth knew, they all knew, that when they found him it would be too late. After his abrupt and furious exit it had taken long moments before Security reacted fully. The show was a shambles. The audience had enjoyed the entertainment hugely, unaware of the ghastly price Palmer-Dent was now paying for all he had done. Boardman's eyes were cold with disappointment. They had Diana, but the killer had slipped through their fumbling fingers and now had the Home Secretary at their mercy. He doubted there would be any shown to Palmer-Dent.

Molineux had arranged a briefing room; they were ordered to stay until Buchan, the Home Secretary's PPS, arrived. Fergus was quieter than normal. He looked around the disintegrating set of the primetime show with contempt; the sets were as thin as the politician's sincerity. He looked at his watch: 4 a.m. and Buchan was still not ready for them. Beth too was impatient. The hours of inaction had dragged past. There was other business to attend to: Maddy. Molineux had reluctantly told her about the trial. There was only the final stage of the summing-up and then it would be too late to call any further evidence. *Her* evidence. Beth wasn't going to let Maddy down, but there was something she had to do first. She pushed open the door to Molineux's command centre and walked into the presence of the sweating policeman. He replaced the phone in its cradle. Every minute the HS was missing was another step further away from his knighthood.

'What now?' he said wearily, rubbing perspiring hands over his tired features.

'Where is she? Where is Diana? I want to speak to her.'

'No. There are other people who need to speak to her first.'

Beth winced at the hint in his words; somewhere the Orchid woman was being interrogated by Special Services.

'She won't tell them where he is, you know. I doubt she even knows herself. She is too clever to want to know, she wouldn't endanger the killer.' Beth was almost certain she now knew the killer's identity, but needed confirmation of the truth. Molineux simply nodded his head in grim agreement at Beth's appraisal of the situation.

'It was all leading up to this point, the Perfect Day. We just didn't realise that the Perfect Day would involve the violation of Palmer-Dent in public; it was her retribution for the rape he'd carried out on her, all those years ago.'

Her words trailed away as Beth attempted to understand the level of bitterness Diana had experienced over long decades. Beth herself had hated Middleton for what he had done, had wished him ill, but had never really wished him dead. Was it Beth who was wrong? Should she demand the ultimate penalty for the crime, like Diana and the assassin? Was she weak, too weak to assert her own rights? Beth thought not: not in the end, not really, not truly. It took more strength to allow the law to take its course, whatever the outcome, than it did to escalate the violence by revenge rather than justice.

Diana was wrong, Beth knew that now: she had known it all along but she had put the argument so well, so convincingly, and Beth had been betrayed by the system she was seeking to protect. The thought made her focus on Molineux. He had selected her in much the same way a serial rapist would stalk a victim. He had looked around until he found the one he wanted, and had 'fucked' her in just as brutal a fashion as Middleton had. You could be raped of your rights as well, but you could regain them in the right circumstances.

'Our agreement still stands.'

'I don't suppose I have anything more to lose,' Molineux conceded. 'If you are willing to go back into custody and run the risk of a conviction, I'm not going to stand in your way.' His eyes held a vague mischievous light as he spoke. 'After all, it's life if you go down and that would certainly get you out of my hair.'

'Not thinking of rigging another trial, are you?' It was Boardman, and his face contained a hint of menace that Beth had never seen in the normally mild-mannered policeman. 'If so I will ruin you, Molineux. This is your only chance to keep this under wraps, otherwise the whole plan will be revealed and you could get life yourself. Conspiring to pervert the course of justice is a serious offence. All Beth wants to do is to stand her own trial. All Madeline wants is to be released from a trial she has no real part in. Do the decent thing for once, Molineux. And, remember. We have the letter, the blue print.'

Beth thought Boardman's appeal to Molineux's better nature was a long shot, but the threat to his position seemed to hit the mark.

'Can I trust you, Boardman?' he said quietly, sitting back in his chair.

So, Beth thought, he's ready to talk.

'I will hold the letter. Remember, I was involved too. I will only release it should you contravene the conditions that Beth and I spell out . . .'

Fergus had been sitting for half an hour wondering where Beth had gone to. Eventually she appeared with Boardman: they were followed by an unhappy Molineux, his face pinched with anger. Beth, however, looked relaxed and confident.

'It's all arranged, I go back in first thing this morning.'

The Irishman was unhappy.

'You don't have to go back in at all,' he spat, glaring at Molineux. 'That twisted bastard,' he shouted, 'knows you didn't kill Middleton. He could have the trial stopped.'

'Fergus,' she said gently, staring into the frightened eyes of the man she now knew she loved, 'don't you see? That would be as wrong as what they did at Middleton's trial. This has all been about the law and whether we can trust it to reach the correct judgement. It's not perfect, but when it's allowed to act fairly and without interference, at least it stands a chance of getting things right.' He was starting to turn away before his tears shamed him. Beth reached up to his face and felt its roughness between her hands.

'I know, I know,' she whispered, the warmth of his tears on her hands. 'If we sweep it under the carpet, people will always wonder. I can't live like that. I need people to know the truth.'

Molineux coughed nervously at this last reference.

'The truth that I didn't kill Middleton. He raped me, but I didn't kill him.'

Her words went unanswered. Boardman reached out a hand and squeezed her shoulder. Molineux seemed for a moment to drop his head in shame, then appeared to reject that ludicrous emotion for the stranger it was.

'This is all very touching, but there are matters to attend to.' Beth moved in front of Fergus and smiled bravely at him. He relaxed a little as she nodded.

'You can have five minutes with her,' Molineux conceded. 'Try and get her to talk about Palmer-Dent, we'll be listening. They've tried sodium pentathol on her and you were right, she doesn't know where he is, but she may know something.'

He led her away, up into the heights of the cathedral. Eventually they reached an armed man in black standing outside a door. After she and Molineux were searched by the guard, Beth entered. She could see Diana in a comfortable chair, and whilst there were restraints they were loose and did not look painful. Molineux nodded to the guard and they both left the room. Beth was left face to face with the Orchid woman. She pulled a chair across the light green carpet. Diana had had her eyes closed until that moment. Now, they opened and focused directly on Beth.

'I thought I might see you again, but not quite so soon. They have given me something that makes me talk rather more than usual so do forgive me if I seem to be monopolising the conversation.'

Beth could see that Diana's pupils were dilated.

'You know, you really mustn't be too angry with me, Beth. Remember, I didn't select you, they did.'

'But you used me.'

'I was always the practical one, you see, of the two of us, we sisters. I could always find a use for things, a purpose. You were meant to be a tethered goat for us to consume. Instead I made you a smoke screen for the Perfect Day.'

Beth listened to the woman's voice: whilst it had lost none of its intelligence, something was absent from it that had been there before . . . passion. Her passion was now spent.

'Why didn't you just kill him once your sister passed away? It would have been simpler, it would have avoided all these complications.'

The older woman smiled.

'But it wouldn't have been perfect that way, it would have been just another death. No. That would not have done at all. Rape is murder of the soul. I wanted to take from him in the same way that he took from me. He robbed me of my right to choose. Silence is not consent. Women have the right for their silence to mean no. Only yes will suffice. I wanted his humiliation to be public, so that whenever his name is mentioned now it will be linked to his crimes, not his success.'

Beth was conscious that she would not be allowed much longer with this intense woman.

'And what about your own crimes?' She asked. 'How do they sit with your judgement over Palmer-Dent?'

'What crimes are they, my dear? I didn't kill anyone, which is more than I can say for you.' Diana was smiling broadly. 'At least, that is what the prosecution are saying. So are the public.' Diana paused for a moment, deep in thought, before she said, 'Of course,' and smiled afresh at Beth, 'it's Madeline who is refusing to attend your trial, isn't it? You have been very clever, Beth. I always knew you were a marvellous choice. As for my crimes, as you put it, they are what they are. If the police can prove I did any more than shout at a politician on a television programme, I shall be very surprised. You see, I too have the right to silence.'

Beth considered the woman's statement carefully. Diana meant more than she had said. The words were an echo of her own at the police station when she'd refused to answer their questions, but they meant more to Diana than that.

'You have silenced him now haven't you? Whatever happens, he's finished.'

Beth paused to think of the photographs she had seen of the previous murders then shuddered at the woman's impassive expression.

'You must have dreamed of him laughing at you. What he did to you all that time ago.' The narrowing of the Orchid woman's eyes told her she was right. 'But you had to wait, didn't you? You had to wait until your sister died before you would make your move.' There was no further response than a gentle shrug of the older woman's shoulders.

'Would you have waited forever?' Beth nodded her own head slowly. 'Yes, you would.' She hesitated momentarily, the truth now clear. 'You must have loved her.'

'She loved him, you know, even after all those years, all that misery, she did.' Diana hesitated. 'She chose him. It wasn't that she didn't believe what he had done to me, she could not help herself. Always the weak one.'

* * *

Two days before the society wedding of the year, Lady Diana Chalmoley walked the lush gardens of the family home. Lavender hedges lent their scent to the still air and their colour to the vivid landscape as the pre-nuptial garden party moved languidly into its fourth hour.

Over to her right, where the land sloped to the ha-ha, a knot of revellers listened intently to Anthony Palmer-Dent's scurrilous tales of life in Parliament. She had met him a year before at a point-to-point in Rutland. As the son of a textile mogul he had talent-spotted the girls who would provide a perfect passport to a higher strata of social acceptance.

Diana rejected him.

His reputation as an orator was well known, but there were other, darker tales that passed around the dinner tables after the port began to flow. He was charming, in the way that junior politicians are, believing that because the public cannot see through the thin veneer of their intent, that other, more discerning, spectators also share that myopia.

He had attempted to court Diana's affections then, once rebuffed, turned immediately to her sweet younger sister. And she had fallen for the thrusting young politician. Where had Diana gone wrong? At every stage of the courtship she had attempted to sabotage the relationship, even to the point of introducing her sister to more trust-worthy and acceptable suitors. It had all failed. Palmer-Dent's smile grew increasingly confident as the wedding approached. That was the problem. Juliet always fell for the open smile that masked the closed heart.

Diana was not in the mood for company. She would have spoken to her sister once more but she was miles away in London, undergoing the final fitting with Norman Hartnell, couturier to royalty. Diana moved away from the crowd to the hothouse.

She could smell the warmth of the humidity before she felt its wet, sensual embrace. The blooms, her blooms, leant towards each other in the dampness. White orchids bent from their rows and pulsed a heavy musk into her nostrils. She loved them. She adored their fragile nature and impermanence. Diana had first felt their enslaving effect high in the mountains of the Andes, with Benedict. That was four years earlier, and two years before he had fallen to his death in the Pyrenees.

She could no longer see the guests or hear the stale gossip

dripping from weak, strawberry-stained mouths. She hadn't heard him come in.

'Not in the party mood, I take it.'

Anthony Palmer-Dent stood, glass in hand, at the doorway. His ash-blond hair had fallen from its parting over one eye and Diana noticed a grass stain on the knee of his cream Oxford bags.

'I don't believe it's anything to celebrate.'

Palmer-Dent clicked his tongue disapprovingly.

'Not very sporting, not really pukkah, not the attitude that won us the Empire,' he sneered, referring to the origin of her wealth.

'Precisely what did win it. People with vision. Not grubby grammar school boys with ambition.'

'I didn't go to a grammar.' Then he paused and smiled. 'But you're teasing me, of course. I have so much to learn, Diana, and I will. You could have taught me, showed me the secret things that your class accept as the norm.'

'You will learn anyway; it will just take a little longer this way. I hope you can learn to be patient.'

He moved a little closer to her, sweeping aside his foppish hair.

'You were the one I wanted. Proud Diana, haughty Diana, dry brittle Diana. But you may as well have been tied to that idiot fiancé of yours when he hurled himself off that mountain. You may as well be called Haversham for all the good that fine body will do for mankind.'

'Shut up, Anthony. It isn't too late to convince her what you're really like.'

He began to laugh in her face. Diana could feel the spittle from his baying mouth.

'But it is. She loves me, she worships me.' He opened his eyes wide in mock astonishment. 'You would be amazed at the things she will do for me – dirty, filthy things – and she loves those too.'

Diana's uppercut caught him in the throat. Palmer-Dent grabbed for her as the blow reduced him to guttural gasps. One of his hands clamped her mouth as the other spun her around and began to lift her white summer dress. She saw the orchids, and the orchids saw her and him joined together. And her despair.

'She will never believe you.'

Before Diana passed out the orchids seemed to turn to deathly black before her eyes: row upon row of black velvet treachery.

*   *   *

'She refused to accept the truth, Beth. She knew but couldn't acknowledge it. She claimed that I would do anything to ruin things for them; that if it did happen it was my fault. In a way, I suppose she was right.'

Beth watched Diana look away towards a blank wall as she smoothed an invisible wrinkle in her skirt. Beth could hear movements outside the door. 'What about Eve?' she said quickly. Diana was rocked by the mention of her daughter's name.

'How did you . . . ?' she began, then faltered in her question.

'It was with the file you sent me about Middleton. *Ezekiel 16:44.* "As is the Mother, so is the Daughter",' Beth quoted from memory. I never knew what it meant until we found out about you adopting a little girl.' She paused. 'But she *is* your daughter, isn't she? Yours and Palmer-Dent's.'

Diana suddenly looked old, lost and lonely in this place; just another elderly human being with too many unhappy secrets. Eventually, her voice a little less confident, she replied, 'She is a clever and resourceful girl, Beth, just like you. Come and visit me some time before my release.'

The door was opening and the guard began to walk towards them, indicating with a nod of his head that Beth's time was up. She rose from her seat. Diana's face wore a puzzled expression. Molineux entered the room. It was only at that moment that the Orchid woman's formidable mind provided the solution to the vexing question: How?

'The document from the hothouse, of course.'

Diana looked pleased; she beamed at her as Beth began to walk away.

'You will be all right, my girl, whatever happens. But look out for Eve. She doesn't share my affection for you.'

'Goodbye, Diana. I have a trial to attend.'

'About the blood,' She said calmly, 'the blood at the scene of the murder. Did you ever think how sloppy that was? So unlike a professional assassin to make such a basic error. Unless it was deliberate . . .'

Beth thought through the cryptic message until it became clear. She smiled broadly at the unfathomable woman, who returned Beth's show of understanding. Then the Orchid woman turned her gaze on Molineux and, smiling loftily, sat back exhausted. Her journey was now at an end.

CHAPTER FORTY-SEVEN

Maddy couldn't sleep. Her levels of trust were exhausted, hope bankrupted by Beth's silence. And now at 4.35 a.m. her strength was dissolving into panic. It wasn't that the trial had gone badly. From what Paula the prison wardress had said, D'Stevenson had performed remarkably in the circumstances, without a client, without instructions, without a hope in hell; at least it had started that way.

Paula marvelled at the forensic skill the mature barrister had shown in cross-examination. First he had attacked the powder burns found on the jacket's sleeve. The scientist called by the prosecution eventually conceded that the visit to the gun club witnessed by the police could account for their presence. It was a start at least. Next he challenged Agnes Middleton's ability to recognise the voice that had lured her away from her house shortly before her husband's killing. He played five tapes – an audio identification parade – and she was decent enough to admit that she could not pick out Beth's voice. D'Stevenson had continued to whittle away, always the snapping terrier at the prosecution's heels. He continued on a daily basis to beg an audience, to give him weapons to fight the allegations with; to give him blood. That was what the case now turned on.

'It was quite exciting,' Paula admitted as she took the lunch tray away. 'The prosecution are left with the blood sample at the scene, it's all that remains of their case. They've said to the jury that because you won't give a sample for DNA then it's got to be yours.'

She looked slightly disappointed that there was no sample to prove things one way or the other. 'It's soon going to be too late, you know. They'll just accept you murdered him.'

Paula was kind, in her way, her cropped hair hardening naturally soft brown eyes. It was an uneasy friendship, but one that Maddy was grateful for – like Beth's friendship. But where was she?

It was 5 a.m. on the day a jury would decide the guilt or innocence of Beth Gamble, the day that Madeline Milton would have to own up to her true identity, before the jury retired; it was the only way if Beth failed her. Maddy could not believe that she would. Or could she?

What would they do to her when she told them who she really was?

Charge her with the murder of Billy McCabe? Assisting an escape, perverting the course of justice? Maddy knew it would be more than a smacked wrist, it would almost certainly mean a lengthy spell of imprisonment. She didn't think she could bear that any more. So she fretted the lonely frightening hours away.

Beth sat in the debriefing room, furious at the delay.

'Molineux, the press are all over the place and I need to be at the Old Bailey in two hours' time. What are they going to do if I go out and announce just what has been happening?'

The Commander had his orders from Buchan.

'You'll get there the same way you came. The chopper's waiting at the field, You know how long the journey is. It's all arranged.'

Beth expected him to add the pointless words 'Trust me'. Boardman interrupted.

'Beth, we should be leaving shortly. I won't let him renege on the agreement.'

The atmosphere reeked of distrust and ill temper all the way to the waiting helicopter. Short moments later they were airborne. Beth was anxious about Maddy's state of mind. By this time, she would be terrified by the lack of activity.

'Come on, hurry up,' she shouted through the deafening noise of the aircraft. 'If we are too late now, it'll be too late for ever.'

Beth knew that the public only remembered a jury's verdict and rarely paid attention to the Court of Appeal's decisions years later. If she was convicted and appealed successfully then to many she would remain convicted, just another rich girl with a clever lawyer taking advantage of technicalities.

'Hold on, Maddy, hold on,' she whispered to the night as the helicopter sped above the M3 to the capital.

They came for Maddy at 8.30 a.m.

'You're early this morning,' she commented to the grim-faced prison guard. The woman ignored her completely as the handcuffs were secured, her wrist twig-like against the escort's forearm. The customary coat was placed over her face as she was driven out of the gates and towards the last day of the trial. It usually took about twenty-five minutes. Maddy reached up to remove the garment from her upper body.

'Leave that where it is,' the wardress ordered. Maddy could not think why, unless photographers were lining the route, but the tone of the stern command invited no disagreement.

'Who are you?' Maddy's voice became edgy. 'Diana sent you, didn't she? You're going to kill me.'

'We are running out of fuel.' Beth heard it over the pilot's intercom. Her eyes glared accusingly at Molineux, but his own face was a picture of confusion.

'How long do we have left?' he barked.

'A couple of minutes, no more. We can't make it without refuelling.'

Molineux grimaced. If they didn't make the trial it would be over for all of them, particularly him.

'Get as close as you can.' He adjusted his radio to a different frequency. 'Dobson, the pilot is going to get us some co-ordinates. Have a car, a fast car, with full escort to meet us. We're going by road. Inform the other operatives of the delay.'

'What about the court?' Beth screamed as the chopper banked steeply down to the right. Molineux's body fought for balance against the sharp dive.

'Don't you understand? I can interfere with evidence but not a High Court Judge. The trial goes on.'

Beth pulled back her sleeve to look at the watch on her wrist: it was 9.45 a.m., three-quarters of an hour before the jury in the Crown v. Gamble retired to consider their verdict.

Maddy sat silent and afraid next to the terrifying wardress. She doubted that was her real occupation. The woman's mute refusal to answer any questions only drove her further down the path of terror. As yet she had been too frightened to remove the coat from her face and now the sweat ran from her to it and back again, chilled and clammy. The van had driven for what seemed an age. The journey never normally took this long. Maddy was more convinced than ever that something was wrong.

Time passed slowly and she had the feeling that she was travelling in circles. So what was new? It had all been one big hoop, she thought, one lousy orb of suffering, beginning with her father, continued by McCabe, and ending today with a bullet in her head.

The landing was smooth but Beth felt shaken up inside. The common at Windsor, in sight of the castle, accepted the helicopter easily, but they were still miles from London. Nobody spoke as the party all craned their eyes for the transport. They heard it first then saw a Jaguar XJS pull swiftly on to the common land. Beth ran towards it. She could sense Fergus and Boardman alongside moving at the same pace and with the same thought: they were going to be too late.

Moments later, sirens screaming in the morning air, the convoy of conspiracy struck out for London.

'We're never going to make the Bailey in time,' Boardman said, looking to the clock on the fascia of the Jaguar. 'What's the van's position? We have to intercept it.'

Beth watched, her mouth dry through the panic of the moment as Molineux clicked open a frequency.

Maddy could hear the order: her final destination, where they would do it. The crackle of the message reduced her to utter stillness. The vehicle swung sharply and accelerated away. She began to move her arm; it was snapped close to the woman.

'Keep still. I am only following orders.'

So that was it. Diana had decided it was the end for her. What gave her the right to do that? Maddy was brought up short when she thought of her own involvement in the death of Billy McCabe. What gave *her* the right? She felt strangely calmed by the clarity of her revelation.

As the van continued its journey, and though her eyes were still covered with the coat, she could see clearly for the first time in years. What she did was wrong: understandable, but wrong. It didn't make things better, it just served to fuel the hatred.

Her calm left her as the vehicle drew to an abrupt halt.

The Jaguar was only a mile from the City of London. It was 10.15 a.m.

Beth was surprised when the car swung away from the road and up the ramps of a multi-storey car park.

'Where the fuck are you taking us, Molineux?' Fergus shouted to the front-seat passenger.

'Shut up, Finn, I know what I'm doing.'

The vehicle continued at speed up to the third floor, accompanied by the rubber-smearing shriek of tyres on tarmac.

In the corner was a van.

Maddy could feel the tears of fear roll down her face and on to the inside of the coat. She heard the sound of the van door sliding open, expecting the searing pain at any second.

'Get it over with,' she said, more bravely than she felt, 'but I'm not going to die with this over my face.' She ripped away the coat as a familiar voice interrupted her.

'You're not going to die at all.' She swivelled her head quickly to the right where Beth Gamble stood, arms outstretched.

'No time for this,' barked a tall figure to Maddy's right.

'You're right, Molineux,' Beth concluded.

'Maddy, listen to me, it's over. At least, for you it is.' A short man standing by Beth approached Maddy with a slightly worried frown. 'This is Boardman, you can trust him, he's a policeman,' Beth told her.

'Only a policeman but you can trust me,' he said quietly.

'He is also a friend.' Boardman took Maddy by the arm and began to lead the confused girl away to the waiting car.

'But, Beth, what about you?' Maddy shouted over her shoulder. Beth slipped into the prison van and handcuffed herself to the prison wardress.

Me? thought Beth. I have a trial to attend.

Court two of the Old Bailey was not merely full. That description would not do justice to the shortage of available space. Hacks elbowed and needled, bribed and persuaded, to win their positions on the bench.

The public gallery appeared to bulge sideways from the mass of professional trial oglers. Court officials, delighted that they were involved, attempted indifference but failed through pride. Ancient oak, highly polished beyond normal diligence, lent the courtroom a warmer look than usual.

It was 10.30 a.m. when D'Stevenson strolled into the room and down the barristers' bench; he looked tired, felt tired, was tired. All that remained was for the judge to remind the jury of the brief facts then that would be that. He swivelled around to the dock, hoping that she might have repented, might have given him the vital information to counter the one remaining piece of evidence: her blood. Only the wardress attended; D'Stevenson noted with surprise that is was not Paula. She had helped him get information into the cells; it was strange that she would choose to miss the end of this trial. The jury shuffled into their seats before the judge was announced and entered the room, an imperial expression on his austere features.

'Produce the defendant,' he ordered, aware that this was merely a request, and one which the defendant had declined since the trial began; it was up to the jury to make of her refusal what they wanted. His face held only slack boredom. D'Stevenson watched the High Court judge, noting his professional indifference to Beth Gamble's decision. He watched the man's hooded eyes narrow at the sight of the single figure of the wardress appearing behind D'Stevenson's back, then heard the gasps and hushed murmurs of the public gallery. He saw the judge's eyes open in astonishment as they settled on a figure in the dock.

'Miss Gamble,' he said a little nervously, 'so pleased you could join us at last.'

Beth stood upright. D'Stevenson spoke, his head twisting back and forward between the judge and the dock, his starched bands flapping as much as he.

'My lord, may I have a moment to take instructions?' The judge nodded gravely to the barrister's request.

'Miss Gamble.' Beth smiled at the man who had cross-examined her so mercilessly at Middleton's trial. 'Will you give them the sample?'

'May I say something, my lord?' Beth asked. The man inclined his head, eyebrows raised in surprise at the unusual request.

Beth didn't wait for permission. 'I was in this very courtroom as a victim and I return as one. I am not ashamed of what happened to me, I have learned that it was not my fault. Middleton took my blood, this blood.' The court watched in stunned fascination as she produced the phial she had demanded from Molineux as part of the agreement, then shook their collective heads as she produced a pin and pricked her thumb until it ran red into the waiting container.

'Now the blood will tell you the truth about this murder, about everything. Your sample, Mr D'Stevenson,' she said quietly, suddenly shattered by the events of those past months. Beth leant forward to him with it outstretched in the palm of her hand, aware that once the sample was matched against the blood left at the scene of Middleton's murder, her innocence would be established beyond doubt.

She turned to the faces of the audience, the witnesses to everything that had occurred since she was raped. Fergus smiled shyly at her, now convinced by her arguments that it would be all right in the end.

Boardman's face was smoothed of worry by Molineux's full co-operation. Then there were the faces of the others: the interested, the inquisitive, the desperate, whose own sad lives were illuminated briefly by a daily dose of justice, confirming that there were some worse off than themselves. Her eyes fixed upon one who did not fit that description: Eve. A familiar face, younger but unmistakable, flat eyes devoid of warmth or compassion. Beth was stunned by the girl's appearance and, whilst the hubbub of the court continued around her, saw Eve lift her index finger to her lips, which were lightly pursed, and urge her to silence. Beth understood and nodded once, and once only, to the slight girl who returned the gesture. She walked away without difficulty through the packed gallery; it seemed to peel away in front of her.

Beth now knew that justice was in the eye of the beholder. It had to be seen to be done and be done to be seen. If one corner was cut, one right sacrificed in the name of expediency, then everybody lost, but in the short term the losers would be those less able to help themselves. She had been lucky. Beth took a rich lungful of her future.

EPILOGUE

They met in the arrivals lounge of Geneva airport. Diana, tired by her journey, hugged her fierce daughter tightly. She had known they would never, could never, press charges without evidence, and they had been careful, very careful, and it had worked. Diana had been remanded in custody for a month before they saw reason, her reason, and decided against the embarrassment a show trial would create. She followed her daughter from the terminal to the car and Hans, its driver. Her luggage was stored in the spacious boot of the Bentley. Hans held the door for her and she climbed into the rear seat.

Eve produced a newspaper and presented it proudly to her mother. It was over four weeks old but in pristine condition. It was dated the day of Beth Gamble's acquittal and carried the news of that and a photograph of her and her cameraman leaving the Old Bailey. But it was not that item that had been highlighted in blood-red marker pen. Inside the newspaper, an obituary column was headed 'Anthony Palmer-Dent.' The announcement said that after a brief illness, the Home Secretary had died suddenly at his family home. It concluded by stating that he was a widower and never blessed with children. Diana turned to look at his blessing. Eve watched the traffic with hungry, avaricious eyes. What had Diana left for her daughter? What was left?

Diana returned her attention to the paper. Underneath the face-saving account of his death, and the plans for a thanksgiving service for his life and works, there was a personal announcement: 'Here endeth the lesson'.

Diana turned to Eve. The lesson was over for Palmer-Dent and for herself, but for Eve?

Oblivious to her mother's thoughts she watched the streets of

Geneva flash by and smiled at the thought of all the dark places
the world possessed and all the dark men in them.

'Behold I was shapen in iniquity; and in sin did my mother
conceive me.'

Psalms 51:5